A Distant Field

A Novel of World War I

RJ MacDonald

WARRIORS PUBLISHING GROUP
NORTH HILLS, CALIFORNIA

A DISTANT FIELD: A Novel of World War I

A Warriors Publishing Group book/published by arrangement with the author

PRINTING HISTORY
Warriors Publishing Group edition/October 2018
All rights reserved.
Copyright © 2018 by RJ MacDonald (rjmacdonald.scot)
Cover art copyright © 2018 by Gerry Kissell

ISBN: 978-1-944353-20-9
Library of Congress Control Number: 2018957810

10 9 8 7 6 5 4 3 2 1

You fell;
and on a distant field,
shell shatter'd,
Soaked with blood

—*For Francis Ledwidge* (Killed in action, July 31, 1917),
Norreys Jephson O'Conor

For John MacDonald—Grampa

Who served with the Scots Guards, the Cameron Highlanders, and the King's Own Scottish Borderers in Egypt, North Africa, Canada, the Rhine Crossing, Germany, Palestine and Cyprus. He enlisted as a piper in 1931 and fought throughout WWII, retiring as a highly decorated lieutenant colonel.

He seldom spoke of his wartime experiences.

CHAPTER ONE

RMS *Lusitania*

2:10pm, 7th May 1915
11 miles off the Old Head of Kinsale,
the south coast of Ireland

"Torpedo! Starboard side!" The lookout grasped the cold metal handrail tightly, his knuckles white, staring helplessly as a 20-foot torpedo, travelling at 60 feet per second, disappeared from his view to ram 400 pounds of high-explosive TNT-Hexanite into the majestic ocean passenger liner.

The detonation rocked through the ship, instantly killing those below decks where the torpedo hit. Passengers and crew braced themselves against whatever they could hold on to or fell to the deck. A column of water powered into the air and cascaded over the ship, damaging lifeboats and leaving the surfaces slick with water and punctuated with debris. Then a second, much larger explosion ripped through the doomed vessel.

The blast reverberated through the metal hull, buckling metalwork and shattering glass. Smoke billowed from the forward funnels, and soot rained down onto the decks below. Stokers in the forward boiler room screamed inhumanely as pressurized steam erupted from fractured boilers, blinding and scalding them. Within seconds, steam burned their bare sweat-drenched torsos, plunging them into a sensory hell before they found a merciful death from shock and drowning.

No one near the first or second explosions lived. They were either incinerated or trapped in the forward boiler rooms, far below the waterline, as the cold dark waters of the Atlantic rushed in through the ruptured hull to drown those who lay blinded, bleeding, and damaged on the industrial metal deck. On the bridge, Captain Turner ordered a hard turn towards the Irish coast in a desperate attempt to reach safety, but just after the ship altered course, the steam lines ruptured, and the liner's four Parsons turbine engines failed to respond. RMS *Lusitania*, once the world's fastest ship—the greyhound of the seas—suddenly had no power.

***

Stuart McReynolds struggled to comprehend what was happening. He lay sprawled on the port-side upper promenade deck, near the stern, his ears ringing from the shock of the explosion. As he struggled to his feet and looked around him, the stunned silence was split with screams. Panic swept through the crowd as injuries registered pain and alarm. Deck officers began to bellow urgent orders to crewmen. An icy realization gripped McReynolds—his family were below decks. His mother and father, twin sisters, and younger brother had gone back to their cabins after lunch to prepare for arrival in Liverpool later that day. Stuart had been about to join them after his walk along the promenade deck.

He began to run, dodging around people until he reached the stairwell leading three levels down to second-class accommodations. Groups of passengers were forming, packing into the narrow corridors and stairwells in the ship's interior. Even as he forced his way down the stairwell, McReynolds realized that ship was already listing dramatically and he was fighting against a flow of passengers trying to escape up on to the open decks—and he was losing. He began to shout, barging into people, pushing people aside, politeness gone in his desperation to get to his family.

As he reached the first level down, Stuart's way was blocked by those surging towards him. He forced his way into the crowd, only to be roughly pushed back by a large, wild-looking bearded man, shouting at him and leading a large family group of women and children. Stuart tried again and felt the hard jab of a fist striking him as the bearded man lashed out without warning. Stuart stumbled back, carried by the crowd, and just as he thought he would lose his balance and be swept backwards by the desperate flow of passengers, he heard his brother yelling his name, "Stuart!"

The bearded man turned to the sound of the shout and his head snapped backward as Stuart's brother connected a punch to his chin. The man glared at the new threat, instinctively wanting to fight, but hands were grasping his sleeves and pleading in a foreign language as he was pushed forward by his family. It was not the time to fight; it was the time to live. The big man pointed a threatening finger at his attacker before pushing forward again with the large group of women and children behind him towards the exits. Stuart's knees buckled, but then his brother was next to him, pulling him into a recess and letting the panicking horde sweep past.

"Jesus Christ. You're a mess," his brother Ross shouted, concern on his face.

Stuart's face was burning where he'd been hit. His cut lip bled inside his cheek and down his chin, but there was no time to dwell on it. "What's happened?"

"They're saying we've been torpedoed."

"Torpedoed?" Stuart struggled to comprehend what he was hearing as Ross reached out to feel his bloodied face.

"I'm all right." He realized his brother was alone. "Where are they?" he asked in alarm as he searched the crowd for the rest of his family.

"Dad sent me on ahead. They couldn't keep a hold of the girls in this crowd, so they're going for the elevators. We need to help them get out when they reach this deck," Ross shouted back over the noise of the panicked passengers sweeping past them.

Only eight years old, the twins had arrived ten years after Ross, an unexpected blessing as his mother would say. Their parents would have been terrified of losing them in the crowd of frantic passengers. The elevators were beyond the throng. He looked at his brother. Ross McReynolds was younger, 18 but built big. Where Stuart was strong and lean, Ross was muscular and heavyset, a wide chest leading to a thick neck and large muscle-bound arms. Both boys had grown up spending a great deal of their time outdoors and playing sports, unwittingly strengthening their bodies as they grew into early manhood. Although both were six feet tall, Ross had first equaled, then grown in strength past his older 20-year-old brother.

The deck below their feet lurched. The ship was no longer moving forward, but it was listing more and more to the starboard side. Stuart looked at Ross who looked back in alarm. Through the screams and shouts, they heard deck officers relaying orders to abandon ship.

"We need to move now!" shouted Stuart.

"Stay behind me," Ross replied before turning into the crowd and wading against the on-flowing crowd of passengers. Even in their panic, the crowd parted as Ross, face set in fierce determination, cleared a temporary channel which lapped around and closed behind them. From deep within the ship, they heard a series of ominous rumbles as the ship shuddered and they pressed on towards the elevators. Eventually, they reached the elevator shafts, one on either side of the main staircase. The first elevator reached their deck. As it rose up, the brothers saw frightened passengers coming up from second class. When it reached the level of the deck and stopped moving, the gate clicked as the double locks holding the gate in place released. Stuart yanked open the doors and the passengers hauled back the heavy concertina interior metal gate and spilled out. Stuart looked but couldn't see any of their family as the occupants poured out and ran down the passageway towards the exits.

Then Ross ran past him yelling, "Over this way! The other one's coming up!"

They reached the next elevator moving slowly upward towards them. Stuart and Ross shouted, "Dad!" They heard shouting as the elevator came towards them. "Dad! Are you there, Dad?" Stuart heard a hint of desperation creeping into his brother's voice as Ross bellowed, "Dad!"

His father's deep voice came back to them, "We're here, boys! We're coming up!" They heard their mother and young sisters calling their names, hope in their voices. The brothers, despite the panic around them, smiled with shared relief. They'd made it; the family was together. They just needed get out and reach a lifeboat.

Suddenly, the great ship lurched, tilting up at the stern while the bow dipped towards the starboard side. As both boys staggered, the lights flickered once, twice, and then died. The area at the top of the stairs, which straddled the width of the ship, plunged into semi-darkness, lit only by light coming in from portholes on either side of the ship. The elevator, which had just broken the plane of the deck by 12 inches, creaked and stopped without electricity to power it. A shout of alarm came from inside. Stuart pulled on the door, but it remained closed until Ross grasped the brass handle with him and together they forced the exterior doors open and outwards. The boys both crouched down, just able to see into the elevator and to reach through the metal concertina gate to touch their father's hand. Then they heard the water.

"Get the gate open, boys, and you can pull us through the gap!" shouted their father. Both sons stood. Gripping the metal concertina gate, they began pulling it open, but the gate held firm. Working together, they counted to three and pulled sideways with all their combined might, but the gate remained closed. They heard the twin girls scream and then their father's voice, "Boys, there's water coming up fast. Get that gate open and we'll pass up the girls!"

Ross braced himself against one side of the elevator door and heaved with all his might, the muscles in his arms and the veins in his neck both bulging as he applied all his strength. Stuart grabbed a hold of the metal and strained with his brother. By now, their hands were bleeding, cutting into the metal, but the doors refused to open. The RMS *Lusitania* was built on docks that lined the river Clyde in Scotland and was built to last. The ship was only eight years old. From its hull to its masthead, from its bow to its stern, construction engineers, welders, metalworkers, ordinary workmen, and craftsmen had done their job with pride and had done it well, including the Glasgow firm that had taken great care in installing the elevator gates so that they would only open when the lift floor was fully level with the deck.

The gates were concertinaed to make them strong. They bent and shook with the combined might of the boys, giving the brothers the belief they could force them open if they just tried harder, but the gates held fast as the water flooded in unabated. Each parent had one of the twins in their arms. The girls hung on to their necks, small arms and feet wrapped tightly around their parents, each wailing in alarm and fear into the murky darkness, seeking some sort of comfort from their parents that all would be well.

Hearing the girl's crying, Ross swore at the gates, heaving his body and bracing his feet against the elevator opening to gain leverage, ignoring his battered hands as he sought some way to open the doors. Stuart looked frantically around him. There were no fire axes on the wall, there were no other passengers—they'd all fled.

Water began pouring out of the elevator and the stairwell beside them, covering the deck. The parents looked at each other in the gloom, their eyes meeting, filled with desperation before a silent, calm resignation formed between them.

The brothers then heard their mother's voice for the first time. "Boys."

She wasn't shouting as they all had been. Her voice was clear and calm, "Boys, there isn't any time, now listen to me."

Ross heard his mother but replied by heaving more frantically on the doors, yelling over and over again, "No, no, no!"

His father cut him off. His voice had changed, sounding strangely distant. "Stop, boys. It's time for you to go, find help if you can, but go. There's still time. We'll be fine."

As he spoke, both boys dropped to the wet deck, pushing their hands through the elevator gate and feeling for their parent's hands. Their mother's voice was trembling but clear. She was holding one of the crying twins, whispering softly, trying to reassure her wee ones that whatever was going to happen, they'd be together—that Mummy and Daddy loved them and to close their eyes and hold on as tightly as they could.

The water was up to their necks, the twins inching their way up their parent's bodies to keep their heads out of the water, trembling and sobbing as they clung on. Tears of frustration welled up in the boy's eyes as they pleaded with their parents not to give up. Then their mother's voice reached them once more and stilled them.

"Listen to me, boys. No more of that shouting. Stay together; find a way off this ship. Go, please, and don't turn back." Her voice wavered as she spluttered water. The boys continued to reach through the gate, holding their parents' hands and feeling the twin's wet clothes as the small girls gripped their parent's bodies ever more tightly in desperation.

They heard their father's voice, straining and half-muffled. "We're in God's hands now, boys. Save yourselves. Live. We..."

He began to say more, but whatever it was, it was cut off as the water rose above his mouth. They heard their mother struggling for breath as the water reached within inches of the elevator's ceiling, still trying to soothe the girls who had stopped crying as they gasped for breath. Their father, choking as water covered his face, refused to panic or struggle and turned away to embrace his wife and children in the last seconds of his life.

Stuart strained against the gate, reaching out towards his family in the flooded compartment. He felt a small hand latch tightly around his own, fingers digging in, one of the twins, he didn't know which, and then a larger one, his father's, and then unmistakably his mother's kiss on the back of his hand, and then no more. The grips loosened and then broke, floating away into the gloom.

Abandoned or embraced by God, their family was gone.

The guttural scream from Ross was beyond pain; it came from beyond human endurance for pain. He held his hands to his face, kneeling in the rising water, moaning in anguish. Then he grabbed the gate again and started to shake it, cursing and swearing at the unyielding metal. Diluted, watery blood ran down his wrists and dripped off his arms.

Stuart reached out through his numbness and put one hand on his brother's shoulder. "They're gone, Ross. They're gone."

They stared at each other, tears rolling down their faces, soaked to the skin, and felt the great ship begin to tilt downwards. For a moment, neither of them moved. Stuart looked at his brother and saw no will to live. He felt it, too. Without question, they both could have stayed and let the water take them. But then his mother's voice came back to him, "...find a way off this ship."

Despite his desperation, he felt something else emerge deep inside him, an anger so overwhelming it lent warmth to his pain-filled soul and sent a pulse of energy through his battered and soaked body.

"We've got to live," Stuart said, staring into his brother's tear-filled eyes. "We've got to try for them, and we've got to try together. I need you with me. I can't do this alone."

Ross looked back into his brother's eyes and nodded slowly, wiping away tears before looking back at the elevator shaft, now submerged in oily dark water that bubbled up from below, and added in a voice void of grief, "And God show mercy to those who did this."

***

The brothers stood almost waist deep in water, staring at the elevator shaft until they heard an explosion below. The remaining boilers were rupturing violently as cold seawater came in contact with white-hot furnaces. With one last backwards look, they began to wade against the water, seeking an exit. The water pulled against their legs as they struggled through the darkened passageway. Just as they were reaching the exit, the ship's bow sank underwater, tilting the stern upward so the brothers were now struggling uphill to escape. The water rushed down the passageway and Ross grabbed Stuart's shirt to stop him from falling backwards. As they reached the door, the brothers looked out onto a scene of sheer devastation and panic.

The ship was now sinking at the bow and rising in the stern, its four massive propellers emerging from the water as it listed hard to starboard. The lifeboats couldn't be lowered on the rotating hull of the ship without simply smashing against the hull or swinging inboard to crush passengers and crew.

The passengers staggered about in front of them trying to keep their balance, trying to hold on to the railings, and desperately looking for a way off the rapidly sinking ship. Families were trying to stay together, desperately looking for a way off the ship. Children were crying, and crewmen were rushing past, yelling commands at each other and trying to launch any lifeboat or raft they could. Some passengers had life vests on and some didn't. Some people were praying, and some, overwhelmed by the scene they found themselves in, just stared about them, unable to think, unable to function.

A warning yell from above was followed by a lifeboat crashing down past the brothers from the deck above as it attempted to launch down the hull of the ship. The one-inch rivets dug into the wooden hull, up-turning the lifeboat and spilling its occupants, cart-wheeling them down the hull like bloody ragdolls to disappear into the sea below, leaving smears of blood where women and children had once been.

Out on the water, they could see small groups of people, some clinging to debris, circular lifebuoys, or each other. Others floated, face down, and arms spread wide as if to embrace the ocean, hair gently fanning out in the sea. Looking down from above, women's white skirts and petticoats billowed out in the water, and for a moment Stuart thought they looked like white magnolia flowers or lilies in a pond. There were no lifeboats among them.

Stuart looked down the length of the ship. As far as he could see, passengers and crew were frantically moving about, trying to cut away lifeboats in a vain attempt to float them off the ship. As he stood staring, the stern began to rise even more. If they stayed, the brothers would be trapped and go down with the ship.

He turned to Ross, "We have to jump, now!"

"How?"

"We need to get closer to the water. If we stay on this side, we won't get hit by the funnels or masts as the ship rolls over, but we'll need to run down the outside hull," Stuart replied, a vague surreal plan forming in his mind. Ross nodded.

"Let's go!" Stuart shouted over the sound of screaming and the ship tearing itself apart. Metal fittings succumbed to gravity and pressure, and began to tear through the doomed liner.

They moved downward towards the bow and towards the water. The brothers stayed close, but as they moved down the passageway, a door to their right flung open. A large woman rushed out, grabbing Ross by the arm and yelling for help hysterically, pointing towards the open door. Ross stepped back, trying to break the woman's grip on his arm, but she hung on even tighter, wet clothes clinging to her body, pleading for his help.

Above them Stuart heard a loud, sharp metal crack, one of the steel cables supporting the orange-red funnel above tore loose and came whip-lashing towards them. He shouted a warning but there was no time for Ross to react before the cable cut through the air and sliced into the woman, missing Ross's arm by an inch.

The weight and speed of the cable cut the woman in two like a cheese wire. Ross stepped back stunned as blood spayed over him and the remains of her eviscerated body fell to the deck in a bloody unrecognizable mess. Stuart looked into the open door, but could see nothing but darkness. No one answered when he shouted, Whoever the woman had wanted Ross to help rescue would remain unsaved.

He grabbed Ross, shaking him out of his trance, "Keep moving!" he yelled. Metal groaned and he could hear more of the deadly cables whipping though the air. The ship lurched forward and another explosion rocked the ship as the final boilers blew apart below decks.

Stuart looked at his brother, "We're out of time!"

He began to climb over the railing onto the upturning hull, shouting for Ross to follow. He grabbed the railing and hauled himself over. Looking down, he could see the slope of the hull, curving its way to the churning sea below. Stuart looked into his brother's eyes, "Together on three?"

Ross nodded, "Together on three."

They both counted down and then let go the railing, running awkwardly down the side of the ship as it rolled up towards them. Stuart could see rivets sticking up proud and then barnacles and willed himself not to trip over. To do so would be a death sentence. Then they both reached the sea and dived the last ten feet as far out as they could into oil slick-covered cold water. Both boys were strong swimmers and they came up together, quickly kicking off their shoes to help them swim. The ship continued to roll and looking up, they could see it begin its last plunge into the sea.

"Swim! Swim before it drags us under!" yelled Stuart, and both of them swam away from the ship as hard as they could, lungs burning from exertion. The oily water stung their eyes and tasted foul, but they matched each other stroke for stroke, desperate to get away from the sinking ship and its undertow. Desperate to live.

Behind them, the great ship, once the largest in the world, went into its final dive. The stern rose up angling to the right and then, gathering momentum, slid towards the ocean floor. The brothers could hear the screaming of hundreds of people, either still trapped within the doomed ship or being swept overboard into the sea. The brothers kept swimming, only slowing through sheer exhaustion. The *Lusitania* gathered speed and then, throwing out one gigantic circular wave, disappeared below the waves, crushing those in the water who lay in the path of its four funnels and superstructure, sending out one last tortuous, deafening, metallic wail of pain.

CHAPTER TWO

The O'Connells

Old Head of Kinsale Lighthouse,
the south coast of Ireland

Seamus O'Connell loved nothing better than spending a day fishing. He liked it even better when he was out with his three childhood friends, Connor, Aiden, and Liam—all O'Connells.

They were distantly related as extended cousins once or twice removed, none of them really knew for sure. They liked that they shared the same name, and perhaps because of that, they had remained close. Their schoolboy gang of friends had weathered the storms and squabbles of puberty, and now they were young men. Ready to join their fathers at work and in the pub, ready to court the girls they'd gone to school with, ready to try out for the local hurling team, ready to become adults—but there was always time for fishing. Some things just had to take priority.

They had decided to enjoy the day fishing while making some money for their family and themselves by bringing home food for the table, which kept everyone happy. They had rowed out to An Seancheann, the Old Head of Kinsale, to a favorite fishing spot off the black-and-white-striped tower of the Old Head Lighthouse which punctuated the headland. The day was perfectly calm, and the morning mist had burned off by noon to reveal a blue sea bathed in sunshine. *One of the first days of summer*, thought Seamus, as he sat with his friends and let the warmth of the sun shine down on his pale face.

They'd gone out to the sands at low tide the evening before and dug for lugworm, and a tin of the large thick black marine worms lay in the bottom of their red skiff, which drifted over the rocky seabed. They'd baited their hand-lines and had landed about three dozen fish between them, mainly pollock, coalfish, and six of the big-mouthed green-brown Atlantic cod. Conner had just caught a cuckoo wrasse—small, tropically colorful and pretty, but absolutely no use for the pot. He'd thrown it back amid some good-natured ribbing from his pals.

While Seamus was wiry, pale, and red-haired, Connor was tall, dark, and handsome and very popular with the girls, not that any of the others would ever acknowledge it. He had wide, strong shoulders, and Seamus liked having him in the skiff because he could row effortlessly for miles. Perhaps the endearing trait that had kept any jealousy from the others at bay was that Connor seemed completely unaware of his good looks and their effect on the girls. His thick dark hair was usually unkempt, and he had a shy, almost clumsy manner, as if he hadn't quite figured out where his long limbs had grown to.

By two o'clock in the afternoon, the boys would head back to the shore, keep the best fish for the plate, and then go door to door through their small coastal village, selling their freshly caught fish. There was always a market for freshly caught fish on a Friday in Ireland.

That afternoon, the boys were into a run of mackerel, hauling them in two or three at a time, laughing and calling to each other. The blue-grey fish were built for speed and two or three on a line could put up some fight before they fell flapping into the bottom of the skiff to form a writhing pile, gulping air and bleeding through gills and mouths where the hooks had been yanked out. The late shoal of oily fish was a bonus, filleted and rolled in oatmeal and then fried they were a prized dish for both supper and breakfast. Seamus looked up at the lighthouse, 240 feet above sea level, and knew it was probably time to time to head in, but a few more minutes wouldn't hurt. He wound in his handline and stared out to sea. He had another reason for lingering—his brother.

The first battalion, Royal Munster Fusiliers, their local regiment, had been sent to Gallipoli. The allies were trying to open up another front through what Winston Churchill, as First Lord of the Admiralty, had called "the soft underbelly" of Europe. No official word had come back, but bad news travels fast, even during war, and folk over in Cork were whispering about casualty lists a mile long. *Surely it was all gossip*, willed Seamus.

The campaign against the Turks didn't seem to be going well, but it was early days yet. The Royal Navy, together with the French Navy, had been forced back by sea mines and shore batteries as it had tried to pass through the Dardanelles Strait towards Constantinople. So the British Army, along with the French and troops from Australia and New Zealand, had been sent in to clear the way. Along with them went Irishmen—including the Royal Munster Fusiliers—and along with them Patrick, his older brother, and Frank, Connor's older brother.

Seamus was worried, and fishing was an escape from those worries. His brother had always been there for him. They were close despite the six years between them. It had been his brother who made sure Seamus had the pocket money he needed, that he had the right clothes for school, that his shoes were decent, if not new, and had defended him from their dad when the old man flew into a volatile rage for no good reason after coming home late from the pub. Patrick and Frank had joined up together, despite, or maybe because of, both their fathers' objections to "good Irish boys fighting for the British Army."

But the British Army provided a pay packet every week, three square meals a day, a bed, a uniform, a roof over their heads, and the promise of adventure, so the older brothers had taken the Queen's shilling and had signed up alongside tens of thousands of other "good Irish boys" for five years. After that, Patrick would come home with savings and soldier's stories, or that had been the plan until war had been declared ten months ago and the first battalion, Royal Munster Fusiliers, had been given orders to deploy overseas. Seamus could still remember walking his brother to the station for the train that would take Patrick and Frank to the regiment's depot in Tralee. Conner had been there, too, seeing off his brother. There had been a Salvation Army band playing *It's a Long Way to Tipperary*; folk were cheering and waving flags as steam bellowed from the train's boiler in preparation for the journey through Cork and Kerry. But Seamus had had to fight to keep the tears in as the moment came to say goodbye.

His big brother had known it. "I can read you like a book," he'd say to him often with a smile. Perhaps it was because they were so alike and so close. When the time came, his brother grasped his hand and squeezed the back of his neck with the other hand and lent in.

"Be brave, Seamus. Take care of Ma, finish school, and I'll be back before you know it." He'd winked, and as Seamus had let go his hand he'd found a small brown paper bag of aniseed-ball candies in it, his brother's favorite, along with one worn silver crown coin.

"Don't tell Dad about the money. That's for you and a rainy day, and don't tell Ma about the sweets or you'll have to share them." His brother had smiled, reached out with a hand to playfully ruffle Seamus' red hair, and then had turned quickly and was gone into the train. Seamus had often wondered if he'd been fighting back the tears as well. The last memory he and Connor had of their big brothers was of them waving and yelling together from the open window of the train as it blew its whistle and steamed out of the station. Seamus had waved as long as he could see his brother, and then he was gone in a cloud of steam and smoke.

***

Seamus had been daydreaming, and as he'd being doing so, he'd been staring out to sea at a huge ocean liner coming in from America and likely heading for England. He could just see its four orange-red funnels and graceful lines breaking the distant horizon and wondered what it must be like to cruise in luxury without a care in the world. Just as he was about to turn away, something caught his eye. It looked like a great geyser of water had washed over the ship, but that made no sense. The ship must be massive to be seen from so far away. As he tried to see more clearly, he heard the first ominous bang rolling in from the direction of the liner.

"There's something wrong," he said, pointing out to sea.

The others had heard the sound and were looking in the direction that Seamus was pointing, trying to figure out what had made it. And then the big ship seemed to leap in the water, black smoke bellowing from the front two funnels and seconds later a louder, deeper boom came towards them from across the sea.

"Sweet Jesus. What's happening?" asked Connor.

"I'm not sure," replied Seamus. "I thought I saw a great column of water break over it, but that can't be right. Let's get those lines up and get ready to go in."

They wound in the lines while looking out to sea. It was clear something had happened, but the boys had no idea what. Then the ship turned towards the coast.

"Is it trying to come in?" said Liam to no one in particular.

They all stared at the ship. It had turned towards them, smoke billowing from the front two stacks.

Aiden had the best eyesight. His piercing blue-grey eyes could see v-shaped flocks of geese in the air coming in for their winter migration from Greenland before anyone else; he could also hear them calling before the others. His mother said he had his grandmother's sixth sense about things, and that it was a God-given gift.

"Aiden, what can you see?" asked Seamus.

Aiden stood up on the skiff and stared out to sea, the boys keeping quiet as if their silence might improve his eyesight.

"Keep her steady," he said, as he stepped carefully up onto one of the four rowing benches that bisected the skiff, spreading his feet wider to help him balance and stabilize himself. He was tall and fair and not one to be hurried. He had a quiet, almost gentle manner. One of the brightest boys in school, he had helped scribble down answers to homework for all his friends at some stage in their adolescence.

But he was no bookworm. All the boys had seen him play hurling or stare down bigger bullies in school. Below the calm placid exterior, Aiden could be single-mindedly determined and disconcertingly fierce when he needed to be. He took his time in most things that he did, be it answering a question, eating his supper, or asking out his childhood sweetheart Mary McCafferty—which he still hadn't quite managed—or in this instance, trying to figure out what was happening in front of them far out at sea.

The boys waited. They were used to Aiden's ways, and knew it was worthwhile waiting and listening to him. He was rarely wrong. Aiden stared, isolating his senses and focusing his gaze towards the ship out at sea. The external noises of the water lapping against the skiff and the fulmars wheeling overhead receded as he stared into the distance. And then he spoke. "She's sinking."

The others just looked up at him in disbelief.

"Are you sure, Aiden?" asked Seamus quietly.

"Yes," he replied. "She's sinking. She's going down at the bow. Looks like she's leaning to one side as well."

A few seconds passed as the boys processed the information, accepting it as fact. "What's happened to it?" asked Liam.

"I'm not sure," Aiden replied, still looking out to sea, "but we all heard the bangs and Seamus saw water rising up over her deck." He looked at the others for confirmation; they all nodded in reply. "So I'm thinking it's another submarine attack. I think she's been torpedoed."

The boys looked at each other. There had been increasing submarine attacks since the Germans had declared unrestricted submarine warfare around the British Isles three months earlier, and in the last two days alone, three ships had been sunk off their coast.

Seamus looked at his friends. Connor looked back at him and then up at Aiden. "How far away is it?" he asked quietly.

Aiden shielded his blue-grey eyes from the sun above them and pursed his lips. "It's hard to tell. She was definitely coming towards us, but I think she's either slowed right down or she's already dead in the water. I think the leaning is worse already. Whatever's happened, she's settling fast. It must have been torpedoes." He paused, "I think she's nine, maybe ten miles away, and she must be gigantic for us to see her from here."

Connor looked back at Seamus. "What should we do?"

Seamus looked around him. There were no other boats out. He had thought they would head in to spread the news, but looking out at the ship in the distance and weighing up Aiden's thoughts, a new course of action was forming in his head.

He looked at his friends. "All right, here's what I'm thinking. I'm thinking we can head in, let our folks and Police Constable O'Hare know what we've seen, and they can raise the alarm. Courtmacsherry's lifeboat at Barry Point can be launched, and the fishing boats and lifeboat from Queenstown can be launched. We'll have done our job." He hesitated. "But I'm also thinking that ship, whoever she is, will have sent out radio messages and is probably still doing so."

He looked at Aiden, who nodded in affirmation. "In that case, we're here, we're already offshore, and even if others get there before us, we can still help. If that ocean liner really is sinking, they'll be hundreds of folk in the water soon."

Aiden sat down. "I agree with Seamus. We're already out here, and we can probably even beat the lifeboats. They'll have more rowers, but won't be able to use their sails in this weather. There's no wind at all, and we'll have a head start; we're closer."

Liam rubbed his face with his hand, blew his cheeks up, and expelled the air. "It's going to be one hell of a row."

Seamus smiled, "You're not wrong there, but if we're right, they'll be fishing boats heading out behind us and we can get a tow back to the village from a Kinsale boat down the coast if we're lucky."

They all looked over at Conner, who looked out towards the stricken ship and then down at bottom of the skiff and sighed. "I think the days of us running to our parents or PC O'Hare are over." It was a simple statement, but the boys knew he was right. He looked up and, perhaps taken aback by what he had just voiced, said, "Well, what are we waiting for?"

"All right then; let's get ready to row," said Seamus, and the friends began to sort out the skiff.

"If I'm home late, I won't be able to come out to play tomorrow," Liam joked and despite the ordeal ahead of them, the boys laughed and grinned back at him, shaking their heads.

That was Liam. He always had the knack of making them laugh. It wasn't that he told jokes, he just had the gift of finding the humor in most situations. Liam always had a deeply dimpled grin on his face, with shining brown eyes and a mop of spiky brown hair to match Connor's mop of black. He wasn't tall, but he was quick and tough and could hold his own in the fights that were always erupting outside of school.

He liked whistling, although that often got him into trouble with Father Foley, who didn't approve of it and would clip him about the ear for reasons they didn't understand. It didn't stop him whistling for long as he had a stubborn streak as wide as his smile. That same stubbornness could be seen emerging now as Liam pulled out his oar and began fixing it into the oars locks. For all his humor, Liam was right about one thing—it was going to be one a hell of a row.

The skiff was clinker-built, constructed from overlapping six-inch wooden planks of ash bracketed into a strong larch wood keel. It was 22-feet long and six-feet wide at the middle, and tapered to a point at both the bow and stern. The worn faded paint was red with an off-white interior and matching stripe below the gunwales, the colors of Cork's hurling team. It was beautifully suited to the coastal waters, strong and seaworthy and able to ride even the choppy waves. It was common property, owned by the village for the purpose in the summer months of rowing against the other coastal villages, who all had similar skiffs.

While perhaps not as pivotal as hurling, each village took pride in its skiff and its rowers were selected for each race with great deliberation. For the past two years, the rowing had been dominated by the O'Connell boys who'd formed a team so strong and fluid that they won every race they entered.

The small boat had four rowing benches, one for each of the boys, and each boy had one 14-foot oar, two each side, set alternatively. Seamus always rowed from the bow, looking over his shoulder to see where they were going and to call out any adjustments. Connor and Aiden took up the middle two benches, the powerhouse of the crew, and Liam, the lightest of them all, sat facing the stern. It was his job to set the pace that all the others would follow, pushing them hard but knowing when to conserve energy for the final sprint.

The boys were ready, flexing their shoulders and arms as they sat on their benches, double-checking oars were securely pinned onto the kabes, clearing their throats, spitting over the side and establishing their own individual double-grip on the Sitka spruce oars.

Seamus took one last look in the direction of the sinking liner. "All right then; ready to row?"

Conner replied, "Ready to row." He was followed in turn by Aiden and then Liam. Seamus looked once more in the direction of the smoking funnels then up to the lighthouse to get a back-bearing, so he would know the rough direction they needed to go without swiveling his neck all the time. As he looked up, he could just make out the lighthouse keepers looking seaward from top of the lighthouse, obviously looking out with binoculars to the big ship in distress. He raised his arm in a wave and one waved back, at least someone would know where they'd gone.

It was time to go. To Seamus' command of "Oars in the water," all four oars dropped into the calm sea, burying their blades underwater.

"Connor, Liam, bring us around, two strokes each." The boys, their oars on the same side of the skiff, pulled gently two times and the bow of the skiff pointed out towards the sinking ship.

"Liam, on your call," said Seamus, handing over control to Liam.

Liam cleared his mouth one last time and braced. "Right boys, four short ones and then long and steady and we'll build it up as we head out. Ready to row..." Four sets of arms stretched out, heads held high, backs straight, stomach muscles tensed, and four oar blades sat deep in the water poised to be pulled back. "Row!"

The oars were pulled back in short strokes four times, jerking the skiff into action and building up the momentum.

Then together they lengthened their pull, leaning forward and then pulling back in a continual series of long powerful strokes, keeping the blades in the water as long as they could to power the skiff forward and then quickly recovering in unison to begin again. Within ten seconds they were moving fast, the streamlined skiff cutting through the millpond flat surface of the water. Used to racing for a mile or two, Seamus had to reign them in. "Long and steady, Liam!" Liam responded by fractionally lowering the tempo, giving the boys a miniscule rest during the recovery between pulls.

Then, coming from the headland, they heard the loud blast of the foghorn up by the lighthouse, followed by another. They looked up and could just make out all the lighthouse men now waving to them, the fog horn blasting two more times. "That's quite a send-off!" Seamus yelled, surprise tinged with a hint of pride in his voice. All the boys impulsively raised an open-palmed hand back towards the lighthouse before quickly resuming their two-handed rowing. The fog horn sounded three more times as the skiff headed away from the point and out to sea.

It wouldn't take long now for their entire village to know about the stricken ocean liner, and that the O'Connell boys were rowing out to it.

CHAPTER THREE

Into the Water

Ten miles off Old Head of Kinsale Lighthouse,
the south coast of Ireland

The final circular wave thrown up by the *Lusitania* hit Stuart and Ross, tumbling them farther away from where the ship had been, making them fight for breath. The vortex caused by the 800-foot liner careening towards the seabed below began to draw those near the churning water into its grip and under the water. People who had struggled successfully to live now were drawn into the vortex along with the liner's flotsam and jetsam. Once underwater, there was little chance of escape before the victims ran out of air, unable to swim back to the surface against the downward current. They followed the great ship down into the depths, trapped in its final death hold. Others were hit by the wreckage around them, driving them under the water or knocking them senseless to drown in blissful ignorance.

Stuart and Ross felt the immensity of the pull and panic shot through their bodies. They swam with renewed vigor, at first being drawn back, then simply holding their own against the current, pulling away from the mortal whirlpool behind them. The wave had helped push them beyond its deadly embrace, but it had been close. The brothers were exhausted. The lack of life vests had in its perverse way saved them. With them, they would never have been able to swim fast and hard away from the sinking ship and would have been drawn down into a cold, unforgiving watery grave.

Without them, just to keep afloat, they had to tread water—and they were getting cold.

The water in early May off the south Irish coast was 50 degrees Fahrenheit, almost half the normal human body temperature. Their bodies' heat generated by their swim had escaped into the cold water, cooling down their core temperature, and they couldn't replace it. The more they moved, the more heat they would lose; the more heat they lost, the colder they became. Unless they could get out of the water, they'd either die from the cold, or, being physically unable to swim, they'd drown.

The brothers looked around and were surprised to find themselves relatively alone. The scene before them bore no relation to the past 20 minutes. The water was cold but completely calm, just a gentle swell rocking them up and down, and it was sunny. They could feel heat on their faces, but their bodies were cold. There were no more explosions, no more screams, no more crowds, no more smoke, or soot, or rendering of metal, or passengers fighting desperately to find a way off the ship. There was no more ship. The survivors were battered, shocked, and cold. Those who couldn't swim had already drowned.

Stuart and Ross were isolated away from the other survivors, who had crowded to the opposite starboard side of the ship in their flight. Through the gentle swell, they could glimpse a handful of lifeboats far away and larger groups of survivors in the water, but neither were nearby and they seemed to be drifting apart. Around them, large bubbles of air rose to the surface, escaping pockets of oxygen from the sinking ship. And along with the bubbles came the bodies. The vortex was giving up its dead. Bodies wearing cork life vests rose to the sea's surface. They came up slowly, in ones and twos, and then in small groups—men, women, passengers, crewmen, children, and babies. Their faces were white, eyes and mouths open, heads thrown back, supported in their life vests. The brothers were treading water amid a sea of corpses.

Stuart looked at his brother. "Get a life vest on, Ross."

"What?"

"Get a life vest on, unless you want to join them. We need to float, not tread water." As he spoke, he took a few strokes over to the nearest body. He tugged at the vest, untying the cords. The body slowly sank back below the water, arms reaching upwards, until it had disappeared, reclaimed once more by the depths. He threw the life vest to his brother and reached out to another victim for a vest of his own. Nearby, he saw a circular lifebuoy, part of the jetsam. He swam the short distance to retrieve it, and both brothers linked their arms through the ropes. Now they could stay afloat with their shoulders and heads out of the cold water.

"Stay as close to me as you can," said Stuart. "We've survived this long; we're not giving up now."

Ross nodded back. "We need to live for them," he said simply, looking back at where the ship that held their family had once been. And then he looked past Stuart's head into the distance. "We need to live for those bastards as well, because I swear to God someone is going to pay for this."

Stuart turned about and looked into the ocean's expanse. Moving away from them, barely visible but with its conning tower still above the surface, was a submarine of the German Imperial Navy—an *Unterseeboot*, or U-Boat. It had surfaced briefly to inspect the damage it had wrought. No thought of help was considered for the hundreds of innocent civilian survivors dying in the cold water. Submarine warfare was all about gross tonnage sunk—not passengers saved.

As the brothers watched the submarine disappear, anger burned within them, lending warmth and determination deep within their souls. Stuart reached out to bring his brother closer. He looked at Ross, staring into his eyes. "We live," he said, a command from one grieving, battered, and traumatized brother to another, echoing their parent's last wish.

Ross gripped his brother's hand tighter in reply. "We live," he answered.

With life vests on and clinging to the circular lifebuoy, they could conserve some energy, feel the sun on their faces and shoulders, and retain a modicum of body heat, but without help, they could only challenge death, not escape it. Very soon both brothers would begin to shiver as hypothermia began. It was all now just a matter of time.

***

In the past 30 minutes, Seamus and the O'Connell boys had rowed close to three miles and were beginning to work up an honest sweat. Used to working in unison, they'd settled into the steady pace dictated by Seamus and set by Liam. Their movements were relaxed but powerful, muscles moving smoothly, their breath taken during the split-second recovery before the oars went back into the calm sea to propel the skiff forward once again.

The conditions could not have been better. The sea was flat as a pancake, and the skiff, perfectly trimmed, planed over the calm water leaving a trail of small diverging waves in her wake. While it was a little disconcerting to be so far off-shore, they soon got used to it, confident in their small boat and in their own abilities to row her.

Seamus looked back at the lighthouse to get a rough bearing. It was barely visible, and he wondered if the lighthouse-keepers were marking their progress through their binoculars. He looked over his shoulder to check their course and gasped. His rhythm gone, his oar clashed into Aiden's and the skiff slewed around, powered solely for a stroke and a half by Connor and Liam whose oars were both on the same side.

"What the feck's going on?" Liam yelled, angry at the disruption, and utterly unused to oars clashing.

"Look at the ship!" Seamus replied in response to Liam's outburst.

As the skiff had slewed around, the boys could all see the ship far into the distance without having to crane their necks. Aiden stood up, balancing himself with a hand on Liam's shoulder, and stared out to the ocean liner. "Sweet Jesus, she's already going down."

They could all see the stern of the ship unmistakably angling skywards. As they watched, scrunching their eyes to try and focus better, it disappeared from view, followed seconds later by a loud ominous rumbling coming over the water, and then silence. The ship they had been rowing out to was no longer there.

"Oh, mother of God. How in earth did she go down so fast?" asked Connor, but no one replied—they had no answer.

Liam who snapped them out of their trance. "Right. Enough of this long-and-steady shite. There's folk probably drowning out there, hundreds of them, and we've got another four or five miles to go. We can either sit here with our thumbs up our arses, or pull them out and do some proper fecking rowing!"

Seamus couldn't help but grin. When Liam got angry, he really was something to hear, but he was also right. "All right, lads. I hate to do it, but throw out all the fish; the bait, too."

Connor shrugged and started picking up the stiff fish from the skiff's bottom and dropped them over the side. The others joined in, understanding the logic of lightening the load, but hating the waste as they washed their hands in the sea and watched a day's catch float away.

Liam picked up the homemade anchor and looked at Seamus. Seamus nodded. "And the anchor. It's all dead weight and it's no use to us this far out."

Liam dropped the small anchor overboard and watched it disappear in a trail of bubbles into the depths.

Seamus looked, but there was nothing else to throw out. "All right. We row hard, stop when we think we're halfway there, switch positions, and then row the rest. Keep a lookout for other boats—we can't be the only ones out here."

He looked at his friends and saw a new seriousness in their faces, a steely determination to see their self-appointed task out, and he was proud to be one of them. "Get ready to row."

Forty minutes later, the boys were exhausted. They'd rowed flat-out, as if in a race. Liam had set a hard, punishing, and unrelenting pace. The boys had pulled back on long strokes until their hands had hit their stomachs, pulling the oar blades from the water to push them quickly away and back into the sea for yet another long hard pull. Aiden had seen the first boats, far out to their right, probably fishing boats from Queenstown. It was hard to know if they were still heading in the right direction, but by keeping Old Man of Kinsale Head directly behind them and keeping the engine-powered boats to the right, they knew they were roughly on the right course.

Seamus called a halt when he saw all their heads down, the pace slacking despite the strain they were applying to the oars. They were all drenched in sweat. They were relieved by the fishing boats. Others would reach the wreckage before them, and they wouldn't be alone. Connor and Seamus switched positions, as did Aiden and Liam. They'd now all be rowing on the side opposite from where they had started, resting some muscles, taxing new ones, but using most of the same. It was as much a psychological as a physical change, but it wouldn't last long. Aiden, now stroke, handed around an old ceramic-topped water bottle and while they quenched their parched throats, he pointed left.

Far, far away they could just make out another rowing boat, level with their own, but bigger, longer with more rowers—the Courtmacsherry Lifeboat. It was making headway, with long powerful strokes.

"All right, boys," Seamus said to get their attention. "Let's follow the other boats. We can't be that far now, and if the lifeboat crew can row this far, so can we—we're in good company."

Aiden pushed out his oars and took a deep breath. "Enough sightseeing. Let's finish this."

The others slid out their oars, adjusted to their new positions, and took some deep breaths. Aiden called out, "Ready to row?"

They responded and braced, pulling hard. "Row!"

It took them another half an hour—half an hour of blistered hands and pain and then more pain. Their short rest didn't last long. Soon they were straining, grimacing as they pulled back, letting heads sink on the recovery, but never letting the pace slack. Individually, they were at the edge of exhaustion. Even Connor with his broad shoulders was in pain, broken blisters on both his hands now rubbing raw and bleeding. No one was going to let the others know how tired they were. No one was going to be the first to say, "I can't go on." No one was going to let down his pals.

The boats were converging. The boys could see a handful of boats already heading back towards Queenstown to their right, low in the water, decks crowded with huddling survivors. The boys rowed on, backs towards the point where the *Lusitania* had gone down. Then the first of the dead bodies fouled their oars.

They were startled. They looked around—bodies floated everywhere. Liam swore gently, as if not to offend the deceased. "Holy mother of God. They're everywhere."

They stopped. Having rowed so far, for so long, they were now unsure what to do next. Conner began to fish in one of the bodies until Seamus stopped him. "Wait," he said. "These poor souls are beyond our help. Let's row on and see if we can find anyone alive." The sea was carpeted by the dead. More fishing boats arrived from the coastline and others headed back in. They rowed slowly, further into the wreckage, gingerly working their way around the dead, calling out every now and then but receiving no response.

A yellow-painted fishing boat crept up from behind. It was a local boat from down the coast, the *Marina Kinsale.* An old deckhand looked down at them. "By Jesus, I told them I thought it was the O'Connells in their red skiff, but even I didn't really believe it. Did you row all the way out here, boys?" he asked in disbelief.

"We did that," said Seamus. He looked around and added, "But I think we're too late."

The old fisherman shook his head. "Not too late, boys. We've been passing Queenstown boats full of folk heading back to harbor, some even towing lifeboats. The sea's cold, but folk can still be alive if they have faith in the good lord above and something other than themselves."

The skipper leaned out of the small cabin. "We'll go on straight ahead, boys, and then reverse our course when we reach open water. We'll look for you on the way back. If we can't find any of the living, we'll take back as many of the dead as we can for a good Christian burial. Do you have anything warm with you? We have extra blankets."

"We have some water, but nothing else," replied Seamus.

"Throw them over a couple of those blankets, will you, Paddy," he called to the old deckhand that had greeted them. The craggy-faced fisherman grabbed two old green army woolen blankets, bundled them up, and threw them towards Connor's open hands.

On seeing them, the skipper shook his head. "God bless you, but your hands are some mess, boys. We'll sound our horn three times when we want to go in and we'll keep a lookout for you; you'll not row back in. It's the least we can do."

Seamus nodded his head in thanks. "We'll search that way then," he said, pointing out towards the west. "When we hear your signal, we'll row towards it."

"God bless you all," the skipper said before slowly moving his boat past the skiff and then ahead into the sea of debris and bodies.

Seamus looked about him. "All right, then, we row out to the west. There's no boats out that way that I can see. Search for anyone that looks alive."

The boys slowly pulled the oars, picking their way through the dead, calling out but receiving no replies. They stopped to check on a woman, still holding tightly on to a child, which gave them hope that one, if not both, were alive, but their faces were both blue-white, and dead expressionless eyes stared back at them as they reached down. They felt despair tinged with anger. They had rowed all this way, thinking they might save someone, thinking that their presence could make a difference, and all they could see were bits of debris and dead people, like discarded ragdolls floating in the gentle swell.

They reached the end of the visible wreckage and stopped rowing. Dejected, they looked around. Liam voiced their frustration. "All this way and for what? There's no one left alive out here. They're dead already, poor souls. We're just too late."

Seamus paused. "We came because it was the right thing to do, and it still is. Like the skipper said, if nothing else, we can bring some of these poor folks back in, let them be identified, give their families some sort of peace of mind and a proper Christian burial. We'll start with that woman and child if we can find them again."

The boys turned the skiff about, ready to head back towards the center of the wreckage and to link up with the *Marina Kinsale*. Aiden stopped and looked out to sea, beyond the point at which they'd stopped searching. Seamus was about to say something when he saw Aiden raise his hand palm out to silence him. That got Liam and Connor's attention, Aiden was staring hard, turning his head to focus his senses, and then stood up. As always, he took his time, then said, "There's someone out there. I'm sure of it."

Coming from anyone else, the boys might have questioned him, even dismissed his statement, but that was exactly what it was—a statement, and coming from Aiden, that made it a statement of fact.

"Which way, Aiden?" called Seamus, the boys now electrified into action.

Aiden turned his head and pointed seawards. "There, that way. I'm sure of it now. I can hear someone," and that was all the boys needed.

Seamus began shouting commands. "Connor, bring us about. Liam, get ready to row. Aiden, stay up and keep us heading in the right direction!"

The boys obeyed quickly. "Row!" was all Seamus said, and they moved off towards the direction set by Aiden.

Rowing with their backs to the bow, they all looked up at Aiden, standing in the stern, peering out to sea with his blue-grey eyes. They'd gone about 100 yards when Aiden pointed and yelled, "There! Over there! I can see someone!"

The boys pulled hard on their oars, pain gone, adrenaline now coursing through their bodies as they adjusted their course without speaking and increased their pace. "There's two of them!" shouted Aiden. Glancing over his shoulder, Seamus could see something in the water, and for the first time could hear what Aiden had sensed—a fading call for help. Someone was alive.

"Keep it straight; keep it straight. Keeping rowing for ten!" shouted Aiden, and the boys pulled ten more times before easing off. "They're coming up on the port side. Slow it down."

Connor and Seamus dipped their oar blades in the water to slow the skiff, and the rowers glanced over their shoulders to see two men in the water, holding on to a lifebuoy, the cords of their lifejackets intertwined to keep them together. The boys pulled in their oars and reached down, grabbing the men's cork and canvas life vests. The bigger one could barely move, and from his blue lips kept repeating, "Help" as he grasped the other man with one hand.

"You're safe. We've got you. Just hang on," said Seamus. "Get them in."

The skiff rocked as Liam and Aiden tried to pull the men over the side, but it was difficult to lift the sodden men. Connor leaned over, telling the others to counterbalance the skiff to keep it from dipping. He grabbed the bigger of the two men and pulled, his cut hands bleeding and arm muscles straining, and the man came half out the water. Connor heaved with his remaining strength and the man fell into the skiff with a start, as the life vest cords holding him to the other man broke under the strain.

The man still in the sea bobbed back down under the water, and then began to drift away and slip out of his life vest now that it was no longer tied together, his eyes flickering and the hand that had held on to the other man opened, searching. For a second, Connor thought they'd lost him as he struggled to sort out the man he'd just pulled in, and then the skiff rocked as Seamus dove into the sea.

He surfaced and grabbed the man's outstretched hand just as he began to sink under for the last time. "You're not going anywhere, mate; not after all we've been through," he said. He turned and pulled the man back towards the skiff and the outstretched hands of his friends.

The two men were freezing to death. How they'd survived in the cold sea was beyond the boys. Both were deathly white with pale blue lips and shivered uncontrollably. The boys put them both together in the stern and covered them with all their spare clothes and both blankets, covering their heads to try and keep whatever warmth was still in their bodies from escaping. Aiden tried to give them water, but they were shivering so much it was difficult, and the water ran down their chins.

"We need help fast," said Aiden. "If we can't warm them up, we'll lose them both to the cold."

Seamus was shivering from his dive into the sea, and couldn't imagine how cold the two men must be or how close to death they were. "We didn't come this far to lose men now. Get ready to row. We need to find the *Marina Kinsale*, or any boat, to save these men, and we need to find them *now*."

The boys returned to their oars, and on Seamus' word, began rowing back into the floating wreckage. They couldn't help but knock into the dead, but Liam said they'd be forgiven for it as they were trying to save the living. Aiden saw the yellow fishing boat among the wreckage, pulling in corpses from the water, and they rowed hard for it. As they drew near, Paddy saw them and called out to the skipper, "It's the O'Connell boys coming in, and they look in a hurry."

Seamus called, "We've got two survivors with us, but we can't warm them up! They're dying of cold!"

As they got alongside, the skipper starting barking orders and they manhandled the two freezing men up to the fishing boat. The boys boarded the boat and used their rope to tie the skiff for towing. Paddy took control of the two men, stripping them of their clothes and then ordering the boys to rub them hard with the rough dry towels before cocooning them in several blankets.

Finally, the two men squeezed into the small cabin with the skipper, where heat from the engine below entered through a pipe. It wasn't that warm, but it was warm enough. Neither of the men moved, and while they had winced at being rubbed down, neither had spoken a word. Paddy produced some hot tea from the engine compartment below and added a generous nip of Irish whiskey from a flask and squeezed into the small cabin, trying to get some of the warm drink into the freezing men.

The boys looked around. After rubbing down the men, they'd done the same to Seamus, and now they all had green blankets draped over their shoulders. Exhausted, they slumped together on the deck as the boat turned for Kinsale. A pile of dead bodies lay across from them. More were stacked by the stern, a grim catch for the fisherman who'd set out hoping to rescue survivors. The two remaining fisherman on deck came up to them, one with more mugs of whiskey-laced tea, the other with a bundle in his arms. Seamus looked up. "Did you find no one alive?"

The men shook their heads. "Not a soul. They were all dead; the cold got most of them, we think, but we saw some terrible sights." Seamus thought of the woman embracing her child, both dead, and felt a pang of guilt that they'd not brought them in. But the living had to come first.

"We did find this, though..." said the man with the bundle, and pulled back a corner to reveal the head of a small brown and white dog, a Jack Russell. "Perhaps you boys can look after it while we head in?"

Connor reached up for him and gently took the small bundle. The dog was still shivering, and he tucked the small body under his blanket and held it close for mutual warmth. "Where did you find her?" he asked.

"We heard her barking. The poor thing was standing on a small red wooden door shivering away. Where the door came from we don't know—maybe the ship, maybe it was just there in the sea waiting. As the dog was out of the water, it was alive, surrounded by folk who were not," said the fisherman, shaking his head at the wonderment of it all.

Cupping has hand on the cup of tea, Aiden reached over and ruffled the dog's head, "She's got no collar on. I wonder what she's called?'

Looking around him, Liam smiled, "Isn't it obvious?"

They all looked at him, waiting.

"There's only one name for a dog that's survived all this..." waving his arm at the grim scene around them before smiling again. "Lucky."

And with that the boys grinned, then despite everything, laughed. That was Liam.

Paddy came out of the cabin and the two fisherman and boys looked to him. "I think they're going to live. Their bodies are warming up very slowly, and I managed to get some tea into them. We still need to get them in quickly. They could lapse back and be gone; I've seen it happen before. It's as if the body can recover, but the will to live can't." Then he looked back. "Mind you, I'm thinking the will to live was all those two men had out here, so it must be strong."

He looked down. "I'll tell you something else boys. I don't know how you rowed all the way out here, or found those two men in there..." He nodded over to the cabin. "...but you saved their lives today. There's no doubt about that. No doubt at all. You did well, boys; you did very well," and with that he headed back to the cabin to nurse his patients, keeping them alive until they could get them ashore.

The boys, warming up, exhausted and rocked by the boat, fell asleep one by one next to each other, heads flopping on each other's shoulders. The fisherman took the mugs back from limp, damaged hands, and gently piled more blankets over them. If the lighthouse men had spread the word that the O'Connells had rowed out to the sinking ship, the fisherman would soon spread the word of what they had done, and who they had saved.

The light began to fade as the *Marina Kinsale* chugged its way back to its harbor with its dead, and with its living— six boys that had become men that fateful afternoon, and a small brown-and-white dog named Lucky.

CHAPTER FOUR

Angus Rhuairi MacIntyre

Kinsale, the south coast of Ireland

For the next two days the fishing boats brought in the dead; for the next two months, they'd wash up by themselves on remote beaches. Makeshift morgues were set up in Queenstown, and the mass burials began on Monday morning. Of the 1,959 passengers and crew aboard the *Lusitania*, 1,198 had died, 128 of whom were Americans. Those not trapped within the ship—or pulled down as she sank—died in the cold sea. In the 18 minutes it took for the ocean liner to sink, only six lifeboats had successfully launched, but the remaining collapsible lifeboats and life-rafts had saved many as they floated free of the ship. Without doubt, those in the water owed their lives to the Irishmen who had fished them out. Some had still died after rescue, too cold to live on, but two men had stubbornly clung on to life.

Stuart and Ross knew none of this. They had slept for two days, tended to in the local inn by the innkeeper's wife, and looked in on every now and then by Paddy. "Just to make sure they're still with us," he'd say in the pub downstairs. Rest and warmth had been enough, along with hot broth spooned into them and a peat fire that was kept lit throughout the night and day. Early Sunday evening, Ross awoke first. He looked about, and fragments of the past days came back to him—the cold, the rescue, the fussing as they'd been brought to the inn, and not much else. His brother was next to him, in the same bed for comfort as much as for warmth.

Looking over at him, Ross couldn't hold back a tide of sadness, remembering now that his brother was all the immediate family he had. Stuart's face was bruised, and he looked gaunt. Running his hand over his own face, he felt the same. Both his hands were bandaged, and he remembered batting to open the lift doors as the cold sea had enveloped his parents and the twins. A groan escaped him, full of sadness and remorse.

The door handle turned and in walked Mrs. O'Sullivan. It was her husband's inn, and she had nursed the two men as best she could, while politely refusing all well-wishers and do-gooders with their miracle cures. She did allow Paddy to visit. He had enough sense to keep quiet and would sit watching the fire and the two sleeping men. From what she'd heard, the men owed their lives to him—and to the O'Connell boys who'd rowed out to rescue them.

Ross watched her walk over to Stuart and put her hand on his forehead, tutting slightly. "He's running a slight temperature still, but he'll be fine in a day or two." She came over to his side of the bed.

"You're looking fine," she said, and in response Ross cocked a questioning eyebrow. "Well, let's say you're looking a lot better than you did when you arrived, then."

Ross smiled. "Where are we?" His voice was hoarse.

Mrs. O'Sullivan handed him a glass of water from the side table. "You're in Kinsale. The fisherman brought you here on Friday, and it's now Sunday evening." She looked at Ross with concern. "Do you remember what's happened to you both?"

Ross nodded. "Some of it." He looked down and was surprised to see his big hands trembling.

Mrs. O'Sullivan sat down and gently reached for his bandaged hands. "Don't fret about it, lad. It's just your soul catching up with your body. Now, you tell me who you are, and what you remember, and I'll fill in the rest as best I can," and she held his trembling hands as Ross began to tell her their story.

***

When she came downstairs, her husband knew she'd been crying, which is not something she did often. Paddy was there, to check on his boys and maybe have a pint of Guinness XX while he was at it. She walked over to her husband who put an arm around her.

"They're brothers, Stuart and Ross McReynolds. They were travelling to visit family in Scotland. The younger one's the bigger one and he's awake now; his brother was just beginning to wake as I left, so I thought it best to leave them for a while," she said, taking a deep breath. "You see, they watched their parents and eight-year-old twin sisters drown in front of their eyes out there." She looked out through the small windows towards the sea beyond.

Paddy looked down, shaking his head. "God bless them, but that's not something anyone should ever have to witness." Following her stare out the window, he also wondered if that shock had given them the will to live when so many others had perished in the sea.

Drawing her eyes back to the room, she said, "I told them about you and the O'Connell boys, Paddy. The big one would like to meet you. I'm sure they both would, and the boys, maybe we can get them over from Ballinspittle?"

Paddy nodded. "I'll get word to the O'Connell boys to come over tomorrow."

Mrs. O'Sullivan looked up at her husband. "We could give them a bite to eat."

"That we can," he said with a smile. "Those boys deserve a decent meal at the very least. Should we get the other one over, too?" asked Paddy.

The *other one* was a third, lone survivor, brought in an hour before the *Marina Kinsale* had arrived at the quay and staying at a different inn across the inlet that formed the Kinsale harbor. There had been others, but they'd gone on to Cork. The solitary survivor had stayed.

He was a big, tall man who spoke very little. He had spent Sunday at St. Multose's church, not inside it, but sitting outside on a bare wooden bench, his back against the outer stone wall of the church, staring out to sea. He had politely refused the entreaties to join the congregation in prayer. When pressed, he had held up his hand with a glare, silently fending off those who wished him inside, until folk had left him alone with his thoughts as they entered the church to pray for the dead and the living. The inscrutable wild look about him scared folk, and he'd been left to himself, awaiting the train that would take him away.

"I'm not so sure he'd come, from what I hear. He seems to stay to himself and his thoughts," replied Mrs. O'Sullivan.

Her husband nodded. "That's true enough. I'll tell you what, I'll send word that he's welcome. Whether he turns up or not is up to him."

***

Late the next morning, Stuart and Ross walked the edge of the river Bandon under Paddy's watchful gaze. He pointed out the *Marina Kinsale* moored at the stone quayside with the red skiff still tethered to its stern. A round-faced harbor seal surfaced and stared up at them with unblinking curiosity before diving under the water in search of fish.

The brothers stopped as locals came up to say hello and pass on their condolences. The sad news had travelled fast, as did word that Mrs. O'Sullivan didn't want them bothered for too long. The last thing the men needed was strangers wringing their hands and reminding them of what they'd lost, so some just nodded their heads or tipped their caps in acknowledgement as they passed by.

PC O'Hare had informed the authorities in Queenstown about the three remaining survivors, and the Cunard shipping line was paying for train tickets and ferries on-wards to Liverpool. The train would take them down the South Coast Railway to Cork later that day.

The two men were staring over the inlet out towards the sea when Paddy spoke up. "It's the O'Connell boys," he said, pointing down the quayside to four young men coming to-wards them.

Stuart looked up, appraising them as they neared. It was clear that they were good friends. They walked together, al-most touching each other as their arms moved, easy in their close proximity. One was tall, broad shouldered, dark and handsome, with a small brown and white dog at his ankles. One was short but wiry, with spiky unruly hair and a broad grin. But Stuart's gaze was drawn to the two others: one was tall and slim, with delicate features and piercing blue-grey eyes; the last one was pale, with red hair, and was walking a bit in the lead, straight towards the brothers.

The red-headed man smiled as he came closer. Stuart smiled back as he realized all six of them had bandaged hands.

"I won't squeeze too hard if you don't," said the redhead, holding out his hand towards Stuart.

Stuart and Ross smiled, holding their hands out. "That sounds like a good idea," replied Stuart. "Just make sure to tell your big friend here that," he said, looking up at Connor.

They all smiled as Connor dipped his head in embarrass-ment, looking down at Lucky who stayed by his adopted master's feet. They all shook hands gently, nodding and smiling as they did so, not sure what to say next.

"I'm Stuart, and this is my little brother, Ross."

"Little brother?" said Liam, looking over at Ross. "He's a bit big for a little brother, don't you think? Did he steal your food when you were growing up?" All six of them laughed, easing into each other's company.

Stuart looked over at his brother, and then towards the Irish boys in front of them. "We both wanted to thank you for saving our lives." He nodded towards Paddy. "Paddy told us what you did." He paused to look at all the boys. "Thank you."

The O'Connells looked down, embarrassed by the situation. "It was nothing," said the redhead. "And anyway, it was Paddy who kept you alive. We're just glad we could help."

Aiden stepped forward. "We heard about what happened out there—with your family. We're sorry for your loss. I wish we could have been there to help."

It was Stuart and Ross' turn to look down. Stuart looked up first. "The last thing our parents told us to do was to save ourselves. Without you, we wouldn't be here. Thank you all for what you did. It certainly wasn't *nothing*. What you did for us saved our lives." He looked around at the Irish boys. "Which one of you is Seamus?"

Liam nudged the pale redhead in the ribs. "This is your man."

"I heard you dived into the sea to pull me out of the water."

Seamus smiled. "Well, now, I couldn't let you swim all the way back, could I?"

Stuart pursed his lips as emotions welled up inside him. "I don't think I was doing much swimming," and he held out his hand again. "Thank you." As he shook Seamus' hand, he choked up and Ross put his arm across his brother's shoulder, drawing him close.

They all looked at each other, embarrassment coming over them, until Paddy broke in. "Now, look. You've a lot to be sad for," he said, looking at Stuart and Ross. "But you've a lot to be grateful for as well. You're alive, you're with friends, you're in Ireland, and Mr. O'Sullivan's promised us a free meal and a drink to go with it. Which doesn't happen every day, if ever—so no more tears for now."

Liam smiled. "Now that sounds grand," he said before hesitating and holding up both his bandaged hands. "But no arm wrestling, mind!"

Stuart smiled, recovering his composure, and held up his hands to show his own bandages. "That's fine with me," he laughed. As he turned with the others towards the pub, Ross's hand gripped his shoulder to stop him. Something in his brother's grip sent him a warning, and as he looked up, he took an involuntary step backwards, a gasp escaping from his lips.

Unnoticed until now—not ten feet away—was the third survivor, the big man with the short hair and wild reddish-blond beard. The same man who had punched him hard as he had tried to reach his family on the sinking ocean liner three days ago. The same man who had swept by with his large family towards the exit, lingering only to point a threatening finger at Ross. And now that same finger was pointing at Stuart.

Stuart could sense, rather than see, the O'Connell boys closing ranks towards the stranger, ready to protect the brothers from the unexpected threat that they had no way of understanding. Ross began to pull his brother back and to move forward to the big man he'd protected his brother from in the mayhem of the tightly packed ship's corridors. As he did so, Stuart gently held his forearm.

The big man in front of him was no threat. Stuart could sense something completely different—pain.

Still pointing at Stuart's bruised face, the man spoke. "I did that, and I'm here to ask your forgiveness." He spoke perfect English, but with the gentle melodic Highland lilt that characterized a native Gaelic speaker. He dropped his hand and clutched his cap, bowing his head.

For a few moments no one spoke, all taken aback by the man's presence and his simple declaration. Then Stuart walked forward, holding out his bandaged hand. "I can't forgive you if I don't know your name."

The big man sighed as if dropping a great weight. "My name is Angus Rhuairi MacIntyre."

Stuart looked into his eyes, and felt his stomach lurch as he guessed the source of the man's pain. "Your family, all those folk that were behind you...?"

The big man shook his head and said one word, "Gone."

"Gone? Not all of them; surely not all of them?" Stuart asked, hardly comprehending the extent of the man's loss.

"The lifeboat tipped over before it reached the water. I watched them all..." but he could say no more about it. "I saw you both the night you came in. I've stayed to come and say sorry. I didn't mean it. It was all madness when the ship went down, and I was trying to get my family and my sister's family through the crowd to a lifeboat. I'm sorry I hit you." He paused and then added, "I heard what happened, and I've come to ask forgiveness if I caused your family to die out there."

Stuart looked at the man and understood the turmoil within him, the pain and sadness of losing so many that might match his own grief, added to remorse that he may have caused others to die. He held out his hand. "It made no difference, Angus. We got there in time; there was just nothing we could do to save them."

Angus nodded in understanding as only another survivor could, stuck out his hand, and gently shook Stuart's, looking relieved. He turned away to walk down the quay. Stuart watched him go before shouting, "Wait!" The big man turned. "Are you hungry?" asked Stuart.

"I could eat."

"Then join us, please."

Angus looked surprised. "I'd be welcome?"

Ross answered, "Look around you. We're a long way from home, and I'm guessing you are, too. It's time to thank those who saved us, and to look to the future if we can."

"The future?" replied Angus. "I'd be glad to join you, but my future is set." He paused, staring seawards, then in a voice that startled the boys in its vehemence, said, "I've been called up. I'm going to kill those who killed all mine."

***

Angus Rhuairi MacIntyre had grown up in the windswept Outer Hebrides, a chain of small narrow islands off the west coast of Scotland. North Uist was at the center of the chain, and the low traditional croft that had been his home had weathered the Atlantic storms with grim determination, much like its occupants. Life on the croft was hard, and his childhood was spent carrying seaweed up from the beach to fertilize the poor soil, cutting peat for the fire, and taking whatever work could be found to supplement the meagre family income. The biggest source of employment on the island was on the laird's estate, and the laird favored those men who had military service; so, at 17, Angus had joined the local army reservist unit of the Lovat Scouts in Lochmaddy.

They called themselves *territorials*, part-time soldiers drawn from the same geographic location, with pride in their community and pride in their local battalions. There were similar territorial units throughout Great Britain. Many had been raised during the Napoleonic Wars with France for home defense. In 1908, they had been reorganized into the Territorial Force, and even understrength, it was larger than the regular Army. Now, they were needed as reinforcements for war in France and elsewhere, so parliament had allowed their voluntary mobilization and deployment overseas.

Trained to varying degrees, they could mobilize quickly and provide a stop-gap until the inexperienced volunteer units of Kitchener's New Army could be formed and trained from scratch. But it would take time for those brand-new volunteer units to reach France, and until then, the Territorials would have to hold the line—next to their regular army counterparts—against the might of the German Army and its allies.

The Lovat Scouts' specific role was reconnaissance and sharpshooting. Often working in small detached groups, they were the only such unit in the British Army. They were drawn from the highland estates, whose gamekeepers and ghillies were expert marksmen, and who knew how to stalk the red deer unnoticed and kill with a single shot from long distance. Angus had learned well. He was inordinately patient, could remain motionless for long periods of time, and heeded his instructors. He had even won his unit's coveted marksman badge with star and wreath for best shot in the junior ranks.

At 21, he had left to go to Lewis, the northernmost island in the Outer Hebrides, to the main town of Stornoway in search of work. There, he had met and married his wife and began to raise a family. He'd transferred to the local Territorial Force unit in town, the Fourth Battalion, Seaforth Highlanders. They'd stayed in Stornoway for four more years, and then he and his brother-in-law had responded to a need for forestry workers in Canada, with the promise of good pay for hard work. The agent had not mentioned the dangers, and his brother-in-law had been killed when a stack of logs had broken loose and had come tumbling down a hillside he was clearing, crushing anything and anyone in their path.

Angus chose to return home. He'd been in New Brunswick for three years when word had come that all reservists were to report for duty. He could have joined a Scottish-Canadian regiment easily enough, but married with children and a widowed sister and her small family to support, he'd decided to go home to North Uist where his family would be looked after in his absence.

They'd booked a cramped third-class passage on the *SS Cameronia*, sailing from New York, but at the last minute the ship had been requisitioned by the British Government. The passengers had been transferred at no extra cost, and amid much excitement, to the far more luxurious and prestigious RMS *Lusitania*, fatefully delaying its departure from pier 54 by two and a half hours.

And now his family was gone. The image of them spilling out of the lifeboat that he had struggled so hard to get them in, before helping to launch it, was seared in his mind. And with that image came the hate. He'd tried to pray it away, to forgive those who had taken his family from him, but the forgiveness wouldn't come. In his grief and turmoil, a clearer, darker, way forward emerged. He'd pick up his rifle again and take revenge until the hate and pain went away. He didn't know long that would take, nor in truth did he care. He'd survived when all with him had died, so living held none of the same importance to him that it had before.

***

Stuart sat across from him as they ate their lunch at the inn, watching the big man lost in his thoughts, thoughts not that far from his very own. As he had drifted in the numbing cold sea, watching the German submarine submerge, he had promised retribution on those who had done this to them. And now the formulation of a plan seemed to be in front of him.

"Angus." The big man looked up at him. "Where will you join up?"

Angus looked at Stuart, as if sensing the purpose of the question. "I'm a Seaforth Highlander, a Territorial, a reservist, so I report to my battalion." Now the others around the table were listening. "I need to tell those at home what happened, and then I'll report to Fort George. They'll find a place for me."

"Fort George?" asked Stuart.

"It's near Inverness, up in the highlands of Scotland. It's where our headquarters is."

Stuart looked over at his brother. They hadn't talked about it, but the encouraging looks his brother gave him and the imperceptible nod said, *ask more.*

"Angus, could anyone join up there? Could we join up there?"

Angus stared at the brothers, weighing them, and making a decision on what he saw. Eventually, he spoke. "I am in your debt. I shouldn't have hit you the way I did, and you both forgave me, so here's what I can do. I will be at Fort George on Friday, in five days' time. I'll wait for you at the main gate at noon. If you are there, I will do everything I can to help you join my battalion; that much I promise. I still know at least one of the recruiting sergeants there." Angus drew his breath. "Just mind this: *if* I can get you in, it'll be tough going. You'll have to catch up fast, and there won't be time for weeks of basic training."

Looking at his brother, Stuart smiled. "We understand, Angus, but thank you all the same."

The silence that followed was broken by Liam. "Well, that all sounds like a grand idea. Imagine: kilts, no underwear, and all the haggis you can eat!"

They all laughed, even Angus, drawing smiles from Mrs. O'Sullivan behind the bar, who was glad to see the two boys recovering. After finishing their meal, it was time to go. Angus left first, shaking all their hands, and solemnly thanking the O'Sullivans for inviting him to eat. The O'Connell boys left next, shaking hands and batting away Stuart's and Ross's renewed thanks for saving them.

Seamus looked at Stuart. "Are you serious about joining up?"

"Yes," replied Stuart, Ross nodding his confirmation.

Seamus understood. "Then take care of yourselves and the best of luck. You've lost at least one of your nine lives, if not a couple more."

Stuart and Ross said goodbye to Mrs. O'Sullivan last, arranging to send payment for their time at the inn. Stuart held out his hand formally, but Mrs. O'Sullivan pulled him close and embraced him as she would a son. Ross smiled before being engulfed himself.

"Now I heard some of what you were asking the big man at the table, boys," she said. "Don't be hasty. The war is a terrible thing, and it will go on with or without you. I hope to God without you. Whatever you decide, remember you always have a welcome here and may God look over you both." She kissed them on the cheek and turned away towards her husband.

Paddy walked them up to the station where Angus was waiting for them. "Take good care of each other now," Paddy said as they waited at the platform for the train to depart. "And remember this—those boys didn't save you for you to go and throw your lives away. Keep them precious; they're special now."

The guard blew his whistle and the men jumped up into the open carriage door. Stuart and Ross waved to Paddy as the steam engine slowly picked up momentum and pulled out of the station, until they disappeared into the clouds of steam.

CHAPTER FIVE

A Call to Arms

County Cork, Ireland

The O'Connell boys headed home. The skiff would remain in Kinsale for a while until hands had healed enough to row again. It had been a good afternoon. Good to have met Stuart and Ross—they'd been fine men, and the young Irishmen were proud that they'd saved them. The lunch had been nice, too; the O'Sullivans had treated them well, and with full stomachs they were bantering with each other as they walked the last few hundred yards to their village.

Just as they turned the corner into the main street, PC O'Hare caught up with them on his bicycle. "Boys!" he called out. They stopped to eye him warily as he came towards them. Years of youthful misbehaving had given them a healthy suspicion of the policeman. He rarely brought good news, but today was different.

"Boys, I've been looking for you. I have four letters for you, from the Cunard line," he exclaimed, holding out the envelopes.

"Letters?" asked Connor. "I've never had a letter in my life. What does it say?"

"Well, open them up, boys. Open them up. I don't know what's in them. They arrived at the police station two hours ago from Queenstown, each addressed to one of you, so I brought them down myself."

The boys looked at each other in astonishment then began to rip open the envelopes, gasping. Inside each envelope was a letter from Cunard formally thanking them for their role in rescuing the two survivors and praising their "Initiative, decisiveness, endurance, and courage." But that's not what the boys were staring at. Each of them was tenderly holding up a five-pound note, a token of appreciation from the board of directors.

Liam simply whistled. "Would you look at that? I've never held a note before. Coins, yes, but never a note."

Five pounds was four to five month's wages, more money than either of them had ever held at one time. PC O'Hare smiled. "We've had our differences, boys," he said with a nod, "but you deserve that money for what you did. You've made the village proud, but no wasting that money in the pub. Put it to good use!" He wagged his finger at the boys and walked away to his bicycle.

Liam looked at the others. "Well, surely we could waste just a little of it in the pub," he whispered, and the boys all laughed, still shocked by their windfall.

***

Seamus was still smiling when he opened the door to the small cottage where he lived. "Ma!" he shouted, eager to share his news, but when he entered the small kitchen he stopped. Father Foley was there in his worn black cassock sitting with both his parents, his mother crying softly and his father holding a yellow telegram in his hands.

A wave of fear came over Seamus. "Ma?" he asked quietly.

Father Foley stood up and came over. "It's your brother, Seamus," he said, looking into the boy's eyes. "Patrick's been taken, Seamus. He's not with us anymore."

"Not with us anymore?" Seamus asked, repeating the words back to the priest. Father Foley maintained his gaze. "He's dead, Seamus. Killed in action. Patrick's with God now."

Seamus just stared, tears brimming in his eyes. "Where?"

"Gallipoli," said Father Foley. "I think the Royal Munster Fusiliers took heavy causalities. There are telegrams arriving throughout Cork, Kerry, Clare, and Limerick—boxes of them."

Seamus nodded dumbly. He walked over to his mother, sat down and held her hand. "It'll be all right, Ma." The words meant nothing; no words could.

Father Foley picked up his black biretta hat. "I have to be going," he said, looking at Seamus. "I'm sorry to tell you, Seamus, but Connor's brother Frank was also killed—the same day as Patrick."

Seamus looked up, "Frank as well?"

"I'm afraid so. If there's any comfort in it, I'm sure they were together at the end. Those two always were inseparable as schoolboys. I see no reason to believe they weren't side-by-side when God took them. I'll look in tomorrow, and we'll say a prayer for the all the boys at mass."

He inched the door closed—other grief-stricken families to visit, other grief-stricken families to try and comfort with inadequate words. It was a trial of faith, he told himself as he walked towards Connor's small house down the street. He'd christened the boys whose names were now on war office causality telegrams, and his heart was heavy with the duties ahead of him.

Seamus could only think of his brother's smile when he'd said goodbye. He still had the worn silver crown coin his brother had given him at the station. "I'll be back before you know it," his brother had said with a smile and a ruffle of his hair. Only he wouldn't be back, ever, and the pain and sorrow welled up in Seamus until he'd had to leave his mother and go sit in the bedroom he and his brother had shared through their childhood. His brother's other words came back to him as he sat on his brother's bed, head held in his hands: "Be brave, Seamus...."

***

Father Foley had been right, and as the next day dawned, so did the realization that the men of the First Battalion Royal Munster Fusiliers had been in a catastrophic fight. If they'd known the real truth, *fight* might have not been the word used to describe it; *slaughterhouse* would have been closer to the truth.

Landing at V Beach on Cape Helles, Gallipoli, on the 25th of April alongside the Royal Dublin Fusiliers and the Royal Hampshires, the Royal Munster Fusiliers had walked down gangways into the converging fire of four hidden Maxim machine guns each firing over six bullets per second. Those who tried to wade to the beach were cut down. Those who dove into the water to escape the bullets drowned under the weight of their service wool uniforms and 60 pounds of equipment, entangled by barbed wire placed underwater on the orders of German military advisors.

The aging steamer that had tried to land them, the SS *River Clyde*, had been filled with the dead and dying lying on her blood-strewn decks—killed by concentrated machine gun fire raking the packed ranks of men before they had even stepped off the ship. By the day's end, the Royal Munsters had lost 70 percent of their men—over 700 soldiers, among them Patrick and Frank. Their blood turned the sea red around the landing beach.

The anger, shock, sorrow, and disbelief within the small Irish communities needed a focus. For some the church provided it. For a few fathers of dead sons, solace was found at the bottom of a glass in the pub, Seamus's dad among them. For others, it took on two diverging forms. The first: A path for immediate Irish self-determination to rid them of the British Army and British rule. Home rule for all of Ireland had been voted for the previous year, then suspended for the duration of the war.

The second: A desire to enlist to fight based on revenge. And so the four O'Connell boys found themselves in a long line of volunteers at the Royal Munsters Fusiliers recruitment office in Kinsale.

For such a monumental step, they hadn't needed much discussion. Seamus and Connor had come to the same course of action in their mutual grief, and Liam and Aiden wouldn't be left behind. "Someone has to look after you two, after all," Liam had said, "and I can't do it all myself." He looked over at Aiden who just shrugged his shoulders and gave a crooked grin.

Recruiting Sergeant Flynn knew his job—to refill the ranks—so when four young men stepped in front of him as a group, he smiled. If the O'Connell boys hadn't been known to the sergeant beforehand, they were now. Everyone knew what they'd done and how they'd done it. Aside from the envelopes from the Cunard line, the coxswain of the Courtmacsherry Lifeboat had been over to offer them a place on his volunteer crew anytime they wanted one. It was a high honor for the young boys. So Sergeant Flynn welcomed the boys into his office, already counting the two shillings and sixpence each new recruit would earn him.

"I'm proud to have you here, boys," he said in a booming voice. "Truly I am." Looking at Seamus and Connor he bowed his head. "I'm sorry to hear about your brothers, sorry indeed. They were good men, the best, they all were," and he paused before looking up. "But you'll be as good as them, better even, by taking up the cause they fell for. I only wish I could go with you boys. By god, we'd show them what Irishmen can do in a fight, wouldn't we?" The boys smiled, embarrassed but proud at the same time. Looking about his small office, they could see recruiting posters, one asked, *A Call to Arms! Irishmen, don't you hear it?* Another poster declared, *An appeal to gallant Irishmen: Join an Irish regiment today,* and between them a big map of the United Kingdom of Great Britain and Ireland.

"Now then, we just need a few things tidied up first, and then we'll attest you and get you up to the depot for uniforms. The ladies do like a nice smart uniform on a young man now, don't they lads?" he said with an exaggerated wink.

"Now let's see. Stand up straight now, lads, chests out, arms to the side. Fine, fine, that's it. You're looking like fusiliers already, by god, so you do!" He looked down at his paperwork. The boys were all over five-foot-three and their chests were easily 34 inches wide. "The doctor will check you over later, boys, but all seems in order here." He made a show of arranging four sets of paperwork.

"Now, I just need to confirm your full names and your ages." He made a dismissive gesture with his hand. "It's just a formality boys," he said, before looking at them all and saying in a slow clear voice, "I know you are all nineteen; isn't that the truth?" He didn't wink at them this time, but the inference was clear. With birth certificates rare, as you had to pay for them, the recruiting sergeant would simply take their word for whatever age they claimed to be. The ranks did need filling after all, and if they were here to enlist, it was his job to enlist them. It was not his job to turn them away over a trivial detail.

Seamus spoke up, "We're all nineteen, Sergeant Flynn," and the boys all nodded in solemn confirmation.

"Well, that's grand boys, that's just fine. I was sure you were. I just had to check, you understand. Now, if you just sign your names, we'll be done."

"No!"

The voice came from the doorway where Seamus' father stood.

"Dad, what are you doing here?" asked Seamus in alarm, but his father ignored him, looking at the recruiting sergeant instead.

"You can't have them. I'm not sending any more of my boys to die for the British Army. Not now, not ever!" Seamus could tell his dad had been drinking. Not too much, but enough to make him even more stubborn and argumentative than normal.

"Now, now, Mr O'Connell," Sergeant Flynn replied holding up his hands, sensing a disaster to his recruiting bounty about to happen. "Did your first son not join up to fight the Hun? And would you not allow your next to do likewise for the same good cause?"

"Good cause! What good cause?" shouted his father. "Yes, my son joined up, without my permission, to die on a beach in Gallipoli alongside hundreds of other Irishmen. Now what cause was good about that?" he demanded, staring at the recruiting sergeant. "Don't try to tell me my own son died for a good cause. It certainly wasn't Ireland's cause. He just died in a godforsaken war, in a godforsaken country, on a godforsaken beach I couldn't even point to on a map!"

Sergeant Flynn grasped at one last straw, "They've passed selection Mr O'Connell, and they can all join if they want without your permission."

"No, they can't." A finger pointing at Seamus first, and then at the others, "He's only seventeen, they're all only seventeen, and you well know it Barry Flynn," pointing a last accusing finger at the sergeant.

Sergeant Flynn knew he was beaten. They all knew the boys were 17, but the charade would have worked until the father had arrived. He looked at the boys, "I'm afraid you'll have to come back when you're older," then looked at the father and said, "or go somewhere else were you're not so well known..."

Seamus' father stared belligerently at the sergeant. "I've stopped them here, and I'll stop them in Cork, or Limerick, or Waterford, or Dublin; by god, I'll even go to Belfast if I have to. If they try to sign up anywhere in Ireland, I'll stop them or be there to pull them out of that bloody uniform when I find them!"

Then he pointed at Seamus, "I should take my belt to you! If you ever try this again, don't bother coming home. I should wash my hands of you just for being here!" With that, he turned and walked out of the office and down the road.

Seamus looked at his friends, stunned and embarrassed. "I'm sorry."

They all looked down, deflated and unsure what to do next. Sergeant Flynn could see their disappointment. "Boys, remember what I said. If you want to join up, go far away from here. It'll not work in Ireland, I'm thinking." He looked at the back of the irate father walking down the street.

Aiden had been quiet the whole time, which wasn't unusual. He was now staring at the map of Great Britain and Ireland behind Sergeant Flynn's desk. The constituent countries that made up British Isles were colored: pink for England, yellow for Wales, green for Ireland, and purple for Scotland.

Just as his friends were turning to go, Aiden looked at the recruiting sergeant and pointing towards Scotland on the map asked, "Sergeant Flynn—where's Fort George?"

CHAPTER SIX

Nell

The East Neuk of Fife, Scotland

Large wooden herring drifters crowded into Anstruther's busy stone harbor. Fishermen in tightly knitted navy-blue Gansey sweaters and black caps worked to square away their decks, calling over to other crews and greeting new ones coming into the harbor as they mended their nets. Bold gulls patrolled the gunwales in search of scraps, while more timid kittiwakes and terns circled above or settled on gently swaying mast heads.

Up on the harbor, rows of expert fisherwomen dressed in oilskin aprons gutted and packed herring into barrels, salting each layer until they were full. Their work was hard and unrelenting. Their fingers were individually bound to help them grip the oily fish. But there was women's laughter, too. Some of it was undoubtedly directed at the two handsome strangers looking at the scene before them.

Stuart and Ross smiled awkwardly and moved on, while the laughter behind them roared. Towards the center of the harbor stood the town's sandstone volunteer lifeboat station. Next to it was the cooper's yard, which was owned by their family and managed by their uncle, John, and their grandfather, Alistair McReynolds.

The McReynolds had arrived three generations ago from the Northwest Highlands. They had come with whisky barrel-making skills and soon began producing the barrels needed to pack and sell herring to Dutch traders, who then exported the protein-rich preserved fish to the Baltic and beyond. In May, the spring herring shoals were running in the Firth of Forth sea estuary off the east coast of Scotland. The chain of small coastal fishing villages that comprised the East Neuk of Fife took advantage of the currents, fisherman setting their nets at dusk and hauling them in at dawn. Later in summer they would follow the shoals north to the Shetland Islands, and then down the coast to East Anglia, the fisherwomen following them by train to gut and pack wherever the fishing boats went.

The herring fisheries had expanded from the late 1800s into the early 1900s due to the increased demand from Russia and Eastern Europe. In one year alone, two-and-a-half million barrels of herring had been exported. Those in the barrel-making cooperage business, including the McReynolds, had made good profits.

Alistair McReynolds, with memories of harder times in the highlands, gave generously to the volunteer lifeboat, and to the Fisherman's Mission. The latter supported fisherman in need—the widows of lost fisherman and their families. Fishing was a dangerous business, especially at night when the boats were normally out. Individuals were swept overboard by ropes and nets, or entire boats could flounder and sink in the sudden storms that blew in without warning from the North Sea. In 1881, directly across the mouth of the sea estuary, 189 fishermen had drowned in a single disastrous storm.

The war brought its own perils. Drifters were being requisitioned by the Admiralty to serve in the Royal Navy Trawler Service and were as far away as Gallipoli, with their volunteer crews often falling victim to the sea-mines they were trying to help sweep. The McReynolds helped where they could. More than one disabled fisherman had found a job at the cooperage when they were no longer able to go to sea and earn a living for their families.

Alistair had bought a modest Georgian mansion above the harbor with views southwards across the wide sea estuary towards Muirfield Golf Course and the Lammermuir Hills of lowland Scotland. He had continued to look for opportunities to expand and consolidate the family business. In 1895, he'd been approached by a visiting American businessman called Palmer Jackson with an interesting proposition—wine barrels.

The wine-making industry in California was beginning to expand from its small established base to meet growing demands. As the number of vineyards expanded and acres of grapevines grew, barrels were needed to store, mature, and transport wine, just as barrels had been needed to store and export herring.

Intrigued by the possibilities, Alistair had sent off his younger son, Jack—with his pregnant daughter-in-law, Mary—to California in a joint venture with Jackson to make wine barrels. He had given Jack limited funds and three years to turn a profit. It had taken less than two. Within a decade, the Jackson-McReynolds Cooperage controlled a growing proportion of the wine barrel business throughout California. Twenty years after leaving Scotland, Jack, Mary, Stuart, Ross and the twins, Jenny and Mavis, had taken the Union-Pacific Railroad towards the East Coast. They had boarded the RMS *Lusitania* in New York—upper second class to travel in style. Only the boys had made it back to Scotland.

Stuart and Ross walked down the main street facing onto the harbor, absorbing the sights, sounds, and smells that their parents would have both known. They were heading to meet their cousin Joanne, who as a "very smart young lady," according to her mother. She volunteered to help with tuition at the Murray Library, set in a tall red sandstone building overlooking the town's stone market cross.

Stuart pushed the door open and entered the library. Ross closed it behind him. Jo was the same age as Ross, and she greeted both boys with a warm smile and a kiss on the cheek. There had been tears at the homecoming, but those had now passed. Jo liked the company of her cousins and had taken it upon herself to make their stay a happy one despite the tragedy that had befallen the family. She had suggested a picnic for lunch out at the rocky point just to the west of town.

"We'll go out to the Billowness. Our fathers spent many happy hours there as children. I've packed a hamper and I hope you don't mind, but I've invited a friend along."

Stuart smiled—he liked to tease his younger cousin—and said, "As long as it's not another dowdy old librarian. One's enough!"

Someone coughed close behind them and Stuart turned to see a woman glaring at him. "Gentlemen, this is a library, and we dowdy old librarians do like it to be quiet."

The young woman facing them was neither dowdy nor old. She was slightly shorter than Stuart, with light brown hair, a button nose, and sparkling green eyes, which had more than a touch of mischief behind them. Stuart stared, dumfounded, unsure what to say.

"That's better!" said the woman, looking at Jo for a couple of seconds before both women burst together into laughter, their faces radiant.

Jo came forward and linked arms with the young woman and made the introductions. "These are my ill-mannered cousins. Ross...," she said, looking up at her cousins in turn, "...and Stuart. Ross and Stuart, this is Nell Abercrombie."

Nell smiled and held out her hand, "I'm very pleased to meet you both."

Stuart held her hand and tried to speak, unsuccessfully, "I'm so sorry, I didn't mean to. I mean, it's a pleasure as well, to meet you that is," before he turned bright red.

Both women laughed again, reveling in Stuart's discomfort. Ross just looked towards the ceiling and rolled his eyes, which made the girls laugh even more.

"Let's get some sea-air into you. You're looking a little flushed, Stuart," said Jo, still giggling at her cousin's embarrassment.

They walked down to the beach and across large stepping stones which at low tide offered a shortcut over a shallow stream to the western edge of the town. As they passed the last sandstone houses, they walked the path that led out to the point. A curved sandy bay sat to their left, and a small golf course to their right. Ross and Jo were walking ahead together, arms linked and chatting away. Stuart and Nell followed behind, the picnic hamper swinging between them.

Nell explained that she and Jo helped those who wanted it with their reading, writing, and arithmetic. "It's often that pupils leave the local school at fourteen to earn a wage. To progress to the better paid clerical jobs, the girls especially, are encouraged to further their education as and when they can. The men also come in for help in the subjects they need to pass their masters certificate that allows them to skipper the herring drifters."

As she talked, Stuart couldn't help but look at her. He found her easy to listen to and liked her casual and relaxed manner. It was easy to see that she and Jo were good friends, and he liked the way she laughed as she clamped a hand down on her head as the wind tried to blow off her hat. They reached the point and settled down in the lee of a stony outcrop as Jo and Ross unpacked the hamper.

Stuart looked back towards the fishing village. "I've seen this."

"You remember this place?" asked Nell.

"No, I wasn't yet born when we left, but we had a watercolor painting hanging above the fireplace, and it must have been painted from near here. My mother used to point to it and tell us that's where we came from and would describe the beach, the rocks, and the coldness of the water."

Remembering his mother and the coldness of the water, he drew silent, and Nell could see the controlled pain inside him. Impulsively, she gently took one of his bandaged hands in hers. "I'm so sorry about your family. It must have been truly awful. I didn't know what to say, so I haven't said anything at all." It was now her turn to be embarrassed and she let go of Stuart's hand just as Jo turned towards them to announce that the picnic was ready.

It was a sunny afternoon and the heat radiated off the red sandstone outcrop. Stuart had asked Nell about her family. She said they lived in Crail, another fishing village three miles further down the coast at the very tip of Fife. "My grandfather served aboard a tea clipper, the *Taeping*, sailing from China to London with cargos of tea. They used to race all the way back. He loves to tell the tale of when the *Taeping* and *Ariel*, both crewed and captained by local men, raced for ninety-nine days from China arriving within twenty-eight minutes of each other. Can you imagine that? Twenty-eight minutes after ninety-nine days! And do you know what? The captain of the *Taeping* shared the bonus for first ship to reach London with the crew of the *Ariel*. Isn't that a great story? With his share my grandfather bought our house in Crail."

"What do your parents do?" asked Stuart.

Nell hesitated and looked down. "My mother died when I was very young, from leukemia. I don't remember her at all. I have her photo and sometimes I stare at it and will myself to remember, but I can't, and then I feel guilty."

Stuart took her soft hand in his and gave it a gentle squeeze, "I'm sorry, I didn't know. I'm sure your mother wouldn't have wanted you to feel guilty. You were just too young, that's all."

Nell looked up at Stuart and smiled as he stared back into her green eyes. He squeezed her hand again before letting it go. "And your father?"

"He's at sea. The days of sailing are fading fast but don't tell my father that. It's in his blood. He captains a merchant sailing schooner, the SV *Broughty Castle*. It trades between

Scotland and the Scandinavian countries across the North Sea. He takes wool, linen, and burlap from Dundee, twenty miles up the coast, and brings back things like timber and cured pork."

"Who looks after you when he's away?"

"My grandfather. Well, we look after each other, really. He spends his time walking the coast and looking out to sea. He misses being out on the ocean but loves when the storms roll in and pound the rocks. He stands there letting the sea-spray soak his face. I think it lets him imagine he's still out at sea crossing the Cape of Good Hope or running before a typhoon, sails tight, battling the wind."

Stuart couldn't help but smile. Nell was babbling away again about storms and names and places he barely knew. He loved listening to her voice, his mind losing itself in the images she conjured up. As he listened to her he realized for the first time since the *Lusitania* that he was relaxed, at ease, and happy.

By mid-afternoon it was time to head back. They packed up, finished the last of the fiery ginger beer that always accompanied picnics, and began walking into town. Ross held the empty hamper, swinging it playfully with Jo. As Stuart followed them he felt Nell's hand tuck under his arm, and they walked back to town together, quietly contented in each other's company. Jo glanced back at them and smiled as if she'd planned it all along, which she had. She was, after all, a very smart young lady.

***

After dinner, uncle John sat Stuart and Ross down, and grandfather Alistair joined them. John and Alistair had stern faces and were seen as serious, taciturn men within the town, a required business demeanor. To the boys, they had always been kind and loving. Stuart and Ross had told their family about their plan of joining the army, and both guessed that they'd been called in to further discuss their intentions.

"We've been talking," said their uncle John, looking over at his father.

"We'd like you to reconsider your plans. There's a home here for you both if you want it. The cooperage is doing well, exports are down due to the war, but that's been offset by an increase in demand for food at home. We're agreed that in time you could both take over the management of the family business. Palmer Jackson has confirmed by telegram that he will either manage our interests out in California, or that over a period of time he will buy out our half of the business. Either way, we've also agreed that the majority of that money will be split between you both—its only right—which will give you both a healthy income. Jackson also sends his regards, with his condolences."

The boys looked at each other. They'd just been told they'd be wealthy men. Maybe not exactly rich compared to those they'd seen travelling first class on the *Lusitania*, but comfortable. But there was no smile between them. No recognition that the rest of their lives could be spent in relative ease while running the family business.

Perhaps their grandpa Alistair saw this as he shifted in his chair and said, "Boys, I've lost a son and a daughter-in-law both of whom I loved dearly. And two grandchildren I never was able to meet. I'm an old man now, and I don't want to lose two more grandchildren, not now I've just got them back safe under my roof. This war kills indiscriminately. Those who come back from it are silent. Silent because they've seen and done things we can't imagine. Thousands are being killed in France. If you stay you can make a difference. If you go, your fate will be out of your hands." He sat back in his chair, looking at his two grandsons.

It was Stuart who replied, his voice wavering as he spoke, "We saw our mother and father drown in front of our eyes, keeping calm even as the water rose above their heads to make it easier on the twins holding on to them." He paused, tears beginning to flow down his cheeks. "Perhaps we should have died out there with them. There were times it would have been easier to give up, but we didn't. We lived for them." Looking over at Ross, he added, "And as we drifted in that cold sea, and watched the German submarine disappear, we made a vow to make those who murdered our family pay."

Ross nodded, his jaw set firmly, "This is something we have to do. Please understand that."

The grandpa, eyes now brimming, stood up and came over to the boys, sitting by each other. Slowly kneeling in front of them, he took one hand each. "I'm proud of you both, but promise us this, promise us as you promised your parents, that you'll live. That you'll protect each other, and that you'll find good men to surround yourself with. I don't know much about war, but I do know that in the thick of battle it isn't fought for ideals or politics or revenge. It's fought for the men beside you. Make sure they are the best you can find."

He stood up and the boys stood as well, embracing their old grandpa. Uncle John came over to put his hands on their shoulders. "Know this too, boys. When you come back, and I pray its soon, everything we've promised will be here waiting for you. In the meantime, if there's anything we can do to help, we'll do it."

The men stood apart, not used to showing their emotions, until Uncle John blew out his cheeks and said, "Right. Who wants a whisky?"

***

Aboard the SV *Broughty Castle,* the crew looked out towards the U-boat lying in the water 100 feet away from their port side. The U-boat's commander, Kapitän von Breunig, watched through powerful brass Leitz naval binoculars from the conning tower as a German boarding party rowed a small collapsible towards the schooner. Its sails were down, sitting dead in the water.

Von Breunig came from a family that valued tradition, honor, and courage. His orders were to sink every enemy merchant vessel encountered within the restricted zone. While he had no hesitation in torpedoing naval vessels, he considered merchant sailors as non-combatants and thus applied prize rules whenever possible. These rules dictated that submarines stop and search merchant vessels to confirm their identity and cargo before sinking them. They took every effort to allow the crews to abandon ship in an orderly fashion under safe passage.

Captain Abercrombie had had little option in stopping. The U-boat had placed itself perfectly ahead of them, slightly off to the port side. Rising out of the sea, its gun crew had raced to the 88-millimeter deck gun, ramming in a shell and firing it across the bows of the SV *Broughty Castle* to explode in her path. The warning was clear—stop or we'll sink you.

Kapitän von Breunig had another reason for watching the progress of the boarding party—Oberfähnrich Hans Breunig, his son. He had connections from his rank and a privileged background. Hans, in his last stages of being an officer cadet, needed experience, and von Breunig had taken the opportunity to have him on board during this voyage. Von Breunig had promised his wife that he would take good care of their son. This boarding party was Hans' first, and Von Breunig looked on with the same paternal concern that any father would.

Crewmen lowered a rope ladder over the side to allow the German sailors to board the sailing ship. Hans came up on deck first. He looked around as Captain Abercrombie walked towards him.

"Kapitän?" asked the young German officer.

"Yes; my name is Abercrombie, captain of the SV *Broughty Castle*."

The German saluted and introduced himself, "Oberfähnrich Breunig. My commander sends his compliments and demands your cooperation." Behind him stood two German sailors, with four more boarding the vessel, all with rifles and black leather webbing with full ammunition pouches.

Abercrombie looked back at the youth. They were both playing a deadly game. There were no other ships in the vicinity, and the U-boat lookouts would warn them if any were sighted. The sailing ship carried no radio, and therefore had sent no distress message. No one knew where they were, and no one was coming to their rescue. The safety of his 24-man crew was paramount. "I would like a guarantee that my crew will be treated as non-combatants."

Hans nodded in reply. "I assure you as a German officer that no harm will come to your men as long as you comply with our demands."

Abercrombie looked around at his crew. "No heroics, gentlemen." Then, looking at the naval officer before him, said, "Our cargo is timber from Bergen, Norway, a neutral country. I can show you the manifest if you wish. It might take some time to find."

Although it could be considered a harmless cargo, wood was needed in increasing demand to shore up the trenches in France.

"That will not be necessary, Captain." The German officer barked an order and four of his sailors disappeared below decks. The two men looked at each other, feeling the rise and fall of the sailing ship as the wind picked up and the sea swell began to increase. After a couple of minutes, a call from below disturbed the awkward silence. One of the Germans reappeared, holding an oily rag in his hands. He came to attention in front of his officer and reported in German. Abercrombie winced when he heard the word, "Fischöl."

Hans questioned the sailor, took the oily rag, rubbing it in his hand and smelling it. He nodded and returning the sailor's salute, Hans dismissed him with a nod to the rope ladder.

"Perhaps, Captain, you forgot about the fish oil, and the cured sides of pork?"

Abercrombie shrugged his shoulders and smiled, "Perhaps I did, perhaps I did."

The young German returned the smile, acknowledging the failed attempt to hide the additional cargo. He shouted an order and the remaining Germans appeared quickly on deck. Hans looked at Abercrombie, "I have to inform you that you are sailing within the restricted zone declared by the Imperial German Navy on February eighteenth. You are flying a British merchant flag and transporting food and timber—contraband cargos. With regret, I must ask you to abandon your vessel, Captain." Looking down at his watch, he added, "You have exactly twenty minutes. Unless another ship is sighted, in which case we will be forced to sink you without further delay."

Hans barked an order and his men began to descend the ladder, slinging their rifles behind them as they did so. With one final nod to Abercrombie, the young officer swung his leg over the gunwale just as a large swell rocked the ship. Abercrombie could see the young man struggle to find a foothold on the ladder, his hands reached out but still slick with fish oil, they had no grip. It was too late, arms windmilling, crying out Hans fell backwards off the ship towards the sea below.

His father saw it all happen as if in slow motion, gripping his binoculars tightly, immediately shouting out commands to bring the U-boat closer to the sailing ship.

Aboard the SV *Broughty Castle*, Abercrombie ran to the ladder. Hans had fallen onto the edge of the collapsible boat the sailors had rowed over, cracking his head on the side before tumbling face down into the sea. The German sailors, hampered by their slung rifles and webbing, were shouting at each other, but none of them could move fast enough to grab the young officer floating in the water. Abercrombie ran ten feet down the deck, shouting, "Man overboard!" Then he vaulted feet first over the side of his ship, 15 feet down into the cold North Sea.

Abercrombie came up to the surface next to the floating German and grabbed Hans' collar and turned him over, face towards the sky. The boarding party threw him a rope and he grabbed it with one hand, keeping a hold of the young German officer in his other. The sailors hauled Abercrombie and Hans into the collapsible boat. Abercrombie looked over. One of the older sailors he assumed to be a petty officer was thumping the back of the young German, then pumping Hans' arms up and down. The officer's head was bleeding down one side. For a moment, Abercrombie thought Hans was dead, but then the man began to cough violently, retching up seawater as he struggled to get air into his lungs.

Ten minutes later, Kapitän von Breunig stood in front of Abercrombie. They were both on the deck of the *Broughty Castle*. "I wanted to thank you. Not only for saving a German naval officer, but also for saving my son."

Abercrombie looked back in surprise. "Your son?"

Von Breunig nodded. "He has a concussion, but he will live due to your quick actions. Do you have a son?"

"No, a daughter about the same age. Her name is Nell," replied Abercrombie.

Von Breunig smiled, "If not for this war, maybe they would have met and become friends."

"This war will not last forever."

"No, it will not, but it does continue, and I still have my orders."

"You're still going to sink my ship?" Abercrombie asked with resignation.

"With regret, yes. I must carry out my duty. My orders state I may not be able to prevent your crew harm, but they also make no restriction on providing your crew assistance if I can."

Abercrombie looked at Von Breunig in confusion.

"It is my intention to tow your lifeboats towards Aberdeen for as long as it is safe for us to do so."

Abercrombie looked in amazement at the German captain. He knew the U-boat commander's actions would mean the difference between floating 100 miles off the Scottish coast, vulnerable to the North Sea storms and strong currents with a good chance of dying from exposure, or living. "You would do that?"

The German nodded. "Yes. You will be given another ship, but no one could have given me another son."

"But when you go back, what will happen?"

Von Breunig shrugged. "Admiral von Pohl is a reasonable man, and you did save a promising young German naval officer at a risk to your own life." He hesitated. "And I believe my days serving in U-boats are over; it is no longer how I wish to fight this war. I will request a post with the High Seas Fleet, though perhaps my next ship will be a staff desk."

Abercrombie couldn't help but admire the man and he held out his hand. "Thank you, Captain, for helping my crew."

"Perhaps in war, it is even more important than ever to have honor. Now, if you can prepare your men, Captain."

Abercrombie issued orders and the merchant seamen were soon in their two lifeboats. They were passed a tow line and looked on as the U-boat's deck gun crew loaded and fired a high explosive shell into the waterline of the schooner, followed by two more. The proud sailing ship splintered apart as the shells ripped through the wooden hull and the sea rushed in. She listed quickly towards them before capsizing and going under. Wooden wreckage and planed timber floating on the water. The death of the sailing vessel seemed particularly poignant to those who watched her sink, as if some crime had been committed against a ship whose sole purpose was to sail with the wind across the seas. Abercrombie shook his head at the sadness and waste of it all.

As the SV *Broughty Castle* was sinking, Kapitän von Breunig ordered the two lifeboats be arranged for towing, one behind the other. The lifeboats and their crews were towed for a few hours until they were 10 miles off Aberdeen, the coastline just visible ahead. The tow line was slipped, and three distress flares arched into the sky, one after another. With a last wave from the conning tower, the submarine submerged.

***

On Wednesday, Stuart and Ross returned to the library. Jo looked up to see her cousins and smiled, quickly telling Stuart that Nell had gone next door to the bakery. He smiled and went to find her. The bell tinkled above the small shop's door as he opened it, and Nell's face lit up in a warm smile when she saw Stuart.

"I'm just on my way home," she said.

Stuart couldn't help but look disappointed, and she saw it. "You could always accompany me. It's a nice day for a walk," she said, her head tilted to the side.

Stuart beamed. "Would you like me to?"

Nell made a show of trying to decide whether or not it would be a good idea, rubbing her chin with one hand. "Well, as long as you don't mind escorting a dowdy old librarian," and she laughed as Stuart began to blush.

Looking at the girl behind the bakery counter, Nell asked for two cold meat pies, two rhubarb tarts, and a bottle of ginger beer. Stuart insisted on paying, and they left the shop to walk down the open-sided main street facing the harbor towards the eastern side of town. They passed the lifeboat station and cooperage and entered the narrow streets where the fishermen lived.

As ballast on the trip from Holland to pick up the barrels of herring, the Dutch traders brought blueware-china plates and cups and thick deep-orange wavy roof tiles, called pantiles. The small white fisherman's houses were tall and narrow, built right up to the sea shore and the pantiles shimmered in the sun from radiated heat. Soon they were past the last of the houses and following a path between the sea and the fields. East Fife was good farming land, and fields stretched all the way down to the shoreline. They passed an old fisherman walking towards them, shoulders hunched, leading an even older white-muzzled black Labrador. Stuart nodded his head by way of greeting and said, "It's a fine day for a walk."

The old fisherman looked at him and then up at the sky. He replied, "Aye, but we'll pay for it!" before walking on.

"What did he mean?" Stuart asked Nell.

She smiled. "It's our dour Scottish Presbyterian upbringing—if we're having fun, we either feel guilty or expect divine retribution."

Stuart laughed before cupping his hand to his mouth as Nell did exactly the same. They both giggled at each other like schoolchildren. Then Stuart looked out to sea towards a small island, five miles off the coast. "What's the name of the island?" he asked.

Nell looked over the sea. "It's called the May Island. At this time of year, there'll be puffins, razorbills, and guillemots out there. It's an important colony for seabirds. In the old days there used to be a monastery on the island, but the Vikings raided it and killed all the monks. If you look hard, you can see the lighthouse. It was built by Robert Louis Stevenson's grandfather—he built them all over Scotland."

"Have you ever been out there?" asked Stuart, impressed at her knowledge.

"No, but sometimes folk go out for a day-trip. I've never been myself. I'd like to one day, maybe if the sea's not too rough!" and she laughed, making Stuart happy once more.

They sat down by a rocky outcrop of honey-colored sandstone to eat their impromptu lunch. Nell said they were called the Caiplie Coves, hewn by the wind and rain into a series of arches and caves. "We should have brought two bottles," Stuart said, waving the single bottle of ginger beer in his hand.

"We can share," said Nell, taking the bottle and raising it delicately to her lips, then handing it back. "If that's not too unladylike, that is."

Stuart took the bottle from her hand and laughed. "You're not like all the other dowdy old librarians I know." She hit him playfully on the shoulder. He pretended to recoil from a gigantic blow and she laughed even more.

"So, tell me about California. What's it like? I've only heard stories of the gold rush and the earthquake that struck San Francisco ten years ago. In the library, we have *Sea Wolf* and *McTeague,* and my father read me *Two Years Before the Mast* at bedtime when he was home, but you've actually been there."

Stuart looked out to May Island and gathered his thoughts. "It's a beautiful part of the world, really. There are redwood trees so tall it's hard to see them properly up close. You have to step back from them to see the tops. And nice weather—warmer than this!" he said with a smile, as on cue, a gentle but cold breeze swirled past them.

"San Francisco is beautiful, too. It's all rebuilt now, with big wooden mansions on the hills and smaller terraced homes stepping down towards the bay. There's a part of the city called Chinatown, where the Chinese workers who came over to build the transcontinental railroads settled. You can walk through it and not hear anything but Chinese; the food is good too. They have this food called *chow fun,* large flat noodles stir-fried with slivered duck and vegetables with something called soy sauce. Ross and I loved them, although I never did get the hang of chopsticks," he said.

Nell watched him as he talked. Both he and his brother had a mixture of soft accents—their parent's Scottish lilt and a relaxed American intonation. It was pleasing to her ear, faintly transatlantic. He had dimples when he smiled, and he smiled a lot, despite many reasons not to. She hadn't asked him about what had happened as the *Lusitania* sank. Jo had told her what she knew, but Nell had glimpsed the pain behind the smile when they'd gone out to the Billowness on their first picnic. His face was still a bit bruised, and his hands were bandaged. She also knew he and Ross were going to enlist in the army.

At first, this hadn't bothered her. They were, after all, at war with Germany. Young men were enlisting to fight throughout Scotland, encouraged to do so as their patriotic duty, but now things had changed. Now the young man smiling next to her as he talked about seeing Caruso singing in San Francisco, sunny vineyards, and sneaking bottles of red wine to drink with his brother, was becoming important to her. At their very first meeting, she had a feeling that he was special. The more she listened to him, the more that feeling took root inside her mind, and more importantly, inside her heart.

After their picnic, they walked along the coastal path to Crail. Approaching from the headland, Stuart looked down at the small stone picturesque harbor, with its own jumble of pantiled, crow-stepped white houses working their way up the sloping road that led from the harbor to the village center. It was one of the prettiest scenes he'd ever seen.

"It's so beautiful here."

Nell smiled, "It is nice, isn't it?" she said with a hint of pride. "Artists come to sit up here and paint in the summer when the weather's not so windy. Every town and village in the East Neuk has its own special character, but I like Crail. But then of course I would; it's my village."

Stuart reluctantly turned to look back towards the way they had come. "Well, I should be heading back. Ross will wonder where on earth I've disappeared to."

Nell twinkled up at him. "I'm sure Jo kept him entertained." She looked down and then up into Stuart's eyes. "Thank you for walking me home. I hope it wasn't too far?"

"I enjoyed it; really, I did." He hesitated, then looking over at her, asked, "Will you be at the library tomorrow?"

"Would you like me to come over?" Nell asked, her chest suddenly pounding in anticipation. She felt his hands take a hold of hers. "Yes, I would like that very much."

She smiled with relief. Slightly embarrassed, she looked at Stuart said, "Then I'll be there."

As he walked away she stayed, watching him go until he turned and waved from the headland. She waved back, aware that she hadn't moved an inch since he'd said goodbye and wondering if for a moment he'd wanted to kiss her. Nell blushed. It would have been very forward of him—but also very nice.

The thought stayed with her all night like a soft warm blanket, comforting her as she slept until her grandfather came into the room and shook her gently. She opened her eyes and sat up with a start.

Her grandfather was clutching a yellow telegram, and he was clearly upset. "It's your father."

Nell sat up. "What does the telegram say?"

"Just that I should go to Dundee, 'regarding your son.' An old shipmate I sailed with sent it. He's a now a watch officer with the coastguard up in Aberdeen. I know him; he wouldn't have sent it if it wasn't important, and he can't breach security with details. We have to read between the lines, go to the Borland Shipping Company, and find out what we can. The *Broughty Castle's* one of their ships."

Nell hugged her grandfather. "I'll pack an overnight bag, just in case we need it," and she kissed his rough cheek.

                              ***

Stuart and Ross looked out of the train, lost in thought, as the enormity of what they were doing hit them both. The local train would take them up to St. Andrews, where they would change for the trip onwards to Perth and then to Inverness and Fort George.

The early morning goodbyes had been hard. Grandpa Alistair had held back tears, but only just, and blamed himself for getting old and soft. Uncle John had made sure they had what they needed and had sorted out bank accounts for them both to draw money out of if required. "Bank accounts might not do you much good where you're going, so here's some cash," he'd said, handing over two brown sealed envelopes. "And some of these might come in handy one day."

He'd handed Stuart and Ross each a small leather pouch secured by a drawstring, each containing a half-dozen gold sovereigns. They had packed light, not expecting to need much in the way of clothing. Jo insisted in walking them along the harbor and up the hill to the station and waited on the platform for the train. Stuart was surprised when after hugging and kissing him on the cheek, Jo embraced Ross. Tears streamed down her face and she had to go, but not before kissing his lips tenderly.

Stuart sat opposite Ross. He caught Ross's eye and asked, "Kissing cousins?" with an upraised eyebrow and a smile.

Ross blushed and looked down in embarrassment. "It just sort of happened. Anyway, what about you and Nell? The last time I saw you two, you were arm in arm and you both looked quite happy about it."

Stuart shrugged. In truth, he didn't know. In the short time they'd been together, Nell had come to dominate his thoughts, but despite her promise, there'd been no sign of her on Thursday. He'd lain awake during the night thinking of her, trying to batter down his disappointment. There had been no sign of her during the morning, and Jo had been unable to help.

The train stopped at Crail and he scanned the platform hopefully, but she wasn't there, and he felt more despondent than ever. He must have imagined the closeness he'd felt between them and tried unsuccessfully to think of something else as the rolling countryside passed by. After a while, the train began a gentle descent towards St. Andrews. Looking out of the windows, the brothers could see the ruined cathedral's elegant spires, the town's churches, and the university, one of the oldest in the world. The train slowed as it approached the station, and as it passed the famous Old Course, Stuart could see tweed-clad golfers on the penultimate 17th green, called the *Road Hole*. The brothers grabbed their bags. They had three minutes to catch the Perth train, waiting patiently ahead of them on the same track.

They stepped down onto the platform and hurried towards the next train. Stuart started to step up onto the Perth train behind his brother when he heard someone calling his name. He turned, and there was Nell, running down the platform towards him, holding on to her hat with one hand. He threw his bag after his brother and stepped down. Nell ran towards him. For a second, he was unsure what to do, until she threw her arms around his neck in an embrace. At that very moment he realized two things—that he felt whole again, and that he was falling in love.

Nell looked up at him. "I was so worried I would miss you. I couldn't come; my father's ship was sunk...."

Stuart cut her off. "Is he all right?" he asked with a note of genuine concern in his voice.

"Yes, yes; he's fine. All the crew were rescued, but we didn't know, so my grandfather and I stayed in Dundee. My father arrived late last night and then this morning I came to try and find you before you went. I knew you'd have to stop here, but I was so afraid I'd missed you already."

Nell was beginning to cry. Stuart didn't know if she was choking up from relief or sadness. Then the train guard blew his whistle. "All aboard for Perth! All aboard!" Steam escaped from the massive engine as it prepared to leave the station.

Stuart drew Nell closer. Looking down at her, he kissed the tear away from her right cheek, and then the left one, and holding her face tenderly in his hands, kissed her softly on her lips. "I have to go, sweetheart. I'll write; I promise."

Nell clutched him. "Darling, we've had no time, I'm so sorry!"

The train began to crawl. Stuart squeezed her to him one last time and then heard Ross shouting as the train moved down the platform, "Stuart! Come on!"

Stuart kissed her quickly once more and then ran down the platform, jumping onto the train as his brother grabbed his hand. They both looked back at Nell waving at them and waved back. Ross shouted, "I'll take good care of him!" and then the train picked up speed, and they were away.

Ross looked at his brother and raised a questioning eyebrow.

Stuart shrugged and smiled. "It just sort of happened."

CHAPTER SEVEN

The Seaforths

Fort George, the Highlands of Scotland

Fort George was built on a cold exposed promontory that pinched into the Moray Firth sea estuary, whose waves crashed onto its weathered battlements. It had been used as an army barracks since 1757 and was at present the regimental headquarters of the Seaforth Highlanders. With a proud history, its soldiers were recruited from the remotest settlements in the highlands and islands of Scotland. The McReynolds stared at its foreboding entrance set across a long narrow heavy timber bridge.

Stuart glanced over at Ross. "Are you ready for this?"

Ross smiled. "Well, I'm not sure what 'this' is going to be yet, but yes, I'm ready. We owe it to others to be here."

"We do." He looked at the entrance ahead of them beyond the bridge, remembering how they had run down the side of the *Lusitania*. "Together on three?"

Ross nodded. "Together on three."

They began to walk across the bridge. Ahead, they saw a Scottish soldier. He was tall and wearing a khaki green-brown wool service army jacket with a single stripe on the arms, a dark-green MacKenzie-tartan kilt, diced red-and-white thick socks or hose under khaki military spats, and heavy-soled army highland shoes. On his head, he wore a diced glengarry, with the silver-metal stag's-head badge of the Seaforth Highlanders on its side. He looked formidable.

Ross whispered to his brother, "I think the world as we know it is about to change."

As they drew closer, the soldier surprised them by grinning. "So, you're here after all. Good."

Stuart looked at the soldier. "Angus?"

Lance Corporal Angus Rhuairi MacIntyre held out his hand, shaking Stuart's and then his brother's. Ross looked at him, stroking his own chin. "No beard?"

Angus smiled. "No beard. It's against regulations nowadays, and I was tired of it anyway." He looked at the two brothers. "As you're both here, I'm assuming you're still wanting to join?"

Stuart and Ross nodded and together said, "Yes."

Angus smile. "Then I have good news—we need you."

Major Sinclair had two problems. The first was that he needed men, eight of them, to make up a section.

In the British Army, four sections made up a platoon, four platoons made up a company, and four companies together with headquarters and other supporting units made up a battalion. The current territorial battalion in the Seaforth Highlanders was below strength. Given time, he might have been able to fill the gaps, but time was one commodity he didn't have.

It was May, 1915, and the 51st Highland Division was being sent to the Western Front in France, and most of its battalions were there or on their way. Major Sinclair was now sending a territorial battalion of Seaforth Highlanders to join them. However, the battalion was short one company, because the company was short one platoon, because the platoon was still short one section of eight men.

Sinclair's other problem was Colonel Lyall, the battalion's commanding officer. The colonel was on his way from a meeting at Cameron Barracks in Inverness. Together, the Seaforth Highlanders and the Cameron Highlanders comprised one brigade within the Highland Division, and

Colonel Lyall had given assurances that his battalion was ready to deploy to France; assurances based on Sinclair finding one more section of eight men for his battalion—by hook or by crook.

At present, he had one man, Lance Corporal MacIntyre, so like all good officers, Sinclair had delegated the task of finding seven more men to a sergeant.

Stuart and Ross were sitting outside Sergeant Harris' office in a cold drafty corridor. One man sat a few seats down, his arms crossed, hands tucked into his armpits for warmth. His face was hidden from the brothers by a protruding architectural support. Before Stuart could engage him in conversation, Angus came out of the office and beckoned the two brothers inside.

Sergeant Harris looked up at them from behind his desk. He had short dark hair, graying at the sides, and the lines on his forehead creased into a questioning look at the men as they entered. He was lean and wiry and looked every part the career soldier. "MacIntyre here has been telling me how it is you met, and that you want to join our territorials. It's quite a story, I have to say. Do you see all those men outside?" He pointed towards the fort's main parade ground.

"Yes, Sergeant," Stuart replied.

The square was alive with formations of men. Non-commissioned officers, the corporals and sergeants that actually ran the daily tasks that allowed any military unit to function, were barking clipped orders and haranguing individual soldiers for reasons they couldn't quite ascertain.

"They're under orders to depart to France today, but we're short one section. Make no mistake—the battalion will depart today. If it departs minus one section, the colonel will get a bollocking from the brigadier, so he will give the major a bollocking, and the major will give me a bollocking. You wouldn't want that to happen to me, would you?" asked Harris.

Stuart and Ross replied in unison, "No, Sergeant."

"Excellent," said Sergeant Harris, nodding. "If, however, I can tell the major we have a section in final training, and he can show the paperwork to the colonel, then all will be well. And you want all to be well, don't you?"

Stuart and Ross replied together once again, "Yes, Sergeant."

"Excellent," he said. "If you agree to join, you will depart for France next Friday to catch up with the battalion. That's in seven days, Gentlemen." He looked at the men to gauge their reaction, but the brothers showed no signs of alarm. Both men simply nodded.

"Excellent. Your training will continue once in France. Don't worry; I promise we won't throw you into the front lines. Over the next week, you will be trained in the basics." He looked over at Angus, standing by the door. "Take them to the doctor for the once-over, and then run back here for paperwork."

Angus stood to attention and replied, "Yes, Sergeant."

As Angus opened the door to the corridor, Harris muttered, "Now, I just need to find five more men."

In reply, a strong southern Irish accent came from the corridor. "Then I'm thinking we came at the right time then, Sergeant?"

Stuart and Ross stood dumbfounded. Outside the door were the four Irishmen they'd last seen in a Kinsale pub a week ago and had never expected to see again. Angus stood speechless—they all did—until Sergeant Harris asked, "Well, do any of you know these men?"

"I hope so, Sergeant. I certainly hope so." The Irishmen parted, and Sergeant Harris stood to attention as Colonel Lyall strode into the office with Major Sinclair behind him.

Lyall sported a salt-and-pepper moustache under a red nose and red cheeks. The complexion of the nose was helped along with regular amounts of gin and tonic, and he had a rather unmilitary round stomach. Despite his paternal looks, he fiercely protected his troops against anyone who would try to interfere with them. He also took an interest in his soldiers and their welfare, which made him a popular commanding officer. Right now, he was looking for a section of soldiers to complete the battalion's roster, which had been asked for by the division staff.

"At ease, Sergeant," he said, looking at Harris. "How are we doing with that missing section? Surely you've eight men by now."

Sergeant Harris made a show of looking at the paperwork on his desk before answering, "We are forming a section around Lance Corporal MacIntyre, sir."

The colonel looked around the room, noticing Angus for the first time. "And who are you forming around him, Sergeant?"

"These two men have been recommended, sir," replied Harris, nodding in the direction of Stuart and Ross.

"Recommended by whom, Sergeant?"

"By MacIntyre, sir."

Lyall looked back at Angus who was standing at attention and staring into the vacant space above the commanding officer's head.

"Service record?"

"Four years Lovat Scouts, four years Fourth Battalion, Seaforth Highlanders, sir."

"Lovat Scouts?" repeated Lyall with a meaningful look at Major Sinclair.

"Yes, sir."

"With a marksmanship award, I see?" Lyall looked at the rare junior ranks' Best Shot expert marksman qualification on Angus' lower-left sleeve.

"Yes, sir," replied Angus with a hint of pride.

"And how do you know these men, Lance Corporal MacIntyre?"

Angus hesitated. He didn't know if the McReynolds brothers would want their story known, but the question had to be answered. "We were aboard the *Lusitania* together, sir."

Lyall peered at Angus and then at Stuart and Ross. "Well, bless my soul. And you all survived?"

Thinking that their presence in the office was proof enough that they'd survived, Stuart paused. Then a thought came to him. "Yes, sir; thanks to the four men standing outside. They rowed miles out to sea to rescue us, sir."

Lyall peered around Major Sinclair to the four men still standing outside the office. "Rowed, you said?" he confirmed with Stuart.

"Yes, sir. In a small red skiff, sir."

"Well, bless my soul. Bring them in, Sinclair. Bring them in, and let's see them."

Sinclair ushered the four men in, and they stood in a line before the commanding officer who asked, "And where are you from, men?"

"Ireland, sir. County Cork," said Seamus.

"Ireland? Well, well, well, this is a strange gathering isn't it, Sergeant?"

Harris replied with a perfunctory, "Yes, sir," not entirely sure what else to say but beginning to crave a cigarette.

"And where are you from?" he asked, now looking at Stuart and his brother.

"We grew up in America, sir, but our parents were both Scottish," replied Stuart.

"America. We can enlist Americans can't we, Sergeant?"

"Yes, sir. We've checked."

"And you men want to join up together, is that it?" asked Lyall, now reaching for the pipe in his right pocket while looking at the McReynolds and O'Connells.

While there was much more to the story than that, Stuart decided brevity was probably the best way forward and answered for them all, "Yes, sir!"

Tapping his pipe, and finding the whole situation amusing, Colonel Lyall looked at Angus. "And do you recommend these men as well, Lance Corporal?"

Angus looked flustered, unsure what to say. Seamus spoke up first. "Sir, if you'll beg our pardon, we have recommendations from the Cunard Line," and he held out a letter in his hand.

Sinclair took it and started reading and while he did, the Irishmen shared nods and badly hidden smiles with Stuart and Ross. The O'Connells had used the money from the Cunard Line to buy ferry and train tickets after leaving some behind for their families, and some for themselves to find their way up to Fort George.

Seamus hadn't told the rest that the morning he'd left home, he'd come downstairs before anyone was up to find his mother waiting for him in the kitchen. She had donned a green shawl to keep the morning's cold air at bay.

She wasn't there to stop him. She'd simply said, "There you are, Seamus. I knew you'd be down, and I know where you're going. Be careful, son. I don't say it that often, but I've always loved you as only a mother can."

His mother had hugged him, and then had tried to dry both his eyes and her own with a handkerchief.

"Are the others going with you?" she'd asked.

"Yes, Ma."

"I thought so. Then take care of each other, and God go with you all. Take this—and you'd better be on your way before your father knows."

She'd handed him a small thick pocket-sized bible, a plain cheese sandwich wrapped in waxed paper, and an apple. With one last hug and a mother's fierce kiss on his cheek, her trembling hands holding his face, she'd turned to go upstairs. He'd left the house with tears streaming down his face.

Finished reading, Major Sinclair looked up at his colonel. "It's a letter from the Cunard Board thanking these men for their rescue effort and praising their initiative, decisiveness, endurance, and courage, sir."

"Just the men we need, Sergeant. Just the men we need," said Lyall before disappearing into a cloud of white smoke from his pipe.

Sergeant Harris nodded. "Yes, sir."

"But that still leaves us one man short, Sergeant. Doesn't it?"

"Yes, sir," agreed Harris.

"Well, that's no good. No good at all. I need to send the battalion roster off now, right now, confirming we have who I said we did. That's why we came over. Are you telling me there's not one more man willing to join these men today?"

A cough came from down the corridor, outside the open door.

Sergeant Harris looked up in alarm towards Sinclair, who took a deep breath. "There is one man, sir, but I'm not sure he's suitable...."

"Not suitable?" echoed his commanding officer in irritation. "Not suitable? I need one single recruit in order to rubber stamp my battalion's move to France, and you're saying he may not be suitable? What's his name, man. What's his name?" Harris began leafing through his paperwork, but the question was answered by a deep voice coming from the office door.

"Munro, sir, Murdo Munro."

Lyall turned around, took the pipe out of his mouth and silently stared. Sergeant Harris looked down at his desk, and Major Sinclair looked at his shoes.

Before them stood a mountain of a man, larger and far more muscular than Ross, Connor, or even Angus, and they were all big men. He had close-cropped tight black curly hair and deep, kind brown eyes. Despite his size, he seemed gentle and non-threatening. But it was neither his size nor his features that had drawn their attention, it was his dark-brown skin.

Colonel Lyall said, "Well, bless my soul, indeed."

***

Murdo Munro had been sitting outside Sergeant Harris' office for three days. He had arrived on Wednesday, and after a short interview with Harris, had been told to wait outside, so he had. All day. On Thursday he came back and sat on the same chair in the corridor. Towards lunchtime, Major Sinclair had spoken to him, and after talking with Harris, had told him to wait, so he had. All day. When the two men had come in on Friday, he was still there. No one was quite sure if he'd ever left. Neither Sinclair nor Harris were sure a black man could join the British Army.

Murdo came from Nova Scotia, a maritime province off the Canadian eastern seaboard, and his family history was complicated.

His ancestors had been slaves in the American Colonies and had worked on a plantation in North Carolina for a Scottish master. The foreman had taught them Gaelic instead of English, to prevent them from speaking with slaves from other plantations and planning escapes. When the colonies had declared independence in 1776 and began fighting the British, many American slaves had been liberated by British soldiers. As a consequence, some had become Black Loyalists. His ancestors were among them. They became freed African-Americans fighting for the British Colonial forces in return for certificates of freedom.

Evacuated to Canada after the war, they had founded Birchtown, Nova Scotia, the largest settlement of freed black Africans in North America. Those who survived the harsh winters persevered to hack and forge an existence from the land and sea, taking up farming, forestry, and fishing for cod. Murdo's family had found itself felling trees.

When war was declared with Germany in 1914, many
Nova Scotian blacks, including Murdo, volunteered to join
the Canadian Expeditionary Force. At the time, the Canadian Department of Militia and Defense's policy towards recruitment was to leave the matter entirely up to the whims
and prejudices of commanding officers. As a result, the vast
majority of blacks, facing institutional discrimination, were
rejected. Including Murdo. Unperturbed, he'd worked his
passage on a Halifax cargo steamer across the Atlantic to
Glasgow and had been rejected from three Scottish regiments so far. At least the Seaforths had let him sit down and
wait. The others had told him to bugger off, only they hadn't
been quite so polite.

Lyall looked at Murdo. "You're black," he said.
     Murdo hesitated before saying, "Yes, sir."
     Lyall inspected Murdo while Murdo stared at the wall in
front of him, copying Angus' stance. "Where are you from?"
Lyall asked.
     Murdo replied, briefly outlining his lineage to everyone
in the room.
     Lyall looked at Harris, who looked at Sinclair, who
looked back at Lyall, who asked in exasperation, "Well, can
we even enlist this man?"
     Major Sinclair tightened his lips, as he did when he was
vexed by some administrative problem, of which Murdo
Munro was one of many. "Sergeant Harris and I have made
enquiries, sir. There are no regulations pertaining to this situation. Although the updated Manual of Military Law does
say that 'negroes or persons of color' can't be promoted past
the rank of sergeant. Which does infer we can enlist him.
The general opinion is that the decision to train him rests
with the commanding officer."
     "And who's that in this sort of case?" asked Lyall.
     "Well, you, sir," replied Sinclair.

"Well, of course I am. Of course I am." He started relighting his pipe, looking silently at Murdo while weighing his conflicting thoughts. He knew of no black men in the Seaforths, and he was slightly worried at what the reaction might be to one appearing in their midst. On the other hand, he thought with a chuckle, Clan Munro was one of the Seaforth's historic clans for recruitment, and he did need one more warm body, right now.

Murdo sensed his fate was in the balance and said unbidden: *Beannaicht' gu robh Iehòbhah treun, mo charraig 's mo threòir; mo làmh a theagaisgeas gu cath, 's gu còmhrag mhaith mo mheòir.*

Angus turned and stared open-mouthed, before catching Sergeant Harris's disapproving eye and snapped his eyes front.

Lyall looked at Murdo. "What was that you said?" he asked.

"It's Gaelic, sir. We retained it within the family from the days in South Carolina, and it was useful for talking with the Scottish settlers in Nova Scotia. 'Blessed be the lord my strength who trains my hands to fight and my fingers to battle.' It just came to me, sir." And then in further explanation, said, "Psalm 144." Murdo paused, unsure of the situation. "I'm sorry for speaking out of turn, sir," he said, and then stopped talking.

Murdo looked at the commanding officer, who stared back at him, repeating slowly, "Blessed be the lord my strength, who trains my hands to fight, and my fingers to battle." He smiled and suddenly patted Murdo on the shoulder. "And in Gaelic. Well done; very well done, my lad. Very well done indeed."

He turned to Sergeant Harris and said, "Well, I think we have our section, don't you, Sergeant?"

Harris looked utterly perplexed, but with nothing further to add, replied as he had all day. "Yes, sir."

"Very well. Major Sinclair will sort out the paperwork. Let me have it as soon as you can." He turned to go, and Harris sprung to attention. The others followed suit as best they could.

"Carry on, men. Carry on." The men relaxed fractionally as their commanding officer left the room and walked down the corridor.

Sinclair said. "Sort out the paperwork, Sergeant Harris, as soon as you can." Then he left the room to go to his office.

"Yes, sir," said Harris, now left in his crowded office with Lance Corporal MacIntyre, Stuart and Ross, four unnamed Irishmen, and as far as he knew it, the only black soldier in the entire Highland Division.

**

Cigarette smoked, Sergeant Harris walked down the corridor to Major Sinclair's office with the paperwork squared away. "We don't have anyone to train them, sir," he stated as he handed over the paperwork.

"Ah, yes. Colonel Lyall had an idea about that. You see, the Mounted Highland Brigade has its own independent unit of sharpshooters. The Lovat Scouts."

Harris nodded. The Lovat Scouts had had a mounted role in the open veldts of the Boer War and had kept their reservist yeomanry cavalry status ever since. As such, they were now attached to a mounted unit, not the infantry.

Sinclair continued. "It's the colonel's idea to form his own sharpshooters for his battalion. Given MacIntyre's marksmanship skills and background, he suggests we begin with his section." He looked up at Harris expecting resistance but was surprised to see the sergeant thinking the proposition over carefully before answering.

"Sir, I fought with our second battalion at Magersfontein and Paardeberg, during the Boer War in South Africa. In both battles, the Boers pinned us down. There was no cover; we just laid flat on the dried earth and dead grass. I saw men shot through the head two or three times by Boers firing German Mauser 95 rifles from five hundred yards. You see, the Boers could only see our pith helmets. They didn't know if we were alive or dead, so they just kept shooting at us all day as if we were targets. We lost so many men at Paardeberg they called it Bloody Sunday. I lost a good friend there. We'd joined up together from Gairloch. When we eventually recovered our dead, he had four holes in his pith helmet.

"If we can train men to do that, sir, I'll support in any way I can. We've both seen how good the Germans are at sniping, sir."

Sinclair nodded. The major was middle-aged, tall and lean. He wore metal-rimmed glasses that lent him an academic look that matched his intelligence and modern outlook—unusual traits among his peers. He and Harris had fought together in France at the battles of the Marne, Aisne, and Messines in 1914, before being recalled to help mobilize the Seaforth's territorial battalions for deployment. They had mutual respect and a bond forged in action.

"I'm glad you agree, Sergeant, because I'd like you to spend a few days with them if you can."

Harris looked at his major in surprise. "Away from the desk, sir?"

"Away from the desk, Sergeant," agreed the officer with a smile before adding quickly, "But not before you tidy up the loose ends. Why don't we have MacIntyre show them the basics for three days while you clear your desk, and then you can take over. We only have seven days to make them look like soldiers."

Harris smiled, his mind already thinking of the challenge ahead. After a few moments he came to a decision. "Sir, an awful lot of initial training is about marching up and down the square, kit inspections, uniform inspections, cleaning stuff that's already clean, polishing stuff that's already polished, and making your bed so perfectly you don't dare sleep in it, all while being yelled at in a military fashion. I can do that, but with your permission, there's always time for that later. They're all fit men by the look of them, so no need to build them up physically for weeks on end to get them into shape like some of them we get. I'd like to concentrate on the stuff that might actually keep them alive on a battlefield, not looking pretty on the parade ground."

Sinclair smiled. "That's pretty unorthodox thinking, Sergeant. You do as you see best. I'll back you up if needed, and remember it's the colonel's idea, so quote him as your authority." As an afterthought, he said, "I'll type up a letter for you to grease the wheels, with a copy for MacIntyre."

"Thank you, sir." Harris nodded, happy to have the leeway he wanted. "Speaking of MacIntyre, sir, he seems solid enough. He has eight years' service and from the badge on his sleeve obviously knows how to shoot. If he's going to train men and assist me, an extra stripe would help."

Sinclair nodded. "Corporal seems appropriate under the circumstances. Do the paperwork and I'll sign it."

Harris looked thoughtfully at his officer, "The sergeant major, sir, he may take an unhealthy interest in what we're doing. You know what he's like."

"I think Sergeant Major Skaig will be busy enough right now without sticking his nose into our business. You just get those men looking and thinking like soldiers. Only the battlefield can do the rest."

"Yes, sir. I agree with you on that point."

Harris brought himself to attention before being dismissed, but then added, "Just one more thing if you please, sir."

Major Sinclair looked up with a barely concealed look of exasperation, "Yes, sergeant?"

"The dog, sir."

"The dog?" asked the major. "What dog?"

"The one tied up outside, sir. I believe it's called Lucky...."

CHAPTER EIGHT

Misfits

Corporal MacIntyre surveyed the seven men in front of him. They all wore basic British green-brown khaki service uniform with boots and puttees—no kilts. That had been Mac-Intyre's suggestion, as he had explained to Sergeant Harris. "We'll be crawling a lot, sergeant, literally slithering on the ground, lying down and firing from the prone position and then disengaging to fire from another. Have you ever tried crawling backward in a kilt? It's embarrassing."

Harris had laughed out loud, quickly warming to his newly promoted corporal, and had agreed to the standard issue uniform worn by the majority of the British Army with tunics cut in the Scottish style. On their heads they wore green-brown khaki Balmoral caps, 'Tam o' Shanters,' the sloping headgear that highland regiments wore in the field, pulled down to the right, exposing the Seaforth regimental crest on the left under a swatch of tartan. On one sleeve, they wore a square patch of MacKenzie tartan; the other sleeve bore the stylized red-and-black round HD patch of the 51st Highland Division.

Corporal MacIntyre looked at the section in their new uniforms. "Right! Listen in!" he shouted. Before continuing, he shook his head in mock despair. "Looking at you lot is like listening to the beginning of a bad joke. Four Irishmen, a black Canadian, and you two," he said, looking at Stuart and Ross, "I don't even know what you are. Americans, Scots, Scots-Americans or American-Scots? I suppose it doesn't really matter. You speak funny, but you're here.

That's what counts. What a bunch of misfits," he said with a smile, before carrying on.

"The colonel has a special role in mind for you. You'll be working independently, which is good, as you won't really fit into the main battalion for a while. We're going to train you as sharpshooters. You will learn to shoot and shoot well, so you can kill accurately up to and beyond six hundred yards. We don't have time to teach you everything, so we're going to be selective. I'll take you through three day's initial training, then Sergeant Harris will take over for the rest. Any questions?"

No one answered.

Angus scanned the section, his section, and outlined the rest of the day. If the new recruits had expected an easy time, they were in for a nasty shock.

"I've been given three days to teach you misfits the basics, and it's already 3 o'clock on day one. The good news is we have sixteen hours of daylight in the highlands right now, and we're going to use every single minute of it—and then some. I want you in two ranks. We're going to begin with a run to test your fitness."

Avoiding the main entrance, Angus took the men out the western gate. The gate opened onto a wooden bridge that crossed a wide stagnant pond, four feet deep, the remains of the old disused harbor once attached to the fort for resupply by sea. They moved at a slow but steady pace until they had cleared the fort down the old military road, where Angus took them onto a trail into the Carse Wood. After about three miles, Angus halted them. It had been Harris' idea to train them here, away from prying eyes, hidden in the pine trees.

The men, as Harris had correctly surmised, were all fit. They were all used to working hard and had stayed together. It didn't take them long to catch their breath.

Angus stood before them. "It's my job to teach you what I know, quickly. We'll keep the shouting for the parade ground because we need you to learn and learn fast. Help each other out. Don't be afraid to ask for help if you need it. If you need clarification, just ask me. I'm here to teach, not to harangue you. First, I'm going to teach you to march. It's not difficult, but it is very easy to mess up. Messing up attracts the wrong sort of attention in the army, because the army does love their marching up and down the square."

Angus began with standing in formation and how formations were comprised. They stood to 'attention,' 'at ease,' and 'stand easy.' They did left turns and right turns, and 'about turns.' They saluted, learned how to report in a loud voice, avoiding eye contact, how to 'fall in,' 'fall out,' and 'dismiss.' Angus had the section open and close ranks, using his hands to alter incorrect positions or movements.

"Don't anticipate the order. Wait until it's given, then move," said Angus as he taught them the drill movements. Two hours later, they were sweating yet hadn't moved far from the same spot.

Then began the marching. "The standard quick march is one hundred and twenty paces a minute. The actual pace is thirty inches, and this gives a normal rate of march of just under three and a half miles per hour. Marching isn't hard; it's just walking together in the same rhythm and swinging your arms high. It's slower than you think." Angus went over the various commands, demonstrating the associated move and having the section practice up and down the length of woodland track they were on.

The small section was easy to instruct. Most of the time, Angus stayed outside the small formation, but sometimes he joined it to demonstrate the pace he wanted. They all caught on quickly with even a few laughs as the inevitable happened and grown men mixed up their left from their right for the first time in their lives. Angus, eager that they learned, passed on tips when he could.

"When I say *right*, pinch your right thumb and forefinger together, that way you'll know which way to turn; the same for the left. It's a simple but easy trick."

When he thought they had the basics, he brought them to attention and ordered, "Section will move to the right; right turn!" at parade-ground volume, followed by, "By the left, quick march!" They marched for another mile, practicing halts, about turns, left wheels and right wheels. To their surprise, feet and backs began to ache, as bodies protested the stiff movements imposed upon them.

Angus halted them in a clearing next to a small stream. "Take a break, ten minutes, drink some water, go pee in the trees if you need to."

He was pleased with the progress. They weren't The Scots Guards, but they were picking up instructions fast, faster than he'd hoped. It was a good omen, he thought. He had them take off their boots and soak them in the stream after they had had a drink. "The wet leather will take on the shape of your feet quicker, which will save you pain and blisters later on," he explained. "If you want to make the leather softer, pee in them, although they're going to stink to high heaven for a while, so it's up to you."

He ended their break by ordering them to fall in, and then began marching them back towards Fort George. At a crossroads inside the woods, he halted them. "Regulations say we need to feed you, unless you volunteer to carry on with training. It's your decision, gentlemen."

The men all looked around at each other. They were hungry, but they knew every hour was precious. Nodding, Stuart said, "We'll stay, if it's all right with you, Corporal."

Angus nodded at the decision and at the proper use of his rank. "Good. Let's go have some more fun, then." Angus' idea of *fun* was relative, relative to what they weren't sure, as they learned to double-time, run in unison, and listen to the cadence their feet made as they struck the ground. He didn't continue it for long, though. "I don't want your feet to blister. There's no point to it, so let's march in, slow and steady pace, remember. You've got to learn to listen to the sound of your feet and *feel* the rhythm." They returned to the fort by the same side entrance, to an eight-man billet in the empty barracks vacated just a few hours ago by the departing battalion.

Their room contained eight metal-framed single bunks, each topped with a bare pin-striped pillow, their bedding, and a mountain of kit. Being inside didn't stop the training. "Right. Ablutions are down the corridor to the left—that's the toilet if you didn't know. Showers are down to the right. I'm in the room next door by myself if you need me. Take a ten-minute piss break, and then back in here."

Hearing footsteps behind him, he turned to see a soldier loaded down with his newly issued kit in the doorway. On seeing Angus, the soldier gently laid down his kit on the last empty bed nearest the doorway and came smartly to attention. "Reporting for training, corporal!"

The section scrutinized the new arrival with curiosity, who stood still. He was medium built, much the same as Aiden, but with straight short blond hair that flopped down and threatened to cover his blue eyes. He had a certain air of assurance about him, and if he was uncertain of his place within the new situation he found himself in, it didn't show.

"Who told you to report here?" asked Angus curiously.

"I arrived on the late train," the new man said by way of explanation.

"At ease. What's your name?" He noted that the new man had come to the correct position of *stand at ease*.

"Morley, Corporal. Giles Morley."

"Any previous military experience?"

"Army cadets, Corporal."

Angus nodded. From his brief introduction, Angus noted a few characteristics about the newcomer—he was well spoken and confident, and given his accent and cadet background, undoubtedly the successful product of an English boarding school education. Angus didn't know how he would fit in with his section of misfits, but the new recruit obviously knew his basic drill, which was good.

"Stand easy, Morley. I'm Corporal MacIntyre. Welcome to the section." He glanced back at the room. "Right. I'll be back in ten minutes. Sort yourselves out."

Stuart walked over and held out his hand to the newest member of the squad. "I'm Stuart, and this is my brother, Ross."

Ross came over and shook his hand, followed by Seamus who introduced Connor, Aiden, and Liam. Finally, Murdo came over and very self-consciously held out his hand. Giles stepped forward and shook it firmly. Exactly ten minutes later, Angus reappeared at the door.

"I need to teach you how to iron your uniform for tomorrow, and how to sort out your webbing. We should be done by eleven o'clock, so if you're lucky, you'll be in bed by midnight."

Good to his word, Angus showed them how to assemble their webbing, leaving his for them to copy. He told them they were very fortunate to have the new pattern 1908 Mills webbing instead of the older leather issue. Then he showed them how to press out their uniforms with military creases, and how to make their beds the accepted military way.

He checked his watch and asked them to gather round. "You've done well. Sunrise is at five-fifteen, so reveille will be at five o'clock. At half past five, I want you all standing by the end of your bed, ready for inspection. Help each other out; work together. Goodnight, misfits!" he said, and then he left the section to sort themselves out.

At five in the morning, Angus opened the door and greeted them with a loud, "Rise and shine—the sun's burning your eyeballs!" before flickering on the ceiling's two bare lights. The section stumbled out of bed as he left, smiling to himself. Half an hour later, he was back. Giles saw him first and called the room to attention.

Angus inspected each individual and then their kit. They were all shaved, clean, and had their uniforms squared away. Giles' kit was perfect. The rest were acceptable, except for Murdo's webbing, which was in disarray. "What's happened here, Private Munro?" asked Angus.

"I ran out of time, Corporal," Murdo replied apologetically.

"Did anyone help you?"

Murdo stared at his feet, keeping silent. Angus changed his tactic and looked at the others. "Did anyone help Private Munro with his webbing?"

After a moment's hesitation, Stuart said, "No, Corporal."

Angus stared at them all in obvious disappointment. "I told you to work together, not as small groups," he said, looking at the O'Connells.

"Not as pairs," he said, shooting a look of disappointment towards Stuart and Ross.

"And not looking after number one." This time, he fixed his gaze towards Giles, who flushed red with embarrassment.

"Seven sets of webbing and one shambles means everyone fails. That's how it works in the military. If I had the time and the inclination, I'd have you all doubling around the ramparts until you dropped, but we don't have time for those games, do we?"

"No, Corporal!" the section replied in unison.

"Do not let this happen again, understand?"

"Yes, Corporal!" the men replied.

"Good. Lesson learned, hopefully. Remember it, and let's move on. Form up outside, full kit, five minutes. Move!"

The morning was cold. The fort jutted out into the estuary, and the sea air lent a shroud of fog to the fort's stone ramparts. The plaintive cry of a curlew echoed through the morning mist. Angus marched them to the back of the kitchen, where they collected three packed meals each and put them in their rucksacks. Next, they went to the armory, where they each drew a rifle and ten rounds of blank ammunition. Murdo drew questioning looks from the junior armorer on duty.

Only MacIntyre knew these were no ordinary rifles.

***

Color Sergeant Tom Murray, the fort's armorer, was an old friend of Sergeant Harris who had gone to speak to him the day before. Drawing heavily on a cigarette, Harris outlined what he had in mind for the section, and the armorer had grasped his intention immediately, helped by a bottle of 12-year-old Dalwhinnie whisky passing hands and disappearing under the counter. They'd both served in South Africa and France and had lost friends to sniper fire.

"I'll hand pick the rifles myself, don't worry. And I'll book the range for your men," said the white-haired color sergeant, standing behind his wide workbench which was laid out with various weapons and weapons parts. "But I'll need authorization for your men to keep them, and I'll have to charge your battalion. The Territorial Force has only paid for the older Charger Loading Lee-Enfields, not these beauties."

Sergeant Harris nodded. "I'll talk to the major. I'm sure we can pay the difference out of battalion funds, and I'll type up the authorization for his signature." Then he noticed a medium-sized wooden box on the workbench behind his friend, pried open and filled with packing material. "What new toys have you got to play with, Tam?" he asked with a smile, knowing how much Murray loved his trade.

The color sergeant smiled, and sticking his hand in the box, pulled out a leather tube. He unclipped an end and gently shook the container until a sleek twelve-inch long metal optic tube slid into his hands, protected in chamois. "Two dozen Periscopic Prism telescopic sights with offset dovetail side mounts," he said in obvious reverence, handing it to Harris with two hands. Harris saw the scope was stamped with *Periscopic Prism Company London, Patent 1915.*

"These are brand new?" he asked with a hint of disbelief. The army was rarely issued with anything state-of-the-art.

"Those, my friend, are very, very new. They are, in fact, the first I've ever seen within the army. The optics provide two-and-a-half times magnification, and it has a range drum from one to six-hundred yards, specifically calibrated to the trajectory of the new .303 Mark VII bullet," he explained as he pointed to a small brass drum on the top of the telescopic sight. Harris squinted through the scope to see a single post and rail type graticule—the aiming point. Handing it back with care, he raised a questioning eyebrow towards Murray, "I don't suppose...."

Before he could continue, Murray grinned and wagged his finger. "I'm sorry, but you'd have to buy these at cost. I can't issue you them as they're special items—very expensive special items." Special items referred to pieces of kit held by stores or the armory that had to be paid for before being issued: luxury military goods. It was equipment that would be very nice to have and was in demand operationally, but only available once paid for through individual battalion or officer's funds.

Harris shrugged. "How much is expensive?" he asked.

Color Sergeant Murray rummaged through the paperwork that had come with the scopes and held up the War Office invoice, whistling as he did so. "£12 each; that's almost four times the cost of the rifle for which it's designed."

Harris slowly shook his head and exclaimed, "£12!" It was almost a year's salary. "I see what you mean. We can't pay that for scopes and have anything left over in the battalion's spare-cash kitty, which would make a lot of folks upset." He shrugged and shook Murray's hand before turning to go. "Thanks for the rifles, Tam. I mean it."

"I'll remember that next time I see you at the sergeant's mess bar," laughed Murray, and he smiled as Harris walked away. It was good to help old friends; they were getting fewer and fewer nowadays.

***

Angus and his section exited from the side gate over the bridge and the murky water of the disused harbor, as they had the day before, and they marched down the road into the morning mist. They headed towards the Carse Woods, rifles over their right shoulders.

As they went, Angus picked up their drill practice from the previous day, reviewing what they had been taught. To this, he added 'compliments on the march'—saluting officers as the section moved in formation. Once back at the clearing with the stream, they went through standing rifle drill, 'order,' 'slope,' and 'present arms.' Angus patiently instructed them: "Move the rifle around your head, not your head around the rifle." He had been correct about Giles, who knew his drill, and that in turn helped the others who would look at Giles for a reference as they went through their drill movements.

After an hour of marching and drilling with rifles, Angus had them fall out and eat. Finished first, he had them remain sitting while he stood and picked up his rifle. "Has anyone fired a rifle before?" No one answered. "Good. That means no bad habits to break."

"Let me introduce you to Smellie," Angus said as he held the rifle out in both hands. "This is the 1907 Short Magazine Lee-Enfield, bolt action, .303 Mark III rifle; SMLE for short, known as *Smellie* to one and all. The 'short' refers to the length of the barrel, twenty-five-and-a-half inches, which is five inches shorter than the 1895 Lee-Enfield which it replaced."

"In fact, by all rights, you should be holding the older model. Sergeant Harris has pulled some strings to have these issued to the section instead. They've been hand-picked for accuracy, and all of them have been used in regimental shooting matches." He paused to let that titbit of information sink in before continuing.

"The magazine can hold ten rounds of ammunition, and this can be re-filled five bullets at a time by using five-round charger clips that notch into the top of the breach for quick loading. You can also load and fire bullets one at a time, while still retaining ten bullets in the magazine, as it has a cut-off that keeps bullets in the magazine until you really need them." He noticed a few confused looks and stopped.

"We'll all go over this slow-time later on. This is just a quick introduction," and he smiled. "Don't worry. You and Smellie are going to become very intimate," he said with a knowing smirk before continuing.

"The rifle weighs eight-and-a-half pounds, add another pound for the bayonet, but we won't be playing with those until we reach France. The sliding ramp rear sights can be set anywhere between two-hundred and two-thousand yards. The effective range of these particular rifles, the maximum range you can confidently aim and shoot at a single target with skill, is six- to eight-hundred yards. Its rapid rate of fire is around fifteen aimed rounds per minute. It fires the .303 Mark VII bullet, a new pointed round with a smooth trajectory, which means the bullet should hit exactly where you aim."

Angus looked at the faces in front of him, seeing a mixture of apprehension and confusion, and he smiled reassuringly. "Right. Enough of me talking. Tidy up and unroll your groundsheet flat. That's where you'll lay your rifle parts. I'm going to strip my rifle down and put it back together. Then we'll all do it together slowly a couple of times. Then you will pair off and help each other, before doing it alone. With the blanks, we'll practice loading and unloading and using the five-round charger. By the end of the day, you'll be doing it all blindfolded," and he wasn't kidding.

They worked all day on their rifles. At midday, they ate their packed lunch and went for a march as much as to practice drill as to stretch their legs. Then they were back to their rifles, stripping and assembling them quickly. Angus broke them into two teams and had them race each other. Giles had certainly handled a rifle before, but not the SMLE III, so he had no advantage over the others.

Angus was relieved that no one seemed to be having a problem with training so far, and they all seemed to be getting along with each other. The latter observation frankly surprised him. Potentially, there was a volatile mix within these misfits, but the smallness of the unit worked in its favor. There was a shared sense of commonality and purpose against a limited time frame regardless of backgrounds. The four O'Connell boys were sticking together which was to be expected, as were Stuart and Ross, although Stuart was always first to answer or take the initiative when needed. Murdo was keeping his head down and was definitely the most reticent of the section.

Giles seemed outgoing, confident, and embarrassingly polite, which bothered Angus. There were lots of Englishmen in the Scottish regiments, drawn by their elite status and smart highland uniforms, but Angus suspected there was more to Giles than met the eye. Given his education and cadet experience, he should be commissioned and training somewhere in southern England, close to home. Instead, here he was in the furthermost regiment he could be within the British Isles, training in the remotest military barracks as a private. And that to Angus raised a lot of questions regarding their late acquisition to the section.

Towards the end of the afternoon, the blindfolds came out and went on. They were allowed to practice alone before pairing off and racing against each other. Angus allowed a bit of leeway when he saw Liam pinch Aiden's firing pin. Aiden was left blindly trying to find it as they all silently laughed before Aiden realized the joke being played on him, pulling up his blindfold and pointing at Liam, swearing good-natured retribution.

As promised, by the end of the day, they could strip, assemble, and load their rifles blindfolded.

They ate their last meal leisurely, Angus telling them to soak their boots once again to help mold them to their feet. He wandered over to Murdo and asked him about his forestry work. Soon, they were contrasting and comparing methods of tree felling. They'd both been lumberjacks in neighboring Canadian provinces, and Murdo seemed to relax more and more as he talked, and towards the end of the conversation, both men were sharing a laugh and few words in Gaelic.

"Right then, gentlemen, time to head back. Make sure you don't leave anything and fall in at order arms."

Angus brought them to attention followed by 'present arms' and 'slope arms,' and soon they were marching back towards the fort as the sun faded below the horizon. Once home, as the section increasingly viewed it, they returned their rifles and blank rounds to the armory and returned to their billet. After a ten-minute break, Angus spent an hour with them going over full kit inspection and polishing boots, then bid the section, "Goodnight, misfits," and left them to plan the next days' training.

***

There were many things Sergeant Major Skaig disliked, including everyone that he came into contact with. He was the senior ranking non-commissioned officer in Fort George at present, feared and hated by all for the tirades he could administer to the enlisted men and NCOs—and he liked it that way. Junior officers learned to keep their distance from him, and he liked that even more. Junior officers were the bane of his life, technically superior to him in rank, but worthless, interfering, supercilious idiots.

He was small in stature with close-cropped black hair and a black mustache, waxed to opposing points that he habitually rolled and preened. Under his arm, he carried a slim sergeant major's baton and was unafraid to use it to administer swift punishment when he deemed it in the recipient's interest.

Skaig knew everything and everybody within Fort George's ramparts, or so he thought. So, when a rumor came to his ear about a section disappearing into the woods every morning, and reappearing every night without his knowledge, he disliked it. When he heard a rumor about a big black man in uniform within his fort, he disliked it even more. He had no reason to hate black people, he just did, and nothing in his narrow upbringing or military service had changed his deep-rooted prejudices.

Attempts to locate the mystery section had failed, and this increasingly frustrated him. They were never seen in the mess hall, they were never seen on the parade ground, and no one knew where their billet was. He began to doubt that they existed until he questioned a junior armorer working late, poking his baton into the man's chest until the soldier hesitantly confirmed nine men had drawn rifles that day. He didn't know where they were from, but they were due back tomorrow at a quarter to six in the morning—and yes, one of them was black.

The next morning, Angus opened the door to the section's room and began to shout, "Rise and shine, the sun's...."

He stopped in surprise as Stuart called out, "Section, section 'shun!" and the room echoed as the remainder of the room came to attention, crashing their feet down in unison. "Section all present and ready for inspection, corporal!" Stuart called out, and so they were.

Each man was standing by his bunk, fully dressed and kit laid out. Their boots were shined, and their uniforms squared away. Angus stared at them and then walked into the room. He could see that they were more than prepared. Their bedding was taut, their kit placed in the prescribed manner, and each man stared straight ahead, at attention. He couldn't help but smile, and the section couldn't help but smile back.

"Well then, it looks as if we're ready to start early today, which means we'll end early as well. The good news is, as its Sunday, we'll take it easy today and finish in time for a hot meal. You all deserve one. Now, once you've stopped grinning like a bunch of smug idiots, and if you're ready, gentlemen...," he said with false deference, "outside in five minutes."

Sergeant Major Skaig stared at the section disappearing down the old military road into the morning mist. He methodically tapped his baton against his leg in frustration and annoyance. They'd been early, and he'd missed them. But now he knew which gate they used, and he'd be waiting for them, no matter how long it took. Someone was making a fool of him and someone was going to pay.

The section reviewed the drill they had learned and raced each other through stripping and assembling rifles. The only additional training Angus had them do was first aid. They learned how to rinse out a wound with water and then apply a battlefield bandage to stop bleeding, and then paired off to practice fireman's carries, laughing as Giles struggled under the weight of Connor. At midday, they ate their packed lunch in the sun and relaxed in their clearing, listening to the melodic call of the wood pigeons surrounding them. The pungent smell of gorse bushes, heavily laden with yellow flowers, hung in the air.

"Tomorrow we'll begin firing rifles," said Angus. "All soldiers have been taught rapid fire first and foremost, but we're going to concentrate on single well-aimed shots, and we'll cover rapid fire later on. I want you to get a good night's sleep tonight. You did well this morning so no inspection, just be ready to go at five-thirty."

He stood up and looked at the section, "I know it seems a lot to take on board, but it's only been three days, and you've grasped the basics well. Good job, and I mean it. Now let's pack up and march back. You've earned a break, and it is Sunday after all, a day of rest," he said with a smile.

At the side entrance, Angus halted the section and had them turn to the right so they faced the wooden bridge to the fort over the old stagnant harbor basin. Angus turned to face them to give them some last instructions before heading to the armory when Stuart, standing in front of him caught his eye and hissed, "Behind you, Corporal." Angus now heard studded highland shoes approaching down the bridge. He turned to see Sergeant Major Skaig in full Sunday best, red dress highland uniform, bearing down on the section.

"Report!" barked the sergeant major with menace in his voice as he approached Angus.

"Fourth Section, 4th Platoon, D Company, Territorial Battalion, Sergeant Major," answered Angus, wary of the senior NCO now standing in front of him.

"Territorials," said Skaig with scorn in his voice. "They deployed three days ago. What are you still doing here?"

"Training, Sergeant Major," said Angus, not giving anything away.

"No one trains without my knowledge. No one. Who ordered this and who," he asked, tapping Angus' rifle with his swagger stick, "issued you those rifles?"

"I have authorization, Sergeant Major," said Angus, reaching into his uniform and bringing out two letters prepared by Harris. The first authorized training by Colonel Lyall, the second authorized SMLE III rifles and was signed by Major Sinclair.

"Authorization?" mimicked Skaig sarcastically, snatching the letters and giving them a cursory look before dismissively crumpling them up and stuffing them into his tunic.

"Only I can authorize training on this fort, and I sure as hell didn't authorize you to train anyone, sunshine." He bypassed Angus and stood in front of Murdo. "And who put this black bastard in a uniform?" he asked, prodding Murdo in the chest with his baton.

The section remained silent. "Colonel Lyall, Sergeant Major."

Skaig prodded Murdo's chest harder with the baton, "Shut up, boy! Did I ask you to speak? Well, did I, blackie?"

Murdo remained silent.

"A negro in a uniform—someone's having a joke, but the joke's over now, let me tell you that." He hit Murdo's chest hard this time with the baton, and Murdo rocked on his heels.

"He's part of our section, Sergeant Major," replied a distinctive southern Irish voice defensively.

Skaig whirled around to face Liam, standing next to Murdo. "Shut your trap, you Irish piece of shit! I might have known I'd find a Fenian bastard next to blackie here."

This time Angus cut in. "Sergeant Major, I was dismissing the section. They're finished with training."

Skaig took three steps right up to Angus, his face inches away from Angus', staring up at him with contempt. "You aren't dismissing anyone, *Corporal*. Training? Do you want training? Oh, we can train, we can train right here, right now."

He turned to face the section pointing to the stagnant dank water between them and the fort, "In! Get in and touch the wall, then back here." It was a regular punishment meted out frequently to those who incurred the wrath of the sergeant major, often for no cause.

The section stood motionless and the sergeant major turned red with the rage. He grabbed Liam and propelled him towards the old harbor basin. Liam turned quickly, eyes flaring in anger ready to strike back, and then Connor engulfed him. "Don't do it, Liam," he whispered urgently in his ear.

Skaig stared at Connor, "Get into the bog, you shitheads." He grabbed Giles and physically pushed him towards the water.

Slowly, the section climbed down the muddy embankment and into the cold water, which rose up to their chests, and began to wade towards the fort. From above, the two sentries on duty gazed down in sympathy and motioned to others, and within minutes word had spread—Sergeant Major Skaig had a section in the water, and one of them was black.

Skaig noticed none of the growing numbers of spectators as he hurled insults at the men in the water as they reached the base of the fort wall for the third time and turned. It was physically hard work to wade in the water. The churned-up mud clung to their boots, and the stagnant water stank as it seeped inside their uniforms. They held their rifles high above their heads, adding to the pain and gritted their teeth, enduring the sergeant major's tirade.

"Faster, you scum, double time! Come on, you Irish Fenian bastards, you should be used to living in a bog, it's just like being at home with your whore mothers!"

Murdo was ahead of the others and reached the embankment first. "Crawl up here, blackie. Time to teach you a lesson." Murdo began to crawl up the muddy embankment towards Skaig, but could find no grip for his boots and fell face down, and then the sergeant major was on him. He lashed out at Murdo's shoulders and back with his slim baton, spittle coming from his mouth as he poured down insults and hatred upon the prostrate recruit. A downward lash caught Murdo's ear and he howled in pain as blood spurted from the cut.

"Let me hear you cry, blackie!" shouted Skaig, a manic look filling his hate-filled eyes.

"Enough!" a voice shouted to Skaig's right, "Stop this right now, Sergeant Major!"

Skaig turned to see Giles coming up the embankment to his right.

"And who the fuck are you to give me orders?" he raged.

"I am Second Lieutenant Morley, and you will address me as sir!"

Giles shouted clearly with authority in his voice, so even the audience on the wall heard it with shock and amazement. But Skaig was past rational thought. He was seeing red, and now he now had a new target for his wrath.

Just as Giles reached the top of the embankment, Skaig's baton arched in a vicious backswing, catching Giles along the jawline and sending him back down the embankment as Skaig yelled, "You pompous shit!"

Then Murdo was upon him. He snatched the baton from Skaig's hand and snapped it in two before stepping towards the sergeant major, who back-stepped and fell to the ground. Murdo grabbed one of his arms, twisting it behind him, pinning Skaig's cheek to the ground. Skaig's rage was incandescent. "Get your hands off me, you black ape!"

Seamus helped Giles up the embankment, blood seeping from the cut along his jawline. Angus came up to him, "Are you really an officer?"

"Yes, well. I am now."

Angus looked at him questioningly before coming to a decision and bringing himself to attention, saluting Giles. "Now what, sir?"

Giles glanced at Murdo still pinning Skaig to the ground. "Are you all right, Murdo?" he asked with concern in his voice.

Murdo nodded. "I'm all right," he said, then quickly corrected himself, "I mean, yes sir."

Giles nodded, looking at the rest of the section. "I'll explain later, but we need to take care of that first," he said nodding towards Skaig. "Connor, Murdo, stand him up please."

"Yes, sir," said Connor, reaching down to help Murdo pick up the sergeant major.

"Get your black hands off me! I'll have you all whipped for this, by God, I will," ranted Skaig his voice dripping with venom.

Giles walked up to Skaig and simply said, "Shut up!"

Skaig stared at Giles in pure anger at the unheard-of affront to his position, "How dare you speak to me like that?"

Giles' jaw tightened. He turned to Angus, "Corporal MacIntyre, escort this man to the guardhouse. Inform the duty NCO that he is under close arrest for striking a recruit and for striking an officer. I want him placed in a cell. Then please escort Private Munro to the garrison hospital." He reached up to his jaw and glimpsed blood on his hand. "I will meet you there. In the meantime, I will inform the Officer of the Day of what's happened here."

"Yes, sir!" replied Angus, still reeling from the events and revelations of the past half hour. He nodded at Connor and Murdo. "Escort the prisoner to the guardhouse." Then looking at Stuart, "Private McReynolds, ensure all the rifles are returned to the armory and give them a quick clean before turning them in. We'll meet you there."

"Yes, Corporal," replied Stuart, and together with Ross, Seamus, Liam, and Aiden he gathered up their rifles.

"One more thing, Corporal," called out Giles, "Make sure the guard searches him and records everything they find."

Angus, somewhat perplexed, nodded and said, "Yes, sir," before motioning for Skaig to be moved.

Connor and Murdo, each with a firm grip on Skaig, began to walk him over the bridge to the side entrance of the fort. Perhaps the sight of it, or of the men looking down in utter amazement, triggered one last desperate rage in him. He lashed out a heavy hob-nailed thick-soled shoe at Connor's shin making him yell out in pain and stumble. One hand now free, he swung it hard and hit Murdo on the side of the face. "You fucking black bastard, I'll kill you. I swear to God I'll kill you all for this!"

Murdo reeled and then grabbed Skaig by the throat with one hand, squeezing hard. Skaig's hands went up, trying to pull Murdo's clenched hand away. Failing, he began clawing at Murdo's face.

"Murdo!" shouted Giles, "Throw him over!"

Murdo hesitated before Giles yelled again, "Now!"

Murdo, still gripping Skaig's throat, leaned down, grabbed Skaig by the crotch with his free hand and picked him up. Skaig was now suspended in the air, yelling and swearing.

Murdo looked over at Giles, who simply said, "Do it."

Murdo then threw the senior ranking non-commissioned officer of Fort George, in his Sunday dress highland uniform, over the wooden railing and down into the filthy mud-churned water below.

It was at that same instant Sergeant Harris appeared at the fort's side entrance for a quick cigarette, just in time to see Sergeant Major Skaig flying through the air. The complete and utter silence that followed was only broken by Giles, who shouted up at Angus. "Get him out and get him to the guardroom. Have Ross help, and add "resisting arrest" to the charges, Corporal."

Harris stood still in utter disbelief. One of the first things that entered his head—after muttering 'bloody hell' to himself—was that 'quietly training the section' hadn't entirely gone to plan.

The guardroom was by the entrance to the fort. To reach it, Angus, Murdo, Ross, and Connor had to escort Skaig, dripping wet and covered in stinking mud from head to toe, diagonally across the length of the fort's parade ground supervised by an increasingly amused Sergeant Harris. Skaig once again attempted to break the hold of his escort and ranted at Sergeant Harris. Harris stepped in close to Skaig and whispered in his ear, "If you don't stop your whining right now, I'll make sure you 'fall down' the guardroom steps, repeatedly. And we both know the guardroom doesn't have any steps. Now for god's sake, shut up and at least try to act like a soldier."

By the time they had delivered their prisoner to an astonished Corporal of the Guard, most of the soldiers within the fort had witnessed what had occurred. Those few who hadn't had certainly heard about it by dinner time, and the enlisted mess fell deathly still as the section entered through its doors for their first hot meal.

Giles wasn't with them. The rest of the recruits followed Angus into the mess, uniforms damp but cleaned, a bandage around Murdo's ear and Connor walking with a distinct limp. The silence was palatable, and for a moment they thought there was going to be more trouble. Then a soldier somewhere began to bang the table in front of him with his knuckles followed by another soldier, and then others. Men began banging plates and cups until the whole mess rocked to the sound, now joined by a growing cheer coming from the men of Fort George.

Angus proudly shouted to his section over the noise: "They're saluting you, so stand tall. You all deserve it. Trust me, you deserve every second of it."

And then a chant emerged from the cheering crowd towards the man who had picked up and thrown Sergeant Major Skaig into the stagnant water, and whose name was now known to all. It began softly and then gathered strength. "Murdo, Murdo, Murdo, Murdo!" until the chant reverberated from the walls.

If Private Murdo Munro, the only black soldier in the 51st Highland Division, had been worried about acceptance into the Highlanders, his worries were over.

CHAPTER NINE

Sharpshooters

Back in their billet, the section relaxed, collapsing onto their bunks with full stomachs. Liam interlaced his fingers under his head and stared up at the ceiling. After a minute, he said, "You know, I've been thinking, so I have. It might just be me, but I don't think Sergeant Major Skaig likes us very much."

After a moment's hesitation, the room burst into loud laughter, Murdo laughing along with the rest. It was good to hear, thought Angus, as he walked into the room motioning to the section to remain as they were, and sat on Giles' empty bunk.

Stuart wiped away the tears of laughter and smiled at Angus. "What now, Corporal?"

"I'm not sure, to tell you the truth. Major Sinclair's talking with the colonel, and I believe the Brigadier is now involved. It depends what kind of courts-martial they opt for. If it's a district courts-martial, Skaig could be looking at hard labor and reduction in rank. If it's general courts-martial, striking an officer could carry the death penalty. I suppose a lot will depend on Giles—or I should say, Officer Morley."

"Giles sounds right, given what we've been through. But I'm afraid the army may not agree," said Giles, standing in the doorway. The section made to spring to attention, but Giles quickly said, "As you were gentlemen, as you were, please."

He entered the room and checked on Murdo and Connor. Ross moved over to sit beside his brother and offered his bunk to Giles, who thanked him and sat down. He was now dressed in an officer's uniform with a Sam Browne leather belt and holstered pistol. Instead of a kilt, he had opted for subdued Sutherland tartan trousers known as *trews*, worn by the regiment's territorial officers, tucked into knee-high brown-polished leather boots. He carried a black glengarry hat in his hands, with the Seaforth's stags head badge. His right-hand jawline sported a livid red welt the length of the jawbone.

"How's your face, sir?" asked Aiden, inwardly wincing at the wound.

"I'll be fine, thank you. The doctor says it may leave a slight scar, but that will just attract sympathy from the ladies," he said with a smile, and the section smiled back awkwardly. "It's going to be a district courts-martial, by the way, no death penalty. Skaig is a nasty piece of work, don't get me wrong, but the Brigadier doesn't want this going any higher than it has to and neither do I."

He looked at the section. "I wanted to come and see you," he said, pausing for a moment before continuing.

"By all rights, I hold a temporary commission in the territorials by way of my schooling and officer cadet service. But I didn't tell anyone this when I arrived. You see, for various reasons, I didn't want my commission and thought by traveling as far away from home as I could and enlisting in the Seaforths, I could just serve in the ranks without being an officer. That was my hope, at least until Skaig changed things." He gently rubbed the welt along his face before continuing.

"It was never my intention to claim officer's rank, but it was the only way to stop Skaig. There was nothing else that could have been done, so I made the decision to end Skaig's madness." He glanced down at the floor and then up to the men surrounding him who were listening in silence.

"I'm afraid I'm not very popular in the officer's mess right now. 'Not the done thing,' it was explained to me. I've been told to lie low until they can confirm my commission, but I'm glad I was with you, because I was able to stop what was happening."

He stood up, "I suppose it's also 'not the done thing' to apologize to the men, but that's why I'm here. I wanted to apologize to Corporal MacIntyre for my deception. I meant no harm by it, and it did allow me to see what a splendid section leader you have. It was never my intention to cause any offense, and I hope none was taken."

He hurried on. "I also wanted to apologize to Private Munro." Murdo gazed up at Giles with a look of confusion. "I wanted to say sorry that I couldn't stop Skaig sooner, but until he physically hit you, I knew that there was nothing I could do, and no charges I could press that would stick. I'm sorry you had to take abuse at all. You're the first black man I've ever met, and all I've ever seen you do is try your best in a quiet, unassuming way. Why some folks are offended by the color of your skin is beyond me. I'm sorry to have witnessed it, and that it happened—it makes me feel ashamed."

Not waiting for a reply, Giles went on, "And I came to say it's been suggested that I be reassigned, given the circumstances. Sergeant Harris will talk to you later. I just wanted to say for the brief time we were together, it was a pleasure, and that I wish you all the best in France." He turned and began walking to the door.

"Just a moment, sir," said Angus, standing up. He looked around at the section who sensed his purpose and nodded. "It seems to us, sir, hearing what you've said, that you're a bit of a misfit over at the officer's mess. Well, that seems exactly the right kind of officer this section needs. And besides, if you can stand up to someone like Sergeant Major Skaig, we'd love to see you in action against the Germans. As far as we're concerned, sir, you'll always be welcome with us."

Giles smiled and nodded. "Thank you, Corporal." Then, looking at the whole section and seeing their smiles, he said,

"Thank you—all of you." He walked out into the corridor before the section could see the size of the lump in his throat.

Angus took his leave of the section soon afterward, telling them to have their uniforms pressed and boots and brass
shining tomorrow. "They'll be wanting to talk to you all, so
look smart and just tell the truth. We've absolutely nothing
to hide. Be on line, ready to go at six o'clock. I think a nice
cooked breakfast would be a novel way to start the day. I
have a feeling it's going to be a long one."

In fact, Angus was wrong. The officer acting in defense
of Skaig didn't have much of a case, and he knew it. A coun-
ter-charge that Murdo had assaulted the sergeant major was
thrown out, as he had acted under direct orders. The claim
that Skaig hadn't known Giles was an officer was also tossed,
as both sentries said they heard him clearly state his rank
from their posts up on the ramparts. Fifty-three other soldiers were more than willing to testify to that, and to witness
that Skaig had resisted arrest. Clutching at straws, the defense lastly argued that Skaig had not been informed of the
section's training. This was quickly dismissed when the Corporal of the Guard confirmed letters had been found on his
person when searched, and once dried out, confirmed that
Skaig had been in personal possession of the written authorization.

Brigadier James was a fair man, but with his brigade of
Seaforth and Cameron Highlanders deploying, he was in no
mood to draw out the inevitable or listen to others defend
the undefendable. While the evidence was all very cut and
dry—including the welt on Giles' chin—the circumstances
muddied the water. Giles should not have been in an enlisted uniform "masquerading as a private." To avoid pro-
longing the process, Giles hesitantly agreed to drop one of
the charges. By late afternoon, Brigadier James was ready to
pass judgment and to go to tea.

"Sergeant Major Skaig. This courts-martial finds you
guilty of two counts: striking a recruit and resisting arrest.

After discussion with Officer Morley, the charge of striking an officer has been withdrawn and replaced with "causing offense," of which you are also found guilty. After taking into account your long service and current rank, you are hereby sentenced to four months' imprisonment and reduction in rank to sergeant. Please understand that if we were not at war, this court would have ordered a dishonorable discharge following your imprisonment."

If Brigadier James had been expecting any gratitude for a lenient sentence, he was disappointed, as Skaig launched into a tirade pointing his finger at the Brigadier. "You think I gave a shit about you and your negro-loving army with its stuck-up arse-wiping officers? You can all go to hell!"

The two military policemen escorting Skaig grabbed his arms and held him tight.

Brigadier James, red-faced with anger, called for order and stared hard at Skaig as if seeing his true colors for the first time. "Sergeant Major Skaig, I find you in contempt of this courts-martial and utterly without remorse. I, therefore, revise the sentence to four months' *hard labor*, reduction in rank to private, and order that your service record for this war be reviewed at its cessation to see if your service warrants anything other than a dishonorable discharge. Take him away!"

Within the harsher punishment, Brigadier James had hidden some small incentive. If Skaig served well in the war, he could at least avoid a dishonorable discharge, which would leave him penniless. But serving well was not what was in Skaig's mind as he was marched back to the guardhouse—revenge was. Revenge against the section that had brought his military career crashing down around him in such a humiliating fashion.

Skaig swore that he would make them pay, however long it took, whatever he had to endure—he would seek them out and make them suffer.

***

After breakfast, the section gave their statements, and then Sergeant Harris came to see them, ordering them to stay within the fort. He also asked about Second Lieutenant Morley and whether they wanted him as their section commander. It wouldn't be their decision, obviously, but it would be useful to know. When Angus said they'd be proud to have him as their officer, Harris nodded. "Excellent. I thought you might. I'll let the major know."

Angus marched them to the armory where they drew their weapons once again. For a while, Angus marched them on the parade square, just so they had the experience of marching on the hard surface with room to maneuver. Then he marched them to the rear of the fort beside the chapel where there was some open ground within the ramparts.

"We've got some time to kill, so let's use it productively. We'll go over the various shooting positions, but I want to concentrate on the lying-down prone position. It's the one you'll use the most for what we have in mind." He had them all lie down with the rifles pointing towards the ramparts.

"Pick a target and get comfortable. Now close your eyes and move to and fro a wee bit. Get comfortable again, now open your eyes and look down the barrel. Do not move your rifle! If you're still aiming down the barrel at your target, you have found your natural point of aim. If you're pointing slightly away from your target, move your body until you are aligned again. Don't just move your rifle. Once you've found your natural point of aim, you can fire and reload without having to search for your target again. You're also not stressing your arm muscles trying to hold your rifle at an angle."

He had the section practice and then went over the importance of bone structure—using one's own skeleton to form a solid firing platform. "Your muscles will tire; your bones won't. You'll see what I mean when we go to the standing position. You won't be able to hold your rifle without some sort of movement, which deteriorates your aim."

For the rest of the day, he had them practice the various positions including sitting, kneeling, and standing, and finding their natural point of aim in each one. He taught them how to reload while watching the target, not their rifle. "That way, you'll always know where the target is. As soon as you look down at your rifle, you'll have to spend a couple of seconds re-acquiring your target, which could be fatal. Always keep your eye on the target. The great advantage of Smellie is that you don't have to move the bolt up ninety degrees to pull it back. It'll slide back at sixty degrees, allowing you chamber a new round while still looking through your sights. It also cocks as you close the bolt, which improves your rate of fire."

Late that afternoon, Harris informed them of the courts-martial verdict and that Skaig would be leaving the fort that evening under darkness. "Good riddance, if you ask me. He's had that coming for a long time. I'm just sorry you had to be the ones that got involved, but never mind. You'll never see him again."

He then had them go to the armory and draw live ammunition. "You've been running about with those rifles for two days. It's about time you fired them. We still have daylight, so let's use it."

The ranges were outside the main fort, and Harris had Angus fall in with the section, so he could march them together. He gave them a few different commands and rifle drills on the march, and he was both surprised and impressed at what he saw. The section knew their commands and was moving as one. They certainly didn't look like they were recruits. Corporal MacIntyre had done a good job.

At the range, they were joined by Color Sergeant Murray from the armory. Harris halted the section and had them stand at ease. "Color Sergeant Murray and I, along with Corporal MacIntyre, are going to run the fifty- and one-hundred-yard ranges, to get you used to firing the rifle. The rifles you are holding were all hand-picked by the color sergeant.

They will hit exactly where you aim. We'll know pretty soon if this section has the potential to be sharpshooters." He brought them to attention and had them fall out.

Downrange, they could see seven bulls-eye targets. After going through range safety and how to properly align the sights with the target, Harris had them load with one round and assume the prone position. They were all told to fire at the bottom left-hand corner, "Just to get used to the bang and kick," explained Harris. "The SMLE rifle has a two-stage trigger. As you pull, you'll feel a slight hesitation in the action. That's the first stage. Keep pulling—the second stage takes a bit more effort."

Next, he had them load three bullets into the magazine. "I want you to fire at the dead center. It's important you maintain your aim throughout, which means aiming at exactly the same point each time. There's no hurry. Take your time and remember what MacIntyre taught you this morning about the natural point of aim—move your body to the rifle, not the rifle to your body."

When the section had stopped firing, Harris had them walk to their targets. "What we're looking for is three bullet holes tightly grouped. I'm not fussed whether they are in the center of the target—we'll adjust for that as we go, but we do need to see you can fire well-aimed shots."

They repeated the procedure two more times, Color Sergeant Murray expertly adjusting sights to create a 'zero' for each shooter—the ideal point at where the group of three shots was hitting the center of the target. They used glue and paper to put up new targets and then loaded with ten rounds each.

Harris glanced up and down the line of shooters. "I want you to fire all ten rounds at the bullseye. Again, we're looking for tight groupings, not bullet holes all over the target like the spray of a shotgun. In your own time, fire." The rifles began to bark out unhurriedly, as the section settled down to their task. The smell of cordite hung in the air, and the men became used to the kick of the rifle and blindly working the bolt to chamber a new round after each shot.

Once it was confirmed all the shooters were finished, they walked downrange to the 50-yard line to inspect their targets. Harris walked down the line with Murray, pointing out grouping and discussing the results. All 70 shots were within the wider bullseye, with the exception of three or four shots. Certainly not bad for an initial effort, but none of the groupings were tight. Angus walked over to Harris and asked if he could try something, who nodded. They pasted on new targets and then Angus ordered them back on line.

He had them load ten more bullets into the magazine from two charger clips. "Your groupings are good, but we need to make them a lot better. There's a couple of wild shots—that's due to you jerking the trigger as you pull, and the same is true for your loose groups, which tend to drift to the right of target. When you get to the second stage of the trigger pull, I want you to slow down into a steady, unhurried, gentle-but-firm pull. Don't pull quickly—you'll move the barrel, and the shot will go wide of your aim. Ideally, I want you to be surprised when your rifle fires. You shouldn't know when that's going to happen unless you're pulling too hard."

He nodded to Harris who gave them the command to fire. The groupings were better, and Angus had them repeat it again. "Good, but remember your breathing. Use deep slow breaths to settle yourselves down. If you have your natural point of aim, the tip of your front sight should gently move up and down your target as you breathe. Not sideways, not diagonally, just gently up and down. If it's really moving up and down a lot, try moving your chest off the ground a little. It'll dampen down the movement. Take a couple of minutes and adjust yourselves." He walked the line, tapping a few legs to open them wider to provide a more stable base.

"Some of you are pulling the trigger with the tip of your forefinger. Try using the inside of the middle digit of the forefinger instead. It has more cushioning and strength, which helps prevent tugging. All right, take a deep breath and start pulling the trigger. When you feel the trigger's first hesitation, let your breath out slowly and keep pulling gently. Remember, you should be surprised when the rifle fires. If you need to take another breath, stop pulling, take a breath, and when you let it out start pulling again, slowly."

Shots started going downrange, more paced than before, the section taking its time and controlling its breathing and aim. Harris was impressed with MacIntyre's marksmanship instruction and his calm manner on the range. He was even picking up some marksmanship tips himself.

The results of Angus' tuition were impressive. Harris walked down the line of targets to see 70 shots on target, no wild shots, and some very close groupings. Stuart, Seamus, and Aiden seemed to be shooting very well, with the others not too far behind. They switched to the 100-yard range for the rest of the session, constantly applying their marksmanship principles. Angus tirelessly worked the firing line, adjusting positions to make them more stable and giving them helpful tips. "Don't move the barrel or let go of the trigger until your bullet has gone down-range. Just keep still and observe your target. Remember, once you've shot, the enemy is going to be looking for you, so remain completely still."

Harris brought the session to an end before they got too tired and lost their edge. "Tomorrow, we'll go out to two- and three-hundred yards. We'll just keep working on those marksmanship principles, so go over them in your head tonight. Color Sergeant Murray will bring out one rifle with a telescopic scope for you to try out. I wish we could issue you all one, but they're simply too expensive," and he shrugged his shoulders apologetically. "Corporal MacIntyre, have the section clear up the range, pick up the spent brass cartridges, and then back to the armory for weapons cleaning."

The entire next day was spent shooting. The section increased the range to 300, and also worked on firing from standing, learning to lean backward with their weight on the back foot and tucking in their left elbow to provide a more secure support for the rifle. The emphasis was on well-aimed single shots. Towards the end of the day, Color Sergeant Murray came out with a rifle mounted with one of his new telescopic sights. Each of the men fired ten shots with it at targets 500 yards away. "Don't get your eye too close to the rear lens of the scope," he warned them. "About two inches away is right. Any further away and you won't get a full field of vision; any closer and the same thing will happen, plus you could earn yourself a black eye from the recoil."

The results with the scope combined with what they'd learned exceeded their instructors' expectations. Harris was relieved. All the men were good shots and Stuart, Seamus, and Aiden were getting better and better all the time.

Stuart and Ross had talked earnestly during a break, and after a nod of agreement, Stuart went to talk to Sergeant Harris and Color Sergeant Murray. "Excuse me, Sergeant, but the telescopic sights—how much are they?"

Murray smiled. "Too expensive for a private to buy, let me tell you that, son."

Stuart smiled indulgently and then asked, "But how much is 'expensive'?"

Murray glanced uncertainly at Harris, sensing something amiss. "Twelve pounds each, my lad," thinking that would end the conversation.

Stuart nodded. "Is there a paymaster in the fort who can cash a banker's check, Sergeant?" he asked Harris.

Harris knotted his eyebrows in confusion. "Yes, yes there is, but are you really thinking of buying one of the scopes with your brother?"

Stuart shook his head. "No, Sergeant. My brother and I would like to buy them for the entire section."

Harris and Murray gawked at Stuart, seeking some indi-
cation of a joke being played on them, but saw none. "You
want to buy eight scopes? That's almost a hundred pounds.
You could buy a small house for that sort of money," said
Harris in astonishment.

"I don't think a small house will do us much good in
France," said Stuart with a smile. "We recently inherited
some money; it won't do us much good sitting in a bank, and
it seems if we're going to be sharpshooters, we need those
scopes. If nothing else, just to look the part until we can
prove our worth."

Murray shrugged, "If the lad can pay for them, I'll have
them fitted for you tonight."

Harris gazed at Stuart remembering what MacIntyre
had told him about the brothers losing their family aboard
the *Lusitania,* and he began to put two and two together.
"Are you and your brother sure about this lad? That's a lot
of money."

"Yes, Sergeant," replied Stuart. "Like I said, money
won't do us much good in France, but those scopes will. If
Color Sergeant Murray can help, we'd like a half dozen binoculars as well," he added, nodding to the binoculars hanging from the necks of Harris and Murray for inspecting the
targets. "We do have one condition, though..."

Somewhat baffled, Harris and Murray stared at Stuart,
both expecting anything at this stage, but not what came
next. "We don't want anyone to know we bought them, if at
all possible. Perhaps you could just say the battalion found
some extra funds or something?" he asked, looking hopefully at Harris.

Harris looked at Murray who shrugged, and they both
nodded. Harris simply smiled, finished the cigarette he was
smoking and said, "Then we'd better get you to the paymaster, lad. Give your rifle to Color Sergeant Murray and follow
me."

Stuart gave his brother a quick thumbs-up gesture, and then followed Harris towards the fort.

Color Sergeant Murray held Stuart's rifle in his hands and watched them leave with bewilderment. *Only in the territorials*, he thought, *can a private have a general's bank account, and a vicar's modesty.*

***

The next morning, the section stood at the armory in confusion as their rifles came back to them mounted with brand new Periscopic Prism telescopic sights.

MacIntyre questioned the junior armorer, who just shrugged his shoulders. "They were fitted last night, Corporal, no mistake here. All signed for by the color sergeant. They're all yours now."

The section marched out to the range where they met with Harris and Murray. Sergeant Harris had the section load and fire at the 100-yard range with their new telescopic sights. Color Sergeant Murray adjusted each scope carefully until they were calibrated properly, then left them to it.

Once satisfied, Harris had them firing at the two, four, and 600-yard targets, calling out which target he wanted them to engage, and then having them use the top drum on their scopes to adjust to the correct range on their rifles.

Towards the end of the day, Harris called a halt and gave them a break. Afterward, he had them paste up new targets at the 100-yard line. It was time for rapid fire.

"So far as we promised, you've concentrated on single shots, but if the enemy is attacking you, you will need to switch to rapid fire. Every soldier is trained to place fifteen aimed shots downrange in what we affectionately now call a 'mad minute.' That's five rounds from your magazine and reloading five rounds at a time. Your scope is offset to the left to allow you to reload quickly if needed. Let's see how you do. On my command, begin, and then stop on my whistle." Harris had them reload and then barked out a command.

"Ready! Section, enemy to your front, one hundred yards, ra-pid fire!" and seven rifles exploded into action.

After 60 seconds, Harris blew his whistle. They had all fired 15 rounds. The men walked down to the targets. There were a few wild shots, but overall the results were good. "Not bad, but remember don't jerk the trigger, even in rapid fire. Let's do it a few more times, see if you bunch of misfits can reach twenty rounds each, all on target."

By the time they marched back, the section was in a good mood. Each recruit had a sense of accomplishment. They were shooting well and had covered a daunting array of military skills in a very short time—a testament to their intelligence and motivation, and to Angus and Harris' calm methods of instruction.

Harris halted them at the armory. "Tomorrow afternoon, Color Sergeant Murray and I will run the rifle qualification range. We'll be using open sights for rapid fire at the three-hundred-yard range targets, then single shots at a twelve-inch bullseye on the three-hundred-range targets. We'll also sort out targets for the scopes at six-hundred-yards, as you all have them. Major Sinclair will join us to see where you are in your training, so don't let us or yourselves down. We'll run through a practice in the morning, and then shoot for real in the afternoon."

As promised, the next day was filled with the sound of rifle fire and the pain of sore shoulders as the section absorbed the repeated recoils of their rifles.

By the afternoon, they were ready. Connor was sitting down with Seamus, Aiden, and Liam, eating his pack lunch, when he was assaulted by Lucky. The little dog had run up quietly behind Connor and leaped onto his lap, and began licking the Irishman's face, the dog's small stump of a tail wagging furiously. Major Sinclair smiled as men stood up at attention. He waved at them to relax, and looking down at Lucky, said, "He'll sleep under my desk all day, but as soon as I leave, he comes with me and stays by my side. I don't even need a lead."

Connor laughed. "Thank you, sir, for looking after him."

"Well, we didn't have much choice, did we?" he said, with a look of mock annoyance at Connor. "And he'll go to France—as long as he catches rats. Now, whether you men will join him depends on your shooting today." He returned Angus' salute and walked over, clipboard under one arm, to Harris and Murray.

Soon afterward, Harris called the section to fall in. With Sinclair looking on, the veteran sergeant went through a half an hour of marching and rifle drill with them. Then, switching with his friend, Murray had them strip down their rifles and reassemble them, naming parts as they did so and quizzing them on rifle maintenance, cleaning, specifications, and performance, including that of the scope. Harris then had them fall in, open ranks, for inspection. He then accompanied Major Sinclair, introducing each man before Sinclair asked each one a few questions, ending with Angus.

"From what Sergeant Harris says, you've earned that second stripe, Corporal. No doubt about it—well done."

After inspection, Harris had the section line up on the firing line. "Just as we practiced this morning, we'll begin with ten shots at the twelve-inch bullseye on the three-hundred-yard targets, open sights, and then ten shots with the telescopic sights at six-hundred-yards with telescopic sights only, then lastly twenty rounds rapid fire at three-hundred-yards, open sights. You each have eight charger clips of five rounds each—forty rounds in total." He glanced up and down the line and at the concentration on their faces. "Remember your marksmanship principles, remember your breathing, and try to remember everything Corporal MacIntyre has taught you. Don't rush. Settle yourselves down quickly, and whatever you do, do not jerk the trigger!" The last instruction elicited a few smiles. If they'd heard it once, they'd heard it a hundred times.

"Section! With two clips of five rounds, load!" shouted Harris.

"Make ready!" and the section pulled back their rifle bolts to chamber their first round.

"Assume the prone position!" and they dropped gently to the ground, protecting their rifle as they'd been taught.

"With ten rounds at the three-hundred-yard target bull-seye, in your own time, open fire!" Harris was relieved that no one fired. Each man checked his natural point of aim, settled the rifle into his cheek, sighted down the barrel, controlled their breathing and then began to slowly squeeze the trigger. The first shot went downrange after ten seconds, followed by others until a steady, slow rate of fire built up within the section. When they were finished firing, each man checked and cleared his weapon and then looked towards Harris, so he knew they were no longer shooting. He shouted, "Cease fire! Cease fire!"

Sinclair, Color Sergeant Murray, and Angus then walked down to the targets and recorded the scores for each shooter, double-checking each one and confirming hits before Major Sinclair scribbled numbers down on his clipboard. The range flags were limp in the air and there was a slight cloud cover, perfect shooting conditions—no wind, no glare. Once finished, they moved away to the side and signaled Harris to continue.

"All right lads, slow and steady using the scopes this time," he said in a deep calm voice. "Standby. With ten rounds at the six-hundred-yard target line, in your own time, open fire!"

Once finished and given the order to cease fire, Harris walked down range to inspect the targets.

Murray nodded as he came towards them. "They're doing very well. The results from the three-hundred-yards targets, open sights, were much tighter than I expected." Harris smiled with relief and a small amount of pride. "And look at these," said Murray, pointing at the six-hundred-yard targets. All the bullseyes were peppered with holes, with only a couple of shots outside the twelve-inch black circles.

"Those scopes are in the right hands, I'd say," came Sinclair's voice from behind him.

Harris turned. "Yes, sir. I'd agree with you there. They're shooting better than I dared hope."

Sinclair nodded at both sergeants and at Angus, who had finished papering up the targets, scores having been confirmed and recorded. "Gentlemen, we still have rapid fire, but I think it safe to say we have our battalion's sharpshooting section. Well done to you all." Looking at Angus, he said, "Especially to you, MacIntyre. They've accomplished a lot in a short time. I've seen that this afternoon. Very well done, Corporal. Now, let's finish shooting."

Harris walked back to the firing line, while the others stopped well to the side of the three-hundred-yard rapid-fire targets.

"You are doing well so far. Relax and concentrate. You have twenty rounds to fire in one minute at your target. Each round counts, but you only have to shoot fifteen. Begin with five rounds and then reload, five at a time. Do not fire off the last five blindly, either aim and fire, or leave them. They can improve your score, but they could also damage it.

"Right, listen in. Section, with one charger of five rounds, load! You will fire a minimum of fifteen rounds at your target within one minute. You will have to reload after the first five shots have been fired, so be ready to do so. You may fire up to a maximum of twenty rounds if you have time. When I blow my whistle, you will immediately stop firing. You can use the post in front of you to rest your arm on."

He repeated the instruction and then said, "Make ready. From the prone position...ra-pid fire!" and as he clicked his stopwatch seven rifles fired, followed by seven bolts being palmed backward and pushed forward, loading the next round to be fired. At the 15-second mark, the quickest began to reload with five rounds, by 45 seconds, everyone had reloaded three times. Just as Harris began to move his whistle to his lips, the firing had petered out, and as he blew his whistle, one last shot rang out followed by silence.

"Unload and clear your weapons for inspection!" called Harris, as Sinclair, Murray, and Corporal MacIntyre went to inspect the targets. Harris walked the firing line, ensuring weapons had no rounds in them. "Did anyone not fire twenty rounds?" he asked, looking at the ground for live ammunition ejected during the unloading procedure. The section remained silent, "Excellent."

Harris let them relax as he walked down to the rapid-fire targets. He knew the news was good by the grin on Angus' face. "All in the black! Everyone single one, Sergeant!" Angus said as he walked up, unable to contain his delight.

Major Sinclair came over. "Twenty shots each on target?" he said questioningly, "Correct me if I'm wrong, Sergeant, but I thought they only had to fire fifteen?"

Harris smiled. "I just wanted them to be ready for the real thing, sir. And they were all on target with one minute."

Sinclair smiled back, "And here I thought you were showing off...."

"Showing off, sir? Me, sir?"

Sinclair laughed. "Heaven forbid, Sergeant, heaven forbid. Right, march them to the parade square, and we'll have a little ceremony. After that, have them thoroughly clean their rifles and hand them in. Give them the evening off—no more instruction for now. Tomorrow have them back in the parade square after breakfast. Make sure they have a good dinner, a good sleep, and a good breakfast. It's going to be a long two days."

Harris saluted his officer and then yelled for the section to fall in before marching them back towards Fort George. Once inside, he had them march up and down the square before halting them in the center. The men, including

Angus, formed two rows, open ranks, facing their sergeant, who pivoted 180 degrees to salute the major as he walked towards them.

Major Sinclair stood in front of the section. "You have learned the basics well—better than we expected, if I'm honest. But it has been just the basics. There's a lot more to becoming a soldier than marching and shooting. The rest will come later, in France, but you've done what we've asked of you and more. I can tell you now, with not a little surprise, that all of you have qualified for your first-class marksmanship badge, and along with it, an extra six pennies per day onto your wages." The section couldn't help but smile at each other.

Sinclair continued, "Your scores on the range were all very good, but some were exceptional, especially when it came to using the telescopic sights," and he glimpsed down at his clipboard. "There is no specific award for infantry sharpshooters, not yet anyway, but if there were the following three individuals would undoubtedly have earned it today: Private Aiden O'Connell, Private Seamus O'Connell and..." he paused to survey the section before continuing, "Private Stuart McReynolds." Stuart's face lit up with genuine surprise and delight.

Sinclair reached into one of the large pockets of his officer tunic and brought out a small brown paper bag. "Given your outstanding performance today, in all aspects, I can confirm you are now officially the battalion's sharpshooting section. While you are no longer recruits, you are still under training, make no mistake. Well done, each and every one of you." He hesitated before nodding towards the rear of the small formation.

"All that is left for me to do is hand out your badges, but perhaps that is best done by your own officer." As he spoke Stuart saw Giles march into view from behind the section to salute Sinclair. On each cuff, the young officer wore the single diagonal pip of a 'subaltern,' a second lieutenant. The major returned Giles' salute before addressing the section again.

"Despite his somewhat unorthodox entry, Colonel Lyall has persuaded the brigadier not only to allow Lieutenant Morley to remain, but also for him to serve as Officer-in-Charge Sharpshooters." He looked sideways at Giles before shrugging his shoulders. "We didn't really know what else to do with him," he said with a smile as he peered over his glasses at the blushing officer before him.

He walked up to Giles who stood at attention, and reaching into a small paper bag, he brought out a pair of gleaming brass metal shoulder titles and handed them to the young officer. Each badge had 'SEAFORTHS' on it, curving upwards in a gentle semi-circle surmounted by a 'T' standing for Territorials. "Please hand the rest out to the section, and well done." He shook Giles' hand meaningfully.

Taking a step backward, Sinclair said, "I will see you tomorrow when we depart for France. I have left some forms with Sergeant Harris. That is all."

Giles called them all to attention and saluted the major. As Sinclair left, Giles turned to face the section—his section—and couldn't help returning the poorly hidden grins that met him.

"It looks like we're staying together for a while, gentlemen," he said before walking down the small formation, handing out the new shoulder titles and shaking each man's hand as he did so before turning the section over to Harris and walking away back to the fort with a determined stride.

Harris marched them back to the armory for weapons cleaning. "I'll be back in an hour. In the meantime, I need you all to sign Form 624 Imperial Service Obligation." He left a stack of forms with a pen on a table. "That allows the army to send you as territorials, overseas; and that, gentlemen, is where we are now heading."

CHAPTER TEN

Quintinshill

Quintinshill, near Gretna Green, 22nd May 1915,
the Scottish-English border

The train journey had been a pleasant one, thought Stuart, as he'd gazed out of the window at the majestic highland scenery. At times when the dark clouds came in from the west, it had seemed harsh and foreboding, but when the clouds had cleared and the sun had shone, chasing the cloud's shadows over the craggy, heather-covered mountains, it had been breathtakingly beautiful.

They had returned after dinner to find a crate of McEwan's Ale in their billet. No one could be sure, but Giles' hasty departure from the parade square suggested his involvement, and they'd toasted him with their first bottle. In the morning, they had cleared and cleaned their billet before heading to the armory with all their kit to pick up their rifles along with six Aitchison No. 3 Mark 1 binoculars from Color Sergeant Murray, who had wished them all a safe return from France.

Major Sinclair had seen them again on the parade square and had given each soldier a silver metal Imperial Service badge surmounted with a crown, to pin above their right breast pocket. This badge let everyone know they were territorials who had volunteered to serve overseas. He'd looked approvingly at their polished Seaforth T shoulder titles on the men's epaulets, and then had handed Angus a brown envelope. "Perhaps you should hand these out."

Barely hiding a smile, Angus saluted and turned to the section and called Liam, Connor, Murdo, and Ross forward, giving each man a crossed-rifle, first-class, skill-at-arms marksmanship badge, shaking their hands, and telling them to sew it on their lower left sleeve. Then he asked Aiden, Seamus, and Stuart to come forward. "Major Sinclair found these in the back of a drawer. We haven't issued them since the war began, but instead of letting them gather dust, he suggested we award them in recognition of your exceptional scores yesterday."

He presented each man with one of the badges surmounted with a five-pointed star. The award signified 'best shot' within a unit. Stuart inspected his badge as the train trundled along, already sewn with pride above his left cuff. For the rest of the morning, it had been a case of hurry up and wait—being rushed to complete a task only to stand around for ages afterward while nothing else happened. Angus had just shrugged his shoulders and said, "Welcome to the army."

They'd eventually boarded the train to travel to Inverness then down through the highlands towards Perth and Stirling. Sergeant Harris was with them, sitting by Angus. Giles and Sinclair were in first class. They had passed Stirling with its imposing castle on the hill above the town, now home to the Argyll & Sutherland Highlanders, and had continued to Larbert.

Larbert was a small village with a railway station close to where Scotland's 52nd Lowland Division was mustering to mobilize southwards. The plan was to join territorials from the Royal Scots Regiment headed for Liverpool docks, travel by train with them as far as Crewe, and then change trains for France. It was a standard joke within the British armed forces—wherever you were going, you always had to change at Crewe.

They'd arrived at Larbert to be told there were delays. There were always delays, so they'd just sat down and waited. The word came that the troop train wouldn't leave until midnight, then one o'clock in the morning, but it wasn't until three am that an old train appeared on the platform. Train carriages were in demand to transport troops, and so old, obsolete wooden carriages had been pressed back into service. Each passenger compartment held eight men and was lit with gas lamps.

The section sat towards the end of the station while Sinclair and Giles went to check on the arrangements. A few soldiers chatted with them when they saw their territorial insignia. These other men were also territorials from the Royal Scots, recruited from Leith, the port of Edinburgh. While their original orders had them heading for France, rumor had it that they were now heading for Gallipoli to reinforce the regular army for a big push.

One of the soldiers glanced over at Murdo, "He's not the one that threw the sergeant major over the parapet at Fort George and into the sea, is he?" he asked the other members of the section.

"Yes—but how do you know about that?" replied Stuart in surprise.

The man smiled. "You have to be joking! The whole of the Lowland Division knows about that by now." News of a black man throwing a sergeant major off the walls of Fort George and into the sea was too good a story not to share, and it had spread quickly.

"My name's Corporal Hicks," he said, sticking out his hand towards Murdo, who shook it self-consciously. "This is my section. We're part of A Company." He nodded to the men behind him, who all came up to shake Murdo's hand. "Wait till I tell the rest of the lads about this!" and before anyone could stop him, he was off towards other groups of soldiers, pointing in Murdo's direction.

Groups of men came up, some just to get a better look at Murdo, some to shake his big hand and confirm that he had indeed thrown a sergeant major into the sea. There were a few jokes about him being in the wrong Scottish regiment. "You should have joined the Black Watch, mate!" and another involving kilts and sheep at night, but they weren't aimed to hurt him and were self-effacing.

"Don't mind them, Murdo. It's just a bit of banter," said Hicks. "They're from D Company. Not too bright, if you know what I mean." He circled a pointed finger next to his head, rolled his eyes, and stuck out his tongue. The men laughed, and Hicks effortlessly deflected the banter now aimed squarely at him from the rival company's soldiers.

At 3:45 am, the train finally left Larbert Railway Station. Sinclair and Giles were sharing with some Royal Scots officers in the carriages reserved for the Headquarters Company. Harris had secured his men a carriage within D Company, much to the dismay of Hicks and his section, who were at the front of the train with A Company. "Don't fall asleep, or you'll wake up with no wallet or coins in your pockets! And Lord help you if you have any gold teeth," Hicks shouted as he walked past their compartment. The D Company men hurled a few choice words of friendly abuse in return.

Stuart checked at his watch. It was almost four in the morning, and despite Hicks' warning, all eight men were soon fast asleep.

***

Quintinshill was a small non-descript section of a vast railway network.

It lay on the west-coast line, one of the two main north-south railway lines that connected Scotland to England, and thereafter the rest of the world. It was comprised of an elevated railway signal box and two sidings, one on each side of the tracks that the signal box overlooked. The siding, laybys for trains to park temporarily, were there in case low-priority trains were impeding the progress of urgent ones. The signalman working the night shift was due to be replaced at six o'clock, but an arrangement was in place where whoever was coming on shift could catch a ride with a local train and arrive half an hour late. It suited everyone, and the books were kept in such a way that no one in authority knew it was happening—or turned a blind eye if they did.

That morning there was a problem. Two north-bound express trains were running late. The first was bound for Edinburgh, the second for Glasgow. Express trains had priority. The tracks had to be cleared for them, and the signalmen at Quintinshill found themselves with three low-priority trains to get out of the way to allow the northbound express trains to pass without hindrance. A local goods train was parked in the north-bound siding, and an empty coal train was parked in the south-bound siding. So, to clear the northbound track for the express trains, the third local northbound train was parked on the southbound track, on the wrong side, as no third siding was available.

At this stage, the signalmen at Quintinshill should have closed the south-bound track to all trains until the express trains had passed northwards, and the local train was sent after them, leaving the south-bound track empty again. But that's not what happened.

The two signalmen, James Tinsley and George Meakin, had made a litany of fatal mistakes—the late turnover meant paperwork needed to be completed, to cover up the infraction. Railwaymen from the parked trains were in the signal box reading newspapers and gossiping about the war, against regulations designed not to distract signalmen from their job. Physical safety and signal measures—which would have drawn attention to the fact the local train was sitting on the wrong tracks—were ignored.

And as the signalmen received a priority call to let the Royal Scots' south-bound troop-train pass, no one simply looked out the signal box windows to see the third local train still patiently parked outside on the southbound tracks, yards away from the signal box.

Moments later, the first Edinburgh north-bound express train passed the signal box. After a couple of minutes, it passed the troop train heading south. Stuart awoke as the trains passed each other at speed. It was daylight, and everyone else was still asleep, exhausted by the late night and the week of training. He sat dozing, eyes half-closed, looking out the window as the tranquil rolling countryside near Lockerbie passed by.

Quintinshill was situated on a bend. The troop train's enginemen were now on a downhill stretch with a heavy over-loaded train, packed with almost 500 soldiers, traveling at 70 miles an hour. As they came around the bend, they stared in abject horror to see a static train on the tracks in front of them and jumped to the brakes, but it was far too late. There was nothing they could do to avert the unfolding catastrophe.

The troop train's engine smashed into the local train, killing both enginemen instantly. The carriages full of soldiers were crumpled, torn apart, and catapulted over the local train. They landed on the northbound track and accordioned into each other, the old wooden carriages splintering apart with the force of the head-on collision. Within seconds, what had been a 215-yard long troop train had been reduced to a mere 67 yards of twisted metal, pain, and blood.

Stuart's first notion that anything was wrong was the squeal of brakes as the enginemen tried in vain to stop their train. He opened his eyes wide to look out the window in mild irritation when he was thrown forward, and all the rifles and kit cascaded down from the overhead racks, accompanied by a terrific hollow explosion as the troop train smashed into the local train in front of it. The carriage was full of shouts and yells as the rest of the section awoke amid the collision, holding hands up to cut faces and split lips, where rifles had battered them as they fell.

And then the stillness came. Stuart could feel bile rush up to his throat. It was just like the *Lusitania* all over again, and perhaps because of it, he was the first of them respond.

"Get out!" he yelled, "Get out now!"

The door to their compartment had buckled, but Ross, reacting as Stuart had, gave it an almighty kick that blew the small lock open. Their rearward carriage was still upright, sandwiched between others—compressed, but intact. The four rear carriages had separated and rocked backward, absorbing the impact and saving their occupants. Ross and Seamus jumped down to the track below, followed by the others. Harris and Angus quickly handed down their rifles and then jumped. Other soldiers around them were doing the same.

As they looked towards the front of the train, all they could see were train carriages scattered like gigantic fallen dominos. Clouds of steam erupted from the engines' remains, and soldiers were crawling on the tracks, dazed and bleeding. Others, trapped in the wrecked carriages, were crying for help and yelling out in pain. The dead were silent.

Angus checked the section. They were all right, apart from minor facial cuts. "Liam, Seamus, stack the rifles; the rest of you follow me. Those men need our help!" Angus turned to go, but Aiden grabbed his arm.

Angus wondered why Aiden was gripping his arm, but then the Irishman's eyes went wide, and he yelled at the top of his voice, "Get off the tracks! Get off the tracks! Run!"

Aiden started running towards the embankment, away from the trains, and as the section followed they saw why. Coming around the far bend towards the train crash, and towards the men crawling on the tracks and those trapped in the wreckage, was the Glasgow north-bound express train.

"Oh, sweet Jesus," muttered Liam a split second before the express train tore into the wreckage piled up in front of it, the injured soldiers, and their rescuers. The section threw themselves to the ground as the second collision blasted metal, debris, and bodies through the air. The express train mounted the wreckage, trapping those still in carriages below, and causing carnage on the tracks.

As the section began to pick themselves up, a couple of ruptured gas cylinders from the obsolete troop train—used for lighting the carriages and fully charged—contacted hot coals from the destroyed engine furnaces and exploded. Within seconds, the three-way train wreckage was ablaze.

High-pitched screams came from the destroyed carriages of the troop train. Those trapped in the warped and twisted carriages were burning. The buckled doors and windows barricaded those soldiers inside, most of them injured. And now the flames were taking hold of the wooden carriages and spreading fast. Aiden began to run towards the carriages towards the rear of the train, and as Harris and the section followed, they could hear something above the noise and screams around them that Aiden's acute hearing had picked out first - barking.

They ran towards a ruined carriage sandwiched between others. It had crumpled into about half its original size. The compartments at the end of the carriages had almost disappeared and were silent. No one could still be alive. But in the middle, the compartments had remained somewhat intact, although damaged and buckled. From the center one came the high-pitched bark of a small dog.

"It's Lucky!" shouted Connor, "The major and Giles must be in there."

Liam gestured at Murdo and cupped his hands. "Boost me up there!" Murdo meshed the fingers of his big hands and Liam stepped into them, holding Murdo's shoulders as the big black man raised his hands high. Liam grabbed the outside of the compartment door, pulled himself up, and peered inside the carriage.

Immediately, Lucky jumped up from inside the carriage, barking furiously at the fractured glass. Past the frantic dog, Liam could see a bundle of men on the floor or sprawled on the seats, Major Sinclair and Giles among them. Giles was holding his bleeding head in his hands when Liam yelled, "Lieutenant Morley! Lieutenant Morley!"

Giles held up a bloody hand to Liam in recognition. Liam yanked at the door, but nothing happened. He shouted down at the section. "They're both in there, but the door's jammed shut."

Giles shook his head to try and clear it. Whatever had just happened, Liam's call and Lucky's barking had brought him back to the here and now. At that moment, another gas cylinder exploded nearby, and that cleared Giles' head even quicker. Wherever the here-and-now was, it wasn't a good place to be. He stood and walked over to the door, pushing it, but nothing happened. Liam called from the other side, "Try the windows, sir." Giles tried to pull the compartment windows down, but they too were buckled and jammed.

Giles forced down a sense of panic as he smelled smoke from outside. Something was on fire, and he was trapped inside the damaged carriage. He shouted at Liam to move away and began kicking at the window. It cracked and eventually gave way, showering glass down on the section below. He kept breaking the glass until it was all gone, then he lifted up Lucky and held him out through the window to Liam, who passed him down to the others.

"Sir, we need to get you out fast," said Liam, "The train's burning."

Giles looked around at the men with him including Sinclair, all unconscious, and then reached for the leather holster on his Sam Browne leather belt.

"Get down and stand away from the door," he ordered Liam, drawing out his standard issue service revolver, a Webley IV. The Webley fired a large caliber .455 bullet at low velocity, which meant it had very good stopping power, and as Giles fired once into the compartment door's handle, it disintegrated. He re-holstered his pistol and forcefully kicked the door, which flew open.

"I've always wanted to fire my pistol," he stated simply with a schoolboy smile on his face.

Murdo boosted Liam back up, and Giles hauled him in, and then they both worked to pass down the six now-recovering men and Major Sinclair, who was bleeding from a cut above his eye, as was Giles. Liam and Giles came down last, just as two railwaymen appeared. "We're going to try to pull these carriages away with an engine before they catch fire," one of them shouted. Then he pointed towards the wreckage ahead of them, just as another gas cylinder exploded, spreading another ball of flame through the wreckage. "See if you can help those poor bastards trapped down there," he suggested before moving with his colleague to hook up an engine, now backing up towards the rear of the troop train.

They left Sinclair on the embankment with the others and went forward towards the center of the train wreck. They could see the Royal Scots desperately trying to reach fellow soldiers as the flames spread from carriage to carriage, buckling metal with heat, turning it red, and making wood steam before it exploded into flames. The screams coming from within the carriages being engulfed by the fire were inhumane.

They arrived at a carriage which was on fire at one end and on its side. Soldiers were trying to break through the sideways-facing roof with bayonets, knives, and bare hands as the screams from inside increased. Even as the section struggled to comprehend the disaster unfolding in front of their eyes, the carriage next to them exploded when yet another gas cylinder ruptured.

"Liam—up on the roof. It's our best chance," shouted Stuart, and then he turned to Giles, "Sir, if we can get some axes, Murdo and Corporal MacIntyre will make short shift of the roof. They're both lumberjacks."

Giles nodded. "Sergeant Harris, take Corporal Mac-Intyre and Private Munro and try and find some axes. Look in the other trains or the signal box; ask the railwaymen, they must have something, somewhere."

Harris replied with a quick, "Yes, sir," before running off towards the signal box with Angus and Murdo behind him.

Ross boosted Stuart up onto the roof as Connor did the same for Liam, followed by the Seamus, Aiden, and Giles. Connor and Ross stayed below, ready to help. The men felt the heat from the carriage through their boots. It was getter warmer all the time, and the old varnish on the wood was beginning to blister and crack. The end of the carriage nearest the collision's center was already on fire, which crackled and popped, consuming the wood. Standing on the top of the train, the men could see through the row of broken and buckled windows that had once been the side of the open carriage.

Stuart stared down into hell itself. Men were trapped in the wreckage of the carriage, and most couldn't move as the fire crept towards them. Those that could move had terrible injuries. Bones poked out of elbows and legs, some men had multiple compound fractures, and they yelled out in pain as they tried to drag broken limbs away from the fire. The fire was moving quickly, but they couldn't. The unconscious died where they lay, but others were all too aware of the terrible fate sweeping towards them.

As Stuart tried to take in the scene, he saw a soldier closest to the fire take out his bayonet and cut into his leg above the knee, which was trapped beneath twisted metal. His hair and uniform began to smolder as he sawed with increasing desperation, screaming as he did so and then, without warning, his hair and clothing burst into flames. He tried to smother his hair, but his hands were now on fire. With one last scream of pure anguish, he reversed the bayonet and drove it into his chest with both hands, falling back as the fire engulfed him.

Stuart backed away from the row of broken windows, too stunned to watch, but then saw something that focused his stare—a familiar face.

He now remembered A Company had been at the front of the train, and as he looked down, he could see Corporal Hicks, the cheery chap who'd chatted to them on the Larbert platform. Looking around and recognized more faces— Hicks' men, all with debilitating injuries, all unable to stand, let alone reach up to the men above them. At that instant, he heard the smashing of wood below, and Ross called up, "We're breaking through. Just tell them to hang on!"

Below them, Murdo and Angus were both smashing big axes into the train's exposed roof. They worked in perfect synchronicity, one ramming his axe blade into the wood while the other recovered, and then the other would crash his axe into the same mark on the wood. It was a mutual skill and trust that took years to develop, and they both had it in each other.

The fire was working its way up the carriage, and as Stuart watched in horror he saw one of the trapped men plunge his army-issue jack-knife into his own throat, sending blood gushing down his neck as the flames set his boots on fire.

"Hicks!" Stuart yelled down. "Hicks!"

Corporal Hicks gazed up towards the broken glass and recognition flicked across his face, alongside the pain. Both his arms were broken. Stuart could see the bone sticking through both forearms, and his head was bleeding badly. He was kneeling among his men with his arms hanging use-lessly. He couldn't help them or help himself, and there were tears in his eyes as he looked up. As he did, a hole appeared to his side, as ax heads began to rip apart the laminated wood.

"Hicks!" Stuart yelled, "Murdo and Angus are making a hole. Just hang on, we'll get you out! We'll get you out!"

But then the Royal Scots soldiers from the other side of the carriage, the underside, where the wheels and undercarriage were, began to yell. The soldiers could see the gas cylinders begin to smoke as the metal became hotter and hotter. "They're going to explode!" yelled a soldier and then began to turn away just as the first cylinder ruptured, sending a wall of flame through the carriage.

Hicks looked up desperately at Stuart, one broken arm held high, as a wall of fire swept over him and his men. Looking down, the section could see the whole carriage was on fire now. Their own boots were hot, and the flames had singed their clothing and faces.

Stuart and those around him were barely aware of Connor and Harris yelling at them to jump for it. Looking down through the windows, Stuart could see Hicks on fire, his broken arms flailing about, he and his men screaming, writhing in agony, engulfed in flames. Stuart closed his eyes to the horror, and then he heard the shot. He looked over in alarm as another shot rang out, and another.

Giles, face blistering, tears streaming down his face, was shooting into the carriage with his revolver, ending the agony of those burning alive inside. Two more shots rang out, and then the revolver clicked against an empty chamber. Giles turned, grabbed Stuart and yelled: "Jump!" As they did so, the remaining gas cylinders exploded, and so did the train carriage.

Major Sinclair saw what happened from a distance. When he heard the warning yells from the soldiers and saw his section on top of the roof of the burning carriage, he began to run hesitantly towards the train, still groggy from a slight concussion and wiping blood away from a cut on his forehead that was dripping into his eyes. As the first cylinder ruptured, he began to shout and wave at his men to get off the roof. He saw flames surge up from beneath them, and then saw Giles pointing his pistol downwards and shooting. Then an almighty explosion rocked the carriage.

Its sheer intensity saved the men, already in mid-air, as the explosion carried them beyond the deadly metal tracks and onto the soft grass verges below. Harris, Ross, and Connor were blown from their feet, but managed to get up to roll both Angus and Murdo on the ground to extinguish the flames licking their uniforms. Then all of them staggered towards the five limp bodies of their friends ten feet away.

Major Sinclair found them together and was astonished that none of them, if not all of them, were dead. They were bruised and bloodied, and their uniforms were all burnt. Their hair was singed, and their faces and hands blistered, cut and bleeding, from the collision or the explosion, or both. And they were either coughing or vomiting up smoke-filled bile. But miraculously, they were alive.

A Royal Scots soldier came running towards them, took one look, and began yelling for help over his shoulder. Stuart wondered why as he struggled to stand up, then he felt light-headed and his knees crumpled beneath him. The last thing he was aware of before he lost consciousness was Lucky licking his upturned face.

CHAPTER ELEVEN

Edinburgh

Stuart felt the heat on his boots increase until they caught fire and the flames began to lick their way up his uniform towards his face. He tried to beat them down with his hands and run away, but he couldn't move, and the flames kept coming closer and closer until he screamed.

He heard Ross calling his name, and then a merciful coolness descended upon his face and he opened his eyes. He was lying in a bed with his brother looking down at him. A nurse dressed in a pristine, starched pale blue-and-white uniform with a red cross on the sleeve was holding a cool wet cloth to his head.

"Hello there, sleepyhead," said Ross with a smile, but concern in his voice.

Stuart looked around in confusion. He was in an empty hospital ward of eight beds. "Where am I?"

The nurse smiled, relieved to have her patient awake. "I'm Nurse Ellis. It's Sunday, and you're in Edinburgh," she said as Stuart stared at the empty beds. Reading his thoughts, she said, "Don't worry. The rest have just gone out for a walk."

He looked up at his brother, who had bandaged hands, a dressing above his left eye, and whose face was deep red. "Are you okay?"

Ross nodded.

"You don't look okay," said Stuart.

Ross laughed. "You should see yourself!"

Stuart held up his hands and saw dressings on both. Reaching up, he felt his own face, which was red and tender. A dressing like his brother's lay on the right side of his forehead. He smiled. "And the rest?"

"They're all going to be fine, just the same as us—bruised ribs, minor burns, cuts, and sprains. We were very lucky. A moment later and it would have been too late."

"All those men—Corporal Hicks and his section—what happened?"

Ross sat down beside the bed. "It was in all the local newspapers this morning, although there wasn't much in the national papers. There was a train sitting on the southbound tracks and we crashed head-on into it. Then an express train ran into us and set off the fires. I hope to God I never see anything like that again. Those poor souls."

"And Giles?" asked Stuart.

"Giles is in another ward somewhere. Major Sinclair, Sergeant Harris, Angus, Connor, and Murdo are all fine and staying with the survivors from the Royal Scots. Physically, Giles should be fine, but I can't help wonder how his nerves are going to be after what he did."

Stuart stared at him for a moment. "They should give him a medal for what he did. No one deserves to die like that."

"I don't think they give out medals for shooting your own side. The sooner he's back with us the better, I think; don't give him too much time to ponder it all."

"How many died?" Stuart asked.

"They're calling it 'the worst railway disaster in British history.' The newspapers are a bit unclear, but about two hundred and fifty injured, and they're saying another two hundred and twenty-six killed. The fires got so hot they never recovered all the bodies. They were simply incinerated. Less than sixty men walked away unscathed, and only five of those were from A Company. There's a mass funeral in Leith tomorrow—the city's in mourning today."

They heard people coming down the hallway outside and could hear the unmistakable voice of Liam saying, "...and then Murdo just picks him up above his head like this and throws him in!" followed by a gasp and laughter—women's laughter.

Stuart glanced at Ross who smiled and shrugged. "Did I forget to mention Jo and Nell are here?"

As Stuart watched the door, Seamus came in with Jo on his arm, and between Liam and Aiden, there was Nell. Her face beamed as she saw Stuart sitting up in bed. The O'Connells all came to pat Stuart to make sure he was really better by touching him. Jo gave him a kiss on the cheek. "Why is it every time we meet you have bandages on your hands?" she said with a smile.

After a minute or so of banter, Ross stood up and motioned to Jo, who smiled and asked Nurse Ellis where they could get a cup of tea. Liam was about to say he'd join them later when Aiden not to subtlety coughed and arched his eyebrows towards Nell, standing at the end of the bed. Liam got the hint and frankly declared, "I'm parched. A cup of tea sounds just grand!"

"I'll leave you now," said Nurse Ellis, smiling at Nell, and Stuart watched her follow the rest out and then gazed up at Nell, whose eyes were now brimming with tears. He felt them come to his eyes as well and held up his hand. "Come here, you."

Nell sat down on the bed and then fell into his arms, sobbing. "When I first heard you'd been on the train, I thought you'd been killed. So many were. It's just so awful—it's just so sad."

"It's all right. I'm fine, we're all fine."

She looked up at him. "You're not all fine, you're all covered with bandages and you're crying, too."

He smiled. "I'm just so happy to see you. It seems such a long time and it's only been a week and a bit."

She sat up and dried her tears. "I can't let anyone see me like this. I'm a mess."

Stuart just gazed at her. She was more beautiful than he'd remembered. "You look lovely." He held up a bandaged hand to her cheek and drew her close, kissing her lightly on the lips.

"And that's enough of that!" said a stern voice from the doorway. They both turned like naughty children to see Giles walking into the ward, smiling at them both. Like Stuart, his hands were bandaged, and he had a plaster above one cheek, black eyes from what looked like a broken nose, and the same angry red complexion they all did. Despite his smile and informality, Stuart could see something had changed in the young officer, although he wasn't sure just what.

Stuart relaxed. "Sir, may I introduce Miss Abercrombie."

Giles shook her hand formally. "It's an absolute pleasure. I'm Second Lieutenant Morley, but please call me Giles," he said before looking back at Stuart. "It seems like you're in good hands Private McReynolds. Do you know where the rest of the misfits are?"

Stuart told him what he knew and where Ross, Jo, and the O'Connells had gone. "Jo?" he questioned as his eyes went to the ceiling and back. "Honestly, I leave you McReynolds alone for a day, and you're both sneaking women into the hospital!"

Nell laughed out loud before covering her mouth with her hand, taking an instant liking to Giles, who said, "Tea sounds splendid, but I'm afraid I'll have to go join my fellow officers for it, or maybe I can find Nurse Ellis. Please tell them all I came to see them."

"I will, sir. They'll be glad to know you're up and about, sir."

Giles smiled and turned to go, when Stuart stopped him, "Sir, if I may, it's just we were all talking about it, and I just wanted to say, you did the right thing. We all think so."

Giles stared back at Stuart for a few seconds. "Thank you," he said, and then he turned and left the room.

Nell gave Stuart a questioning look. He pursed his lips and after a moment, said, "He did something very difficult, very terrible."

"I like him, but he looks older than he should, like something awful has aged him."

As soon as she said it, Stuart knew that was the change he'd seen in Giles—he'd aged. Nell looked at him, seeing for the first time that Stuart himself had changed. "Tell me about what happened, and tell me what you all did."

She held his damaged hands gently in hers. "Please darling," she asked, and then smiled. "And then tell me who the misfits are."

He took a deep breath and began.

Ross and Jo came back after 20 minutes, followed soon after by the rest. Nell got up and with Jo went to 'powder their noses.' They came back as the boys were all settling back into their beds. Despite their smiles and banter, they were tired. Both Jo and Nell could see that, and they could also see that they were already a close group of men, a quick bond had developed, and they were comfortable in each other's company. Nurse Ellis came in and informed Nell and Jo that visiting hours were over. They left with smiles, promising to return the next day, Nell blowing a badly hidden kiss to Stuart. They didn't have far to travel as the East Neuk was only an hour by train over the Forth Rail Bridge from Edinburgh.

As they left, Liam summed up the Irishmen's thoughts. "If there's any more like those two where you came from, I'm coming home with you next time!" They were laughing as Major Sinclair, Second Lieutenant Morley, and Sergeant Harris walked in with Angus, Connor, and Murdo—the last three burdened down with uniforms.

"At ease, gentlemen, at ease," said Sinclair. "It's good to see you're all feeling better." He went from bed to bed, inquiring after each man, checking that they were recovering and were being cared for. When he was finished, he turned and addressed the section.

"First, I want to say I've been meeting with the Royal Scots today, and I wanted to pass on their gratitude for your efforts yesterday morning. In the midst of tragedy, you all brought credit to yourselves and to the battalion. Well done." He turned to Giles. "Well done, everyone."

"Second, I have some news. As a result of the disaster yesterday, the Royal Scots are deploying without enough men, although soldiers from the Highland Light Infantry have volunteered to fill gaps as best they can. As we are already mobilized, here, and ready to go, a suggestion has been made to have us join the Lowland Division for the next few months. Colonel Lyall has agreed to this, strictly on a temporary basis, and so we will detach from the Highland Division forthwith. What this means, gentlemen, is that instead of going to France, we will be going to Gallipoli."

Seamus and Connor glanced at each other. They had come all the way to Scotland to end up following in their older brother's footsteps.

"I assure you, your skills are needed. The Turks are proving very effective snipers. Just a few days ago, one killed an Australian major general. The Royal Scots will be glad to have a section of sharpshooters out there." And with that sobering news, he and Giles departed.

Sergeant Harris addressed the section. "It's now Sunday afternoon, we leave Tuesday morning. We have a long journey, so there will be plenty of time to recover from your injuries on the way. I'm afraid we can't wait any longer. On Tuesday, we'll go down to Liverpool and then sail to join the Mediterranean Expeditionary Force. The Royal Scots have sorted out our uniforms. They're a bit singed and that's not a bad thing, makes you look like you been around, which you have. They've replaced what couldn't be repaired." He nodded and Connor and Murdo handed out uniforms back to the section, all except one.

Harris looked at Stuart. "While you were having your beauty sleep this morning, laddie, the rest of us had a chat. Corporal MacIntyre here needs a second-in-command, a '2IC,' and with Second Lieutenant Morley's approval, and mine, you are hereby promoted to lance corporal."

Angus came forward with the last uniform in his hands, and Stuart could now see a new white single downward stripe on both tunic sleeves. "Well done," Angus said, shaking Stuart's hand gently. The section all applauded and laughed at the look of surprise on Stuart's face.

"Of course," said Angus, "you now owe us all a round of drinks!" An even louder cheer went up from the section, drawing the attention of Nurse Ellis, who came in and told them all to be quiet.

Harris motioned for them to settle down. "You'll stay here tomorrow, although you can leave in the afternoon for a few hours if you want. Go see a bit of Edinburgh is my advice, you've all earned a breather. Just don't go to Rose Street—too many pubs." After congratulating Stuart, Harris left with Angus, Connor, and Murdo, who said they'd be back tomorrow at noon for visiting hours.

Ross came over to congratulate his brother, as did the others, joking that at this rate he'd be a general in no time. Soon Liam was parading past Stuart's bed and saluting with an 'eyes right.' The section burst into laughter, drawing back in Nurse Ellis who scolded them good-naturedly, but firmly this time, to get some rest.

When she turned to leave, Liam called out, "Sister, just one thing I wanted to ask you."

Nurse Ellis turned expectantly. "Yes, Private. What it is?"

"Can you tell us where Rose Street is?" and the section burst into laughter all over again.

***

As it turned out, Rose Street was ridiculously easy to find, sitting as it did behind Princes Street, the main scenic thoroughfare through the middle of Edinburgh, Scotland's stunning capital city. Nell and Stuart had parted from the rest of the group outside Jenners, a vast seven-story sandstone corner department store and established landmark in the city. Jo and Stuart were heading for the castle, and the rest were heading for Rose Street, with a parting warning from Stuart not to be late—they were due back at four o'clock. Theoretically, the girls were chaperoning each other, but between them, they'd made their own arrangements, and neither Stuart or Ross were going to question them about it

Inside Jenners, Nell had taken Stuart through the grand hall and then upstairs to have lunch in the tearoom. "To celebrate your first promotion!" she'd insisted. She'd held his arm since they'd left the hospital and every now and then would place her head on his shoulder. Oblivious to others, they were about to sit at a table by the window, looking over Princes Street towards the castle, when an officer came up to Stuart abruptly and asked why his tunic collar was not tightly fastened at the neck.

Stuart looked at him without expression. "I have burns to my face and neck, sir," he stated.

The officer's eyes narrowed. "I can see that, Lance Corporal, but that's no excuse for slovenly appearance."

"No, sir," said Stuart, with barely hidden annoyance in his voice. "But if I were to fasten my collar, the wool would rub and chaff my burns, which would then become infected, and I wouldn't be able to leave the hospital, sir."

The officer stared back at Stuart, not normally used to anything beyond a *yes, sir* or *no, sir* reply from an enlisted soldier.

"But you're not in the hospital now, Lance Corporal."

"Actually, I am, sir. We've just been allowed out to enjoy the afternoon, sir." Stuart placed an undue emphasis on the words *enjoy the afternoon, sir.*

To Captain Colin Campbell-Greenwood, the British Army was all about standards, regulations, and discipline. He was irritated that some enlisted soldiers were unable to grasp this self-evident fact. Some enlisted soldiers—including the one in front of him—didn't know their place, threatened discipline, obedience, and the very fabric of society, and had to be corrected.

"Name," he demanded, and Stuart could feel anger well up inside him as he felt Nell's arm tighten on his.

"McReynolds, sir," said Stuart, this time placing undue emphasis on the *sir.*

Captain Campbell-Greenwood's face tightened ever so slightly. There was a hint of impertinence in the soldier's voice, combined with a look verging almost on arrogance, maybe enough to charge him with dumb insolence. "Commanding officer?" he demanded.

Stuart just stared at the officer in silence, his jaw tightening.

"Ah, that would be me, old boy," came a voice from behind Stuart, who turned in surprise to see Giles.

Before Campbell-Greenwood could say anything, Giles took Nell's hand and shook it gently. "Miss Abercrombie, what a pleasure it is to see you again!" he enthused. "I hope you're looking after our wounded hero here?"

Quickly turning to Campbell-Greenwood, Giles continued, "Did my lance corporal here mention he was convalescing?"

Campbell-Greenwood, still on the back foot, said, "Well, yes, but..."

"Splendid!" exclaimed Giles, now looking at the red tabs on the officer's uniform. "Gosh, a staff officer!" he said with undue reverence. "Back to the front soon, I hope?"

Campbell-Greenwood hadn't actually been to the front yet and wished the talkative officer would stop being so, well, talkative. "Yes, but..."

"Back for another crack at the Hun, what?" asked Giles with unbridled enthusiasm.

"Yes, but look here, this man..."

"Were you at the funerals this morning?" cut in Giles.

"Funerals?" asked Campbell-Greenwood, unable to keep up with the conversation.

"Quintinshill, the funerals for the Royal Scots, over a hundred of them buried just today. There would have been more of them, funerals that is, for me included," he said, gesturing towards his own battered face, "if my lance corporal here and his section hadn't been there. A nasty business, what?" asked Giles.

Now thoroughly perplexed, Campbell-Greenwood answered hesitantly, "Yes, yes—a nasty business."

"I couldn't agree with you more, old boy!" over-enthused Giles. "I couldn't agree with you more! You must tell us all about it! Please, will you join us for a spot of tea?" asked Giles, gesturing towards a table with a pinafore'd and quietly amused waitress next to it.

Captain Campbell-Greenwood couldn't think of anything he'd rather not do and wondered seriously if the officer meant to sit with an enlisted man for tea in Jenners, and what he was being asked to tell them all about, and how he could get back to the business of charging the lance corporal. "No, but look here..."

"I understand completely, old boy. Too modest, that's what you are, too modest!" and Giles grabbed the captain's hand and pumped it up and down vigorously. "It's an honor to shake your hand, sir, an absolute honor indeed! Here, take our table. Please, we insist. It's the least we can do for you, the absolute least we can do," and he gestured to the smiling waitress and guided a protesting Campbell-Greenwood towards an empty seat.

"Tea for this gentleman!" Giles ordered in a loud voice, and then bowed towards the officer. "It's been an honor, sir. Wait until I tell the general!" He turned, winked at Nell and Stuart, who stood inert, grabbed Nell by her free arm who still held onto Stuart with the other one, and headed quickly for the door.

Captain Campbell-Greenwood, newly appointed staff officer to the 52nd Lowland Division, sat speechless. It occurred to him that something had just happened that shouldn't have, that a clearly insolent soldier had gone unpunished, that he hadn't even made a note of the talkative officer's name and rank, and that somehow he had a feeling he'd been made a complete idiot, although he wasn't entirely sure.

Just as he was about to get up out of his chair, the waitress stood in front of him, blocking him in. She placed a pot of very hot tea on his table, a bit too close to the edge for comfort, and with a completely straight face asked if he'd like to see the cake trolley. "I'd recommend the gooseberry fool, sir. It's today's special."

Giles hurried Nell and Stuart downstairs and outside. "And my parents said that acting in the school play was a waste of time!" He burst into laughter and so did Nell. Stuart looked at them both in confusion, which made them both laugh even more.

"Lance Corporal McReynolds," said Giles, somewhat regaining his composure, "The Café Royal is a very nice place for lunch. It's just tucked in over there," he said, pointing to a small street across St. Andrews Square. "Oysters are their specialty. It's a bit pricey, mind you, although I have a feeling that may not trouble you too much..." and he raised an inquisitive eyebrow. "And please avoid any more altercations with staff officers. That last one could have spelled trouble for you."

"Yes, sir. And thank you, sir."

"Think nothing of it—but it's probably a good thing we're all away from here tomorrow, so go enjoy your lunch, both of you."

He smiled, and as he turned to go, Stuart said, "If you'll pardon me for saying it, sir, you're not at all what I expected most officers to be like."

Giles smiled. "Under the circumstances, I'll take that as a compliment, and congratulations on your promotion, by the way."

Stuart came to attention and saluted. "Thank you, sir."

Giles returned the salute, saying, "Please, keep him out of trouble Miss Abercrombie," and he turned, walking towards George Street, still chuckling to himself.

If Giles Morley was unlike other officers, he had his reasons. He had a supreme personal disinterest in maintaining the outdated social norms that surrounded him.

He wasn't from an overly privileged background, but his family was wealthy enough. They also had a strong work ethic, and as a boy growing up in Somerset, he'd worked hard at a local cider mill during the holidays. There he had earned his own pocket money, developed a taste for *scrumpy*—unfiltered medium-dry hard cider—while learning that folk from England's west country were some of the hardest working, most friendly, honest, humorous, and caring folk one could ever care to meet.

These were not the same qualities he found in the majority of his peers. While attending boarding school, he met those who exuded superiority, haughtiness, and coldness, and who had made cruelty towards those not as privileged as them into an art form.

As a result, Giles had decided early on to be his own man. He'd rejected etiquette for manners, having been told the former was all about excluding the majority of folk and making them uncomfortable, while the latter was the opposite. He'd battled the bullies at school and had developed a fearless attitude, confronting them wherever he found them. Physically strong and mentally astute, he'd done well at rugby and academics, and although seen by many as an outsider for his egalitarianism, no one ever doubted his integrity.

At the outbreak of war ten months earlier, Giles had been in his first year of university studies at Durham. He had considered a few options—returning home and following tradition, joining the Somerset Light Infantry alongside fellow officers he had gone to school with—but he rejected them. He had wanted nothing to do with his privileged and pompous peers, and although he was entitled through his schooling and a stint in the officer cadets to be commissioned, he had decided to enlist instead. He would go where he wouldn't be recognized, where no family connections would be forthcoming, where no strings could be pulled, and where he would be constantly challenged. He hoped that by doing so, he'd wage war on his own terms, on his own merits. So he had found himself in the remotest of military barracks as a private in the remotest of regiments—the Seaforth Highlanders.

It had been an inauspicious start, but the incident with Skaig had confirmed all he held close—that with courage, he could personally make a difference, but to do so he'd had to re-assume the mantle of junior officer rank.

**

Giles was correct. The Café Royal was very nice and was a glorious example of Victorian and Baroque architecture. It resembled a Parisian café with its elegant stained glass, etched and beveled mirrors, and late Victorian plasterwork, with large painted Doulton ceramic murals on the walls.

The maître d' had hesitated at the sight of an enlisted uniform on an injured man entering his establishment. He made a show of checking his reservations until Stuart had casually asked if they stocked a wide selection of white

Burgundy to accompany the oysters. Nell instantly scolded him, "Oh, of course they do, darling. This is the Café Royal, after all," and had rolled her eyes at the maître d' as if in apology, followed by her most endearing smile. That had been greeted with a nod of appreciation and a table for two.

After they'd both ordered Oysters Rockefeller, accompanied by a very suitable 1911 white Burgundy, Stuart looked inquisitively at Nell, 'Oh, of course they do, darling?' he parroted.

Nell blushed. "Well, I could see he was hesitating, and I had complete faith both in your selection of wine and in the Café Royal's wine cellar."

Stuart laughed. "You do make me laugh sometimes."

Nell smiled. "And that's a good thing?"

"Yes, of course it is, sweetheart," and he leaned over and kissed her hand.

She beamed again and then, holding his hand, asked, "Why was that officer in Jenners so beastly when Giles seems so nice?"

Stuart pondered the question. It would be easy to say one was just a supercilious idiot and one wasn't, but would be too easy. "I'm not sure. Perhaps he just didn't like me being there. Some officers can be like that, I'm certain. Perhaps he doesn't like territorials, or perhaps he was just having a bad day. I'm not sure." He smiled and shrugged. "Ask me later on, and I'll probably give you a completely different answer."

Nell squeezed his hand. "When will 'later' be, darling?"

Stuart sighed. "I'm not sure. We're being sent away, and I know leave isn't given often. It might be some time." His voice dropped. "We're being sent to Gallipoli."

"Gallipoli? I thought you were being rushed to France," asked Nell in hushed tones.

Stuart laughed half-heartedly, "So did we. Apparently, we're now on loan to the Lowland Division, but only for a while. We'll be in France soon enough. I think."

Nell squeezed his hand. "How long do you think the war will last? The papers were all saying it would be over by Christmas, and Christmas was five months ago."

Stuart shook his head. "I think those predictions were all based on optimism and colonial wars, where one side had an overwhelming advantage. I don't see that happening in this war—this is different. There are so many armies involved over such a vast geographic area, it'll be hard for anyone to land a knock-out punch to end it quickly. In school, we studied the American Civil War—big armies, industrialized support, large territories, some of it trench warfare. It went on for four years before one side was ground down. Towards the end they called it a war of attrition. I can see this being exactly the same."

Nell listened to him, afraid of what he was saying, afraid of a long war, afraid for his safety, and afraid of the deep feelings she had for the man across from her, already injured before even leaving the country. She could have quite easily burst into tears at that moment, in despair and worry, but she took a deep breath and did the opposite. She squeezed his hand, smiled lovingly and said, "Then let's not waste any of our precious time together, darling," just as the waiter arrived with a perfectly timed and chilled bottle of Chablis.

They spent the rest of the afternoon leisurely. Stuart enthralled Nell with tales of San Francisco and the wine country to the north of it, clam chowder in bowls made from sourdough bread, sea otters swimming on their backs cracking abalone open in Monterey Bay, and clouds of migrating red-orange Monarch butterflies at Santa Cruz. He told her of the days he and Ross had spent at a small rustic boarding school in the foothills of Santa Barbara. It had been founded by a Harvard graduate named Curtis Wolsey Cate. There, he and Ross had thrived during days spent on rigorous academics, outdoor sports, horse-riding, and daily cold showers.

Nell, in turn, told him of school days spent at Waid Academy in Anstruther with Jo, where the girls had both vied, and then tied, for 'Dux'—the top academic of their year. She described North Sea storms that could send massive sea-grey, spume-covered waves to pound the stone harbor, rocks and shoreline, powerful enough to make the ground shake. She told of accompanying her father on one of his sailing ship voyages to Demark and Holland and then back home to Scotland and of a childhood spent searching tide-pools, beaches, fields, and farms, giving her a knowledge of birds, fish, and animals that was as impressive as it was fascinating to Stuart.

After an excellent dessert of crème brulee, they walked arm in arm down the length of George Street admiring its Georgian facades and elegant shop windows. They strolled towards Charlotte Square, and then across to the Parisian Ross Fountain in Princes Street Gardens, where they sat and ate an ice cream with Edinburgh Castle towering above them. They'd sauntered down the gardens, Nell laughing at the squirrels scampering about, past the towering monument to Sir Walter Scott, and had eventually reached Waverly Station, where Nell and Jo had arranged to meet.

Waverly was a large railway station with over 20 train platforms, all covered with a Victorian wrought-iron and glass roof. Stuart laughed as Nell told him a story she'd once heard as a child. "There was a local deckhand, apparently none too bright, who'd somehow won a return train ticket to Edinburgh. He'd set off in the early morning and had come back in the late afternoon. When folk eagerly asked what he'd thought of Edinburgh, he'd said that it was nice but very busy and noisy, and that he liked somewhere he could see the sky properly and there were trees—he'd spent his entire day in the train station!"

Nell held on to Stuart's arm tightly as he looked up at the central clock. It was time for him to go. "I can't be late," he said, with apologetic resignation in his voice.

Nell turned to face him and let her fingers contour the single stripes on his sleeves. "No, that wouldn't do at all, Lance Corporal McReynolds," she'd said with forced frivolity. But then she'd laid her head on his chest and hugged him, the tears quickly welling up and slowly running down her cheek.

"Promise me that you'll take care of yourself, darling," she said through her tears.

"I will—I promise."

"And no more injured hands."

He smiled and agreed. "And no more injured hands."

She began sobbing, her chest heaving and her breath coming in gasps, as she was hit by the stark realization that he was now leaving her to go to war.

"But most of all, please come back to me, my darling. Please, please, please come back to me," she begged, desperation now creeping into her voice.

She felt the roughness of his army tunic as Stuart held her close, with one bandaged hand around her slim waist and the other tucked under her chin and gently raising her face up.

"I promise," he said, and then she felt him kiss the tears away from one cheek and then the other, just as he had done at St. Andrews station ten long days ago. He kissed her gently, and then more passionately. Nell pressed her lips to his, holding him closer as she did so, willing the moment between them to last forever.

She looked up at Stuart and as he gazed into her tear-filled eyes he said, "I love you Nell."

She felt her heart leap. "I love you too, my darling, I love you too," and as she said it she knew it was completely, wonderfully, and terrifyingly true.

CHAPTER TWELVE

To Gallipoli

Cape Helles, Gallipoli, Turkey, June 1915

Their journey had taken four weeks, from Liverpool to Gibraltar to Malta and then on to the island of Lemnos, only 50 miles from the tip of the Gallipoli peninsula. The Greek Government had offered Lemnos to the allies and was the campaign's major naval base, serving as a staging and transit area for troops, hospitals, and convalescent camps. By the time they reached the island, they'd recovered from their injuries and Sergeant Harris had used the time to continue their basic training, including bayonet drill and hand-to-hand combat.

"There will come a moment when you're faced with someone trying to kill you, or when your job is to kill someone, and you'll naturally hesitate. I've seen it happen again and again, and I've seen good men die because of it. Split seconds count in battle. Hesitate and you give the man in front of you—or his pal—time to kill you." He motioned for the section to sit down on the sunbaked ground before continuing.

"There's a suspension of belief in battle. I remember the first time someone shot at me. I looked at the soldier next to me, he stared back at me, and while we were trying to comprehend if we were really being shot at, he was killed right in front of me with a bullet through the center of his chest. Because we hesitated, we gave the Boers shooting at us another chance to kill us, and they took it.

"In hand-to-hand combat, there is absolutely no room for hesitation. You have to kill or disable quickly and keep going, because they'll always be someone else looking to kill you. If you're wounded, keep fighting. This isn't a game of football or shinty—no referee's going to blow the whistle to stop the game. No one is going to stop the war just because someone's stuck a bayonet through your arm. All you've become is an easier target for the next enemy soldier to pick out of the crowd and kill. That's how it works- weakness is fatal. You keep fighting to stay alive, and to keep the man next to you alive. If you're in pain or bleeding, good- it means you're not dead. And if you're not dead, you can fight, you can reload your weapon, you can pull a trigger, you can swing a sharpened spade, you can stab with a knife, club, choke, batter, gouge or bite, and I've seen it all done. The major and I have done it ourselves, and because of that we're here, instead of rotting in the bottom of some forgotten skeleton-strewn trench on the Western Front."

He looked down at the scout section. He'd become close to them, closer than he'd ever admit. The nature of his training and their small number meant he had gotten to know the section well. *They're all good men, even Murdo*, he thought, and he was ashamed now for his hesitation in enlisting him. They were smarter than many soldiers he'd served with. They seemed to absorb everything that was taught to them and be ready for more the next day.

At the marksmanship ranges at Lemnos, they'd had a chance to improve their sharpshooting skills and had won grudging admiration from a handful of Cameronians watching them- high praise indeed from Scotland's rifle regiment. But he worried that their swift basic training, devoid of the usual yelling and abuse that characterized regular military training, would leave them vulnerable. He'd seen men fight because they feared the non-commissioned officers behind them more than the enemy in front of them. The scout section hadn't experienced that, and he wondered if as a result, they'd have the disciple to stand and fight when the odds were stacked against them.

"Right then; enough of this chit-chatting. Let's go over it all again, and I want to see some real aggression in the moves!"

For the rest of the morning they parried, thrust, slashed, stabbed, and butt-stroked with their rifles and bayonets. "If you get three seconds to yourselves in a fight, reload! But remember, if you shoot someone in a trench with a rifle, the bullet will go clean through them and hit someone else behind him, which could be good- or could kill your best mate. Be aware, use your peripheral vision, use your senses, and do not hesitate to trust in them. Forget any rules you thought or read or imagined applied to warfare- none exist in close combat. If someone has their back to you, bayonet him; if someone's wounded, finish him off; if someone's trying to surrender when everyone else is still fighting, knock them out or kill them- you simply don't have the ability to take prisoners in close combat, and you can't afford to turn your back on them. It isn't nice, it isn't written down, but it's the simple plain truth of it."

After lunch, Major Sinclair visited them, with Lucky still at his heels. After drawing Sergeant Harris aside for a moment, he motioned for Angus to have the section fall-in. "I'm glad to see you all fully recovered. I came to tell Sergeant Harris to prepare you for departure. We leave for Gallipoli tonight."

He paused, letting the information sink in. "Once there, we will attach ourselves to the Scottish Rifles Brigade with the remainder of the Royal Scots- those that weren't at Quintinshill." Looking at the eight men in front of him, he couldn't help wondering how many would survive the next few months, or how many would survive the war.

"Are there any questions?" he asked. When no one answered, he said, "I may not see you for a while, but I'll leave Sergeant Harris with you for now, and Second Lieutenant

Morley will meet you when you arrive. Remember all we've taught you and look after each other." Sinclair nodded to Harris who saluted, and then the officer left them in silence, broken after a few seconds by Harris.

"Right then, time to earn your pay. Corporal MacIntyre, I want uniforms and bodies scrubbed and washed, and rifles stripped down and cleaned. Do not polish your brass. Let it tarnish. No point giving the enemy a nice shiny target, but make sure everything else, including yourselves, is squared away. After that, I want a full kit inspection, each of you with a standard ammunition load: one hundred and twenty rounds, bayonets sharpened, rations, and water for two days. Any questions?"

"No, Sergeant!" replied Angus.

"Excellent. I'll see you in three hours," and he left the section to prepare for the final leg of their journey.

***

The 29th Division was comprised of regiments from across the British Isles: fusiliers from England and Ireland; borderers from Scotland and England; infantrymen from Wales, Essex, Hampshire and Worcestershire; and territorials from Edinburgh and London. It even included a volunteer battalion: the Royal Newfoundland Regiment. The division had landed in Gallipoli on the 25th of April, expecting a quick and easy fight to clear the coastal guns so the navy could push its way through to Constantinople and knock Turkey out of the war while opening up the major maritime supply route to Russia. In doing so, they hoped Romania and Italy would join the allied cause. It was meant to take a couple of weeks. It hadn't worked. From the very moment they had attempted to land on the Turkish shoreline, they had suffered horrendous casualties. A month and a half later, they still hadn't captured the first day's objectives.

At least they weren't alone. The Royal Naval Division had landed with them, sailors and marines, both regulars and reservists. The French *Corps Expéditionnaire d'Orient* held the right flank, attacking up the Dardanelle coastline with a mixture of French infantry and colonial troops: Zouaves from Algeria and Tunisia; Senegalese Tirailleurs from West Africa; and a composite battalion from the Foreign Legion. The Australian and New Zealand Army Corps, known by the acronym ANZAC, had landed further up the coastline on the left flank, a landing designed to cut off and encircle the Turkish troops at Cape Helles. That hadn't worked either. They'd landed on the wrong stretch of coastline and were completely hemmed in and isolated by the Turks, who were dug in on the high ground, dominating what had become to be known as Anzac Cove.

The navy was offshore, providing heavy naval gunfire to support the troops ashore, but the plan for them to cruise full-steam up the straits to Constantinople hadn't worked. In fact, nothing had worked so far, and so General Sir Ian Hamilton had asked for reinforcements- tens of thousands of them.

He had been sent three volunteer divisions: the 10th Irish; the 11th Northern; and the 13th Western divisions together with the 29th Indian Infantry Brigade- Sikhs, Punjabis, and Gurkhas from British India. But the bulk of his reinforcements would comprise five territorial divisions: the 42nd East Lancashire; the 52nd Lowland; the 53rd Welsh; and the 54th East Anglican along with the 2nd Mounted Division. The latter comprised territorial yeomanry cavalry from across Britain who had left their horses at home to fight, begrudgingly, as lowly infantrymen.

The Anzacs were reinforcing, too. The Australians sent another division of volunteers and territorials including Australian light-horsemen, whose horses, like the British yeomanry, had been left behind. The New Zealanders added more men, including mounted rifles, now fighting in a dismounted role and reinforced by the Maori Native Contingent. The French doubled their numbers to two divisions and two squadrons of aircraft, providing reconnaissance beyond and above the lines of trenches. And still more units came: the Ceylon Planters Rifle Corps appeared to bolster the number of riflemen; both the Maltese and the Egyptian Labor Corps arrived to provide extra muscle to dig trenches, fill sandbags, construct piers and dugouts. To reinforce the Indian Mule Cart Transport Unit in moving supplies, water, ammunition, and evacuating the wounded, came the Palestinian Zionists of the Assyrian Jewish Refugee Mule Corps, shortened for obvious reasons to the Zion Mule Corps.

The first reinforcements to reach Gallipoli would be the territorial Scots.

Opposing them was the Turkish Fifth Army; 80,000 well-equipped experienced soldiers sworn by Jihad-holy war-to push the infidels back into the sea. Initially five divisions, the army was rapidly expanding under its German commander, General Otto Liman von Sanders, to meet the allied invasion on Turkish soil. Although the Fifth was ranked the best in the Ottoman Turkish Army, the allies-and the commanding general of Gallipoli forces in particular- had woefully underrated the individual Turkish soldiers that made up its ranks.

General Sir Ian Hamilton had made it known that in his estimation one British soldier was equal to eight Turks, Syrians, or Arabs- but no one had told that to the Turks, Syrians, or Arabs at Gallipoli. Within a month, they'd inflicted 24,000 casualties and had fought the allies to a standstill. Individual companies of 120 Turkish soldiers had wreaked disproportionate bloody havoc on 1,000-strong battalions of British soldiers approaching the beaches.

The Turkish soldiers were defending their homeland- in some cases, defending their very own towns and villages-and they were proving the equal of any soldiers sent to attack them.

The newspapers, fueled by overly optimistic reports from General Hamilton, were reporting success after success where only abject failure existed on the ground. The British, French, Colonial, and Anzac troops were brave beyond reason, courageous in battle and tenacious in defense, but so were the Turks. There was both a stalemate and a mutual respect. Both sides dug trenches, closely contouring each other, mirroring the Western Front and mocking the plans for a quick, easy, fluid campaign.

***

Lance Corporal Stuart McReynolds and the section knew none of this as they jumped off the small landing boat that had taken them onto W Beach, the British Army's logistical landing point for Cape Helles. Stuart landed in warm seawater up to his thighs and then- holding his rifle high- he waded ashore, following in the wake of Angus and Sergeant Harris, his brother close behind him. The beach was a hive of activity- piles of crates were stacked on the beach, supplies of every kind that were needed to support the troops. These supplies were distributed by the rear echelon soldiers of the Army Service Corps. Most of it came from Egypt, including fresh water, although *fresh* was stretching the description of what sloshed around the huge warm sealed metal tanks. As more supplies and troops arrived, naval shore officers directed the mayhem, trying to impose order on those looking for a multitude of units and destinations in the darkness.

Just as the rest of the section was wading ashore, they heard the screeching wail of a solitary shell coming towards them, and they dropped at the water's edge, covering their heads, as the shell exploded further down the beach.

"And what do you think you lot are doing? Taking a nap?" shouted an irate, bearded, and overworked naval petty officer of the shore party. He was standing in front of them, shaking his head in disgust and waving a pace stick, a symbol of his authority. "Get off my beach, now, or I'll give you more to worry about than Asiatic Annie!"

The section picked itself up, now dripping wet and covered in sand, and headed up the beach towards Angus and Harris, who were now standing next to Second Lieutenant Morley. Beside Giles stood a short stocky soldier wearing a faded slouch hat pushed back to reveal pale blue eyes and a mop of blond hair. He wore a collarless pale-blue shirt, a leather bandolier across his chest, and a Lee-Enfield rifle slung on his back, his cord breeches held up with wide braces. Around his calves, he wore knee-high puttees atop brown boots adorned with stubby spurs.

Giles gathered the section together. "This trooper will show you the way, and I'll be up to see you as soon as I can."

The soldier flashed a broad smile. "G'day. My name's Sunny Jim."

On the side of his downturned brim, they could see a stag's head crest, not of the Seaforth Highlanders, but of the Otago Mounted Rifles, a yeomanry regiment from the hinterlands of southern New Zealand.

Giles nodded to Sunny Jim, who nodded back and said, "Follow me." He turned to walk away from the beach. They had gone less than 100 yards when they pulled off the path to let a line of men through towards the beach. As they passed, Stuart could see some of them were wounded, and those who weren't were carrying stretchers.

"Is that you, Sunny Jim?" asked an Australian soldier lying on a stretcher, cigarette dangling from the corner of his mouth.

"Don't tell me you went and stubbed your toe, mate," joked Sunny Jim as the stretcher bearers paused beside him.

"Nah. A bloody grenade thrown over from Johnny Turks' line caught some bits in my legs and arse. Can you believe it?"

Sunny Jim laughed. "You'll be dancing the horizontal polka with the nurses in Lemnos in no time. Just get yourself down to the shore and catch a boat."

"No worries, mate. I'll make it if I have to crawl the rest of the way!" The wounded Australian reached out one hand and shook Sunny Jim's hand. "You take care of yourself."

Sunny Jim nodded. "You too, mate, you too. I'll see you after the war for a tall lager. The first round's on you!"

The Anzac soldier laughed and waved as the bearers resumed their slow walk to the beaches. Sunny Jim watched him go and shook his head in despair, "He'll be lucky if he makes to Lemnos."

"He didn't look too bad," said Harris.

Sunny Jim shrugged his shoulders. "It takes a day to get to Lemnos, and then what? The nurses don't have half the supplies they need and are working out of tents. If he's lucky, he might go by hospital ship. If he's unlucky, it'll be a converted tramp steamer, possibly afterward onto Egypt or Malta. By the time he gets there, infection will have set into both legs. They'll amputate, and he'll die or live in a wheelchair the rest of his life. No more Waltzing Matilda for him, poor sod. It's not the medics fault. They just can't deal with the numbers of wounded—it's worse during a big push. The wounded just lie in rows on the beach until they die. The doctors are overwhelmed, poor bastards."

"Did you know him well?" asked Sergeant Harris.

Sunny Jim nodded. "He was a good mate. We were joking with each other at lunchtime, and now he's gone." He blew out his breath and adjusted the rifle on his back. "Let's go."

Harris walked beside Sunny Jim as the small section of men wound their way off the beach and away from the coast. "I thought all the Australians and New Zealanders were up the coast at Anzac Cove."

"They were, but they brought down two brigades, one Aussie, one Kiwi, for a big push on Krithia. There's some still about, and I arrived late. We should be gone tomorrow if we're lucky; we're not supposed to still be here. You know we were meant to be in Krithia the first day of the landings?

From what I hear, the British made it, but then their officers ordered them back to the beach. Can you believe it? We've been fighting to take it back ever since, but we can't budge Johnny Turk."

Harris listened, hiding the dismay he felt in the pit of his stomach. He'd seen it all before, in South Africa, in France, and now he was hearing it here in Gallipoli—incompetence. The ability to send soldiers into ill-planned, unimaginative attacks with little hope of success and lacking decisive leadership on the ground. When he'd reached the rank of sergeant, he'd vowed to do whatever he could to look after the soldiers under his command, to use a good dose of common sense over blind obedience, and to encourage and reward, rather than to browbeat and bully.

As they walked further up the trail in the dim morning light, they became aware of trails and dusty tracks going off in all directions. They led to artillery batteries, supply depots, rest areas, first aid stations, headquarter and signals units, ammunition dumps, mule stations, and multitudes of battalions of allied soldiers. They all crowded into the tip of land that comprised Cape Helles, six miles square, which ended in three miles of trenches stretched across the peninsula from the Aegean to the Dardanelle Straits. Harris' veteran eyes took it all in and couldn't help thinking it represented the Western Front in miniature.

To Stuart, it reminded him of the Santa Barbara back-country in California where he and Ross had gone to school. It had the same expectancy of heat about to envelop them as the sun struggled to rise above the horizon. His senses picked up familiar smells of wild sage, rosemary, and pine needles. The ground underfoot was baked hard, the poor soil strewn with small stones. He could just make out copses of small pine trees, some standing, some felled for timber, and some shattered into irregular stumps.

As they progressed, he could smell cooking fires and the pungent aroma of curries being cooked by Indian troops. And then a faint sweet smell, that got stronger and more bitter as they walked up the trail until it became an overpowering stink as they walked by the remains of a dead mule team. All six animals were lying by the side of the trail, bellies punctured open, eyes pecked out by birds, teeth bared in a deathly welcoming smile. Stuart glanced back at his brother, who waved his hand in front of his nose to try and waft the smell away.

They came to a crossroads, marked with a crooked wooden sign and followed Sunny Jim to the right. After a few moments he stopped and turned. "Better load those rifles. We'll be getting close to your positions now."

He looked over towards the horizon. "Sun'll be up in just over an hour or so. We'll just have time to settle you in before the heat begins."

They were walking up a narrow winding trail now, and imperceptibly it turned into a sandbagged communications trench, known as a *comms trench*, a tributary bisecting the three lines of trenches that comprised the frontline. They began to recognize the Cameronians that formed half of the Scottish Rifles Brigade, but no Royal Scots. As they followed Sunny Jim, the gaunt shadows of soldiers stared back at them, inspecting the new section, fresh off the boat, with a strange mixture of curiosity and ambivalence.

Sunny Jim paused to ask directions from a sergeant in the Cameronians, who scratched his head. "The Royal Scots? Aye, they just took over the frontline last night, keep going past the support lines and when you reach the end of this comms trench, you should find them there."

Sunny Jim nodded his thanks and with a last look over his shoulder at the horizon, now perceptibly brightening against the darkness, he headed off towards the frontline trenches. "Best we get there soon."

It took half an hour to walk the next half a mile. They had to pull off into bulges in the side of the trench to let soldiers through, either going to the frontline or away from it, usually burdened with supplies and food going to the front or empty containers going to the rear. Stuart noticed with unease that they seemed to be going against the flow of human traffic. He also noticed the sweet smell he'd experienced approaching the dead mules, but this time it was different—more sickly sweet until became an all-pervading stench that caught in the back of the throat. It got worse as they went forward.

Eventually, they reached the end of the communications trench and met the first of the Royal Scots. A section of them was holding the line where the comms trench and the frontline formed a T-shaped intersection, a Lewis light machine gun with a large ammunition drum propped up on a bipod in front of them. Harris told Angus to keep the men slightly back and went forward to chat with the frontline soldiers.

"Seaforth Highlanders?" questioned the corporal in charge in disbelief, seeing Harris' stag's head cap-badge. "There's no Seaforths here, Sergeant. In fact, there's no Seaforths at Gallipoli that I know of- there will be Highland Light Infantry and Argylls soon enough when the rest of the division arrives, but no Seaforths."

Harris smiled reassuringly. "We know; we're attached to the Royal Scots," and by way of explanation added, "we were at Quintinshill with them."

That caught the attention of the rest of the corporal's section. "You were there, really?" the corporal asked.

"Yes," Harris replied, then returning to his original question asked the corporal if he knew where the Royal Scots were.

"Yes, Sergeant. They're down this trench on the left-hand flank, but best go back down the comms trench for a while until 'stand to' is over. It's been quiet, but you never know."

Harris nodded. One of the most likely times of the day to attack, or to be attacked, was first thing in the morning, especially if it meant the sun was shining into the eyes of the enemy. And one of the best times to attack was when a new, fresh unit took over the line before they settled in. 'Stand-to' was the response to this threat- soldiers on either side of no man's land would man their fighting positions in the trenches, ready to repel any emerging attack. After a while, when no threat emerged, they'd 'stand down' and go about their normal morning routine, leaving a few sentries to keep an eye on the enemy, ready to warn others of attack.

Harris went back to the scout section and motioned for them to retreat back down the comms trench. Once they'd gone 50 feet, he halted them and went up to Sunny Jim. "We know where the Royal Scots are now. There's no need for you to hang about. Thanks for bringing us up the line- we'd have been lost without your help."

Sunny Jim flashed his bright white teeth in a smile. "No worries, Sarge. Glad to help. Best I head back to the beach to find my mates, then." He held out his hand to shake Harris' hand, but both men froze as they heard artillery fire beyond the frontline, coming from behind the Turkish lines, followed by the sound of incoming artillery shells screaming towards them.

Harris had just enough time to yell, "Take cover!" when the first salvo of Turkish shells landed on either side of their comms trench. Stuart dropped to the bottom of the trench and found himself lying next to his brother. Earth and stones rained down on them and then they heard more shells. The high explosive shells crashed into the hard, sandy soil, exploding on impact and sending out lethal shards and splinters of hot metal, stones, and flint, destroying trenches, killing and maiming those near the site of impact. Stuart could feel the concussion waves buffering them and his ears were ringing, making it hard to hear. The Turks were using German Krupp 75-millimeter field guns, rapid firing and perfect for laying down a quick barrage.

Harris grabbed Sunny Jim's shoulder and yelled, "How far away are the Turkish trenches here?"

"Not far enough!"

Harris digested the information. A short nasty barrage could mean two things. Either the Turks were letting their artillery cause havoc by itself, or they were softening up the front-line before quickly attacking with infantry. Lightly equipped, it would take the Turks less than a minute to get out of their trenches and make their way across no man's land. The first and fastest of them could be at the Royal Scots' frontline in half that time.

The shells began to recede towards the frontline trench. Harris checked on his men. They were all lying in the bottom of the trench, Angus near to him and Sunny Jim, then the McReynolds brothers, followed by the four O'Connells. He could see the big bulk of Murdo at the end. He felt sorry for them. *This shouldn't be happening to them*, he thought, not on their first day, not on their first look at the frontline, but no one had told the Turks that. Staying close to the trench wall, he risked sticking his head over the top to survey the frontlines, just as a salvo of shells impacted at the intersection of the trenches where they had been standing a minute ago. Two high explosive shells landed inside the frontline trench, and he had a vision of men minus their limbs being blown up into the air as the shells tore apart the trench and the soldiers within it.

Ducking back down, he shouted, his hearing numbed, "They've hit the intersection, it's gone!"

Sunny Jim nodded, immediately understanding the situation. If the Turks attacked, they'd be a gap in the defensive line, and if the Turks got into it, they could not only go right and left down the trench line, but they could also swarm

down the comms trench into the supporting trenches behind them.

Sunny Jim just shrugged fatalistically. "Well, I guess I'm
not going back to the beach, then. What do you want to do,
Sarge?"

Harris looked back at his section. They were raw, half-
trained, and obviously scared, but each one of them was
looking up at him with a look of determination and expecta-
tion. It was time to put them to the test. He had no other
choice.

He motioned for Angus, and told him to quickly gather
Ross, Seamus, and Conner together and to drop their packs,
and then motioned to Sunny Jim. "You take these four men
and cover the right of the intersection. I'll cover the left with
the remaining four." He paused, staring hard at Sunny Jim,
before moving closer and shouting in his ear over the
shelling, "They're mostly raw recruits. None of them have
seen combat. Talk them through it—look after them!"

Sunny Jim nodded. "No worries, Sarge." He motioned
for Angus to follow him up the line.

Harris looked at the remaining men, now grouped with
packs off and crouched together. He had Stuart, Aiden,
Liam, and Murdo with him. "Check your rifles, set your
sights for two hundred yards, and if they charge us, aim low
at the center of their bodies. It'll be rapid fire, but don't
waste your shots. We're going up and to the left. The others
have gone to the right with Sunny Jim. It's up to us to hold
the intersection." He turned and crouched, moving towards
the frontline and the shelling.

When they got there, the intersection didn't exist. It was
just a pile of rubble, broken planks, smears of blood, and
body parts. At the edge of the mess, towards the left, they
found the Royal Scots corporal. Both his legs were missing.
The Lewis gun lay at his side, its bipod and wooden stock
smashed, its outer cooling jacket heavily dented. Beside
him, the one remaining man alive from his section was

trying to tie a bandage around the stumps of his corporal's legs with one of his own arms dangling uselessly by his side and blood running from both his ears. Another salvo of shells landed close by, and Harris shouted for the section to spread out.

Then the shelling abruptly stopped. For a couple of seconds, Harris thought it was all over until he heard whistles and trumpets coming from the Turkish lines followed by a deep throaty yell as the Turks emerged from their line. Hundreds of them. It was the worst scenario he could have imagined, but it was completely out of his control now. For Stuart, Ross, and the rest of the section, their boots still damp from the landing, it was time to fight or die- quite possibly both.

Stuart was lying on a pile of rubble facing the enemy lines. Murdo was to his right, both of them at the apex of the intersection. Liam was to his left, where the trench began to take form again, and beyond him were Harris and Aiden. The smell of cordite still hung in the air from the shelling, and in front of him he saw the source of the acrid stench that pervaded everything- piles of dead bodies decomposing in no man's land. Then beyond them, emerging out of their trenches, came the Turks.

He heard Harris frantically shouting, "Stand to! Stand to!" Gripping his rifle tightly, Stuart pulled back the bolt and then pushed it forward in one easy motion, chambering a round, then thumbed the safety catch off and peered down his open sights. He was scared, more scared than he'd been in his entire life, but then a calm descended upon him as he readied his rifle. He thought of his brother, his family, and lastly of Nell, and then all thoughts left him as he heard Harris barking out a fire order, "Enemy to the front, one hundred yards, ra-pid fire!"

A mass of Turks was charging towards them. Stuart sighted on one slightly ahead of the rest, waving a sword in one hand and a pistol in the other. It had to be an officer. He squeezed his trigger, trying not to jerk his rifle, aiming for the middle of the man's chest and his rifle fired, the recoil punching back his right shoulder and he saw the officer double over and fall. It seemed surreal. He'd just killed a man and his only feeling was one of elation- the rifle, his training, the men now firing on both sides of him- it all worked. He aimed and fired again, unconscious of even having pulled his bolt back and forth to re-chamber another round, and fired again, and again, aiming and watching men falling in front of him.

To his far right and far left, Vickers heavy machine guns erupted into fire, and he saw entire groups of Turks, ten, twenty, thirty at a time, pitch backward under the concentrated fire of the heavy machine guns. He glimpsed at Murdo, firing at his side, making no noise, just mechanically working the action of his bolt. To his left, he could hear Liam swearing away as he fired, a running commentary spewing from his lips, every third word a curse. Stuart fired again and again and then he squeezed his trigger and nothing happened.

It was his time to curse now. He'd forgotten to count his rounds and had run out of bullets, wasting precious seconds. He turned on his side, ripped open an ammunition pouch on his webbing, and grabbed a charger of five rounds, jamming them into the guides at the top of his rifle, fingers trembling slightly, and immediately chambered a round. As he did so, he was aware of the rifle fire around him slacking and knew they were all reloading at the same time, giving the Turks a moment to gain ground unopposed.

Stuart rolled back up into the firing position and the remaining Turks were close now, he shot one down 30 yards from him, and then another, and another, but they still came on, less of them, but still there. He could hear them yelling "Allah" and "Allahu akbar" as they ran towards them, big men, tanned with large mustaches, brave beyond reason in the face of such concentrated fire. They were getting closer. Stuart repressed a growing fear as he saw their bayonets and fierce faces. He shot twice more, men going down both times, and then had to reload. Instead of rolling over onto his side, he got up into the kneeling position, one leg forward to rest his elbow on to stabilize himself.

He jammed another five rounds into his rifle, chambered the first and brought his rifle up to shoot and fired immediately, killing a Turk 15 feet away. He chambered another round and then paused. The Turkish soldiers in front of them were all down, killed or wounded, but unseen by the section was a second wave of enemy soldiers now bearing down on them, already charging across no man's land.

"Sweet Jesus," he heard Liam saying in exasperation, "How many of the bastards are there?"

Sergeant Harris had seen them, too. "Reload! Reload!" he yelled at the men around him.

Stuart had managed to get five more rounds into his magazine, giving him nine in total, but the Turks were coming on fast. The heavy machine guns to the right and left were killing them in neat rows, but directly in front there seemed to be an arrowhead of enemy soldiers coming right at them. Perhaps the first wave had shown some weakness in the line where the shells had done their damage, where the machine guns were less effective, and the second wave was trying to exploit it.

As he raised up his rifle he was aware of the two wounded Royal Scots behind them shouting urgently, but there was no time to listen as Harris barked out a hasty fire command, "Ra-pid fire!"

Again, he aimed at the Turk nearest him and squeezed the trigger, the rifle bucked, and the man was thrown backward by the impact of the bullet. Stuart worked his rifle's bolt and fired again and again in quick succession, but the mass of men in front of them grew larger as they drew nearer. He fired again and then heard Sergeant Harris's urgent voice cutting through the chaos, "Fix bayonets! Fix bayonets!"

Cold sweat now trickled down his back. He reached for his bayonet, withdrew its heavy, long seventeen-inch blade and attached it to the end of his rifle with trembling hands. As he did, he saw Murdo back away and turn towards the rear of the trench. He felt both surprise and rage as Murdo disappeared from his peripheral vision, but there was no time for anything else. He raised his rifle, its muzzle now heavy with the added weight and length of the bayonet and fired at the Turks now bearing down on them. He could hear Liam cursing in desperation. There were just too many enemy soldiers. Stuart fired three more times, almost blindly into the Turkish soldiers charging towards him, and then, one bullet left, he rose to his feet, aware of Liam closing into his blindside with bayonet raised, for mutual protection.

He pointed his rifle at a big Turk now leading the arrowhead of men heading straight at them, 15 feet away. He was splattered with blood, and his bayonet was pointing directly at Stuart. Stuart took aim and squeezed the trigger. The soldier fell back, but the Turk's rifle came arcing towards him, its bayonet planting into the ground at his feet, just as the space beside him exploded with flame and gunfire.

The Turkish soldiers, split seconds away from reaching the trench where Stuart and Liam stood side by side, reeled under the impact of a stream of bullets. Stuart looked to his right and was stunned by what he saw.

Murdo was standing to his right, the damaged Lewis gun cradled in his big arms, shooting from the hip. The 28-pound light machine gun bucked and shook, but Murdo kept firing it methodically into the Turks, stopping their assault just as it was about to overwhelm their position. Murdo wasn't trained, but he was immensely strong, and teeth clenched, he unleashed a continual volley of rounds into the Turks, who staggered under the impact of the bullets.

"Don't just stand there," yelled Harris. "Bloody well reload and fire!"

Liam and Stuart snapped out of their trance, quickly reloaded, and added their rifle fire to Murdo's devastation. As they did, Stuart was dimly aware of more men to the right of them standing beside Murdo, adding their weight of rapid rifle fire to the onslaught, led by a young officer blasting away with his Webley revolver. It was too much for the remaining Turkish soldiers. They had come so close to overrunning the weak point, but the moment had passed and both sides could sense it. As Murdo's machine gun ran out of ammunition and grew silent, the few surviving Turks took the opportunity to retreat as best they could, chased by rifle and heavy machine gun fire, until Harris bellowed at them to "Ceasefire," followed by a cautionary order to "Reload."

Stuart held his rifle at the ready and gazed out towards the Turkish line. He cleared his weapon and then inserted ten new rounds, but the Turks had had enough. He stared at the scene before him, now lit up by the sun rising behind them. Their field of fire was covered in wounded, dead, and dying. The newly killed lay in a field of decomposing bodies, some grotesquely bloated with tight black skin, some blown apart, heads lying separated from bodies, limbs scattered carelessly on the ground, and some reduced to partial skeletons, grinning obscenely at the newly dead who had joined them on the battlefield. The wounded moaned or cried out in agony among the dead, some crawling as best they could back towards their own lines, unwilling to join the carpet of corpses that surrounded them.

Stuart stared dumbly at the scene and at the dying Turk's rifle, sticking out of the ground by its bayonet at his feet. Suddenly he began retching, the stink and sight of corpses sticking in this throat. Leaning on his rifle, he felt a touch on his shoulder. It was Harris, face blackened, but with relief in his eyes. He held out his metal water bottle and

Stuart nodded gratefully, raising it to his lips with trembling hands and swallowing down a mouthful of tepid water.

"Let's go find the rest," Harris said gently.

Stuart nodded, shaking hands with Liam and Aiden, and they walked over to Murdo, the Lewis gun still grasped in his hands.

Stuart reached out his hand and patted him on the shoulder. "You saved our lives, Murdo. You probably saved us all, and the trench."

Murdo turned and stepped down into the trench from the pile of rubble from which he and Stuart had fought. "It was the corporal," he said, looking down at the legless soldier, who stared with lifeless eyes towards them.

His wounded companion was still next to him and looked up at Harris. "He knew you'd need the Lewis gun, you see, so instead of stopping his legs bleeding, he had me clear and check the gun. It was damaged but serviceable. He cleared the drum magazine himself and then readied the weapon for firing. I couldn't carry it, so we shouted and shouted until the big black soldier heard us and took it- all he had to do was point and pull the trigger. The corporal watched the big man firing away, smiled, and then he was gone."

Harris patted the wounded man on the shoulder and watched the growing number of Cameronians coming down the comms trench to reinforce the intersection. The first of them had arrived just in time to add their fire to Murdo, and among them he saw Second Lieutenant Morley, revolver still in his hand. Giles came over to them with a look of alarm on his face. "Where's the rest of the section?"

Harris pointed towards the other side of the intersection as he saw Angus coming towards them, the rest of the section behind him. Stuart turned and after a moment's hesitation embraced his brother, silently holding him tightly until he found his voice. "Are you all right?"

"I'm all right," said Ross, reaching for his water bottle, his hand also shaking slightly, "but that was too damn close."

Harris turned to Giles. "Sir, we need stretcher bearers." He pointed towards the two Royal Scots. "And the corporal there deserves a medal. He died making sure his Lewis gun was ready to go back in action."

Giles nodded. "And the section?"

Harris looked over at his men, all now following Ross' example and sharing water bottles with each other, and explained what had happened when the Turkish artillery had opened up. "They were solid beyond any expectations I had for them, sir. They stood their ground, hit what they aimed at, and at the end were ready to fight with bayonets if they'd had to. And then Private Munro came from nowhere with that bloody Lewis gun and just mowed the Turks down. He saved the day, sir. A few more seconds and we'd have been overwhelmed. I had to split the men, so I only saw my half of the section in action. I don't know about the rest."

"Well, the other half can fight by my side any day, mate, any day." They turned to see Sunny Jim behind them, his rifle slung, and his slouch hat pushed back. Harris explained how he'd taken half the section to cover the right.

"Thank you," said Giles. "I'll make sure your command knows what you did here."

Sunny Jim smile broadened. "No worries, sir. If that's all, I'll be making my way back down the line. It's time I found my own unit before they think I've gone walkabout."

Harris stuck out his hand and gave the Anzac trooper a firm handshake. "Thanks for looking after them. I mean it."

"Me look after them?" he said incredulously. "I thought they were looking after me, Sarge!" and he laughed as he turned to go.

As he made his way past the section, he shook all their hands, patting Murdo on the back as he did so. Just before disappearing around the intersection, Sunny Jim turned to them with his big smile, spread his arms wide, and shouted, "Welcome to Gallipoli!" quickly ducking down as a shot rang out from the Turkish trenches.

Giles turned to Harris and asked with a smile, "What was that trooper's full name?"

Harris just shrugged and smiled. "To tell you the honest truth, sir, I never asked him, but I have a feeling if you contact the New Zealand Mounted Rifles and simply mention 'Sunny Jim,' they'll probably know exactly who you are talking about."

CHAPTER THIRTEEN

Baptism of Fire

Fir Tree Spur, Cape Helles,
Gallipoli, June 1915

The plan of attack, approved by Lieutenant General Aylmer
Gould Hunter-Weston, commanding officer of VIII Corps,
was simplicity itself—after a two-hour artillery barrage,
waves of British infantry would charge uphill over 300 yards
of open ground towards the Turkish trenches, with bayonets, in broad daylight.

In the fourth attempt to advance on Krithia, the British
and French were launching attacks on the Turkish flanks on
the east and the west. The French attacks a few days ago in
the east had been mostly successful, and so now it was the
turn of the British forces. Supported by artillery, the Border
Regiment from the north-west of England would assault an
outpost named Boomerang Redoubt, and then attack up a
deep scar in the land named Gully Ravine. Two ridges stood
on either side of this main attack. On the left ridge, named
Gully Spur, the Gurkhas and Royal Fusiliers would attack
supported by naval gunfire. On the right rose a ridge of land
named Fir Tree Spur. This would be attacked by the territorials of the Scottish Rifles Brigade, the first brigade of reinforcements to arrive at Gallipoli.

The Royal Scots would attack both up the left of Fir Tree
Spur and up the center; the Cameronians would attack up
the right. Artillery would give them what support they could,
but shells were in limited supply, and the attacks on Gully

Spur and Gully Ravine needed the most support. The artillery barrage would commence at nine o'clock in the morning, the Royal Scots and Cameronians would attack two hours later.

The plan had been devised by army staff officers aboard Royal Navy ships anchored off the coast. Major General Henry de Beauvoir de Lisle, who would carry out this plan, had briefed the senior officers, who then passed down the plan to their subordinates. Major Sinclair had sought out Giles after the junior officers' briefing.

"We're here to support the Royal Scots, so you'll be attacking with them up the middle." He looked for a reaction from the young officer and saw him take a deep breath to steel his nerves.

"Find the section and stay with them. Listen to Sergeant Harris. He has experience. Ask for his opinion, but remember you're in charge—you make the final decisions. This will be your first action, so keep it simple. Stay together, but don't bunch up or you'll become a target. Get across No Man's Land as fast as you can. Once into their trenches, consolidate your position quickly—the Turks will counterattack with everything they have. They always do. Keep calm. You're here to lead, so no matter how scared you are—and trust me, you'll be scared—try not to show it. You have to set an example for the men." He stopped, knowing anything else he said probably wouldn't be remembered, so he held out his hand instead.

Giles shook it firmly. "Thank you. I'll do my best, sir," he said with quiet conviction, then saluted and turned to go find the Royal Scots and his small command.

He found them drinking tea in the fading light around a small trench stove with some Cameronians and Royal Scots in the supporting trenches. One of the Cameronians was telling the Royal Scots how Murdo had stood up with the Lewis gun: "...and there he was, standing on this pile of rubble, blazing away at the Turks as we came up the comms trench behind him. Never seen anything like it before." Then Liam told them about Sergeant Major Skaig, and before long they were all laughing as Liam played out the story. Giles listened to them and smiled. They were good men, and now he had to lead them into battle. It was a daunting prospect. He was about to walk closer when he heard someone behind him, and turned to see Sergeant Harris coming along the trench. A cigarette dangled from his lips, a rifle was slung on his back, and he held a bulging sack in each hand. "Good evening, sir," he said as he recognized Giles in the gloom and quickly stubbed out his cigarette.

"Good evening, Sergeant Harris. It's a bit early for Christmas, isn't it?" he asked, looking at the sacks.

Harris smiled. "Helmets, sir," he explained. "The brigade has all been issued pith sun helmets, sir. I thought we'd stick out like a handful of sore thumbs without them on our noggins, so I managed to get some for the section." He put down the sacks and brought one of the pith helmets out and handed it to the young officer. "Begging your pardon, sir, but if you go over the top tomorrow without one, you'll stick out like a nun in a brothel."

Giles reached out for the helmet and inspected it. "Well, it's a good thing we left our kilts at Fort George, then—but shouldn't I be 'conspicuous at the front,' Sergeant?" he asked in mock seriousness.

Harris pursed his lips. "We all know who you are, sir, but why let the Turks know? Put it this way, as soon as any of our lot see an enemy officer leading a charge, waving a pistol or sword about, dressed differently from the rest, we shoot them, don't we sir?"

Giles nodded.

"And you getting shot first doesn't help the rest of us, does it, sir?"

"I sincerely hope not, Sergeant," said Giles with a self-effacing smile.

"Well then, if you'll beg my pardon again, sir, you should probably have this as well." He unslung the rifle from his back, opened the bolt, and handed it to Giles.

"I've checked it myself, sir. I can't vouch that'll shoot like the ones we have, but if you go over the top tomorrow waving a pistol around, you probably won't be with us by the time we reach the Turkish trenches, sir."

Giles took the rifle, checked its chamber, and closed the bolt. "Some might say an officer trying to look the same as his men is cowardice, Sergeant," he said in a questioning tone.

"Sir, you're officer-in-charge of a sharpshooting section, therefore carrying a rifle makes perfect sense. Running at the Turks waving an officer's revolver about, asking to be shot, doesn't. And besides, Major Sinclair told me to look after you, sir, and I wouldn't want to disappoint him."

Giles laughed. "All right, Sergeant, you win. I don't want to disappoint the major either. Hang on to this until I get back," he said, handing the rifle back to Harris, "and I'll go see where they want us on the line." He turned to go and then turned back. "Make sure the men have everything they need. Any problems, tell me and I'll see what I can do."

"Yes, sir," said Harris and raised his hand, saluting Giles.

Giles returned the salute and then said, "Not much point wearing a pith helmet and carrying a rifle to blend in if you're going to salute me, Sergeant. Let the section know that when we're in the trenches, salutes will be assumed, not required."

As he disappeared down the trench, Harris couldn't help admiring the young lieutenant. If he survived, he might become a half-decent soldier—for an officer.

**

Stuart looked at the sunrise painted across the Aegean horizon. It was stunningly beautiful, and he could already tell it was going to be a hot day, but his mind was too full of thoughts to appreciate either. He could smell breakfast cooking along the various trenches, but he wasn't hungry—none of them were. Since arriving, they'd spent their time mainly digging new trenches or expanding old ones. It was hard never-ending labor, but deemed good work for new troops to tone their muscles after weeks at sea. It also got them used to the Turkish artillery, and before long, they learned when to duck and when not to. Not only did the Turks have artillery behind their lines, but they could also fire all the way across the Straits from Asia Minor, and one heavy caliber gun in particular became known as *Asiatic Annie*. Its erratic firing had greeted their arrival on the beach.

Their first few days had also gotten them used to the lack of water, the lack of decent food, the lack of supplies in general, and the lack of any part of the battlefield not being covered in dead and decomposing bodies. Requests for truces to clear the bodies from the Turks had been refused by the British general staff on the grounds that attacking over their own dead would deter further Turkish attacks. It didn't. It simply resulted in bodies from both sides remaining unburied in the heat of the sun, an all-pervading stench, and an utter infestation of flies—great clouds of them. They landed on any piece of exposed skin, on food, on drinking water, on men trying to sleep, and with them came maggots and intestinal diseases, making life miserable for the men in the trenches.

Second Lieutenant Morley had talked to the section in the evening, letting them know the plan of attack and their place in the grander scheme of things. The objective was to take two lines of Turkish trenches. Giles had been told to support the center of the Royal Scots, the very center of the attack up Fir Tree Spur. He had relayed the army's intelligence reports to the section that suggested the main opposition would be to the west, at Gully Spur and Gully Ravine. No major obstacles had been identified at Fir Tree Spur, and

it was considered a less taxing position for the territorial
Scots to attack in their first action.

The brigade's commanding officer, Brigadier William
Scott-Moncrieff, had walked through the lines, pausing to
chat groups of soldiers as he went, stressing the need for
success in the morning's attack and wishing them well. He
had come through their position and had stopped to speak
to them briefly, especially to Harris when he saw his Boer
War ribbons on his uniform, as they had both served in
South Africa.

During the night, they had moved up the line as quietly
as they could. The trenches were crowded with soldiers, and
the section stopped in the support trench behind the Royal
Scots. Once the first wave had left the trenches to attack the
Turk's front line, they would follow them and then move up
through the initial objective to attack the second.

Stuart hadn't slept, or if he had, the brief lapses of sleep had
been so fleeting it felt as if he hadn't slept at all. He'd
checked and rechecked his rifle and equipment and had uri-
nated frequently throughout the night, even when is wasn't
really necessary. He couldn't eat, and when he tried, he felt
nauseated and had quietly retched. By moonlight, the section had talked quietly for a while as night had slowly turned
to dawn, and then had grown silent. Each man became lost
in his thoughts, some waiting for the sun to chase away the
grey mantle of darkness surrounding them, some nervously
wishing the sun to stay below the horizon, for time to stand
still. Slowly the sun's beams split the horizon.

From their elevated position, they could see the outlines
of large naval ships out at sea. Among them scurried the
small boats of the Royal Navy Trawler Service, and Stuart
wondered if any were requisitioned herring drifters from the
East Neuk of Fife, and then all he could think of was Nell. In
his mind, he went over their walk along the coastline together, savoring the memory, replaying it. He'd been

overwhelmingly happy to see her in Edinburgh, and delighted in their lunch at The Royal Café and the afternoon walking through the Scottish capital. He remembered their parting, and how he had held her close: her warmth, the smell of her hair, her lavender scented perfume, and the touch of her lips.

"A penny for your thoughts," said a voice, and he opened his eyes to see his brother's smile.

"Miles away from here, I can tell you that much," replied Stuart.

Ross nodded. "This isn't where I thought we'd be, or the fight we'd be in."

"Do you think it's too late to transfer to the Royal Flying Corps?" asked Stuart with a smile.

Ross chuckled quietly. "I'm not sure Sergeant Harris would approve the paperwork right now." He rummaged in a pocket and brought out a biscuit of hard tack, breaking it in two.

Stuart shook his head. "I'm not hungry."

"Neither am I," replied Ross. "But take it anyway. We need to eat something."

Stuart accepted the biscuit but barely nibbled it. Then he looked at his wristwatch, a present from his parents for his 18th birthday, and showed it to his brother. It was two minutes to nine. He felt his stomach tense, his throat dry. "Not long now."

Ross nodded, then looked at his brother. "Two hours of artillery and no strong points. We'll be all right, you'll see."

"If you say so, but just stick by me, we do this together."

Ross smiled. "We do this together," he said, and he gently reached out and ruffled his brother's sandy hair.

Harris came down the trench towards them, checking equipment and giving reassuring smiles to the section. "Rise and shine, you bunch of misfits. Time to earn your pay! Make sure your rifles are clean and bolts well oiled, make sure your equipment is tied down and not flapping about.

Empty your bladders and fill your water bottles. Don't do both at the same time or you might get a nasty surprise later on!" The section grinned back at him, responding to their sergeant's casual demeanor and bad jokes, the palpable tension easing a fraction.

They decided to mount only two scopes, given the outline of the attack. Stuart had one, and Aiden had the other. The rest of the section had normal open iron sights. All would charge with bayonets when the time came. After a few minutes, Giles joined them, accepting his rifle back from Sergeant Harris, who also gave him spare clips of ammunition to stuff in his pockets and a sharpened bayonet. Giles accepted them in silence. They were all wearing pith helmets and standard wool uniforms, Giles still wearing his subdued Sutherland tartan trousers.

Stuart stood next to his brother, their backs to the front trench wall, looking over the rear of the trench and out to the sea beyond the peninsula. They saw fire erupting from the naval guns and could clearly see the large-caliber shells as they rose into the air and then descended towards Gully Spur. The sound of the firing reached them moments before the shells impacted onto the land. Taking their cue from the Navy, 75 artillery guns opened fire at the Turkish trenches all along the British line. The majority of them were 18 pounders, the mainstay of the British field artillery. Crewed by six experienced gunners, they could fire up to 20 rounds per minute at targets 7,000 yards away.

The brothers crouched down at the sheer sound of the gunfire as the shells screamed overhead into the Turkish positions. More and more guns joined in, and then they heard Aiden yelling at them all to get down. Out of the cacophony, his ears had picked up the sound of shells heading towards their position. An artillery battery, somewhere far behind them, had miscalculated and their shells were falling short.

They dropped to the floor of the trench and covered their heads just as the first misplaced salvo arrived. It landed between the frontline and the support trench, sending great eruptions of hard-baked earth into the air interlaced with white-hot fragments of metal. They stayed crouched in the bottom of the trench as more salvos came towards them. The gunners were working hard, clearing, loading, and firing shell after shell—all into their own lines.

Stuart and Ross heard Liam swearing away. "Bastards! For feck's sake, someone tell them feckin gunners we didn't come all the bloody way from Ireland to be killed by our own feckin side!"

Again and again, shells rained down on them, ripping apart their own trenches, until eventually the gunners paused, readjusted, and began to fire over their heads towards the Turkish lines. In response, the Turkish artillery opened up with a vengeance. The British artillery was ineffective and sparse around Fir Tree Spur, while the Turkish artillery was on target and on mass. It came as little surprise. The Turks held the high ground, and their artillery observers had a panoramic view of the battlefield, especially from the heights of Achi Baba—a sloping hill 700 feet high—that dominated the Cape Helles peninsula. Like the village of Krithia, it was supposed to have been taken on the first day of the landings, and just like Krithia, Achi Baba remained firmly in Turkish hands months later.

As the section crouched in the bottom of the trench, Harris yelled at them to keep their mouths open. Doing so helped to counter the pressure waves that swept across and then back over them. The Turkish shells worked their way from the rear trenches towards and over them to the frontline and back again. Then the Turks concentrated on the front trench, and soon the section could hear men screaming and others calling for stretcher bearers. A captain from the Royal Scots came stumbling into their trench. He was bleeding from a large jagged cut bisecting his forehead and his left arm hung unnaturally limp by his side, his sleeve torn. On seeing Giles, he came forward. "We've been hit

hard by the Turkish artillery. Take your men up the line—
I'm going back for more reinforcements," he ordered, and
he stumbled on unsteadily towards the rear trenches.

Giles looked at Sergeant Harris who simply nodded
once, picked up his rifle, and shouted at the section, "Get up!
We're needed up front." He hesitated and then said, "Load
your rifle with two clips of ammunition, but don't chamber
any rounds. That way you have them if you need them."
Giles nodded in agreement, and the section pulled out two
clips of five bullets each and pushed them into their rifles'
magazines. Once finished, Harris looked over at Giles with
an almost imperceptible nod of the head.

Giles took his cue and cleared his throat, remembering some
of what Major Sinclair had told him. He let out his breath
slowly and shouted calmly over the din of shells crossing
over their heads. "Corporal MacIntyre!"

"Yes, sir!" replied Angus from further down the trench.

"Bring up the rear. Make sure no-one falls behind."

"Yes, sir!"

"The rest of you, follow me and stick together!"

The scene that awaited them was grim. The Turkish artillery had sought out and found the frontline trenches full
of Royal Scots biding their time until the attack commenced.
A shaken lieutenant asked Giles to take his men to the right
of the line. It had been hit badly and the Royal Scots, already
under strength, had a trench full of casualties.

Giles led them through the trench, Turkish artillery still
coming down in salvos. Mercifully for them, the smoke from
previous explosions was masking the trench line from further accurate fire. As they reached the right of the line, they
entered a site of destruction. Shells had landed inside the
trench, obliterating the tightly packed soldiers. The walls of
the trench had been blown outwards, and the sandy com-
pacted earth was sprayed in blood. Lumps of bloody pale
flesh lay everywhere, and the trench floor was crisscrossed

with bluish-red strings of intestines and torn limbs. Walking wounded were limping past the dead and dying, moving slowly to the rear, their wounds hastily bandaged. Giles led his section over torn and mutilated bodies, until they went through a zigzag in the trench line and into a stretch of trench where they found a depleted platoon of Royal Scots.

"Where's your officer?" asked Giles.

A color sergeant came forward. "He was checking our men to the left of the zigzag when the artillery—either the Turkish or our own—found our line. We haven't seen him since, nor a man I sent to find him, sir."

Giles paused. "If they were back there, I doubt you'll see them again soon, Color Sergeant. We were sent to reinforce you."

The senior non-commissioned officer paused to take in the news and then stood to attention. "Color Sergeant Rennie, sir!"

Giles told Rennie to stand easy. "What's your strength, who's further down the line, and what are your orders, Color Sergeant?"

Rennie rubbed his chin. "Thirty...no, twenty-nine men, sir. Down from us, it's the Cameronians. Orders were to attack the first two trenches and dig in, sir. After the artillery had softened them up...."

Rennie stood silently in front of the unknown rifle-carrying officer that had arrived with a section of reinforcements dressed like his men, but Giles could sense he had more to say. "Let's hear your opinion of the situation, Color Sergeant."

Rennie weighed up the new officer quickly. Few had ever asked him for his opinion. He leaned in so the soldiers behind him couldn't hear. "Sir, our artillery has hardly touched the Turkish trenches. There's been no high explosive stuff hitting them, but the Turks are pasting us good and proper. It seems to me all we've done is let them know we're coming."

Giles pursed his lips. "Thank you, Color Sergeant. Get your men spread out as best you can. There should be more reinforcements coming soon." As he was speaking, they heard loud bangs off to their right and then looked in amazement as a large heavy projectile soared slowly into the air, hovered at the apex of its flight, and then descended towards the enemy lines to the left of them, followed by a huge explosion of earth and bodies.

Rennie looked back at Giles. "The French sir, firing *La Demoiselle*, their heavy mortar to support the attack at the Boomerang Redoubt. They say the shells are filled with one hundred pounds of melinite." Melinite was a high explosive containing picric acid and guncotton.

"I wish they'd lob a few of those at the Turks in front of us," added Rennie in a dejected tone.

"Do you think the Royal Scots can't do the job without help from the French, Color Sergeant?"

Giles watched as the senior non-commissioned officer grew in height and scowl at the suggestion. "No, sir!"

It was the response Giles had been hoping for. "Good. Has the platoon loaded their rifles?"

Rennie looked quizzically at Giles. "No, sir. Orders are to attack with the bayonet."

"Yes, but have your men load ten rounds into their magazines anyway. We might just be needing them in a hurry."

Rennie smiled, warming to the new officer. "Yes, sir. Makes sense to me, begging your pardon, sir."

"What does and does not make sense to you is very helpful to me right now, Color Sergeant. Now go get those magazines loaded."

Giles turned to Harris as Rennie started barking orders at his men. "Suggestions, Sergeant Harris?" he asked.

Sergeant Harris licked his lips. "The sun's getting very hot, and this smoke doesn't help. Perhaps let the men loosen their collars, sir. It's going to be a long day."

"Permission granted, Sergeant, and have the men gather any spare water bottles they find while you're at it. Pass the word on to Color Sergeant Rennie."

"Yes, sir. Are you taking command of the platoon, sir?" asked Harris.

Giles took off his pith helmet and ran his fingers through his mop of sweaty, sandy blond hair. "I suppose I am, Sergeant Harris," he said with a hint of resignation. "I suppose I am."

For the next half an hour, the artillery duel between the lines continued, and Giles could only agree with Color Sergeant Rennie's summation—the British guns were doing little damage to the lines at Fir Tree Spur in front of them. The bulk of the barrage was focused on Gully Spur and Gully Ravine. Meanwhile, the Turkish artillery kept probing the Scot's frontline, seeking out the huddled soldiers massed in their trenches, and causing bloody mayhem when their shells succeeded.

At 10:45, there was a crescendo of artillery fire followed by the faint sound of whistles announcing the attack by the Border Regiment against Boomerang Redoubt. The section could hear increased rifle fire as the soldiers assaulted the strongpoint, followed by cheering from the lines. It gave them some hope, and then the British artillery increased in tempo all along the line. Giles looked at his watch—ten minutes to go. He felt the urge to urinate, but didn't—he knew it was nerves. He took out his revolver and checked its stubby rounds, and then re-holstered it. He checked his rifle and beckoned to Harris and Rennie.

"It's time to earn our pay, gentleman," he said, copying Harris' frequent admonition. "We go over together. There's not enough of us to split into two waves, and I see nothing to gain by it. Don't bunch up, and remember our ultimate objective is the Turk's second line, so don't get bogged down in the first trench. Clear it out and keep going. The intelligence reports all suggest the right flank is lightly held, so keep up with the Cameronians to the right of us. Don't let them charge ahead." He looked at the two non-commissioned officers who nodded.

"Right, then. Color Sergeant Rennie, have the men stand to and fix bayonets."

"Yes, sir. And good luck, sir."

"Thank you, Color Sergeant. Good luck to us all."

***

Color Sergeant Rennie filled his lungs, and at parade-ground volume, yelled over the cacophony of shelling, "Stand to! Fix—bayonets!"

Stuart unsheathed the long heavy 17-inch bayonet and after the prescribed pause, clicked it onto the lug of his rifle. Beside him, his brother did the same. Stuart felt physically sick. For a fleeting moment, he wished the shellfire had wounded him—not badly, but enough to not have to charge out into no man's land. He banished the thought and took a deep breath, then looked over at Ross, whose jaw was set in determination. On one side of them stood Murdo, Angus, and Sergeant Harris. On the other side were the O'Connells—Seamus, Conner, Liam, and Aiden. Beyond them, Giles stood staring at his watch, followed by the rest of the Royal Scots with Color Sergeant Rennie in their midst. Smoke, debris, and dust from the shelling covered their trench, the explosions making them wince involuntarily. None of the territorial Scots had charged the enemy before. Gallipoli was to be their baptism of fire.

As the moment for them to go over the top approached, Stuart could hear Seamus on his right muttering to himself, repeating something over and over, flexing his hands as they gripped his rifle and getting louder until he looked at his friends and said in a loud voice, "Ready to row?"

Connor, Liam, and Aiden looked over at Seamus, who looked back at them, gripping his rifle, and repeated, "Ready to row?"

Connor smiled, recognizing the misplaced ritual, and nodded.

Then Seamus yelled, "Ready to row?"

"Ready to row!" replied Connor with fierce intensity.

Then Liam joined in, "Ready to row!"

Aiden, looking at the others and smiling, shouted, "Ready to row!"

Then many things happened at once. The British artillery stopped, and the men could hear bagpipes bursting into play from the trenches to the far left and right of them. Then whistles began to shrill all along the trench-line. Giles blew the heavy cylindrical nickel-plated whistle around his neck and yelled, "Over!" as he left the trench ahead of his men.

Stuart climbed over the fire-step and clambered up the trench parapet. He was part of a huge wave of men now emerging from trenches and bursting into an uphill sprint, rifles held in front of them, bayonets glinting in the bright sun, all yelling as they ran forward. He heard the sharp bang and hiss of shrapnel shells exploding and spaying out their cone of lethal steel balls, the whip-like crack as a bullet zipped past him, followed by another and another, and then further down to the right of the line all hell broke loose.

Massed, concentrated, heavy machine gun fire erupted from the Turkish trenches, pouring a torrent of lead bullets into the Cameronians. The machine gun fire began to creep towards them, and the men around Stuart sprinted even faster towards to the Turkish trench, which perversely—despite the enemy riflemen firing at them—was the only sanctuary from the heavy machine gun fire scything through the ranks of men in no man's land.

Stuart was level with his brother and slightly behind Seamus when the rifle fire in front of them increased as the Turkish soldiers tried desperately to halt the first wave of charging men. More bullets and shrapnel zipped by him, and he felt a tug at his shoulder and for a second, thought someone was trying to pull him back. He could see the

Turkish trench clearly now, devoid of barbed wire, and punctuated with enemy soldiers firing towards them. He felt his lungs bursting, and his running slowed as he side-stepped the decaying corpses that littered the ground. He glimpsed for a fraction of a second to his left and saw Ross, still running with him, but now minus his pith helmet and bleeding from the side of his head. He looked forward and then to his right, just as Seamus pitched backward, propelled by the impact of a bullet to his chest.

Looking back, he saw Seamus land spread-eagled on his back, unmoving and lifeless. To the other side of the gap of where Seamus had been, he saw Conner slow, looking towards the prostrate form of his lifelong friend, then Giles was yelling at them all to keep going. Connor yelled with fierce rage, a rage taken up by Liam and Aiden. Stuart was filled with a burning hate, matched only by a desire to kill the bastards in front of him that were causing this hell.

With 25 yards to go, the first of the enemy soldiers bolted uphill for the rear trenches. Within seconds others were following, leaving their frontline and seeking sanctuary in the trench behind them. The last few yards disappeared and in front of him, Stuart saw a Turkish soldier fire one last shot wildly at him and then turn to try and scramble out of the back of his trench. Stuart yelled as he reached the enemy parapet, he angled his rifle and with his full momentum, plunged his bayonet into the exposed back of the Turkish soldier. He let out an ear-piercing shriek before collapsing back into the trench.

Still holding his weapon, Stuart twisted his rifle and pulled the bayonet out of the dead Turk, staring at the limp body in mute disbelief. Turning to his left, he saw his brother knock aside the desperate bayonet thrust of a smaller Turkish soldier, and then thrust this own bayonet into the soldier's throat. Blood fountained out of the wound, spraying them both with the dying man's blood. Further down he saw Angus, Murdo, and Harris clearing the trench.

Spinning around to his right, he witnessed Connor stamping on a Turk lying on the trench floor, the heel of his boot pulverizing the stricken soldier's features into red pulp, his arms reaching weakly up for Connor's leg, and then falling limply as Connor continued to stamp on his face.

Beyond Connor, he saw a Turk—both arms raised in surrender—facing the point of Liam's bayonet. For a moment Liam hesitated, then swung his rifle to the side of the soldier's head with a vicious butt-stroke, knocking him out cold. Stuart looked towards the Turks running towards their rear trench and then heard Harris yelling, "Get after them! Don't let the bastards get away!" and before he knew it, he was running towards the second line, screaming for vengeance, Harris, Murdo, and Angus in the lead.

As he ran, he could still hear heavy machine gun fire to his right, but it no longer concerned him. With a terrible blood-lust upon him, his sole purpose was to reach their objective: the second Turkish line.

There comes a time in any battle when one side gains the momentum. It's perceptible and intransigent, often defying the odds, and it takes a miracle to reverse it, and no miracle was forthcoming for the Turks in front of them. Hampered by their own men retreating wildly back towards them, their line of fire was obscured and ineffective. As the first of the retreating Turks reached their second line, they leaped over it and kept on running. Seeing this, and just as had happened before, first one enemy soldier, and then more, abandoned the second trench and retreated, their officers and sergeants cursing them as they died under the bayonets of the battle-maddened Scots attacking them.

Stuart jumped into an empty section of trench. To either side, he could see his friends in hand-to-hand combat. A large Turkish sergeant was gripping Ross' rifle, both of them straining to leverage it away from the other. Stuart thumbed open his rifle's magazine cut-off, chambered a round, raised his rifle, and at less than six feet away, shot the Turk in the head, blowing half of it away against the trench wall. He stared at the destruction he'd caused before spinning around, his guard up. He shot another enemy soldier in the back as he fought with Murdo, the bullet going straight through the Turk and impacting on the trench wall. Ross ran past him, yelling at him to follow.

Beyond Harris, the trench opened up, and just as Ross and Stuart joined their sergeant, rifles raised, a small group of Turkish soldiers fleeing from another part of the trench came around a corner towards them. Stuart dropped to one knee and fired. Ross and Murdo fired their own rifles over his head. The Turks, unable to move or seek shelter, died in a bloody pile. One fleeing Turk managed to turn, reaching the corner only to be flung backward by rifle fire further down the trench. Rifles still raised, Angus called out, and hesitantly a young Royal Scot answered back and then edged his way around the corner. The trench to the immediate left of them was clear, but they could still hear machine gun fire and a battle raging to their right, and somewhere down there were Liam, Aiden, Giles, and Color Sergeant Rennie with his platoon of men.

Before they found Liam, they heard him, swearing repeatedly, "Those feckin bastards will feckin well pay," followed by the crack of his rifle as he fired towards the new Turkish line 100 yards away in a support trench, shooting a careless Turkish soldier in the head. "Take that, you feckin bastard!" he shouted as he re-chambered another round and sought out another target.

Just as they approached him, Giles came around a corner from the opposite direction with Aiden by his side. On seeing the rest of his section, he relaxed a fraction. "Sergeant Harris, situation please."

Harris lowered his rifle. "The trench down to the left is secure, sir. The Turks have retreated, but you can be sure their officers will be whipping them up to counterattack soon."

"Seamus is dead," said Connor in a flat tone, drawing a look of disapproval for cutting in and addressing the second lieutenant directly.

Giles saw the look and quickly said, "It's all right, Sergeant Harris," before looking at Connor. "Are you sure?"

"Yes, sir."

"I'm very sorry to hear it. We'll bury him properly later if we can, I promise, but right now we're not out of trouble yet. The Turks have heavy machine guns placed all along the right flank."

"Multiple heavy machine guns? But the intelligence reports said the line was lightly held, and that all the strongpoints were to the left," said Harris.

"The intelligence reports were wrong, as are the maps we have. Most of them date from the Crimean War. As far as I can tell, the first wave of the Cameronians were wiped out. They certainly didn't capture either trench, but I suspect they'll give it another go...."

They heard a roar from the British line—officer's whistles and the faint sound of bagpipes playing forward the wave of men emerging from the Cameronians' line. All sound was promptly drowned out as multiple heavy maxim machine guns opened up on the charging soldiers.

"Sweet Jesus, God help them," muttered Liam as they watched the dreadful scene unfold.

They didn't stand a chance. From their elevated position, the section could see the Scottish Rifles being torn apart, men hit by three or four bullets at the same time, flailing their arms in the air in a macabre dance before tumbling to the ground as the machine guns overlapped their fields of fire. There was no way through the hail of lead, and no mercy shown in the one-sided slaughter. After what seemed like only ten seconds, the machine-gun fire ceased, and all that was left of the Cameronians was a pile of dead and dying broken men, punctuated by rifle fire from the Turkish line at any sign of movement. They stood silent, transfixed by the sight, until Harris coughed loudly to get Giles' attention.

"Begging your pardon, sir, but we need to sort out this trench quickly if we don't want to join those poor sods, and we still don't know where Color Sergeant Rennie and his men are."

Giles turned and focused back on the here and now. "You're right, Sergeant, of course," he said, and paused to collect his thoughts. "Color Sergeant Rennie is holding the right of this position with the remains of his men. They were hit by the last sweep of machine-gun fire and are down to half strength. How many men have scopes?"

"Two sir, Lance Corporal McReynolds and Private Aiden O'Connell, sir."

"Have them keep a lookout towards the Turkish line for any sort of activity and shoot anyone they see. Let's try and keep their heads down at least—it might buy us more time."

Harris nodded, and with a tilt of his head sent Stuart and Aiden to man their posts with the simple order, "Yell like hell if you see them coming."

"The rest of you, we need to re-build this trench, fast."

The parapet and fire step were all on the wrong side, as were the comms trenches which now ran towards the enemy. The men had to build new fire steps and a parapet and block off any comms trenches if they were going to survive the expected counterattack. It would take them all hours to properly move sandbags to rebuild the parapet, and they didn't have hours. They did have lots of dead bodies in the trench.

Angus reached down and picked a dead Turk's awkwardly sagging body up from the bottom of the trench, motioning to Murdo who grabbed the legs, and together they swung the body up onto the lip of the trench. The rest of the section paired off and followed their example. More Royal Scots were coming through the trench to reinforce the right flank where a barricade had been thrown up to prevent

Turks coming through the trench-line, and men everywhere worked feverishly to turn the trench around to face the new Turkish lines. Lewis light machine gun teams came through their position, and one of the sweating machine gunners said their own heavy Vickers were being brought up. The sun was blazing, and the section stripped down to their pale grey-blue collarless shirts and took a quick swig of tepid water before returning to their labor.

Stuart had found a slight depression looking towards the Turkish line. He took off his conspicuous pith helmet, reloaded his rifle, checked his range settings, and slowly eased his weapon up and sighted down the telescopic sights. He panned down the Turkish line, 100 yards away. He could see heads bobbing along the line, men moving along the trench—and clearly, there was a lot of activity. What had been their third trench-line was now the Turks frontline, but it was incomplete, not fully sandbagged, and Stuart quickly identified a gap where, like him, a soldier was looking out towards the enemy line.

He slowly adjusted his body, finding his natural point of aim as he had been taught. He could see the Turk's head and shoulders in precise detail through the scope. He clicked off his safety and began to slowly squeeze the trigger. *Be surprised when it goes off,* he thought, as he felt the trigger move into its final stage.

The soldier turned to his right and disappeared. Stuart cursed until he saw a new face appear to scan their trench-line with binoculars—it had to be an officer. He resumed the slow inexorable pressure on his trigger and his rifle fired. He remained perfectly still as through the scope he saw the officer fly backward and disappear. Unbelievably, the soldier he had seen first reappeared, looking furtively towards the line to try and see where the shot had come from. Then a single shot rang out to his left, and the soldier's head jerked away in a cloud of red mist. Stuart just smiled—it had to be

Aiden. They'd both just made their first kills with the tele-scopic sights, and it felt good.

"That's for Seamus," Stuart muttered, not knowing that 30 feet away, Aiden was saying the same thing.

He chambered a round again and scanned for another likely opportunity. He found it behind the Turkish frontline, where an enemy comms trench was bustling with activity as Turkish reinforcements worked their way forwards. He could see an officer wearing a taller sun helmet than his sol-diers' kabalaks, standing a bit higher out of the trench, wav-ing his men forward. He adjusted the range on his sights and took aim. Once again he controlled his breath, gently ap-plied pressure to the trigger, and was rewarded when his target threw up his arms and fell, his dead body falling half out of the trench.

As he scanned farther down to his right, he heard Aiden's rifle crack followed by Harris shouting, "Keep it go-ing men. Get their heads down, and shoot their bloody offic-ers if you can!" After a pregnant pause, he added in a quieter voice, "No offense intended, sir."

Stuart grinned as he heard Giles' labored voice reply, "None taken, although if they're anything like you, it might make more sense to shoot their sergeants."

Harris smiled as he replied, "Good point, well made, sir."

Giles was working hard with the men to reverse the trench, something he shouldn't strictly be doing as an of-ficer, but the section admired him all the more for it. Stuart's attention was drawn to puffs of dust much farther behind the Turkish line, and then black objects arched up into the air. Before the sound of the artillery had even reached them, Aiden yelled at the section to take cover.

The Turkish artillery knew exactly where they were, and unlike the British artillery earlier in the day, they were spot on and firing high-explosive shells. Harris had just enough time to order Stuart and Aiden to stay at their posts before the section dove for whatever cover they could find. Once again, the Turkish artillery played havoc in the new front-line, sending great mounds of earth, white-hot metal, and debris over the trench. Stuart burrowed a few inches further into the hard ground and covered his ears against the deafening sound of impacting artillery rounds. He felt exposed and vulnerable, but he also understood someone had to warn the others if the Turks emerged to counterattack.

Concussive waves washed over him, and after a salvo fell to the left, he could hear the screams of injured and wounded soldiers calling out in pain. He felt a tremor course through his body and his hands begin to shake, so he gripped his rifle tightly and looked towards the Turkish line. There, in the gap in the enemy sandbags where he had shot his first officer, was another with binoculars, assessing the damage being done by the artillery. With the shells impacting all around him, Stuart eased his rifle out, took aim, noted the officer's red collar, and fired, watching the officer's head jerk back and blood-stained helmet fly off. "I'm still here, you bastards!" shouted Stuart, his voice lost in the maelstrom, and then he worked his bolt back and forth.

As he looked over his sights for another target, he saw the sun glinting off something the length of the Turkish parapet. Puzzled, he looked through his rifle's scope and saw what was causing it—the sun reflecting off a sea of vertical bayonets. He turned and shouted a warning with all his might, "Stand to! Stand to! Here they come!" just as the artillery barrage ceased.

Looking back at the gap in the sandbags, he saw a Turkish officer emerge, only to be thrown back with a bullet in the chest as Aiden's rifle cracked out. Behind him, more men were scrambling up, and Stuart shot a large man with a mustache and red-striped tunic sleeves—a senior non-commissioned officer—aiming 'center mass' as they had been taught.

Giles' voice rang out behind them. "Enemy attacking, rapid fire!" It wasn't necessary to let them know where the enemy was—it was obvious to everyone.

Then the Turkish soldiers poured over their parapet and ran towards them.

The trench erupted in rifle fire. Stuart and Aiden brought down two more men waving swords and leading the others. Two heavy Vickers machine guns blazed into action off to their right, and the higher-pitched quick rattle of the light Lewis guns sounded off to their left. All along the line, soldiers fired their rifles in a mad minute as they had been taught, quickly and efficiently, and the Turkish attack withered under the combined defensive might. There just weren't enough of them, and with all their officers shot, the attack wavered and then collapsed. The surviving Turks retreated to their lines, although few of them made it to safety.

"Cease fire! Cease fire! Reload!" echoed the order down the line, as the noise of gunfire was replaced by that of Turkish soldiers crying out in the new no man's land. A single shot rang out, and Stuart saw yet another officer fall backward from the handy observation gap in the sandbags, followed by Aiden's detached voice saying, "Those poor bastards just don't learn, do they?"

They weren't the only ones. Looking back towards the right of their old front line, Angus called out to Giles, "Sir, I think the Scottish Rifles are having another go."

"Impossible," replied Giles, but looking back from their elevated position, they could all see a mass of yellow pith helmets bobbing up and down the Cameronians front trench line. "Don't they realize the Turks can see them from up here?" asked Giles.

Then they heard the drone of bagpipes and a roar from the lines as the Cameronians emerged to charge the massed Turkish heavy machine guns once more. At their head emerged a familiar figure.

"It's the Brigadier," said Harris with disbelief tinged with awe, staring down at the attack. Despite the utter futility of it, a third attack against the Turkish strongpoint—without any further artillery support—had been ordered.

Brigadier William Scott-Moncrieff, commander of the Scottish Rifles Brigade, a veteran of the Zulu and Boer Wars, led the last attack of the Cameronians himself at 11:47 in the morning. He was cut down by machine gun fire as he left the trenches, alongside the battalion commander and his soldiers. The Turkish machine guns were firing before they even left their positions, and many men were thrown back into the trench they'd just climbed out of.

"Can anyone see any of the Turkish machine guns?" asked Giles with desperation in his voice.

Stuart and Aiden scanned the Turkish lines away to the right of them, and it was Aiden who pinpointed the machine gun closest to them. "There! About fifty yards down their trench from the barricade."

"I see it!" shouted Stuart, reloading his magazine with ten rounds. "Sir, if you can keep the Turks above us pinned down, I can enfilade the gun from that hillock in no man's land." Stuart pointed down towards an exposed rise on the ground surrounded by dead bodies, about 30 feet downhill.

"All right, but..." and whatever Giles was going to add, it was too late. Stuart leaped up, jumped back over the trench, and was running downhill for the hillock, rifle held in front of him with both hands.

Giles stared in disbelief before hearing Aiden's rifle crack out and bullets whizzed overhead towards Stuart in reply. "Covering fire!" he yelled, and the section began to pour rifle fire into the Turkish trench above them.

Stuart ran for all he was worth. He heard bullets snapping by him and then dove feet first down behind the hillock. It offered little cover but elevated him enough to see down the line of the enemy trench towards the machine gun to the right of their position. Bullets continued to zip by and kick up the ground as he chambered a round and settled his breathing as best he could. Sighting down his scope, he found the closest enemy machine gun crew firing towards the Cameronians. He focused on the man firing the heavy maxim and slowly squeezed the trigger.

The Turkish machine gunner's head snapped sideways as Stuart's high-velocity bullet went straight through his skull, spraying blood out the far side. He slumped towards his gun, which stopped firing. Amid all the noise, the gun crew hadn't heard or seen the source of the shot, and presuming it came from the soldiers charging towards them, simply pushed the dead machine gunner aside and the assistant gunner took over. Before the new gunner could depress the trigger, Stuart fired again, and that soldier was knocked sideways, blood pumping from a mortal wound to the neck.

Stuart reloaded and looked towards the gun crew. He saw an officer raise his hand and point towards him. Stuart aimed at his chest and pulled the trigger, watching him fall backwards, arms flailing in the air. Another of the crew turned in his direction, and Stuart carefully took aim and shot him between the eyes. Turkish soldiers in the trench were now firing towards him and he found himself in a crossfire—Turks shooting at him from above, and Turks shooting at him from the right-hand trench. Looking back through his scope at the now abandoned machine gun, he chambered a round and fired into the square side of the exposed maxim, aiming for where he judged the firing mechanism to be. Working the bolt rapidly, he fired, again and again, pumping bullets into the same point until his magazine emptied.

Bullets were now slapping into the dead bodies piled around him. Pain lanced through his body as he felt a bullet cut through his left bicep and then another sear past his right cheek. A desperate thought came to him. He reached out for a discarded rifle strewn on the ground, and then threw himself backward, arcing the enemy rifle into the air and then lay completely still. The firing at his position first slackened and then stopped.

To both the section and the Turks it looked as if Stuart had been shot dead, his body and rifle flung backward in death. The fire from the Turkish line above them stopped, and those in the trench below them to the right refocused on the Cameronians—now reduced to a handfull—retreating back to their trench line. While the machine guns further down the trench continued to fire, the one nearest them remained silent and out of action.

***

As Ross stared at where his brother lay inert, the other members of the section began to look towards him in stunned silence. Then Ross saw Stuart raise one forearm up from the ground, spread out his hand, and point one finger skywards. A second later he pointed another, and Ross snapped his rifle up towards the Turkish trench while yelling, "Covering fire!" as Stuart raised a third finger skywards.

Stuart took a deep breath, said a quick prayer, and burst into life. He rolled and was up and running towards the trench within two seconds. Within three seconds he was running flat out as fast as he could, his rifle held high across his chest and legs pumping. Within five seconds he could hear bullets cracking past him and he began to sidestep, lungs burning. He could hear Giles and Harris yelling at him to run faster. The sound of bullets increased as Stuart covered the last few yards and then dived headfirst for the trench just as a bullet creased his thigh in mid-air and spun him sideways. He hit the inside of the trench wall and landed in a pile, the wind driven out from his lungs, coughing and gasping for breath.

Ross ran over and crouched down. He quickly checked his brother's wounds and then gave Stuart a sip from his water bottle and admonished him gently, "Now that was either the stupidest or bravest thing you've done so far, probably both. Don't do it again. Ever."

Stuart nodded. They heard urgent voices farther down the line calling for them to stand to. The enemy had used the attention focused on the massacre of the Cameronians to their advantage and were already pouring over their parapet towards them.

"Enemy attacking, open fire!" shouted Giles, and the section sprang up to place their rifles over the hastily constructed parapet of dead bodies to face another bayonet charge. Ross pulled his brother up, loaded his rifle with two clips, and handed him back his weapon, muttering "No rest for the wicked." The Vickers and Lewis machine guns burst into action, and the soldiers worked their bolts frantically, firing off round after round. The Turks were attacking in greater numbers and had surprised them. It was a more determined attack than before, and Stuart fired again and again into the mass of men charging towards them. Beside him, he could hear Connor repeating something about 'defending us in battle' each time he worked his rifle bolt to and fro. His ten bullets fired, and he reached for a charger of five bullets, loaded them, and looked over the parapet. He realized a group of eight Turks was seconds away from them.

He stood back in the bottom of the trench and calmly pointed his rifle upwards. A large enemy soldier loomed up in front of Connor and Stuart swung his rifle and shot him, propelling backward, quickly reloading, he shot another up through the chin, blowing his lower jaw and face away, leaving a grotesque mask of blood and bare skull in its place. The man staggered backward, still alive, screaming incoherently through a bloody raw hole leading to his throat. Stuart stared in abject horror as Connor and Ross backed down next to him as the remaining Turks came leaping into the trench. Stuart thrust upwards at the first and impaled him on his bayonet, but the weight of the enemy soldier falling towards him tore his rifle from his hands.

Before he could grab it, a large Turkish soldier stabbed at him with his bayonet and rifle. Stuart turned sideways and the bayonet thrust missed him by inches. He grabbed the soldier's rifle, trying to wrestle it from him, but the soldier was too strong and Stuart was still exhausted from his sprint back to safety. Both gripping the rifle, the two men frantically tugged and pulled, and then the Turk smashed his head forward and Stuart fell with the Turk on top of him, his rifle across Stuart's neck.

The Turk pushed down with all his might. Stuart tried to push upwards, but the man was too powerful, and his rifle came closer and closer until he could feel it against his windpipe. He could smell the Turk's breath, see into his eyes full of hate and aggression, as the rifle cut off his air. He pushed frantically upwards, but it gave him only a second's reprieve before the rifle was choking him again. He tried to kick out, to push his attacker sideways, but the man was too big, and he felt the pressure increase against his windpipe. He looked up and saw two things happen—a pistol appeared at the side of the Turk's head, and then the man's head exploded, blood and brains splattering off the trench wall and onto Stuart's face.

The dead soldier was hauled off him, and a hand reached down to pick him up. It was Connor, handing him back his rifle. "Are you all right?"

Stuart massaged his throat and nodded. "Thank you."

"Don't be thanking me. Thank the boss. He walked down the trench with his pistol out, shot the Turk I was fighting with, then shot your man, and then two more fighting your brother, before reloading and disappearing down the trench, yelling for Ross to follow him. Cool as a cucumber, he was."

"The Turks?" asked Stuart.

"Gone. Aiden's keeping a lookout. They reached our lines, but not in enough numbers to hold any."

Stuart stood on shaky legs and massaged his throat, his other hand supporting him against the trench wall. After a minute or so, he felt his breathing ease and he looked up.

"When we were shooting, you were repeating something the whole time."

"I was?" said Connor perplexed.

"Something about 'defending us in battle'," Stuart explained, still rubbing his windpipe.

Connor knotted his eyebrows and then smiled. "*Saint Michael, the Archangel, defend us in battle, be our protection*....it just came to me. One of the prayers Father Foley used to have us recite before hurling matches with the other schools. To tell you truth, I didn't even realize I was saying it out loud."

Stuart smiled up at the big Irishman, his black shock of hair wet with sweat and covered in grime. "It sounds like a good prayer for a soldier. I may borrow it, if I'm allowed to?"

Connor made a show of stroking his chin and knotting his eyebrows. "Well, I'm not sure—being the Protestant heathen you are—if a good Catholic prayer would be wasted on your soul or not. Somehow I think God won't mind too much. Father Foley, on the other hand, may try to excommunicate you, even if you're not Catholic, and I'm sure he's been around since the Spanish Inquisition."

Stuart laughed and bowed his head. "I have a feeling we need all the help we can get, divine or otherwise. I'm fine now. Why don't you check on the others?"

Connor nodded. "I'll do that, and I'll send your brother over when I find him." He turned to disappear down the trench.

"Connor," called out Stuart, and the big Irishman turned. "I'm sorry about Seamus."

Connor pursed his lips and nodded his head, suddenly unable to speak, and then disappeared down the trench.

Stuart took out his water bottle and gave it a shake, half full or half empty, it didn't really matter right now. He twisted off the cap and took a gulp of warm water, then carefully poured a little into one cupped hand and threw it onto his face, using his wet hand to wipe his face clear of grime and blood and then ran his fingers through his dirty sandy-brown hair. It was hot, very hot, the heat shimmered off the hard-packed soil and he closed his eyes, tilting his head up towards the sun, feeling its fierce heat dry his face in seconds.

"It's just like being on the beach in sunny California," joked a familiar voice, and he opened his eyes to see Ross standing in front of him, a concerned smile on his face. "Are you all right?" he asked.

Stuart rubbed his throat. "I'll be fine, thanks to Giles. He shot one of the big bastards off me at point-blank range."

Ross looked down at the bottom of the trench and saw the bloodied bodies lying in their death throes and knew it must have been a close fight—too close. "He shot two near me and a few more down the trench. Next time we stick together," he said.

Stuart nodded and then looked at his brother, who had a livid scar and dried blood down the side of his head. "How's your head?"

"Its fine. A bit too close for comfort, but an inch the other way and it would have missed me altogether," he replied with a smile. "How's your shoulder?" he asked, poking Stuart's left shoulder with his finger.

Stuart winced and looked down. His tunic below his epaulet was bloody and torn. "I didn't even know that was there," he replied.

"Well, it is, along with others. Let me take a look." Ross drew closer, examining the wounds. "Looks like a bullet nicked the top of your shoulder. It seems fine, but I'm sure it'll hurt soon enough. You've got a nice furrow down your thigh, but it's mostly blood, no damage. You've got another flesh wound through your bicep and a nice crease on your right cheek. That's going to mess up your dashing good looks for a while." He paused and then looked Stuart in the eye. "That was a hell of a thing you did, but no more heroics big brother, promise me that."

"I promise."

"And how did you know anyone would be looking towards you when you stuck your fingers in the air, and that you were counting to three?"

"It's all I could think of at the time."

"Well, don't let it happen again. We stick together, and that's hard enough to do without you leaping around the battlefield taking on the entire Ottoman Turkish Army single-handedly."

Stuart, suitably chastised, looked at his brother as he gently tied a bandage around his bicep. "Did you think it would be like this?" he asked quietly, looking at the dead stacked up on the parapet, and pinching his nose at the coppery stench of blood mixed with feces, urine, dead and decomposing bodies, entrails alive with flies, and upturned eyes already pecked out by hooded crows.

Ross shrugged his shoulders. "How could I? If folk saw this—what war is really like—they'd think us rabid animals. We charge the Turks on the right and die, the Turks charge us on the left and die, for what? A few hundred feet of sun-baked ground in the middle of nowhere. It makes so little sense, it's not even worth trying to make sense of it. It would drive a man mad to try."

Just then they heard Aiden's rifle fire and they tensed, but no call of alarm followed.

"Best we reload and get ready for them. I'm thinking it's going to be a long hot day," said Ross, settling in next to his brother, and he was right. From their position, they could hear repeated massed Turkish counterattacks to the left towards Gully Ravine and Gully Spur, and twice they repulsed bayonet attacks on their own position, the brothers fighting side by side. Towards late afternoon, they ran out of water. It was the hottest day of the year so far on the Gallipoli peninsula. They tried to find shade in the trench, but with little success, and the flies massed in clouds around them. They heaved the rest of the Turkish bodies onto the parapet and, already accustomed to the stench and sights around them, settled down and closed their eyes.

Stuart woke as someone kicked his boot gently. He opened his eyes and saw Giles and Harris standing above him. Startled, he struggled to his feet, inhaling sharply as pain shot through the wound down his thigh.

"At ease, Lance Corporal, at ease," said Giles.

"I'm sorry, sir. I must have dozed off. It won't happen again," said Stuart, his voice hoarse, his throat sore.

"McReynolds, as long as you're not on sentry duty or work parties, you grab whatever sleep you can, wherever you can. That's an order," said Harris.

"Yes, Sergeant," replied Stuart, relaxing.

Harris asked him about his shooting, and Stuart told him about the gap in the sandbags.

"You mean you shot an officer during the artillery barrage?" asked Harris.

"Yes, Sergeant. He was just standing there—red collar, binoculars, looking at our trench. I guess he thought he was safe."

"Red collar? Are you sure?" interrupted Giles.

"Yes, sir."

"That signifies a general staff officer, probably high ranking," Giles said looking towards Harris.

Then they asked him about the machine gun, and Stuart told them about shooting its crew and trying to disable the heavy weapon by repeatedly shooting its firing mechanism, before playing dead.

Giles scribbled down notes in his notebook and then looked up at Stuart, "Good work, Lance Corporal. Perhaps enough heroics for now, though. That was a close call."

Stuart smiled. "Yes, sir. My brother said much the same thing to me, sir."

"Well, then listen to him, because we don't want to lose anyone else today. Is there anything more we need to know?"

Stuart thought for a second and said, "The pith helmets, sir. we can be seen for miles with them on. They're like giant yellow mushrooms. It would be good to have something that kept the sun off, covered our eyes, but didn't stick out so much when we're shooting from cover, sir."

"We'll see what we can do."

"And sir," added Stuart, looking at Giles, "thank you for shooting that Turk off me."

Giles smiled. "You're very welcome, Lance Corporal. I'm sure you would have had the best of him sooner or later. I just hurried things along a bit in your favor," and he turned with Harris beside him to check on the rest of the position.

It was dark before they were relieved. The Turks had attacked once more, but had been driven back. Color Sergeant Rennie passed through their line and paused to chat with Sergeant Harris before leaving. Harris looked behind Rennie and saw nine men with him, two of them wounded and limping badly, supported by their friends, and Rennie himself had a bandage around his head. "Is that it?" asked Harris in a soft voice.

Rennie looked at him, and Harris thought in the moonlight he saw his cheeks glistening with tears. "I had a full platoon this morning—over thirty men—all lads I'd trained myself, knew most of them their whole lives. They went to the same school, did the same work, lived in the same streets, drank at the same pubs, and now I'm down to nine, and two of them won't soldier again for a while, if ever." He paused and rubbed his face. "I lost some to our own artillery before we even left our trenches, about half to machine guns that we didn't even know about, and then more to Turkish shrapnel and bayonets." He shook his head before adding, "And this was their first battle." He looked behind him and motioned for the remainder of his men to follow and continued down the trench.

A few minutes later, Giles came to gather them together. "Quietly does it—no noise." They pulled on their dirty blood-soaked uniforms and adjusted their webbing. They picked up their weapons and followed Giles in a single line, Angus bringing up the rear. Down the section filed, back over the ground they'd raced up in the morning, now covered with the dead being cleared up by work parties as others dug new comms trenches to the new frontline. They reached their start-off position and worked their way back through the trenches to the support area, now teeming with soldiers bringing up new supplies and equipment to reinforce and fortify the new positions.

As they worked their way back, they saw fires with men huddled around them for warmth and comfort, shielded from the Turkish lines by the gullies and ravines that bisected the land. Giles stopped to check directions with a quartermaster sergeant and was pointed towards a fire already blazing to their left. "You'll find hot stew and water. Your man has already started a fire for you."

Giles let Sergeant Harris know he was off to report in with Major Sinclair and to let the section rest for the night. He'd be back with their orders in the morning.

The section plodded towards the fire and saw a lone soldier tending the fire. Hearing their footsteps, he turned and stood up stiffly, looking towards them, and Connor let out a gasp—it was Seamus.

The section stood bewildered until Connor, Liam, and Aiden went to embrace their childhood friend, now resurrected and standing before them. Seamus winced and cried out in pain. "And there I thought I'd have a quiet night to myself," he said with a grimace and a smile.

"But you were dead!" said Connor in disbelief. "I saw you hit. I saw you fall down," he insisted.

"I was hit," agreed Seamus, pointing to a hole in his left breast pocket, "but two things saved me. I'll tell you all about it while we eat, if you're hungry, that is."

As the section quickly pulled tin plates out of their kit, he ladled out greasy tough stew from a square tin next to the fire and passed around stale loaves of bread. They both tasted delicious.

While they sat, Seamus told them what had happened, his face lit up by the fire. "So, there I was, running along with the rest of you, and then *wham!* something almighty hits me in the chest and sends me reeling backward. I thought that was it. I couldn't breathe, I couldn't feel anything, I couldn't move or cry out, and I made my peace with the Lord above and then I realized I was still alive. I had this pain in my chest beyond belief, but when I went to feel for blood, there was nothing there—just pain, but no blood—and then I felt a bullet hole in my pocket. I reached in underneath my tunic but there was no wound below. Then I reached into my pocket, and I found the bullet."

"What do you mean, you found the bullet?" asked Liam, entranced by Seamus' story.

"Here it is..." replied Seamus, and in his hand, he held out a shiny misshapen bullet.

Connor took it in his hand and looked at it. "But that's impossible," he said.

"That's what I thought," replied Seamus, "until I pulled this out my pocket," and he reached in and withdrew the pocket bible his mother had given him with a clear hole punched into its leather cover. "So, you could say that God saved me, with a little help..." and he opened the bible and carefully removed a heavily indented silver crown coin, the same coin his brother Patrick had given him when they'd parted at the train station in Ireland. It had been inside the middle of the bible, and combined with the dense thin paper pages of the book, had absorbed the deadly impact of the bullet leaving Seamus with three bruised ribs—but very much alive.

The bible, the coin, and the bullet were reverently passed around for everyone to see, hold and marvel. It was nothing short of miraculous.

"I crawled back to our trench along with the other wounded. The medical officer wound a bandage tightly around my chest about ten times and told me to report for light duty, if that's all right with you, Sergeant," he added, looking at Harris.

"That is just fine with me, Private O'Connell." He looked at the bullet in his hand. "It must have been fired from a rear trench and hit you without any real force behind it, that, or the cartridge was faulty. This bullet should have gone straight through the bible, coin, and you, make no mistake. You're a very lucky man, O'Connell, and I'm sure I speak for us all when I say I'm glad you're still with us."

"So am I, Sergeant. So am I!" and the section shared a quiet laugh. Seamus stood up gingerly, glad to be with his friends again, and picking up the ladle, asked if anyone would like more stew. Liam held out his mess tin and Seamus ladled more in.

"I could eat a horse!" declared Liam, shoveling in a large mouthful of the greasy stew and biting off a chunk of hard bread.

Seamus smiled. "Good, because that's stewed mule you're eating."

Liam looked at his mess tin in disbelief, his mouth completely full, and looked up at his friends.

Across from him, Aiden whinnied and neighed like a horse, and then the entire section burst into laughter.

CHAPTER FOURTEEN

The Gallipoli Racing Club

Cape Helles,
Gallipoli, July 1915

"Bathing parade, now! You all stink," ordered Sergeant Harris. The section gave no argument. Their uniforms were filthy and blood-stained, and so were they.

In the weeks since their arrival, they had become as gaunt as the rest of the soldiers at Gallipoli. The flies spread dysentery, and everyone suffered from the Turkey Trots to some degree. Many had to be evacuated to Lemnos, where the nurses also fell ill and in some cases, died alongside their patients.

The food was at times inedible. The bully beef liquefied in the shimmering heat and poured out of the tins in an unappetizing molten slop that was immediately covered by flies. The men, for the most part, survived off runny apricot jam, also covered in flies, and Huntley & Palmers Army Number 4 hard-tack square biscuits, supplemented occasionally by stewed mule, bacon, and hard cheese. Water was rationed to two pints a day, for cleaning and drinking, and in the summer heat, drinking took priority.

At the very farthest point, the front trenches at Cape Helles were two to three miles from the sea, often less. Any point on the peninsula could come under enemy artillery fire as the Turks controlled Achi Baba and could observe most of Cape Helles from the hilltop. Nowhere was safe on the peninsula—no rear area for rest and recuperation, no four- or six-day passes home to Britain or 48-hour passes to Paris. If they were lucky, soldiers might spend a few days at Imbros, a small island 12 miles off the coast in the Aegean, which served as Gallipoli's forward supply base for the allies. There was little to do, but at least it gave them a break and some decent food, including freshly baked bread. For the most part, a trek down to the beach and a wash in the sea was all that could be hoped for.

Harris looked at his wristwatch, then up at the morning sun, and finally over to Angus. "Bring them back before sunset, Corporal. Make sure they take some bars of soap and wash their bodies and their uniforms. Find some drinking water while you're down there and make them drink as much as they can, then fill their water bottles. Lieutenant Morley says you can have the rest of the day off."

With high spirits, the section followed Angus down the trail. They could see that more men had recently arrived, including the two remaining brigades of the 52nd Lowland Division comprising the Royal Scots Fusiliers, the Kings Own Scottish Borderers, the Highland Light Infantry, and a battalion of the Argyll & Sutherland Highlanders. The men were obviously nervous of the sound of artillery and were looking around at their new surroundings, which included open stares at the section as they passed. Stuart thought back to their walk up the line when they first arrived and wondered if they now already looked like seasoned veterans—weary and stinking, they certainly felt like it.

Angus saluted as they passed a group of staff officers, and Stuart heard one commenting loudly on the "shabbiness of the soldiers." Glancing towards him, Stuart turned away quickly, drawing the attention of the officer who stared after him as he walked down the trail. Although he couldn't be certain, Stuart thought it was the officer who'd harangued him in Edinburgh. He put the thought behind him as the section stared at the beach. There were no waves and little sand, just stones, and water lapping around the bloated

stinking corpse of a mule and a shoreline of discarded rubbish, an oily grey slick covering the water. With no tide to
speak of, the Aegean was very slow at cleaning itself, and the
detritus that littered the beach would remain for some time.

"This is no good," declared Angus, and they followed
him down the shoreline, back up into the scraggy pine trees,
and further down the coast. They walked for half an hour,
peering down the cliff edge, until Angus halted them and
took a few steps back. He'd spotted a mule-track winding its
way through the shrub and down towards the coastline.
They followed it down through a narrow gully in the cliff until it opened up on a small cove about 100 yards long, where
the water looked pale turquoise-blue against the white rocky
bottom. Too steep and isolated to use for unloading supplies, the pebbly beach remained pristine. After stacking
their rifles, they stripped off and waded into the sea.

It was pure unadulterated bliss.

For the first time since arriving at the front, there were
no flies, just a gentle breeze and the cool water. They
splashed each other and dove under the water. Apart from
Murdo, their bodies were pale, but their arms, necks, and
heads were deeply tanned. They all had cuts and minor
wounds, and the sea water helped to clean them. Seamus'
chest was still painfully bruised and green-yellow. Stuart's
wounds were all livid red and swollen, so Ross made him
scrub off the scabs, squeeze out the pus, and clear out the
wounds under the salt water. It took a while and was painful,
but the results were rewarding and looked a lot healthier.
After a while, Angus had them turn their attention to their
clothing, and they spent an hour scrubbing their uniforms
free of grime, lice, and blood-stains with hard green bars of
sea soap and stiff bristle hand-brushes, pounding them on
the rocks to dislodge the dirt and lice. Once cleaned, they
spread their uniforms on the hot pebbles above the waterline and let the sun dry them, and after another swim they

stretched out on the small smooth stones, letting the sun dry their bodies.

Liam broke the silence by declaring in a loud voice, "All we need now is a steak pie and a nice pint, and I'm not too fussed about the pie!"

"*Bonjour, mon amis*—hello, my friends. A pie and a pint I can't help you with, but would some wine and fresh bread help?" said a slow deep voice behind them.

They looked behind them in surprise to see a tall man standing there, slipping a canvas haversack off his back. He wore loose-fitting khaki trousers tucked into black boots, a wide blue sash under his belt, a sweat-stained white tunic, and a long blue coat with green chevrons on the sleeve. On his head he wore a battered white kepi. He rummaged into his haversack and produced baguettes of crusty white bread and a very large cylindrical cloth-covered canteen designed to hold three-days' worth of water for desert marching. He unscrewed the top, raised it to his lips, and took a deep swig before handing it to Liam. "Help yourselves, *mes amis*. There's more coming."

Liam raised the big canteen to his lips, closed his eyes, and took a deep drink. He let out a groan and then handed it to Connor. The canteen was filled with claret. The tall man then handed the baguettes to Stuart and Angus, who accepted them in disbelief. Stuart inhaled the aroma of the fresh bread and groaned. "Fresh bread and red wine. Have I just died and gone to heaven?"

The man laughed. "Trust me, this isn't heaven—but the French supply their soldiers with a little more than bully beef and hard-tack."

"You're French?" asked Stuart.

The big man laughed, "Not really, *mon ami*, but I wear their uniform, take their pay, fight their enemies, enjoy their food, chase their women, and drink their wine." He took off his coat and then stood melodramatically to attention, palms open and pressed flat against his thighs. "Caporal-chef Jacque Lafitte, 3rd Bataillon de Légion Étrangère, 1st Regiment de marche d'Afrique, at your service," and then bowed to his astonished audience.

"You're in the French Foreign Legion?" asked Stuart with undisguised awe.

"*Oui*," said Lafitte, now stripping off his shirt to reveal a deeply tanned—and equally scarred—muscular body. His hair was cut down to the bone on the back and sides, and what was left on top was blond.

"Where are you from?"

"*Legio Patria Nostra*—the Legion is our Motherland," he said with a smile and pride. "But before the Legion, a life-time ago, New Orleans. I've been in the legion for twelve years now, mostly Algeria and Morocco, fighting the Berber and Rif tribesmen. Now France sends me here to fight the Turks," he said, spreading his arms wide and smiling. "And where, *mes amis*, are you from?"

"Like yourself, far from here—the west coast of America and the east coast of Scotland."

Lafitte raised his eyebrows in curiosity. "And the others?"

Stuart stood up and introduced the section, accepting Lafitte's canteen from Ross and taking a swig of wine.

"Try it like this," suggested Lafitte, breaking off a mouth-ful of bread, popping it into his mouth, and then taking a small swig of wine from the canteen. He closed his eyes as he let the wine in his mouth soak into the bread before chewing and slowly swallowing.

In response to the war, the French Army—including the For-eign Legion—supplemented its strength by adding tempo-rary *regiments de marche* to fight on the Western Front. They were filled with volunteers—in the case of the Legion, foreign volunteers—many of them American. The Legion had formed four *regiments de marche* for service in France, along with an independent battalion which it had sent to Gallipoli, still wearing its late 19th century uniforms, as part of the French colonial army contingent from Africa.

Lafitte had grown up in New Orleans, but his ancestors had been Acadians—French immigrants in the 18th century who had settled in New England and Canada's Maritime Provinces, an area also known as Acadia. During the war with France in North America, the British suspected all Acadians of French sympathies, and as a result, they had been forcibly resettled during the Great Expulsion. Many found their way eventually to the Spanish territory of Louisiana, a third of them dying of disease or drowning on the way. Once in Louisiana, they settled outside New Orleans and become known over time as Cajuns.

As a young man, Lafitte had gambled and drank, a deadly combination in the back streets and bayous of New Orleans. Accused of cheating, he'd been attacked, and in drunken self-defense had fatally stabbed his assailant, who happened not only to be equally drunk but also, more importantly, the spoiled son of a local magistrate. With little hope of a fair trial, he'd fled to France and had enlisted in the Foreign Legion. He had assumed the impossibly swashbuckling name of Jacque Lafitte as his *nom de guerre*. Over the past 12 years, he'd fought and fought hard, and had risen to the rank of *Caporal-chef*, Senior Corporal. He had left his past and birth name far behind. He'd not been alone. During the brutal recruit training, he'd formed an alliance that had lasted his entire service in the legion. That alliance was now walking down the trail towards them in the shape of *Caporal-chef* Ricardo Ramirez.

"I hope you brought more wine!" called out Lafitte.

"*Hola mi amigo*—hello my friend! More English and Australians?" replied Ramirez with a Mexican accent.

"Much, much worse—Scots and Irish this time!"

Ramirez made a show of crossing himself and glancing skywards, "Perhaps we should go back for a barrel?"

"Do you actually get issued wine?" interrupted Stuart in astonishment.

"*Naturellement!*" replied Lafitte, and he wasn't lying. The supply depot for the French forces included stacked barrels of wine, diligently guarded day and night. A near military catastrophe took place when the Turks shelled the depot and spilled over 2,000 gallons of wine into the thirsty dry sand.

Diagonally across Ramirez's chest hung two more large canteens, both filled with red wine, and from his haversack, he produced more baguettes and a block of hard cheese. He sat down and brought out a wooden-handled Opinel pocket knife and carefully sliced into the cheese until half of it was cut into slices, introducing himself as he shared it with the section. He was a French-Mexican, a *Barcelonnette*, descended from French textile workers who had settled in Veracruz. He was good with a knife—and fast. No one knew what had driven him to join the Foreign Legion, and no one, if they knew what was good for them, asked.

"Do you always come prepared for company?" asked Stuart.

"Only on Saturdays," replied Lafitte.

"Is it Saturday?"

"Yes, my friend. It's easy to lose track of time at here, and the days become meaningless, so we began the Gallipoli Racing Club. It gives our weekend some purpose, something to look forward to, and this," he said, spreading his arms wide and looking at the hidden cove, "is our secret meeting place."

"The Gallipoli Racing Club?"

"Ah, now that would be my idea," replied a thick south-coast Irish brogue behind them, and they turned to see a lanky Irishman coming down the trail. He stopped suddenly and looked in astonishment at the section. "Now there's a sight I didn't think I'd see when I woke up this morning.

Don't tell me—the O'Connells have rowed their skiff over just for the craic."

The Irishmen stood up to meet the new arrival. "McAvoy?" asked Seamus slowly in utter disbelief.

"It is indeed, Seamus—the very same, and I see Connor with you, and wherever you two went, Liam and Aiden were never far away." He stepped forward and began shaking hands. As he came to Connor and Seamus, he said, "And there I was just paying my respects to your brothers, so I was, God rest their souls."

In a day full of surprises, Seamus and Connor stood stunned. "Our brothers?"

McAvoy nodded his head solemnly. "I buried them myself, so I did, not half a mile from here." As he talked he walked over and shook hands with Lafitte and Ramirez, he asked, "Still with us?"

Ramirez laughed. "*Sí, Señor* McAvoy."

Much as Lafitte called everyone *mon ami,* his companion called everyone *señor* for the same reason—it made folk feel important and put them at ease, while internally the legionnaires decided if they were a threat or not—and if they were, how to kill them if necessary. Ramirez looked over at the O'Connells and asked McAvoy if he knew these men.

"I do. Good boys from County Cork they are. I went to school with their brothers, Patrick and Frank. We joined up together, trained together, and landed on this god-forsaken peninsula together. Before we even started fighting, I was the only one left standing of the three of us, by the grace of God," and he crossed himself.

"And now I find their younger brothers here in their place, but not wearing the same uniform?" he inquired. Seamus and Connor told him their story and how they'd come to join the Seaforth Highlanders. In turn, McAvoy told them of the Munster Fusiliers landing in the SS *River Clyde* and the massacre that followed.

"We were together all the way to the beach—three of the few that actually made it that far—and just as we dove for cover, a machine gun stitched a line of bullets right across us. The bullets tore the pack off my back, so it did, but we all landed under a slight shelf of sand. I thought we were all fine, and I lay there cursing the Turks for a while. It was only when I looked towards Patrick and Frank I saw they were completely still, faces both down in the sand, lying next to each other. They must have been a fraction of a second behind me, and both were caught in the chest by the bullets. Patrick's left hand was stretched out across the sand towards Frank's right hand, lying on top of it. Whether they landed that way in death, or in the last seconds of life Patrick stretched out his hand to Frank, I'll never know, but I've taken great comfort from it ever since, and so should you both."

The boys were silent for a moment, until Seamus said, "Father Foley said they'd be together, and he was right."

McAvoy smiled at the mention of their parish priest, and then asked, "Would you like to see their graves? They're not far from here."

Seamus and Connor nodded, let the section know where they were going, and turned to follow McAvoy with Liam and Aiden when they heard a voice behind them.

"We'd like to come too if it's all right with you."

Seamus and Connor turned to see the rest of the section all standing and looking up at them, and overcome with unexpected emotion, Seamus nodded his head and said, "That would be just fine with us."

On the way, Stuart quizzed McAvoy about Lafitte. "Wasn't there a pirate from New Orleans called Lafitte?" he asked.

McAvoy looked at him with a raised eyebrow. "Legionnaires are allowed to adopt a *nom de guerre* upon recruitment. Few go by their birth names, and fewer still ask questions if they know what's good for them. If there was a pirate called Lafitte, perhaps it's a coincidence, perhaps not. Best leave it alone, I think."

It took them 15 minutes to reach the military graves, rows of them, each marked with wooden crosses. Some marked individual graves, some marked mass burials in common graves when the bodies had become too many to bury individually, which was common after most battles. Stuart stared at a freshly excavated mass grave, ready for the next big push.

"Sweet Jesus. There are more than I ever imagined," said Liam.

McAvoy shook his head. "This is just one gravesite—there are more. A lot of our lads were buried out at sea by the navy, and even more just lie in no man's land. We haven't been able to bury them, or the Turks." He paused in reflection before continuing.

"You know, before I came here, I was slightly afraid of the dead, all laid out for people to view in their coffins at home, silver coins covering their eyes. Now I've watched one of my mates decompose not thirty feet from our own lines. At first, he went all black and bloated, then his tongue stuck out his mouth, and then it disappeared, and the flies moved in. After a few days, he was covered in maggots, then he sort of caved in. After that, his dried flesh came away in tatters. Now he just lies there, his skeleton still dressed in a tattered uniform, his skull grinning at me from no man's land with hair still attached. I talk to him now, say hello, ask him what the craic is—it's that or go completely insane. It's an offense against God, so it is, but the generals don't live in the trenches. They're living offshore in naval battleships, dinner and drinks in the officers' wardroom, clean linen and a soft bunk, daily showers and personal servants—so what do they care?"

They walked in silence until they came to Patrick's grave at the end of a makeshift row, and next to him at the end of the row, Frank's. Above each, a crude wooden cross was etched with their names, serial number, regiment, and the date they died.

"I buried them as they fell, next to each other."

Seamus and Connor touched the crosses, both with tears in their eyes.

"Ma will take some comfort to know what you did for them," said Seamus, and Connor drew close and put his arm across his shoulder. They stood there, looking down. Liam and Aiden came forward and linked their arms in with their childhood friends, silently sharing their grief.

After a while, McAvoy broke the silence. "Right then, boys," he said. "You know where they are, and I'm glad I could show you, but neither Patrick nor Frank would want us to stand about moping all day. Let's go back to the cove and have our own wake for them and remember them with smiles and laughter."

As they walked back down to the Hidden Cove, Stuart looked out across the calm azure sea. He could see destroyers and smaller vessels, some of them requisitioned fishing boats, but none of the larger cruisers, battlecruisers, and dreadnought battleships. "Where's the Royal Navy?" he asked McAvoy.

"They've buggered off to hide behind anti-submarine nets. There's a German U-Boat out there somewhere. It sunk two ships, and a German-manned Turkish destroyer dashed down the straits and torpedoed another. After that, the navy pulled out and sent their big ships home or to Imbros or Lemnos to protected anchorages and took away our heavy naval artillery support with them."

"But I thought we were here to clear the coastal guns, so the navy could reach Constantinople?"

McAvoy laughed. "We're here to take the next hundred or so yards of this god-forsaken peninsula one bloody battle at a time and to try and stay alive while doing it. That's as far as I can see—anything else is meaningless."

By the time they returned to the cove, there were 40 or so men there. Lafitte greeted them loudly with another full canteen of claret and a wide smile. "*Ah! Mes amis! Mes amis écossais!*—My Scottish friends!"

He was surrounded by soldiers in various stages of dress. Most, like himself, were stripped to the waist and had been swimming. Tunics from a variety of nations and regiments lay washed and drying in the sun. The subsequent lack of rank and uniform added to the relaxed egalitarian atmosphere. Almost all the men had brought some sort of booze, which helped. French wine and Royal Navy rum mixed with lime juice was the most prevalent, the latter supplied by a handful of Royal Marine Light Infantrymen. The British Army had stopped issuing rum early on in the campaign—just another burden for the soldiers to bear. A great cheer went up when down the trail came a string of five mules led by a short squat man named Medved.

"*Allez Oop!*" shouted Lafitte, and he shook the man's hairy forearm in a tight grip. McAvoy laughed and took a swig of rum, passing it to Seamus.

"We didn't bring anything with us but runny apricot jam, hard biscuits, and water," said Seamus in an apologetic tone.

"Don't you go worrying about it," said McAvoy. "You know what to save up and bring the next time, so just enjoy yourselves at the races."

"The races?" asked Connor.

"Care of the Zion Mule Corps. Whenever they can, they ride their mules, you see, so we call them the *Allez Oop Cavalry* because that's what they shout to make the beasts go. You'll soon see."

McAvoy waved at a group of soldiers who wandered over to greet him, and he introduced them to the section. They were Lancashire Fusiliers, and had landed at Gallipoli on the same day as McAvoy but at a different beach. It hadn't made any difference. They'd been machine-gunned as they approached the beaches in large rowing boats. Most had

died, and there was already talk of six Victoria Cross citations being drawn up. Perhaps because of their shared experiences, they had grown an affinity with the Irish Fusiliers
who had suffered the same fate. They were small in stature
with heavy accents Stuart could barely understand. Soon
they were sharing stories and drink with each other and with
men from the London Regiment, the South Wales Borderers, and some artillerymen from a Glasgow-based howitzer
battery who no one could understand at all.

To everyone's great surprise, Angus was soon chatting
away in Gaelic to a small group of gunners, part of the 4th
Highland Mountain Artillery Brigade that had landed on the
beaches along with the infantry to provide what light artillery support they could. A bottle of whisky soon appeared,
but as Angus beckoned Murdo over to join the conversation,
Stuart's attention was drawn to a commotion further down
the beach. A large circle of men had gathered and, in the
middle, stood Ramirez and a tall black Senegalese Tirailleur.
Both had weapons drawn and were circling each other.

The tirailleur was much taller and much bigger than
Ramirez. His face above the eyebrows and along his cheeks
was patterned with tribal scarring, and he was carrying a
coupe-coupe, a long, heavy, wide-bladed West African
fighting machete. The legionnaire, on the other hand,
looked small and wiry and was armed with a Camillus boot
knife. It was a complete mismatch. Stuart stood to watch the
fight and cast an anxious look at Lafitte, who just winked
and smiled without concern.

The Senegalese soldier struck first, his coupe-coupe
raised upwards, and he slashed it across the Mexican's bare
chest, missing by inches. He slashed his knife back across
Ramirez's face, but Ramirez stepped backward and avoided
it. The black soldier came on again fast, feigning with a slash
to the face, then one towards the legionnaire's belly. Again
Ramirez dodged the knife. Each time the colonial soldier
struck, Ramirez twisted and back-stepped, avoiding harm.

Unlike the Senegalese soldier, Ramirez was holding his knife downwards, blade pointing at the ground. He blocked the tirailleur's attack with his blade a few times but quickly stepped back away from his more powerful opponent, who was taunting him openly now. The crowd cheering on both knife-fighters.

From the corner of his eye, Stuart could see bets being placed, with each other and with Lafitte, but the two legionnaires were biding their time. Stuart saw Ramirez look towards Lafitte, who imperceptibly nodded his head.

The big Senegalese Tirailleur came on again and slashed towards Ramirez, expecting him to back-step as he had been all during the fight, but the legionnaire did exactly the opposite. Before the big knife had fully slashed past him, he rushed the black soldier. Hooking his right foot behind the larger man, he struck out with his knife towards the man's throat, punching his knife towards his windpipe. The big Senegalese soldier reacted by arching backward and lost his balance as he tripped over Ramirez's hooked foot. Ramirez fell with him, knife still at his throat until the black soldier was lying flat on his back, arms spread out to his sides, with Ramirez' knife a hair's breadth from his throat.

For a second or two there was silence, and then the big soldier grinned and laughed out loud in a deep booming voice. Ramirez stood up and held out his hand, helping his opponent up to his feet, and calling for his canteen of wine. Soon both men were drinking, the big Senegalese playfully tousling Ramirez's dark hair.

"They're friends?" asked Stuart in confusion.

"But of course," replied Lafitte. "They fight every time they meet, and Ramirez always wins—he always does with the knife."

"How?" asked Stuart, genuinely wanting to know.

Lafitte could see the interest, not only from Stuart, but the rest of his friends, so he came towards them and unsheathed his own fighting knife from his right boot.

"Fighting with knives and hand-held bayonets has to be done quickly. Don't circle for ages, especially in a trench. You don't have the time or space. Let your opponent make the first move and then step in quickly. A cut to the forehead will bleed heavily and blind your opponent. A short stab to the chest will kill or puncture lungs. A stab across the neck could lacerate the jugular vein or carotid artery. A stab to the belly will usually tear into the liver, spleen, bowel, kidneys, or one of several blood vessels—all deadly. Once inflicted, just step away and let them die. No need to expose yourself to any more danger."

Lafitte warmed to his subject. "Assume you're going to be cut or stabbed and don't cry about it. Just make sure your opponent gets no second chance. Hold your blade downwards, not upwards like you're waiting for dinner to be served. Stab. Slashes rarely kill anyone, so don't waste your time waving your knife about. Get close in fast and punch for the throat, pushing in your blade supported by your forearm. You can also stab just under the Adam's apple, and keep stabbing until your man is down, then leave him for someone else to finish off and look for someone else to attack. Better still, pick up a rifle and load it if you can—a knife is only a last resort. And never, ever, throw your knife. If by some miracle, you manage to actually stick it into someone, chances are it won't be fatal, and you've just left yourself completely unarmed—and easy prey, *mes amis*."

Ramirez came up with his kepi full of money, the big Senegalese behind him, with two more of his companions. Stuart was in awe of them. They were tall, ebony-black men, all with tribal scarring on their faces and chests, but they were all smiling, and Stuart had to laugh when Ramirez introduced his opponent as, "*Señor* Innocent."

"Innocent?" repeated Stuart with disbelief.

On hearing his name the big tirailleur smiled broadly and pointed to his chest, confirming his identity, and at the same time holding out his desert canteen towards Stuart, who took it, bowed slightly to express his gratitude, and took a big swig. It wasn't wine. Whatever it was burned his throat and made his eyes water, and he immediately began to cough uncontrollably while grasping his throat. Innocent and his companions burst into deep resonating laughter and Innocent slapped Stuart's back as he tried to regain his breath and composure.

"Raki!" shouted Innocent, and taking his canteen from Stuart, gulped down two large mouthfuls and then beat his chest as the fiery undiluted Turkish spirit set fire to his throat. His companions had canteens of raki with them as well, captured from the Turks, and they insisted all the section had a swig. They were openly curious of Murdo and cheered when he drank his raki, pre-warned by now, and made a show of licking his lips and rubbing his stomach.

For the rest of the hour, the section mixed and mingled with the other soldiers on the beach, sharing water bottles and canteens of drink as they did so. At some stage, Lafitte let out a piercing whistle to get everyone's attention and made a short speech, welcoming new friends, and called for a toast to those who were no longer with them. Then the races began.

The five mules were lined up at one side of the beach. The aim was to ride bareback up the beach, turn around five poles now stuck into the sand, and race back to the finish line. The winners would race each other until, by process of elimination, a champion was crowned.

With great fanfare, Lafitte, Ramirez, and three French Army soldiers in sky-blue trousers raced first. The mules were used to being ridden, but that did not mean they necessarily wanted to be, and they brayed as the men were hoisted upon their backs. Medved, the Jewish muleteer, waited until there was a moment of calm and then shouted, "Allez Oop!" and off they went.

Four mules went racing towards the poles and one towards the sea, throwing one of the soldiers into the water to

loud laughs and cheers. Both of the remaining French soldiers fell at the 180-degree turn, to more loud laughs, leaving Lafitte and Ramirez to race for home, both shouting,
"Allez Oop!" and hanging on for all they were worth, Lafitte
winning by a length.

The section laughed out loud until their sides hurt,
cheering loudly as more men ran the gauntlet, no more than
two or three at most finishing the course. The Royal Marines
outdid everyone by all falling off at the turn and then running to catch their mules, trying to remount them to win
their heat. Stuart watched with his friends, tears of laughter
rolling down his cheeks. In the next race, two Lancashire
Fusiliers mounted, and with three mules without riders,
Lafitte was motioning towards their group.

Seamus, Angus, and Murdo staggered towards the start,
and with some help, managed to mount their mules and almost immediately they were off. Or four were off. Murdo's
mule just stood still no matter what he did and refused to
move until the muleteer gave it a massive slap on the rump,
and with an "Allez Oop!" it shot off down the beach to peels
of laughter. Murdo hung on around its neck but began to
slowly slide off, which dragged the mule into the sea where
both rider and animal collapsed in a spray of water.

Further down the beach, both fusiliers failed to negoti-
ate the turn and tumbled onto the sand, leaving Seamus and
Angus to race for the line, the soldiers cheering them on. For
a moment it looked as if Angus was ahead, but then Seamus
whacked his mule on the rump and kicked its sides, shouting
"Allez Oop!" at the top of his voice. He overtook Angus just
before the line.

Next up it was Stuart, Ross, Connor, Liam, and Aiden.
They mounted their mules, hands tightly gripping the reins,
until the muleteer yelled and off they went. Stuart had two
initial thoughts: one, that he didn't know mules could run so
fast; and two, that his backside hurt like hell, but he couldn't
help laughing anyway. Racing neck and neck with the

others, he hung on with all his might and let the mule race towards the poles.

At the turn, he made the mistake, as did Ross, of trying to remember through an alcoholic haze how to turn a horse. Horses are intelligent, intuitive animals—mules are not. As the brothers tried gently to turn, both their mules continued straight until they had to haul them around with all their strength. To everyone surprise and delight, all five riders made it around the poles, and for the first time that afternoon, a proper five-mule race was on to the finishing line.

Stuart began laughing as he heard Liam cursing and swearing at his mule to "get a feckin move on," and looking to his side, he could see all the riders barreling down the beach. The roars from the crowd increased as the riders approached the finish line. Stuart dug in his heals and with a final "Allez oop!" raced for home, neck and neck with his brother. But it was Connor, right in the middle of them all, with his mop of black hair blowing in the wind, who reached the line first to the cheers of the crowd.

Stuart couldn't think of when he'd been happier to get off an animal's back in his entire life. His back hurt, his backside hurt, his hands hurt from gripping the reins so tightly, and yet all he could do was grin from ear to ear. It had been the ride of his life, and he embraced Ross, Connor, Liam, and Aiden at the end of it, all laughing together.

With the main races finished, the men sat back to watch the elimination rounds. It soon became apparent that winning one race was no guarantee that the same would happen the next time. In fact, the randomness of success became clear as previous winners fell left, right, and center, including Seamus who only managed to get halfway down the beach before he was dumped unceremoniously onto his backside, bruising it and his recently inflated pride. The eliminations continued amid much cheering until only five were left: Innocent, McAvoy, Lafitte, Connor, and Manners. Manners was one of the Royal Marines who had somehow, after chasing and re-mounting his mule, won his race and had made it through the elimination rounds much to everyone's equal astonishment and delight.

The crowd, hasty bets already made, went silent as riders mounted their mules and the muleteer raised his arm. As he did so, Asiatic Annie sent a shell that came screaming in from over the sea and splashed into the cove. The mules, startled by the big explosion in the sea, galloped off the starting line faster than ever. The crowd laughed and roared for their favorites, and the section yelled for all they were worth to cheer Connor on to victory. The first to fall was McAvoy. He claimed loudly afterward that it wasn't his fault, but he had steered his mule for the post, not around it. Being a mule, it crashed straight into the pole sending McAvoy flying through the air and over the mule's tall ears, much to the surprise of the mule who remained rigidly still.

The four remaining riders made the turn, kicking and yelling their mules into the gallop with a chorus of "Allez oops!" Manners was next to go, the Marine's lucky streak deserting him as he slid slowly but surely forwards until he was hanging on to the mule's neck with both arms and crossed legs. It was a credit to his strength and determination that he lasted so long, clinging on to the neck of his mule. But as with Murdo before him, it just served to steer his mule towards the sea. To the dismay of his comrades and to much laughter, Manners ended up crashing head over heels into the water, to emerge spluttering from the sea.

In the final dash for the line it was Lafitte, Connor, and Innocent neck and neck. The section was now screaming loudly for Connor, but it was simply too close to call. As the mules galloped towards the line, Connor gave his mule an extra-hard slap, and with a last desperate "Allez oop," they all thundered across the finish line to the roar of the assembled soldiers. It was Connor who won by a nose. The section went wild, and as soon as Connor dismounted, he was up on their shoulders, the crowd cheering as Connor waved one hand in the air perched atop his friends. It had been, said the regulars of the Gallipoli Racing Club, the best mule races so far. Even those who had lost money on the betting did so without a hint of complaint.

Lafitte came over and embraced Connor. Innocent stood behind him, smiling broadly and waving about his canteen full of raki. Down by the water's edge, the soldiers were gathering up a shoal of fish killed by Asiatic Annie's random shelling. The fish were striped, silvery-blue with upturned mouths. Aiden announced with conviction that they were some sort of mullet. Whatever they were, they were soon roasting over small open fires and proved to be delicious.

As the sun began to descend and the fierce heat abated, the men gathered around the small fires, finishing off their wine and enjoying the moment. A small fishing boat rounded the cove, a Greek caique, painted white and blue. It chugged its way slowly into the bay, and Lafitte smiled and rose to greet its owner as it pulled alongside one edge of the cove by a rocky outcrop. Stuart watched as the two men talked, the boat's engine idling. After a handshake the caique pulled away and Lafitte walked back up the beach.

Stuart asked McAvoy who the fisherman was. "He's called Tomas-the-Greek. I'm not so sure there's another Tomas about, but that's what he's called, and I've never heard it shortened. Some say he's a spy for the Turks, some say he's a spy for us, maybe he's just a Greek fisherman. He often pulls in when we're here, sometimes with food to sell, and sometimes just with news."

"*Dígame qué pasa*—Tell me what's going on," said Ramirez as Lafitte reached the group. He could read his friend and knew something wasn't right.

Lafitte sat down and ran his fingers through his short hair and with resignation, muttered two words. "Kereves Dere."

Ramirez' shoulders slumped. "*Merde* —shit." He looked over at Lafitte. "When?"

"Monday."

Kereves Dere was a ravine on the eastern side of the peninsula, in the French sector. As the British had attacked Krithia repeatedly, so had the French attacked Kereves Dere. Although small gains had been made, they had come at a terrible cost to those doing the fighting, especially in taking the Haricot and Quadrilateral strongpoints. Both had been attacked by crossing the ominously named *Ravin de la Mort*—the Ravine of the Dead.

Lafitte looked over at Stuart. "You too, I believe, *mon ami*—Achi Baba Nullah."

Stuart glanced over at McAvoy, whose face had drained of color. "What's Achi Baba Nullah?"

McAvoy pointed northwards. "Achi Baba is that feckin hill, seven-hundred feet high. From there the Turks see everything. We were meant to capture it the first day we landed, but that was never going to happen once the Turks turned out to be fighters. Achi Baba Nullah is the ravine in front of it, separated from Kereves Dere by a spur of high ground. If Tomas-the-Greek is right, you're attacking up Achi Baba Nullah, and the French are attacking up Kereves Dere at the same time."

"But how could he know? I mean, if we don't know, how could a Greek fisherman know?"

McAvoy shrugged his shoulders. "That I can't answer."

The news cast a sobering pall on the gathering, and as the sun began to descend, the various groups departed back up the trail. Angus stood up and began to sort out his kit, which was the sign for the rest of the section to follow.

McAvoy went up with them. Before they left, each one shook hands firmly with Lafitte and Ramirez, thanking them for such a wonderful day. Lafitte humbled them by saying it had been made all the better by their company, and as they parted he wished them "*Bonne chance et bon*

courage, mes amis!—Good luck and take heart, my friends."
He embraced each of them in turn. After embracing Stuart,
he held out a sheathed Camillus fighting knife. "It was a
friend's knife, but he is gone. It is a good knife—take it and
keep it close, where you can reach it if needed," and he shook
Stuart's hand with a strong grip.

"Thank you, for everything," replied Stuart.

McAvoy stayed with them until he was sure they knew
where they were going and they had replenished their water
bottles. All of them drank two whole bottles before filling
them up again, and then McAvoy took his leave, embracing
Seamus and Connor. "It's been grand to see you both, although I wish you weren't here, if you know what I mean. But
as you are here, take care of yourselves. Each second Saturday we meet at the hidden cove if we can for the races. Sometimes we can't all be there, but it's worth trying to make it.
The craic's always good, and it's good for the soul." He
paused and then looked at them all. "If Tomas-the-Greek is
right about Monday, keep your heads down, fight hard, and
may God be with you." With a final embrace, he left them to
return to the Munster Fusiliers.

It had been a day like no other, full of surprises, and it wasn't
over yet. As they emerged bleary-eyed and smiling out of the
comms trench towards their rough billet, no more than a
hollow surrounded by gnarled pine trees, Sergeant Harris
was waiting for them.

"Where the bleeding hell have you lot been?" he demanded, inspecting them suspiciously. "Actually, never
mind, don't tell me. I don't want to know, and we don't have
time. Lance-Corporal McReynolds, Private Munro—you
have two minutes to be squeaky clean and on parade. The
rest of you help them. Move it!"

Bewildered, the section sprang into action, smoothing
down uniforms, giving dusty boots a quick once over, and

smartening up Stuart and Murdo as best they could. Harris reappeared with Giles by his side.

"About time, gentlemen!" said Giles, giving Stuart and Murdo a quick inspection and brushing of imaginary lint from their shoulders. "That'll have to do, Sergeant Harris. Let's get them to the general." They were off, following Giles down a trench-line towards the 52nd Lowland Division's forward headquarters.

Awaiting them was Major General Granville Egerton, the General Officer Commanding the Lowland Division, a veteran of Afghanistan, India, and the Anglo-Egyptian War, with a reputation as a soldier's soldier. Egerton was not in a good mood. He had arrived with the South Scottish and Highland Light Infantry brigades, assuming he would find the Scottish Rifles intact, acclimatized, and ready for action. Instead, he had found them broken at half-strength, ripped apart at Fir Tree Spur without his knowledge or permission, its commanding officer killed leading his men against massed machine guns.

His ire was not with his soldiers, and when told decorations had been approved and were awaiting presentation, he had taken the time to personally award them. He had still two medals to give and was now conferring with his staff until the two recipients could be found.

Giles hurried the section along until they came to the headquarters and had them fall in outside, with Stuart and Murdo standing out in front. With a nod to Sergeant Harris, he went to find Major Sinclair, who waited for an appropriate moment to inform a staff officer that the latecomers had been found.

Captain Campbell-Greenwood received the news with irritation and was just saying haughtily, "A bit late, I think. Perhaps another time," when Major General Egerton emerged out of the headquarters.

"Another time for what, exactly?" he asked tersely.

Campbell-Greenwood stood transfixed, unsure what to say, and so made the mistake of talking without thinking—something he was very good at. "Sir, just an administrative formality that can wait until another day," he said with a dismissive wave of the hand.

"What sort of administrative formality?"

Campbell-Greenwood felt the heat rise under his collar, but it was less to do with the heat of the peninsula than the icy stare he was now receiving from Major General Egerton, who said, "Well, speak up, man!"

"Ah, sir, it's regarding the two men late for this afternoon's medals ceremony."

"Late? I was informed they were on bathing parade. Hardly their fault if they didn't know about medals, is it?"

"Ah, no, sir. I believe they're here now, sir, outside now, sir," said Campbell-Greenwood, now completely flustered.

"Let me see the citations."

"Ah, yes, sir. I have them here, sir," and he frantically looked through his clipboard, pulling the citations out, and in the process, dropped the rest of the paperwork on the ground.

Egerton scanned the citations and then down at Campbell-Greenwood, still trying to gather up his paperwork. "Tell me, what exactly do you classify as an 'administrative formality'?"

"Sir?"

Egerton tapped Campbell-Greenwood on the chest with his bamboo swagger stick, right where medal ribbons would have been—if he'd had any.

"I have a citation here for a man who it appears single-handedly saved a key position from being overrun by standing up and firing a damaged Lewis gun from the hip at point-blank range into the enemy. He'd been at Gallipoli for just over two hours, and it was his first action. I have a posthumous award for a corporal who died fixing the Lewis gun rather than having his amputated legs tended to. I have another citation for a man who apparently ran across no man's land under intense enemy crossfire to wipe out a machine gun crew and its gun armed with a rifle. He was wounded three times, but probably saved a lot of men's lives. It was his second action.

"Which one of these do you consider an 'administrative formality'? Or would that be taking the time to recognize the bravery of men who have a very real chance, from what I've seen so far, of dying here?" he asked with measured anger rising in his voice.

"Sir, I, I'm not sure that I follow you."

"I don't doubt that for one minute. What's your name and what are you doing here?"

"Campbell-Greenwood, sir. I'm attached to your staff."

"And from which regiment are these two men?"

"Sir?"

"It's a simple question, Captain. Where are these men from?"

It was a simple question, one Captain Campbell-Greenwood should have known as he had been given the task of officiating the ceremony, but he didn't know. Then he made another critical error—he guessed, based on probability that they were Royal Scots. Most of the Cameronians had been killed or wounded.

Egerton turned and left the headquarters, Campbell-Greenwood and a bemused Major Sinclair in tow, to meet the men. As soon as he appeared, Sergeant Harris called the section to attention, and Giles saluted smartly as Egerton walked towards them.

"Always good to meet the Royal Scots!" beamed Egerton. Then he paused as he caught sight of Giles' tartan trousers and the section's Tam-O-Shanters with a very familiar stag's head crest. "Seaforths?" he asked, with a quick frown aimed towards Campbell-Greenwood.

"Yes, sir!" replied Giles with evident pride. "Attached in support of the 52nd Lowland Division, sir!"

"Well, I'm glad to have you with us. I'm a Seaforth myself, you know," said the general, shaking Giles' hand enthusiastically. Because the general had been a Seaforth, Campbell-Greenwood's future role as a staff officer with the 52nd Lowland Division was going to be very limited. There were a few things Egerton could forgive, but combining arrogance and stupidity with getting the identity of Egerton's own regiment wrong wasn't one of them.

For the next five minutes, Egerton spent time talking with Giles and Major Sinclair, finding out about their story, and with Stuart, Murdo, and Sergeant Harris. Giles mentioned the problem with the high visibility of pith helmets for his sharpshooters and took the opportunity to suggest a solution. Halfway through the conversation, and much to the consternation of Major Sinclair, Lucky darted in from nowhere, dog leash trailing from his collar, and bounded up to Connor, barking excitedly at his feet and wagging his stumpy tail furiously. For a moment there was silence, and then Egerton burst out in laughter. "I think, Private, that you'd better pay some attention to that dog. It obviously wants to pay some attention to you!"

Giles nodded, and Sergeant Harris had the section stand at ease, and then stand easy, to allow Connor to bend down and pat Lucky, who promptly rolled on his back and wiggled his bum to and fro, growling playfully, to more laughter from Egerton. After a couple of minutes, he motioned to Campbell-Greenwood who handed him the medals one at a time. As the scouts came to attention once more, Murdo and Stuart were, to their great amazement and surprise, presented with the Distinguished Conduct Medal. It was Great Britain's second highest award for gallantry in action for enlisted soldiers after the Victoria Cross. If Egerton was at all surprised to meet Murdo, it wasn't apparent, and he shook their hands once more, and nodded to the rest of the section. As Giles shot up another crisp salute, the general returned to his headquarters.

Campbell-Greenwood turned to go, and then stopped and looked back at Stuart, and then at Giles with a flicker of recognition. It was them. No longer red and blistered, they were tanned and had both lost weight, but it was them—the impudent soldier from Edinburgh and his officer. He looked at the citation on his clipboard and smiled. Now he had their names in black and white.

Giles nodded to Harris who had the section stand at ease again. "I just wanted to say how proud we are of you all. While McReynolds and Munro have been singled out, be very clear in your minds that each and every one of you— given your brief training—has performed above and beyond any reasonable expectations. We have been told that rein- forcements for the Lowland Division are on their way. Until then, we will support them wherever they see fit. Major Sin- clair is trying to clarify that as we speak. Again, well done, men." Sergeant Harris called the section to attention and sa- luted as Giles turned towards the headquarters, asking Har- ris to wait until they heard from him again.

The section used the time to congratulate Stuart and Murdo and to play with Lucky, who wiggled in excitement as the men patted him and rubbed his warm smooth coat. But his adoration was clearly for Connor, as he jumped around and licked him frantically. After 20 minutes, Giles reappeared with a burlap sack and motioned for the section to remain at ease.

"First, I have presents for you," he said, and upturned the sack. Out tumbled a pile of slouch hats, the same worn by the Australians and some New Zealanders. "In your ca- pacity as sharpshooters, the general has allowed you to wear these in the field. Do not turn the brim up on one side. Lord knows we don't want you misfits mistaken for Australians!" he said with a laugh. "They should keep your profile lower than the pith helmets, and at the same time, provide shade for your eyes and room for you to aim with your scopes." The section stepped forward and picked up the hats, trying them on and exchanging them until they all fitted low on their heads.

"Second, I have news regarding our next assignment." The section grew quiet and looked towards Giles.

"On Monday, there will be a combined push by the Lowland Division and the French with the aim of advancing towards Achi Baba." The section looked at each other, and Giles noted that no one seemed overly surprised, so he looked at his notepad and carried on.

"Our mission will be to support the South Scottish and Highland Light Infantry brigades. The French will attack Kereves Dere, a ravine on the eastern flank. The South Scottish will attack on their left flank at 0730 towards Achi Baba Nullah, preceded by three hours of French and British artillery fire. To their left, the Highland Light Infantry will attack later in the day. The objective for both brigades is the Turk's third trench."

He paused to let the information sink in and then continued. "We will support the attack by suppressing the Turkish fire wherever we can, with an emphasis on targeting machine gun crews, snipers, and officers. Initially, we will work independently in pairs." This raised a few eyebrows within the section. "Everyone will mount scopes. We've been tasked to support the first attack by the Kings Own Scottish Borderers. Are there any questions?"

With no questions, Angus was detailed to take the section back to their billet, while Giles and Harris went over the plan of attack. An hour later, Harris walked into their billet as the section was brewing up tea. "All right, listen up, misfits," he said to get their attention. "The following will pair off and stay with me. Corporal McIntyre and Private Munro, and you two," he said, pointing to Aiden and Liam.

"Lance Corporal McReynolds will pair off with his brother," he said, nodding at Ross, "and that leaves you two." This time, he pointed to Seamus and Connor. "Once the objective is captured, we'll gather back together and await further orders.

"Tomorrow, we'll zero-in our rifles and scopes again and go over the details, so drink your tea and get your heads down. Lance Corporal McReynolds and Private Murdo, I expect those medal ribbons to be sewn onto your uniforms the next time I see you—and well done."

In a day where surprises had piled on top of each other, a final one awaited them, as Harris reached into his pocket and drew out three envelopes. "Oh, and why anyone would want to write to you lot is beyond me, but here you go." He handed out letters to Stuart and Ross from Nell and Jo, and to Murdo from his family in Nova Scotia.

***

The sight and touch of the envelope propelled Stuart into another world, away from the dirt and disease, the stench and the fear, and the explosions of raw violence. He sat down and opened it, and as he drew out the pages, he detected a slight scent. Holding the pages close he breathed it in, his senses flooding with the sweet lavender fragrance—the same perfume he had inhaled when he had embraced Nell at Waverly train station in Edinburgh. He had last written to her on Lemnos, and although he'd tried to write since arriving in Gallipoli, he hadn't known what to say.

Her letter was full of vivid images as she described the changing seasons on the sea and land—the arrival of house martens, a pair of blue herons nesting in the old graveyard, the fields of young barley and wheat swaying like a green sea in the wind, hares boxing comically in the sun-drenched fields, a flotilla of eider ducklings chaperoned by their mothers in the shelter of the stone harbor, a pod of bottlenose dolphins sighted off the coastline as she walked home. She wished he had been with her too see it all, and Stuart felt his heart tug painfully in his chest.

She wrote to him that the day after he'd left, a drifter had returned to Anstruther from deployment with the Royal Navy Trawler Service. It had been at Gallipoli, ferrying stores and troops ashore from the larger naval ships. Its local crew was full of stories of what they'd witnessed which had filled her with abject horror. She told him that she was being brave. She told him to stay as safe as he could. She told him to come back to her, and she told him she loved him.

By the time he had read it through, his hands were shaking and his eyes were filled with tears. The day's events and Nell's letter had released all his suppressed agonies of the past weeks, and for a moment, he could glimpse normality beyond the battlefield and its brutally cruel rules of survival. As he closed his eyes, he could feel Nell's presence—see her smile, picture her green eyes, sense her touch. It made him ache, and he longed to see her again. Giles had said reinforcements were on the way, so the section might be sent back soon, away from Gallipoli, and for a moment Stuart let that thought pervade his mind.

With the light now fading, he unpacked his writing paper and pen from his kitbag and began to reply to her letter. He wrote of the beauty that could be found at Gallipoli, not at the frontline with its carnage and stench, but in the purple flowers of the wild thyme and lavender bushes, the pungent scent of the wild rosemary, the myriad of wildflowers, the stunted pines, the white tips of asphodel in the breeze, the pink oleanders, the sweet pungent smell of fig trees and pomegranates with budding fruit, the harsh chirping of cicadas at noon, and of small lizards sunbathing on the rocks.

He described the sunsets over the Aegean and the cobalt waters of the hidden cove, cooking mullet over the fire, and looking out at night to the bright lights of the hospital ships in the bay, lit up as if some spring soirée were about to commence. He told her they were all fine and keeping well. He didn't mention his wounds, and he didn't mention his medal. He told her how much he missed her and to try not to worry too much—and that he loved her dearly.

When he awoke the next morning, for a few seconds he felt completely at peace, and as he reached for his tunic he saw with a smile that someone had already ready sewn the red-and-blue-striped medal ribbon above his left tunic pocket.

Then, with a sickening feeling in the pit of his stomach, he realized that in 24 hours, he'd be fighting for his life again.

CHAPTER FIFTEEN

No Man's Land

Major General Hunter-Weston's battle plan, as Giles outlined it, centered once again on a frontal assault by waves of infantry on the Turkish lines in broad daylight. It differed slightly from previous attacks in that two brigades would attack at different times, to allow the limited artillery available to concentrate on one section of the Turkish lines at a time, leaning heavily on the French for support. The only available soldiers still capable of mounting an assault were the two newly arrived brigades of territorial Scots, and so on July the 12th they found themselves on the frontline, while the French and British artillery crashed over their heads towards the enemy trenches. Ahead of them in no man's land crouched four teams of Seaforth sharpshooters.

It had been Giles' idea to go as far forward as possible to avoid the Turkish artillery counterfire and to best position themselves to effectively support the attack. During the night, they had occupied the listening posts in no man's land, to the delight of those they relieved. The listening posts were reached by narrow trenches that opened up into small bays, usually old shell craters, halfway towards the Turkish lines. Their purpose was to alert the frontline at night of enemy activity, patrols, or attacks. It had seemed a good idea at the time, but now with shells firing in both directions over their heads, Stuart and Ross looked over at each other with

trepidation, involuntarily wincing and blinking at the cacophony of noise above their heads. Between them crouched
Giles, peering over the lip of the bay towards the Turkish
lines with one of the section's pair of binoculars.

Off to their left, about 20 yards, away Seamus and Connor crouched, waiting to select targets in support of the attack of the Scottish Borderers that would wash over them.
Their orders were to join the third of four waves of borderers, as Giles had made it clear it wasn't their job to clear the
first two enemy positions—their objective was the third.
Further off to their left, somewhere in no man's land, the
rest of the section was similarly deployed under the watchful
eye of Sergeant Harris.

Stuart and Ross could feel and hear the artillery crescendo. Giles glanced at his watch and shouted, "Five
minutes!"

They crawled up to the lip of the bay and settled into
their firing positions, sights set at 200 yards, magazines full,
with the first round already chambered. They'd worked on
their position at night as it gave them both cover and con-
cealment while at the same time affording them a good field
of fire across to the enemy lines. Giles lay between them and
would scan for targets, calling them out to Stuart on his left
and Ross on his right. They'd agreed if a machine gun em-
placement was spotted, both marksmen would engage it.

The shelling was so constant they couldn't differentiate
individual shells, and the noise deafened them in their small
vulnerable outpost. The ground trembled, and they all instinctively ducked as an off-target shell slammed into the
ground 20 feet in front of them. It sent a shockwave through
their bodies, and the three men crouched in fetal positions
as debris rained down on them showering them in dirt,
stones, and decomposed body parts. The stench made Stuart and Ross both retch, but through the noise they heard
Giles yelling at them to stand by. Stuart crawled back into
position, thumbed his safety off, and settled his body and
mind down to the task at hand.

At 7:30, the barrage lifted off the Turkish positions and onto the enemies' supporting lines, seeking to disrupt or destroy Turkish reinforcements. They could hear whistles behind them and bagpipes playing *Blue Bonnets o'er the Border.*

"Target left, two-hundred yards, first trench, eleven o'clock, officer with binoculars!" shouted Giles.

Stuart scanned the Turkish positions in the direction Giles had indicated and found his target, just as described. The officer took the binoculars away and turned to shout something to his soldiers just as Stuart completed his gentle trigger pull. The bullet ripped through the man's head from left to right at ear level, killing him instantly and spraying skull fragments and brains over the men below him.

"Target front, two-hundred yards, first trench, twelve o'clock, officer!"

Ross swung to face straight ahead and fired quickly, his target falling backward, arms flailing.

Now they could hear the brigade leaving the trenches. It was disconcerting to be in their path. The borderers had been told to look out for their own sharpshooters in the middle of no man's land, and most knew exactly where they were. As the men came forward, a Turkish machine gun burst into action immediately followed by Giles' urgent fire order, "Machine gun right! One o'clock, front trench, engage!"

Stuart and Ross shifted their bodies, and both aligned with the new threat. Ross fired first, his bullet ricocheting off the gun and sending metal splinters into the gunner's face. The gun fell silent as the man—hands held to his bleeding eyes—was pulled away by his desperate crew. Stuart's rifle cracked, and the ammunition feeder's head blew apart in a red mist. They could now hear the first wave of the Lowland Scots behind them.

"Targets, enemy in the open, front trench left, suppressing fire!"

Without needing to be told, Ross kept targeting the machine gun while Stuart swung his rifle back to his sector and saw Turkish soldiers firing their rifles as they brazenly knelt or sat atop their parapet. He fired quickly, and one flew backwards as Stuart's bullet hit him in the middle of his chest. Still sighting down the scope, he rechambered and shot the third enemy soldier down the line with the same effect. Rechambering another round, he swung back and hesitated as he saw one and then another enemy soldier fly backward off the parapet—someone else was shooting them, and he could only guess it was Seamus and Connor. He joined in to shoot two more men in quick succession.

It became mechanical. Every soldier he shot meant that fewer of the attacking borderers would be killed crossing no man's land. Even as he fired, he realized his complete detachment. In the confusion of movement and noise as the charge came towards them, the Turks had no chance of seeing the sharpshooters, but they saw the damage. Almost as one, the remaining Turks settled back into their trench, now only exposing their heads, but that was enough, and Stuart shot two more soldiers, watching them disappear backwards.

"Officer! Twelve o'clock, front trench!"

With Ross still successfully suppressing the machine gun, Stuart swung to the front and saw an officer waving a sword above his head and then point it towards the borderers, extolling his men to remain firm and hold the line. Stuart shot him down without hesitation, watching his sword—still tethered to his wrist—fly in the air and fall backward with the body. Out of ammunition, he turned to reload just as the first of the borderers swept past them, bayonets fixed, their faces fixed in grim determination.

For an instant he was afraid they might be attacked, but then a young officer appeared at the lip of their bay and with a wonderfully crisp English accent said, "Keep up the good work chaps!" With a boyish smile, and then with a polite, "Cheerio!" he bounded after his men.

Stuart smiled as he reloaded, wondering just where such men came from. He'd appeared all of 17 at most and was charging an enemy trench with the same enthusiasm, utter confidence, and lack of fear as if he were playing rugby or cricket for his school.

With men now in front of them, the first Turkish trench became obscured, and Giles had them adjust their focus further up the slope. "New targets, three-hundred yards, second line, observe and engage!"

It took the borderers a minute to reach the first enemy position, but before they did so, Turkish soldiers became to stream backwards towards their rear. "Enemy soldiers in the open, engage!" yelled Giles.

Stuart looked through his sights and focused on a retreating Turk. Because he was moving directly away from him and not zig-zagging, it was a relatively straightforward shot, but he held his finger at the halfway point of the trigger pull, following his target but not shooting. Judging from the silence in the bay, Ross was doing the same.

Then they heard Giles' calm voice. "If they reach their second line, they'll turn and shoot our men. Kill them now—that's an order."

Stuart continued to pull his trigger and when the rifle fired, he saw the retreating soldier sprawl forwards, rifle falling by his side. He swung slightly to the left and shot down another retreating soldier. Ross fired at the same time. He knew Giles was right, and by giving them a direct order, he'd tried to shift the moral responsibility onto his own shoulders away from Stuart and Ross. Stuart hated doing it nevertheless.

"Machine gun, two o'clock, second trench!" came a shout from Ross followed by his rifle firing, just as a second wave of borderers swept by them. Stuart scanned to his right as Giles shouted, "I can't see it!"

It opened fire, and Stuart could see what Ross had spied, a Maxim machinegun strongpoint built into the Turkish second trench. It was well camouflaged and protected and

firing through a square aperture in the sandbagged parapet
wall.

"Fire at the muzzle blast!" shouted Giles.

Stuart adjusted his position, and looking at the machine
gun, willed himself to relax. He closed his eyes and opened
them, adjusted his position yet again. Happy that he'd found
his natural point of aim, he focused on his target. All he
could see was the flash of the machine gun's muzzle, and
surrounding it, a black hole about a foot high and two-feet
wide. Taking careful aim at the muzzle, he slowly squeezed
off a round. Nothing happened. The machine gun kept on
firing. Ross was firing at the same time, without stopping
the gun.

Stuart cursed, fired again—no results. He hesitated and
then aimed to the extreme left of the black square and slowly
fired another round. The machine fire stopped. Stuart
chambered another round and waited. After a pause the gun
erupted into action again, and once more Stuart aimed off-
center and fired blindly into the opening, and again the machine gun stopped. He turned to his brother and shouted,
"Aim off-center. I think there's a steel plate in the middle.
You fire right; I'll fire left!"

Ross nodded and chambered a round. The Turkish Max-
ims were sometimes fitted with a small shield of protective
armor, and Stuart had guessed that this was one of them.

Given the distance they were firing, and the fact they
were in the middle of a frontal assault with artillery firing
both ways and men running past them, their shots were difficult. Between them they constantly interrupted the machine gun's fire.

Stuart could only guess they were injuring or killing the
loaders, and this was causing havoc with the smooth flow of
the ammunition belts into the hungry gun. While the machine gun was still in action, its fire was intermittent and
faltering, allowing the borderers to attack the trench without the usual heavy causalities. Stuart slid back to reload
again and saw a third wave of soldiers approaching their

position. Ross stopped firing. With borderers now into the second trench, the machine gun fell silent as its crews sought to abandon the position.

"Prepare to move!" shouted Giles.

Ross slid down and immediately reloaded his rifle. Once done, he nodded to Giles who shouted back over the constant noise, "Follow the third wave!" As the borderers swept past them, he scrambled up the side of the listening post to run forward, Stuart and Ross behind him.

Stuart felt horribly exposed outside the protection of the listening post, and as he ran forward, the Turkish artillery adjusted its fire to rain high-explosive shells down on them. The shells buried themselves into the ground before exploding, destroying trenches, saps, dugouts, and the men sheltering for their lives inside. Other shells exploded upon impact, sending out a blast wave, and with it deadly jagged fragmented metal that ripped through bodies. The noise was unrelenting. The air was filled with the smell of cordite and smoke, and the cries of the men wounded and dying on the ground.

"Run!" yelled Giles, and they jumped clean over the first cleared Turkish trench and sprinted for the second. They had left the listening post at just the right moment as the artillery caught those lagging behind them and then concentrated on the fourth wave emerging from its starting point. It had been sheer luck. Thirty seconds later and they would have probably been caught within the barrage falling closely behind them.

Stuart's lungs burned as he ran forward, his breath coming in gasps, aware of Ross to his right and following Giles who was running with the Lee-Enfield rifle that Harris had given him at Fir Tree Spur held high across his chest. Bullets whip-cracked past them, and Giles began to run diagonally to the right to present a harder target. Just as Stuart feared he could run no more within the killing zone of no man's land, the second trench appeared in front of them and they jumped in, feet first. Stuart raised his rifle and turned quickly left and Ross turned right, but the trench was cleared—borderers faced them, bloody, stained, and dirty, with dead Turkish soldiers at their feet.

Stuart lowered his rifle and gulped air into his lungs as more men jumped into the second trench. Ross came over and put a hand on his shoulder, giving it a squeeze. "So far, so good," he said with a brief smile as he caught his own breath. He was right. Although they'd suffered causalities, the borderers had successfully captured the first two trenches.

"Who's in command here?" shouted Giles.

"Hello there!" came a reply, and down the trench came the young English officer that had stopped by their position briefly during the first wave. As men parted, he made his way towards them until he stopped in front of Giles, his revolver held in one gloved hand. "I say, you chaps did a sterling job for us by taking out those machine guns. Well done, old boy. Well done."

The officer was still full of unbridled enthusiasm, and Giles noticed the smiles from his men who looked towards him with confidence, despite his obvious youth and schoolboy manner. As they stood there, more men poured into the trench—the fourth and final wave of borderers.

"Right, men. On my whistle. The third trench is only a couple of hundred yards ahead. Let's get there before Johnny Turk can eat his breakfast! First one in wins a bottle of whisky—the last one in can buy it!" The men laughed despite the battle around them, obviously fond of their clearly eccentric, yet infectiously fearless officer. He looked over to Giles and said, "Tell your men to pot anyone who sticks their head up, and then please join me afterward. I'm almost certain I can smell Turkish coffee from here!"

Without waiting for a reply, he turned to the men around him. "Righto then, chaps. One more dash!" He put the whistle to his lips, gave it a hard blow, and off he went, shouting "Follow me!" His men streamed over behind him.

It was all over so quickly, the three of them just stared at each other in dumb amazement. Giles shouted, mimicking the courageous officer's accent. "Righto, pot anyone who sticks their head up then!" and they quickly sought out firing positions in the abandoned trench to look for targets in the third Turkish trench, their final objective.

From their position, they could look up at the slopes of Achi Baba, and Stuart saw that the Turks on Achi Baba could look down on them. Their position was horribly exposed, as were the attacking soldiers. As they stood there, stragglers from the fourth wave entered the trench in ones and twos. One of them, a sergeant, moved near Stuart and Giles. "Begging your pardon, sir, but have you seen The Honorable Lieutenant Pickering?" It was a title given to the younger sons of a lord or other titled gentry.

Without needing to clarify, Giles guessed exactly who The Honorable Lieutenant Pickering was. "I believe your officer has gone ahead to the third trench. Is he quite youthful and enthusiastic?"

"That's him, sir," the sergeant said with a smile, and then shouted to those near him, "Right then, lads. The boss is upfront. Get your breath and off we go!"

Giles picked up the binoculars and peered towards the attacking soldiers. They were running almost unhindered towards where the third trench was marked on his map. "I think the Turks have buggered off," he said to no one in particular.

Looking back, he tucked the binoculars back into his tunic and nodded to Stuart and Ross. "Right then. Let's go join them for coffee."

"Begging your pardon, sir, but did someone say coffee?" came an Irish voice from further down the trench, and Seamus and Connor came around a bend, followed by the rest of the Seaforths. Harris went up to Giles. "Sir, we don't seem to have any more targets, so we thought it best we came to you for orders."

"Good timing, Sergeant Harris. We were just about to go up to the third trench. I think the Turks have abandoned it. We can sort ourselves out again once we're there."

"Yes, sir," replied Harris.

Giles looked at the borderer's non-commissioned officer. "Sergeant?" he asked, searching for a name.

"Armstrong, sir."

"Have your men follow me. Anyone too wounded to run stays here."

"Yes, sir!" Turning to his men, he said, "Well, you heard the officer! Pull your thumbs out and get ready to advance. Anyone too poorly to join us will be talking to me when I get back!" He turned to Giles, who took one more look over the lip of the Turkish trench at the disappearing soldiers and shouted, "Follow me!"

The section all heaved themselves out of the captured trench to follow Giles, as did the remaining borderers—about a dozen of them—but as he scanned right and left, Giles saw more emerging from the trench, taking their cue to advance from the group of soldiers. They moved through a scene of destruction caused by their own artillery. Craters pocketed the hard-packed ground. Shattered wooden planks, equipment, and dead men littered the landscape. Some wounded Turks stared at them as they passed by, offering no resistance, the fight long gone from their glazed eyes. They went on for 200 yards, Giles looking at his map and then up ahead, where the borderers seemed to be milling about in the open.

Harris closed up to Giles. "Shouldn't they be in the trench by now, sir?"

Giles nodded. "Yes. Something's not quite right."

The Turkish artillery opened up with a vengeance. Vengeance for their soldiers killed and for the position lost, and it came in the form of shells—shrapnel shells. The shells were designed specifically to mow down men in the open. Fired from light artillery, they arced their way towards the ground and then exploded in mid-air, firing out 300 half-inch steel balls in a deadly cone-shaped killing zone 30 yards wide and 50 deep. As Giles looked on in horror, he saw the first salvo land among the borderers searching for the third trench. It was if some gigantic shotgun had exploded in front of them, blasting pockets of the battlefield clean of men.

"Get down!" shouted Giles, "Find cover!"

Mixed in with the artillery, they could now hear machine-gun fire from the high ground to their right, although no one could see where it was coming from. The men of the Kings Own Scottish Borderers were being cut to pieces in front of their eyes.

Giles glanced about him. There was no cover, but he could see what looked like a trench line 50 yards ahead. Some of the borderers ahead of them were running and jumping into it, their helmets still showing.

"Prepare to advance!" yelled Giles. To reach the trench was their only hope. "On my command, run for the trench ahead of us!" he yelled over the noise of incoming shells. "Go!" The section was up and running hard. They covered the distance as fast as they could, pumping their legs and sprinting for safety, but when they reached the trench they stared down in horror to see it was only a foot deep. Men were already kneeling down in it, desperately trying to dig in deeper.

Giles checked his map, "The third trench should be here, right here!" he shouted in exasperation, but it wasn't.

The borderers before them had found only a shallow dummy trench, either incomplete or abandoned at only a foot deep. From 1,000 or more feet in the air, it would appear to aerial reconnaissance—with a late-morning or evening shadow across it—much like a normal trench, and had been marked as such and then chosen as the objective. But the objective didn't exist. The borderers had ignored the dummy trench and had gone forward to find their real objective, but it simply wasn't there waiting to be found. The trench existed in the staff briefs on everyone's battle maps, but the maps and the staff briefs were wrong.

"Down!" yelled Sergeant Armstrong, as another salvo hurtled towards them, exploding in mid-air and peppering the exposed soldiers with shrapnel. The sound was deafening, and as Stuart hugged the ground, he watched a shell destroy a group of a dozen men not quick enough to get down. They disappeared in a storm of steel ball-bearings, each hit three or four times by shrapnel and propelled backward into a heap of dead bodies. The Turks warmed to their task, mixing high-explosive shells in with the shrapnel. The shells forced the men out from their meager cover and into the open where the shrapnel could tear them apart. The artillery barrage was now sweeping back towards the Scottish Borderers, still out in the open, now giving up on their futile search for the non-existent third trench.

Stunned, Giles watched as men were blown apart by high-explosive shells, their bodies dismembering in midair. The remaining borderers seemed to be moving so slowly back towards them, too slowly, and the Turkish gunners were having a field day, cutting the men down as they retreated. Armstrong pointed out towards a group of men about 100 yards away. "It's Lieutenant Pickering."

He was leading a platoon of his territorial Scots back, his arm raised, palm out, as if to ward off stinging sleet or rain from his face. His left arm was bleeding and tucked into his tunic. Armstrong began to shout, "Come on!" A salvo of shrapnel caught Pickering and his men in the open. Before their eyes, the entire group of soldiers disappeared in the gigantic shotgun blast of steel ball-bearings. As the explosion cleared, one man remained standing in the middle of the carnage—Pickering. He stood wavering for a few seconds and then fell to his knees.

Armstrong shouted "No!" and began to stand.

Giles grabbed him. "It's too late, Sergeant! There's nothing you can do!" As they watched, Pickering fell sideways, and disappeared among the field of dead and dying.

They were on the edge of hell, and Giles knew it. There was only one alternative—retreat to the second trench they'd left just behind a few minutes ago across 200 yards of open churned-up ground, in full view of the Turkish artillery observers. And they had to do it now or die where they lay.

"Prepare to retreat!" yelled Giles, hating the order, but knowing it was their only alternative. "On my command, get back to the second trench!"

He could hear his order being relayed down the line. Giles looked into the dummy trench and saw that many of those who had sought its refuge were dead already, but some moved, cowering in the scant illusionary protection of the shallow ditch. "Retreat on my command!" he yelled, not knowing if he could be heard or not.

Giles waited until the next salvo of shells tore into the battlefield and then yelled as loud as he could, "Fall back at the double!"

Stuart and Ross pushed themselves upwards and turned to run, followed by Seamus, Connor, and the rest of the section. Around them, borderers were doing the same, and as they saw them go, more men joined in, emerging out of the dummy trench and shell craters—and that was their undoing.

A few scattered groups of soldiers retreating might have been overlooked by the enemy artillery observers, but not an increasing wave of men running together in the open. To the Turkish forward artillery observers, that was simply a target too good to miss. Orders were quickly relayed down field telephone lines to shift fire and range dials were turned smoothly on artillery pieces. Five seconds later, lanyards were pulled and shells exploded out of the muzzles towards the retreating men.

"Get down!" yelled Ross, pulling his brother to the ground as the shells impacted in front of them, and then they were up and running hard back towards the second trench. To get there, they'd have to now run through a curtain of death and destruction as the Turkish observer ordered *fire for effect*. It was an order all artillery gunners savored, as it meant they were on target and could kill with every round they could hurriedly fire, the more rounds the merrier.

Stuart and Ross ran after Giles. Seamus and Connor ran after them for all they were worth, along with Sergeant Armstrong and a handful of soldiers. The shelling became incessant, the air filled with cordite, churned up soil, high-explosive shells detonating on impact and sending out concentric circles of wickedly jagged white-hot fragmented shell casing. Distant machine guns joined in, firing at their maximum range, scattering their bullets randomly over the beaten ground, and all the time the shrapnel shells sought out groups of men and blasted them with lethal steel pellets.

With 40 feet to go, Ross and Stuart dove to the ground as a salvo of four shrapnel shells exploded above their heads, sending out one final wave of death and destruction before the retreating men reached the sanctuary of the second trench. Shrapnel thudded into the ground in front of them like steel hail, punching deep into the hard-packed ground and sending up small explosions of sand and stones. Ross heard Stuart screaming in fear and desperation, and then stared on in abject horror as he saw Giles, Seamus, and Connor all go down 20 feet in front of him, red blood spraying from multiple wounds.

Without a word between them, Ross and Stuart jumped up and ran forward, reaching Giles first—who was bleeding from his thigh—and they both grabbed him by his leather officer's webbing straps and dragged him into a crater. "Leave me!" shouted Giles, but Ross simply tore open Giles' field bandage and wrapped it tightly around his leg.

"I said leave me! That's an order!" shouted Giles.

Ross stared at his officer, someone they'd come to respect and admire, someone they now called *boss*, an officer's unofficial rank of acceptance bestowed through time by his men, and simply said, "Stop being so bloody stupid!" and then after a reflective pause added, "Sir."

Stuart peered over the lip of the shell crater to see Seamus bleeding from a head wound. His teeth clenched in pain and effort as he dragged Connor towards the trench. Connor was heavy and limp in Seamus' hands, his breath ragged and labored. Murdo and Angus arrived and effortlessly lifted Connor between them and ran towards the trench, Liam and Aiden following a split second later with Seamus.

Looking over the lip of the crater, Stuart and Ross waited until another salvo of death erupted around them, and then Stuart yelled, "Together on three!" and heaved Giles up, supporting their officer between them. The brothers could see the trench, and in it they could see Harris yelling at them to run, beckoning them on. With ten feet to go, they were all caught in the blast of a high-explosive shell 40 feet behind them, and they fell sprawling at the lip of the parapet. Hands reached out and man-handled them roughly in, ears ringing, covered in dust and grime, Giles yelling out in pain from his injury as he landed at the bottom of the trench.

Beside them in the bottom of the trench, Seamus, Aiden, and Liam all knelt over Connor. His tunic was ripped and soaked in blood. As Aiden tore it open, they could see three gaping exit wounds to his chest where shrapnel had torn through him from back to front, ripping open his body. All three of the Irishmen reached for their field dressings and tried to staunch the flow of blood. Connor stared up at them, fear and pain etched into his face, and with what remaining strength he had, he reached out one hand to Seamus, who gripped it tightly.

"You'll be fine! Just hang on Connor, you'll be fine!" shouted Seamus frantically as more artillery shells exploded around them.

Connor's eyes fought to focus as Liam and Aiden ripped more dressings open to press into his wounds, lifting him to try and wrap the bandages around his chest, but as they did so his body convulsed and a gush of blood erupted from Connor's mouth. He began to choke as internally, blood spilled into his lungs.

"Sit him up," said Harris gently, looking down at the scene before him, resignation in his voice.

Liam and Aiden propped Connor's head up. His blood had soaked through their efforts to bandage him, and Connor coughed up more with each tortuous rasping breath, his pallor now deathly pale.

"Stay with us Connor," implored Seamus. He grasped Connor's hand tightly, his free hand touching his friend's face, pushing back the unruly mop of black hair from his blue eyes. As he looked into them in desperation, Seamus felt Connor's hand squeeze his weakly, and then it fell slack as the gasping breathing stopped. Connor's eyes stared upwards at his, but they could no longer see his lifelong friend kneeling before him.

Seamus cried out in grief, leaning forward he touched his forehead against Connor's.

CHAPTER SIXTEEN

Achi Baba Nullah

Achi Baba Nullah,
Gallipoli, July 12th - 13th, 1915

They gently placed Connor's bloodied and torn body near the abandoned strongpoint and covered it with filled sandbags. The section had been allowed to briefly share their sadness with Seamus, Liam, and Aiden, whose faces were racked with pain and sorrow. Despite their grief, the battle raged on. One by one the section touched the sandbags covering Connor's body before going to retrieve their rifles and walking down the trench towards the old Turkish strongpoint. Seamus slowly followed them to where Giles was conferring with a major from the borderers.

A handful of reinforcements had made their way up to the second trench line from the borderers and fusiliers. Along with them came unarmed stretcher-bearers of the Royal Army Medical Corps, their unending and exhausting task to take the wounded back to the beaches through shellfire. The battered and bloodied remnants of soldiers caught in the open by the Turkish artillery while searching for the third non-existent trench had joined them, leaving half their number dead and dying.

Giles' thigh wound was painful, but bearable with effort. Seamus had refused to have his head wound inspected, but the bleeding had stopped, and Aiden was able to give it a quick inspection and seemed happy to let it be. Seamus was quiet and brooding, and Stuart sensed a great rage building up within him.

The enemy artillery had ceased, and men were frantically turning the enemy trench around to meet the expected Turkish counterattack. At first, men had worked openly, adjusting sandbags, blocking off enemy comms trenches, and digging their own ones back towards the rear, linking up with old listening posts. And then a shot rang out, pitching a soldier backward, followed by more shots. The firing came from their right, from a finger of high ground called Kereves Spur, where the British and French lines met.

Giles emerged and motioned for Harris to join him. After a quick discussion, Harris nodded and then came forward. "Right, then; listen up!" commanded the veteran sergeant.

"We've lost one of our own and we will make time to bury Private Connor O'Connell properly when we're done, but we're needed elsewhere right now," and as if on cue, another shot rang out, followed by a wounded man's scream. "We've been tasked with stopping the Turkish sniper and finding a good position to help defend the captured trench. To that aim, we will move along the trench until we're up on Kereves Spur. Corporal MacIntyre, have weapons checked and replace ammunition, water, and field dressings if you can. Be ready to move in five minutes."

The section rifled through the webbing of the dead to refill their ammunition and medical pouches and to fill their water bottles. There was little hesitation to do either anymore, they needed them, and the dead soldiers didn't. Seamus' rifle had been struck by a piece of shrapnel, its barrel indented, and stock cracked. He removed its scope, and after conferring with Angus, reluctantly discarded the rifle. He then reached down and picked up Connor's instead, clearing and checking it for damage. Its sights would need readjusting, but otherwise it was fully serviceable.

Harris called them together as Giles appeared limping from his wound, blood soaking through his bandages. "I wish there were more of us, but we're on our own, I'm afraid."

A cough came from behind the section and a familiar face came into view. "Perhaps we can help, sir?"

Looking up, Giles saw Color Sergeant Rennie and seven men—the remnants of the Royal Scots platoon they'd fought with at Fir Tree Spur. "Color Sergeant Rennie, it's both a surprise and an unexpected pleasure to see you again," said Giles.

"Major Sinclair sends his compliments, sir. We were sent forward with the last of the Royal Scots and Cameronians to reinforce the trench, and Major Sinclair suggested I find you to see if we could be of assistance, seeing as we'd fought together already and all, sir."

Giles couldn't help smiling. "We could use your help, Color Sergeant. Thank you."

"Sir, if you're moving to the right, so are we," came another voice, and Sergeant Armstrong came into view with eight soldiers from the borderers behind him.

Giles' smile grew wider. "It seems misery likes company, gentlemen. Let's move out before the rest of the circus arrives."

They worked their way slowly through the trench. At times they had to step on bodies, both friend and foe. Everywhere men were working hard to repair and alter the captured enemy position. Sniper fire punctuated their activity, and they passed more than one soldier who had been shot by the Turkish marksmen. After a while, the trench inclined until they found themselves on the lower slopes of Kereves Spur, where they found a wounded lieutenant in charge of a depleted platoon. Giles conferred with him and then came back.

"The French hold the line about one hundred yards further down. We've been asked to go halfway and dig in.

There's no need to tell you the Turks will counterattack soon
with everything they have, so let's work fast, men. We hold
this position until relieved. Sergeant Harris, I'll take the
men plus Munro and both of you," he said pointing at Aiden
and Ross. You stay here with the rest, Sergeant, and see
what you can do about that bloody sniper."

As the mixed platoon of men had passed through, Ross
waved his finger at his brother and whispered, "No heroics."

"Right, you two," Harris said, pointing at Stuart and Seamus, "pair up and move twenty feet down to the left and
spread out. You two," pointing to Liam and Angus, "twenty
feet to the right and spread out. I'm going back down the
trench. I'm going to count to one hundred and then raise a
pith helmet slightly above the parapet. Let me know if you
see anyone firing. It's an old trick, but it works. Ready?" he
asked, looking for confirmation before retreating back down
the trench, counting out steadily.

Stuart found a slight dip in the trench, and pushing
down the collapsed crown of his slouch hat, began to raise
his head very slowly above the parapet until he could peer
out at the spur rising above him. The slouch hats were perfect. They kept the sun off and shaded their eyes and scope,
and they'd collapsed the crowns to minimize their profiles.
To the front, he could see small bushes, shrubs, even small
pine trees, as the spur sloped gently uphill from their position. To the left, he could see over the battlefield to where
they had searched in vain for the third trench and beyond.

Counting silently he focused on the sparse shrub in front
of his position until he reached 100 and then waited. For a
few seconds nothing happened, and then a shot rang out directly in front of him. He stared, looking for movement, but
could see none. Harris came back up the trench and they
gathered together.

"I think he's lying in a small hollow, perhaps a shell
crater, about sixty yards away. It's surrounded by those
scrubby bushes," said Angus.

"Are you sure?" asked Harris.

"I think so, Sergeant. When he fired, I saw small birds fly up, sparrows, but none from those bushes, yet something moved in there ever so slightly."

Harris nodded. "All right. The same drill, but this time I want all of you aiming towards the hollow. Use your scopes to spot his position. Don't shoot unless you have a clear target."

Harris repeated his rouse, and once again it drew fire from the sniper, followed by screaming and a call for stretcher-bearers from the trench where Harris had been. The section didn't know what to think until Harris reappeared. "Well, I had to make it believable," he explained. This time, they had all focused on the hollow, and all four of them confirmed slight movement and the sharp crack of a rifle being fired.

"Excellent," said Harris, "Time to earn our pay. I want all four of you to focus in on the hollow. I want Corporal MacIntyre to shoot first, followed by each of you in rapid succession, then two more rounds rapid fire. If the bastard's in there, let's flush him out or kill him—or both."

Stuart settled back into his position and focused on the hollow, waiting for Angus' shot. He was to fire next, followed by Liam and Seamus. He peered through his scope, letting the crosshairs rest on the center of the thickest of the small thorny bushes. He began to gently put pressure on the trigger until he felt it give gently, and then he waited. Angus' shot rang out and then Stuart fired, rechambering while still looking through the scope as he had been taught.

Just as Angus' second shot rang out, Stuart could see movement in the bush and then the outline of the sniper as he tried to frantically change his position. Stuart fired quickly. As he focused through his scope, he could see a man pitch forward, and two more shots rang out in quick succession. The enemy sniper fell, his upper body clearly seen now, draped in some sort of camouflage netting. As he lay there,

Angus fired a single shot into his head, which jerked back heavily.

Stuart took his eye off his scope, and raising himself slowly, he looked towards the hollow. He suddenly felt a gigantic hammer blow to the side of his temple. Pitching backward to the sound of rapid fire, he slumped to the bottom of the trench.

**

Having cleared the bodies in his section of the trench by throwing them onto the parapet with Murdo's help, Ross was filling sandbags when Liam touched his shoulder. "It's your brother."

He turned to see Harris coming down the trench, followed by Angus and Seamus with Stuart draped between them. Stuart's head was bandaged. Seeing Ross, Harris said, "Good thing your brother's got a thick head."

Stuart was pale, and the bandage was seeping blood on the left side of his head. Angus and Seamus laid him down on an old fire-step cut into the trench. "He'll be fine if he stays off his feet for a while," said Harris.

Ross rested a concerned hand on Stuart's shoulder. "What happened?"

"I don't know," Stuart said. He tried to sit up but gripped his head between his hands in pain and moaned.

"It was a sniper," explained Liam. "We were all shooting away at one of the bastards hidden in a hollow, and then the next thing we know, his mate opens up and Stuart's down with blood all over the side of his head. Angus got the second sniper, but he almost got your brother first. Thank god it just grazed him."

"Stay with him for a minute or two, and then back to work," ordered Harris before disappearing further up the trench with Seamus and Angus behind him.

"I leave for two minutes and just look at the state of you," admonished Ross gently and he sat down on the fire-step, holding his water bottle for Stuart to sip.

"Jesus, my head hurts," said Stuart, his eyes closing tightly as a wave of pain came over him.

"Harris says you'll be fine, although I think it's safe to say you're going to have one hell of a headache." He took a handkerchief out of his pocket, poured a capful of precious water onto it, and gave his brother's face a clean to get the blood off it.

To Stuart, it felt wonderfully cool, and he closed his eyes to let his brother clean them, and then he was dreaming of swimming at the hidden cove and laughing at the mule racing.

"Don't you worry. I'll keep an eye on him," said Liam, taking up position protectively with his rifle opposite Stuart, as Ross gently laid his sleeping brother's hands on his chest and stood up.

"How's Seamus?" he asked before going.

"He's quiet."

"Is he going to be all right?"

"He'll survive, but God help the Turks if he gets his hands on them, that's all I can say. You can see it in his eyes."

"See what?"

"The hatred."

The nakedness of the observation took Ross by surprise. "If Harris is right, the Turks will be paying us a visit soon enough."

"That's fine with me," said Liam, and he settled into his position, scanning the spur in front of them with his rifle for movement.

Ross shook Stuart awake an hour later. "Rise and shine. The Turks are getting busy." He handed him his Lee Enfield rifle, cleaned and fully loaded.

Stuart sat up and immediately felt a debilitating pain in his head. He groaned and stood on shaky legs. He fumbled for his water bottle, and after giving it an appraising slosh, took two mouthfuls of tepid water, replaced the metal cap, and then took his position between Liam and Ross just as he heard Harris yelling, "Stand to! Stand to!"

It had taken the Turks an hour to gather their men and then the trumpets blared, the whistles blew, and the cries of "Allah!" and "Allahu akbar!" came from across no man's land.

The Turkish soldiers emerged from their trench lines on the spur and bore down on them, running towards them in three lines one behind the other, packed in tightly. From farther up the trench, he heard the parade-ground volume of Color Sergeant Rennie, "Enemy in the open, two hundred yards, ra-pid fire!"

Stuart took aim at a large Turkish soldier and fired, hitting the man in the chest and throwing his body backward. The sound and recoil of his rifle sent a jolt of white-hot pain through his head, but he gritted his teeth and focused on the enemy running towards him. He rechambered a round and picked another target, an officer firing a pistol towards them as he ran in front of his men. Again, he aimed for the center of the body and pulled the trigger, sending the officer sprawling to the ground.

To the left and right of him, Lewis light machine gun crews added their fire. Stuart then heard the sound of shells as the Royal Artillery field guns opened up on the attacking masses. Liam was swearing away as he fired as usual and Stuart took comfort in it, and in having his brother by his side, but still the Turks came at them.

Stuart fired again and again and then paused to reload, taking his time despite the on-rushing attack to load two clips of five rounds. He worked his bolt and chambered the first round. Looking up he felt a wave of panic hit him as he saw the Turks were close, close enough to see their faces and sweat on their tunics, but there were few of them left.

As Stuart fired at another enemy soldier, he could glimpse others falling from the devastatingly effective rapid-fire directed at them. But they were brave men—they didn't turn and retreat, they came on until the very last of them dropped within feet of the trench. Stuart scanned the battle-field with his rifle looking for movement, but saw none, apart from the twitching limbs and moaning of the wounded.

Color Sergeant Rennie's voice ordered, "Cease fire! Reload," and then the artillery opened up again, but this time far to the left.

"It's someone else's turn now," said Ross, and as they looked on from their elevated position to the west, they could see an artillery duel develop between the British and the Turks. After a few moments, French artillery fire arced in over their heads from the right to support the British in softening up the Turkish trenches. The enemy artillery, now alerted to a probable attack, concentrated on the British frontline.

Giles came up behind them. "They must be sending over the Highland Light Infantry Brigade soon."

Stuart, Ross, and Liam turned, but Giles motioned for them to relax. "How's the head, Lance Corporal McReynolds?"

Stuart involuntarily touched his left temple with his hand. "I'll be fine, sir. It's just a bit sore."

"I'm sure it's more than that."

"How's your leg, sir?" asked Stuart in reply.

Giles tapped his thigh and immediately regretted it as he winced in pain. "It's just a bit sore," he said with a smile.

The artillery duel continued, but to their eyes, it seemed the Turkish artillery was doing more damage. A flaw was emerging in the British plan of attack. By staggering the attack, it allowed the Turkish artillery to concentrate on one defensive sector at a time, rather than dilute its impact across a wide front, and they had more artillery and more ammunition to fire. The Turks also had a pretty good idea of the objective, having been through one attack already.

The British were woefully short of high explosive shells and were limited to two shells per day, per gun, during routine duties at Gallipoli. They had shrapnel, but that was of little use against fortified trenches. The British artillery barrage, even with the help of the French, just warned the enemy that they were coming. As the section looked on, three battalions of Highland Light Infantry and one from the Argyll & Sutherland Highlanders emerged from their positions.

In response, the Turkish artillery increased in volume, and they could see from a distance the outlines of men being blown into the air. They could hear Turkish machine gun fire, but it was too far to the left of their position to do anything about. The top of the spur was quiet, and it seemed to Stuart that the Turks were watching the attack with the same morbid fascination as they were, mere bystanders to the death and destruction within their view. More waves of Scottish soldiers emerged from the trenches to add their weight to the attack. The Turkish artillery moved with them, continually taking a toll on the attacking infantry. Despite the carnage, two more waves of light infantrymen left the frontline to join in the attack.

They could see the first of the Turks retreating from the second trench, and all along the line, the borderers cheered. The light infantrymen and highlanders stormed into the Turkish trench, establishing a cohesive front that started with the French on the right, the Scottish Borderers in the middle, and the Highland Light Infantry on the left. It lasted for a few moments, until to their horror, they saw the light infantrymen leave the second trench and begin to run forward.

"Where the feck are they going?" asked Liam. They all stared as more and more soldiers emerged to run further ahead.

"They're going for the third trench," said Giles in abject resignation.

"But there is no third trench!" replied Liam in frustration. "We lost Connor and half the borderers trying to find it. It doesn't exist!"

"It still does on the maps, and it still does in the minds of the staff officers. They still think it's there to be captured, that we couldn't do it, but that others can. We reported it wasn't there. I saw the messengers leave with my own eyes. They just don't believe us," replied Giles in a despairing monotone.

In frustration, the entire trench watched as the light infantrymen advanced into no man's land to the same fate that had met the borderers a few hours earlier. They reached where on their officer's maps the third trench should have been, searched for it in vain under machine gun and rifle fire, advanced further, and then the Turkish artillery opened up on them. Stuart could imagine the enemy gunner's disbelief and delight that such an opportunity had repeated itself, and they made the most of it. Soon the light infantrymen were obscured as high explosive and shrapnel shells bracketed them in a deadly metal storm of destruction.

Eventually, they could see small groups of soldiers emerging from the smoke and dust as they retreated towards the sanctuary of the second trench. By the time the artillery lifted, the light infantrymen—like the borderers before them—had lost hundreds of men searching for a nonexistent third trench.

The Turks had lost two lines of trenches, but they still held Achi Baba and they had inflicted punishing casualties on the men caught in the open by their field guns, and they knew it. The second trench was partially destroyed by artillery—British, French, and Turkish—and for the most part, it faced the wrong way for its new inhabitants. The soldiers that held it were tired and wounded. They were also short of water, ammunition, supplies, and reinforcements.

It was the perfect time to counterattack.

Under the cover of their own artillery barrage, the Turks moved up waves of reinforcements. Their own officers and their German advisors impressed on the soldiers their sacred duty under Jihad to protect their land, their people, and their country by pushing the invaders back into the sea. Some of the Turkish soldiers were local militiamen, and the speeches of the officers were no mere words for them. Their own villages and families were but a few miles away or had already been destroyed by allied artillery.

The section gathered to brew up a half a cup of tea in a brief 15-minute rest called by Harris. Giles appeared to brief them and astounded everyone by producing a small hip flask of whisky and putting a dash into each of their mugs. It was a small gesture, but like many of his small gestures, it didn't go unappreciated and made a big impact.

"There's a platoon of borderers between us and the French to the right, then Sergeant Armstrong and his men, then us, and then Color Sergeant Rennie with his men to our left. Beyond them more borderers, and then the light infantry. We hold this position until relieved, which should be in the morning. We're on our own until then. The good news is the Turks abandoned a Maxim machine gun, and as we're on the high ground, it's coming up to us. It's the one that was inside the enemy strongpoint. Any questions?" asked Giles.

Sergeant Harris cleared his throat. "We're short on water and ammunition, sir."

"I know, I know. All I can suggest is we take what we can from those who no longer need it. I'm afraid we can hope for, but we can't rely on, resupply tonight."

"Yes, sir," replied Harris.

Giles turned to go and then stopped. "Make no mistake, men. The enemy will want this position back, so keep digging in and make sure you're ready for them when they come to try and get it. Is that clear?"

"Yes, sir!" came the reply in unison.

Sergeant Harris turned to the section when Giles departed. "Right then, you lot. The tea party is over! Time to earn your pay. Finish off the cream cakes and scones," he ordered sarcastically but with a smile, "and then gather water and ammunition from wherever you can find it. I want this trench ready for action, so get to it. Private O'Connell," he said, looking at Aiden, "keep a watch and yell like hell if you see the Turks coming. Let's move with purpose you bunch of misfits and get the job done!"

The section moved to sort themselves out when Aiden yelled, "Incoming!" and before they'd even stowed their brewing-up kit, enemy 75-millimeter artillery was raining down high explosives on them. The section cowered in the bottom of the trench as shell after shell came screaming in to explode along the trench-line. Deep in his chest, Stuart could feel the waves of concussion wash over him, and he tucked himself into a ball with his hands over his ears. Stabbing pains went through his head as the shells exploded around them, sending up fountains of soil and stones and jagged iron fragments of shell casing.

The barrage was swift and deadly, and to their right—towards the French line—they heard men screaming as an entire salvo of shells found their mark, destroying sections of the trench and blowing apart the soldiers within them. Over the barrage, they heard the trumpets and whistles of the attacking enemy.

"Stand to! Stand to!" yelled Harris, and the section grabbed their rifles and rose to face the enemy. The Turkish artillery still pounded their position, keeping their heads down and trying to give the attacking soldiers whatever advantage they could. Stuart and Ross rose together and peered over the parapet of dead bodies to see a mass of enemy soldiers coming towards them. They seemed endless, and after a short pause Harris shouted, "Fix bayonets!"

The terse order made Stuart feel sick with fear, and he had the urge to vomit. Controlling his nerves, he unsheathed his long bayonet and clipped it onto his rifle alongside his brother just as the enemy artillery abruptly ceased.

"Enemy in the open, two hundred yards, ra-pid fire!" yelled Harris.

Stuart thumbed off his safety catch and aimed at the advancing soldiers, firing towards a soldier ahead of the others and watching him pitch backward as his bullet slammed into his chest. A Lewis light machine gun was firing somewhere off to the left, but its twin was silent on the right, and Stuart could only guess it had been a victim of the Turkish artillery barrage that had hit the trench. He rechambered another round and fired, again and again, each time watching a soldier fall, each time to be replaced by another. As he stood a group of five sweating men pushed their way up the trench with the captured enemy MG09 Maxim heavy machine gun and boxes of linked 7.65mm ammunition.

"Get that bloody gun into action!" yelled Harris, and pointed at the spot next to Stuart and Ross.

Stuart took another shot and then moved aside as the gun crew cleared a space on the parapet by hauling down a dead body and planted the heavy metal tripod in its place, a corporal issuing orders to the others. Stuart paused to top-up his magazine with a clip of five rounds and then moving to the other side of his brother, aimed and fired quickly into the attacking mass of men. The Turks were yelling and running with long bayonets leveled. To Stuart, they seemed unstoppable, and he fired faster, taking less care with his aim, just firing quickly again and again as his brother reloaded beside him. The Turks were closer now, and sensing their momentum was unstoppable, their battle cries increased in volume and intensity, and then the captured Maxim burst into life.

Stuart had never been so close to a heavy machine gun in action. The noise and reverberation shocked him as it rocked on its tripod, sending out a steady stream of bullets at 400 rounds per minute, over six rounds per second. The machine gun had a small plate of armor to protect the gunner, and the corporal stood behind it, looking through a vertical two-inch wide gap, gripping twin handles while depressing the double-butterfly trigger and sending long bursts into the Turks at thigh height. Beside him, his assistants fed the gun, keeping the linked ammunition level and clear of obstruction as the machine gun bucked on its tripod. The impact of the gun on the attacking Turks was dramatic. It shattered thigh bones and muscle and then slammed more bullets into them as they fell screaming to the ground.

The machine gun corporal knew his trade well. He fired in controlled bursts, almost continuous fire, but not enough to overheat the water-cooled barrel. He moved the gun in a smooth arc, left and right, sensing where the threat to the trench was acute and destroying it with an industrial stream of lead before easing off the triggers as he sought out a new target.

The sudden appearance of the captured heavy machine gun devastated the attackers, wiping out the first waves of men on the spur. More men came on behind them, and Stuart could hear the gunners shouting as the gun paused and they linked in the last boxes of ammunition. The rate of fire dropped as the corporal husbanded the ammunition, picking his targets with care and lengthening the pauses in the stream bullets. As Stuart and Ross reloaded, they heard one of crew yelling, "Last ammo belt!" There was no more captured ammunition, and with the last few hundred rounds, the corporal swung the gun wide, sending a stream of bullets left and right down the line and then the gun fell silent.

In the absence of the heavy machine gun, their rifles suddenly sounded inadequate. The Maxim had destroyed the best part of two waves of men, but the Turkish counterattack was massive and desperate in scale, and more enemy soldiers came charging over their own dead and dying with renewed determination and vengeance now the machine gun had grown silent.

Stuart fired into the attacking men and as he did so, Giles repeated the order, "Color Sergeant Rennie, hold the line! Seaforths move to the right! Color Sergeant Rennie, hold the line! Seaforths move to the right!"

"Time to move," said Ross. They fired one last volley and then dropped down to run up the trench towards Sergeant Armstrong and his section of men, and the platoon of borderers beyond them next to the French. Except the platoon of borderers no longer existed. A salvo of Turkish high explosive shells had devastated the trench and the platoon of men in it. Armstrong and his seven men were left holding a half-destroyed trench with a gap to the right of them, held only by a handful of wounded and bleeding men incapable of holding back the determined Turkish attack.

As they rushed up the trench, they met Giles, firing his rifle into the attacking Turks surging towards the weak spot in front of them.

"Seaforths on me!" he shouted, "Rapid fire!"

Stuart swung his rifle over the low parapet and fired three rounds quickly into the enemy ranks. He knew it was too little, too late.

"Here they come!" he heard Harris yelling. Then suddenly the Turks were on them.

Stuart raised his rifle and shot a man leaping toward him, catching him in mid-air and propelling him backward, his arms flung wide. He chambered another round, but before he could fire, a wave of Turks leaped screaming into the trench. Stuart saw a bayonet come towards him from above, he swung his rifle and parried the thrust, and then the Turk jumped towards him. With all his strength he struck out with his right hand and pulled towards him with his left, slamming the butt of his rifle into the enemy soldier's head, knocking his kabalak sun helmet off and cracking his skull with the metal base plate. The soldier dropped his rifle and screamed, holding his hands up to his damaged head, and Stuart repeated the blow, driving him to the floor of the trench and then pounded the Turk's head twice with the butt of his rifle, smashing through the man's hands and caving in his forehead.

Twisting, he saw two Turks cornering Liam. He raised his rifle and fired at point-blank range into the nearest, and then yelling, thrust his bayonet into the side of the other soldier. The blade met no resistance as it sliced through the man's soft internal organs below the rib cage. He twisted and pulled, and the man dropped, blood gushing from his wound, and then Liam bayoneted him through the neck, pausing only to nod his thanks towards Stuart before moving down the trench.

Stuart turned as another Turk jumped down beside him, slamming him into the trench wall and knocking his rifle from his hands. In desperation, Stuart grabbed the man's head in his hands and battered it against the opposite wall, hooking his thumbs into the man's eyes and squeezing tightly, his teeth bared. The Turk tried to raise his rifle between them, but Stuart was too close and screaming in pain. He dropped his rifle and brought his hands up to pull away those clawing his eyes. Stuart battered his head once again against the trench wall, and then with all his might, jabbed his thumbs deep into the man's eyes. His left thumb punctured one eyeball with a sickening squirt of warm intraocular fluid, while his right thumb dislocated the other eyeball from its socket, popping it out, held to the gaping socket only by its optical nerves. The Turk screamed and put both hands up to his ruined eyes.

Stuart pushed the man away and retched, vomiting into the bottom of the trench just as Harris rushed by him and bayonetted a Turk holding a long knife, who had been right behind Stuart.

Turning, Harris yelled at Stuart in anger, "As long as you're alive, you fight or die in this stinking trench—right now that's all you have time for! Nothing else matters, or you'll be dead in the two seconds that Turk would have taken to slit your throat! We're cut off, so pick up your bloody rifle, and find someone to kill!" and he spun around quickly and was gone.

Stung by Harris's rebuke, Stuart picked up his rifle just as he heard Giles' shout over the din of hand-to-hand fighting and gunfire, tinged with desperation, "Seaforths stand fast! Seaforths stand fast!"

"Whatever's happening up the trench, it doesn't sound good." Stuart turned to see his brother beside him, reloading a clip of five rounds into his rifle, his face bloodstained and masked with sweat.

Liam turned to them both. "Well, things are about to get feckin worse here in a hurry." He raised his rifle and fired down the trench as Turkish soldiers came around a corner traverse. They were cut off, just as Harris had said. Turks were in the trench between them and the French, where the Turkish artillery had wiped out the borderers, and now there were Turks in the trench between them and Color Sergeant Rennie's men.

Stuart glanced at the Turks pushing towards them and issued his first order. "Rapid fire! Stagger the reload!"

Immediately, all three men raised their rifles and fired down the trench into the advancing Turks. They fired five rounds, and then Liam dropped to his knee, yelling, "Reloading!" As Stuart and Ross kept firing, Liam reloaded ten rounds and then stood up.

After five rounds, Ross took a step back and shouted, "Reloading!" followed in turn by Stuart. By staggering their reload, they ensured there was no break in their rapid-fire, with at least two or three of them firing at any one time. It gave the Turks no opportunity to rush them.

Within the confines of the trench, the rapid rifle fire was horribly effective, but the Turks kept coming over their dead and dying, and Stuart yelled the second order of his short military career, "Retreat two steps at a time!" As the three of them fired, they slowly backed up, keeping the distance between them and the enemy constant, reloading all the time.

Just as they had managed to hold the Turks back, Liam yelled, "Grenade!" as a small dark object hurtled towards them. Without thinking, Stuart plucked it out the air and threw it back, and it exploded amid the enemy soldiers, wounding two of them of them.

Again, they backed up the trench and again, a grenade came arcing towards them. This time it was Liam who grabbed it from the trench floor and threw it back. The grenades were small crude cast-iron balls crammed with TNT, each with a 19-second lit fuse, and that was the tactical flaw. Although it could be cut down, the fuse was too long and gave the intended victim time to throw it back at the attackers. Seconds later and yet another grenade came over, high, and—to Stuart's horror—over their heads. He turned to look just in time to see Seamus catch it in midair and throw it back far into the Turkish-held trench. It exploded, and over the rifle fire, Stuart could hear screams. No more grenades came their way, and Seamus took his position beside them, saying, "And here I was thinking you lot were taking a nap!"

Before Stuart could reply, he heard Angus shouting a warning from behind: "Above you! They're coming out of the trench above you!" followed by the crack of a rifle bullet zipping over their heads.

Stuart turned to Seamus and shouted, "Hold this line!" before looking over the parapet. Four enemy soldiers had left their section of recaptured trench and were making a dash for them, trying to attack the small band of men from above while others came at them from along the trench. One was already falling backward, hit by Angus' bullet, and as another fell, Stuart snap-fired his rifle into the nearest, who tumbled into the trench on top of him. As he tried to rise, the last Turk leaped into the trench, his boots missing him by inches.

The Turk was wounded but immediately grasped Stuart by the neck with one hand and punched him with the other on the side of his temple, opening up his wound and sending a bolt of searing pain through his head. He tried to grab the Turk's hand, but it just smashed into his temple again. Stuart felt weak at the knees, but then remembered Harris's words: "...fight or die..." and he brought his knee up sharply with all his might into the soldier's groin, who screamed in agony. As the Turk doubled over, Stuart brought his rifle up with both hands, smashing him in the jaw and knocking him backward. He plunged his bayonet into the Turk's chest, stepped on him, and pulled the bayonet out, dripping with warm blood.

Stuart spun to be greeted by Sergeant Harris. "That's better. He's dead, and you're not. Let's keep it that way."

"Yes, Sergeant."

Harris reached up and touched Stuart's temple. "Go up the trench and have Aiden O'Connell look at that. I'll stay here."

Stuart felt as if he was going to be sick. His head throbbed with pain, but he did not want to leave his post. Reading his thoughts, Harris added, "I'll look after them. Now get going."

"Yes, Sergeant." Stuart picked up his rifle and took the time to reload five more rounds.

"Lance Corporal McReynolds."

"Yes, Sergeant?"

"You did well here. We could hear you."

Despite his pain and the battle raging around them, Stuart smiled with pride. "Thank you, Sergeant," and off he went.

He passed Angus keeping a watch for more Turks trying to rush them over the top and nodded his thanks for the warning. He reached Aiden, now providing first aid. He was surrounded by badly wounded borderers, some of them already dead. "Jesus, Lance Corporal, you look a mess. Sit down."

Stuart sat on a fire-step as Aiden tied another bandage around his head, keeping the old one in place. When he was finished, he gave Stuart a small drink of warm water and asked what was happening down the trench. "The Turks have cut us off. Liam, Ross, Seamus, and Sergeant Harris are holding the trench, but we're being pushed back. Angus is just a few yards away looking out for them rushing us."

Aiden nodded. "Same up that way," he said, nodding his head towards the opposite direction. "They overwhelmed the decimated borderers and started attacking down the trench. You had better go and report to Lieutenant Morley. He'll want to know what's happening."

"Are you all right here?"

Aiden grimaced. "There's nothing I can do for most of these poor sods, but like Corporal MacIntyre, I'm making sure the bastards don't rush us over the top."

Stuart felt his new bandage, muttered his thanks, and went up the trench 20 yards where he found Giles, Murdo, and Sergeant Armstrong with four of his borderers. The rest were dead.

Giles was armed with both rifle and pistol, and was reloading both when Stuart reported. "Well done, Lance Corporal. How's the head?"

"A bit sore, sir. How's the leg?"

"A bit sore, Lance Corporal," and they both grinned just as Sergeant Armstrong yelled a warning: "Here they come again!" followed by a volley of rifle fire.

***

As they had before, the Turks rushed madly down the trench into rapid fire. As he watched, Stuart saw two black metal balls arc their way over towards them. "Grenades!" he yelled as the first struck and exploded. In the constricted space, the explosion was deafening and quickly followed by another. This time, the fuses were perfectly timed. A trumpet blared, and with a yell, the Turks surged forward. In front of them lay three borderers, dead or dying, and one young soldier left standing, bleeding from both ears. Still stunned by the impact, the remaining men raised their rifles and fired into the attacking enemy. Stuart was partially deafened but fired quickly into the Turks. They seemed oblivious to the harm being done to them, and with a cry to Allah, they rushed the Scots, sensing blood and victory.

Sergeant Armstrong, Kings Own Scottish Borderers, had seen his entire platoon and most of his company—including his officer—killed in front of him that day. First, by artillery and machine-gun fire while searching for the third trench, and then by bayonets, bullets, and finally by grenades. He was a tough, hardy sheep farmer from the Scottish-English border with close family on both sides. He was proud of his border heritage, proud of his uniform, and proud of his men, and he was damned if he was going to let the last one of them die in front of him without a fight. So he did what came naturally—he exploded into a ball of rage.

Leveling his rifle, he did the one thing the Turks weren't expecting—he charged. Seeing his sergeant sweep past him, the last remaining private turned and charged after him, unable to hear his own war cry through deafened bleeding ears.

"Shit," said Stuart as he saw Murdo shout and sprint forward, and then both he and Giles were racing behind him, yelling, bayonets leveled and ready to fight to the bitter end.

The physical clash of men within the confines of the trench was medieval in nature and accompanied by screams and yells as Armstrong took down the leading Turks with a bullet fired from the hip into one, and then a bayonet through the throat to the next. The private beside him rammed his bayonet into a third, and then Murdo waded past both of them, his sheer physical strength and height overpowering the Turks in front of him. Years of felling trees had given him muscles on top of muscles, and he had one more thing to add to his personal arsenal—pent-up hatred.

Hatred of a life bowing down to others, to saying *yes, sir* to men half his age because they were white and he wasn't. Hatred of being turned away, of being mocked, of seeing his mother and father shamed by looks of contempt, of being made to feel less than others. Hatred of being made to wait three days on a hard wooden chair in a cold corridor before he could even be considered good enough to wear a uniform. But that was then, and this was now, and now was blood and guts and good men beside him who considered him their equal. Men who considered him their friend. Good men who shared their last morsel of bread and their last drop of water with him, who called him one of their own and chanted his name with pride in the dining hall. If he was going to die beside them, there was going to be one hell of a fight.

Murdo waded ahead, Armstrong on one side, the remaining borderer on the other until the private went down with a scream, a bayonet ripping open his stomach. Stuart took his place and fired his rifle over Murdo's shoulder, killing men before Murdo could reach them, watching heads explode from near point-blank range. Calls went out and the Turks rallied, fighting the desperate men to a standstill. Then Aiden was behind them throwing discarded rifles, bayonet first, into the packed enemy soldiers, spearing them and causing dreadful injuries. Beside him, Giles fired his pistol into the faces of the Turks in front of them. Stuart's ammunition ran dry, and battle-maddened, he took his place beside Murdo.

Time stood still as they fought fanatically, bleeding from injuries they didn't know they had. Sergeant Armstrong went down, screaming in protest and defiance, bleeding from multiple stab wounds until he could no longer stand,

and Giles took his place, pistol discarded, bayonet flashing. Aiden was yelling for help, and then Angus was beside them, the tall highlander firing at the Turks beyond the deadly melee. Then with a cry, Giles collapsed, blood pouring from his thigh wound, his strength spent.

With a yell of anguish, Angus stepped over him into the frontline. If Murdo had his own hidden demons, so did Angus. He had watched his entire family die in front of his eyes, cartwheeling down the side of the *Lusitania*. He'd been helpless then—but no more. If the Turks were allies of the Germans, they were his enemies, and with a fierce war-cry, he launched himself at the enemy in front of him, taking his place next to Murdo. Standing side by side, the two lumberjacks simply went berserk.

Stuart saw Murdo swing his rifle butt plate so hard against an attacking Turk that the man's skull caved in. He saw Angus plunge his bayonet so deep into the soldier in front of him, it erupted out of his back, pulling the trigger he then killed the next Turkish soldier down the trench before pulling his bayonet out and charging ahead, Murdo by his side.

The enemy soldiers died before them, unable to resist the men's combined strength and fury. But the Turks fought hard, draining Stuart's strength, and he felt himself weakening. Just as he thought it must be his turn to collapse, he heard something. It was faint at first, but then with increasing volume, someone, behind the Turks, was yelling, *Venez à moi legionnaires, à moi!*—"To me, Legionnaires, to me!"

The French were attacking from the other direction to close the gap, to recapture the trench, and the men doing the attacking were battle-hardened legionnaires.

The Turks became instinctively defensive, no longer attacking, but it made no difference to Murdo and Angus, or the legionnaires fighting towards them. Stuart was swept up in the battle fever alongside them, somehow finding strength where he thought there was no more, giving no quarter and trampling the dead and wounded below his boots. He winced as from the corner of his eye he saw a soldier block the sun above him on the parapet, and then realized it was Seamus, and behind him Liam, Ross, and Sergeant Harris, pouring fire directly into the trench from above, slaughtering the Turkish soldiers like rats in a trap.

But the Turks were no rats, and trapped as they may have been, they fought on for their country, for each other, and in the end for their right to die as soldiers and proud men on their own soil. In their midst stood a German officer, trapped like the soldiers he had been sent to advise. He unholstered his pistol and fired at the four soldiers working their way along the parapet towards him. The German fired three shots in quick succession before pitching backward, shot through the head by Liam.

Seamus worked the bolt on his rifle, firing again and again into the trapped soldiers below him, aiming for those just behind the battle-line within the trench. Oblivious to the danger, he walked above the trench-line, shooting down at the Turks through cold unfeeling eyes, scorning the danger at being so exposed. He could hear the others behind him and from his elevated position, he could see the legionnaires in their blue coats and white kepis, working towards them. Looking down, he could see Aiden behind Angus, Murdo, and Stuart, fighting with their bayonets, pushing back the enemy in front of them. He felt invincible and elated, each soldier he killed was payment in kind for Connor's death—and the Turks seemed helpless to stop him.

He turned to see if Liam was still behind him when he heard the sharp crack of a small-caliber bullet pass him by, followed by another, and then he felt a hammer blow as a bullet ripped through his left shoulder muscles. He staggered backward and fell to his knees, dropping his rifle and grasping his torn shoulder. Liam stood protectively beside him, rifle at the ready, but the fight was over. A handful of Turkish soldiers had surrendered, their hands in the air—the rest were dead or wounded.

CHAPTER SEVENTEEN

Could Your Land Forget

Achi Baba Nullah,
Gallipoli, July 13th, 1915

Stuart sat exhausted on a sandbag in the trench bottom in front of a pool of vomit. The adrenaline coursing through his veins made him gag and throw up, retching on green bile and shaking with cold.

"Try this, *mon ami*," said a familiar voice. He looked up to see Lafitte holding out his canteen.

"Wine?" asked Stuart cautiously.

Lafitte smiled. "*Non,* cold water."

Stuart took the big canteen and drank in the cool water, taking three big gulps before handing it back. Lafitte noticed he was sweating profusely, and his hands were trembling. Stuart had never been so grateful for a drink of water in his life. Lafitte poured a precious cupful over Stuart's head and down his neck. Stuart groaned with relief. "Thank you. Was that you yelling at the head of the legionnaires?"

Lafitte shrugged. "Someone had to come to the rescue, and I couldn't see the cavalry."

Stuart stared up at him with vacant eyes. "One of my friends is dead, another wounded, and we've probably lost our officer."

"I'm sorry to hear that."

Stuart looked up at the legionnaire and after a long pause, asked, "Is it always like this? The killing I mean? I've blown the face off a man and watched him scream through half a jaw. I blinded a man with my bare hands today. I've already lost count of the men I've shot, killed, or maimed.

I've seen hundreds of good men die because someone somewhere can't read a map, or doesn't know men with bayonets can't charge heavy machine guns in broad daylight, or accept that a third trench doesn't exist over there," and he pointed vacantly towards the slopes of Achi Baba. "And I've been here what, a month? This is madness. Does it ever end? Can no one stop it?"

Lafitte could read the pain, frustration, and desperation behind the exhaustion. "Wars are hard to stop once they get going. They develop their own momentum."

"Doesn't anyone know how many men are dying out here? Doesn't anyone care?"

"That becomes the reason it's hard to stop," replied Lafitte with a shrug.

Stuart stared up at him.

Lafitte paused, exhaling loudly through his nose and pursing his lips. "The more men die, the harder it is to stop. Neither side wants their deaths to be meaningless, so they keep fighting, hoping to win the war, hoping to give meaning to the death and destruction through victory."

"Then we're all insane," replied Stuart in disgust before pinching his nose and blowing, flicking his fingers and sending a stream of snot and mucus to the ground at his feet.

"You are a soldier now," replied Lafitte. He reached down and pointed at the medal ribbon above Stuart's left pocket. "And a good one to be awarded that. As for the rest? We live for the moment—it is all that matters. At the end of the day, the parades, the bands, the medals, and the uniforms are all there to mask a very simple fact—soldiers kill and are killed, maim and are maimed. You live, *mon ami*, that is enough. It is all there is on the battlefield, that and endurance."

"Endurance? I'm sick of this already," said Stuart, gesturing to the trench full of dead. "How can you endure this?"

"Because the alternative is death, so endure, *mon ami*, endure."

"Then we should just pack up and walk away from this madness."

"They shoot people for that," he said with concern.

Stuart laughed. "Look around you, Lafitte. People have been trying to shoot me since I got here. If someone wants to shoot me for walking away, they'd better get in line behind god knows how many Turks. At least they're fighting to defend something." He cradled his bandaged head in his hands. "I have no idea what we're doing here."

"We're here because they sent us here," replied Lafitte matter-of-factly. "Did you volunteer to join the army?"

"Yes."

"For your country, for the adventure, for a uniform to impress a sweetheart?"

"No."

"Why then?"

"I watched my family drown on the *Lusitania*."

The Cajun stared at the young soldier in front of him and softened his voice. "You were there?"

"Yes."

"Then at least you have a better reason than most for being in uniform." He looked about him and then back down at Stuart, "Didn't some American general once say, 'War is hell'?"

Stuart nodded. "Sherman. He also said, 'war is cruelty' and a crime against civilization."

"Then he knew what he was talking about. Now you know it, too."

Stuart looked up at the veteran legionnaire. "When will it end, Lafitte?"

Lafitte just shrugged. "I can't answer that. I don't know. No one knows anymore. This war has become something different. Something terrible."

Ramirez came up behind Laffite and talked quickly in French to his friend. Laffite nodded and picked up his rifle. "We are to hold here. You are to move back down the trench and hold about a hundred yards away. The Turks will be back."

Lafitte reached down, and holding one of Stuart's hands, pulled him up to his feet. He shook it with a strong grip. "I have to go now." He stared into Stuart's eyes. "Remember—endure. Live. Fight for the men to the left of you, and for the men to the right. That is all you can do. *Oui*—yes?"

Stuart nodded, then smiled. "*Oui.*"

"Then *bonne chance mon ami, bonne chance*—good luck, my friend." Shaking his hand firmly one last time, he turned to return to his men, barking orders in French that spurred the legionnaires into activity.

Stuart saw Harris walking towards them. "The French will hold this section of trench. We go back to where we started and dig in," said the sergeant.

Stuart smiled, as the news was already old.

Harris looked up at the sky and then stared at Stuart. "The sun will set soon. Follow Lieutenant Morley to the aid station."

"I'm all right, Sergeant. I want to stay with my brother."

Harris looked Stuart up and down. "You're covered in blood."

Stuart looked Harris up and down. "So are you, Sergeant."

Harris looked at his own uniform and pursed his lips. "Good point; well made. All right, stay if you want."

"How's Seamus?"

"His shoulder looks a mess, but he won't leave, either. Liam's given him the German officer's pistol, a Luger. Not a bad keepsake." Stuart smiled at the news. Lugers were highly coveted.

"And the boss?"

"Not good. Lieutenant Morley lost a lot of blood from his leg. He shouldn't have been running about on it like he was."

"He didn't have much choice at the time, Sergeant."

"No, I suppose not," said Harris, surveying the trench. "Right, let's prepare to move out."

Liam stared at the trench full of dead, and then after a while, looked over at Aiden. "They look like the mackerel."

"What do you mean?" asked Aiden.

"The day we went out, the day of the *Lusitania*, remember we caught all those mackerel? They lay in the bottom of the skiff, all bloody, open-eyed, and stiff. The bodies, they look like them."

Aiden nodded, not knowing what else to say. The two men turned and went back down the trench. They went past the scene of their battles, over dead bodies they had known as living men, Sergeant Armstrong and his borderers among them. When they reached the captured Turkish maxim gun, they halted. The machine gun crew were all dead, overrun by the Turks and bayonetted beyond recognition in vengeance for the casualties they had inflicted. No one on the battlefield from either side gave mercy to machine gunners. The gun lay in the bottom of the trench. Color Sergeant Rennie was still there. He had organized the counterattack with the light infantry that had cleared the Turks from his section of trench, freeing up Seamus, Harris, Liam, and Ross to rejoin the section. He came over to Harris, and after a brief discussion, left to go back down the trench, barking out orders to his section of Royal Scots to dig in next to the Seaforths.

Harris had retrieved Giles' service pistol. He opened it up, let the empty cartridges fall out, and reloaded it, snapping it shut and stuffing it into his webbing. Then he reached down and picked up a couple of stray bullets lying in the trench bottom next to the dead machine gun corporal. He rubbed them together in his hands, cleaning the dirt off them, then looked at his section.

"We hold this position until relieved. Gather up rifle ammunition from the poor sods that no longer need it. I want each of you to have a full load, one hundred twenty rounds at the very least, two hundred forty would be better. Check your weapons. I want scopes off and stowed away. We'll use good-old iron sights from now on. I want bayonets gleaming and sharpened, so they'll scare the shit out of the Turks just by looking at them. Trust me, it works. See if there's any water in the bottles, and fill your own up as much as you can."

He motioned towards the machine gun and tripod at the bottom of the trench, "Get that back up and checked. Corporal MacIntyre, send two men down to the old enemy strongpoint to search for any machine gun ammunition you can find in or around it. I don't care how little there is. Bring back every single round you can find, or don't come back at all. I want two of you here on your hands and knees. Find me more machine gun ammunition—gunners are always dropping it. There's always two or three rounds left lying around," and as he said it he held up the two rounds he'd picked up as evidence. "I want it all."

He paused, looking at Angus, who after a moment's hesitation snapped to attention and said, "Yes, Sergeant!"

"Lance Corporal McReynolds, get that bandage around your head replaced and then sort out a sentry-duty roster. I want two men on for two hours each throughout the night. Put Seamus on now and then let him get some rest. Then I want you to parley with your legionnaire friend and let them know where we are, our strength, and see if they'll send some men down our way. I don't want us isolated again, and I'm not too proud to ask for help. Is that clear?"

"Yes, Sergeant."

"The rest of you sort out this trench. I want the dead bodies out. I want this parapet higher—use the bodies. I want fire steps. I want this trench six inches deeper, and I want it all done about an hour ago."

He took a step back and surveyed the section.

"All of you, square yourselves away. You look like shite. You're Seaforth Highlanders, so smarten up. Use sand to rub the blood off your uniforms. Before it's dark, I want faces wiped clean, and I want you shaved; use spit if you have to, preferably your own. Find your slouch hats. The boss pulled strings to get you them, so get them on. When you're all done with that, eat whatever you have and stand by."

He stared at them with hard, stern eyes. "Listen to me and listen to me well—*this is not over*. We've lost one good man today, and the stretcher-bearers have taken away the boss. I don't want to lose anyone else, so stop your day-dreaming, pull your thumbs out, and get to work unless you want to join them," and he pointed to the dead machine gun crew at his feet before walking away down the trench.

He had been harsh. But he also knew he had to keep the men busy, keep them sharp, and keep them from replaying the death and horror of what they'd just been through in their minds until they became hardened to it through time. The sun would set soon. The Turks would be back. They still had a battle to fight.

Harris walked past Color Sergeant Rennie who was giving his own soldiers an earful, and then he went further down the line. He wanted to see the condition of it and the men within it as they secured his left flank. He stopped just past the old enemy strongpoint and lit a cigarette, letting himself relax for a moment, looking at the detritus left around the bunker.

As he stood there, the first of a trickle of men were making their way to the front line against the flow of walking wounded and stretcher-bearers working their way to the rear. Infantrymen, pioneers, and laborers had completed the first communication trench, and through it came a very thin line of weary stretcher-bearers looking for more wounded to carry, Vickers machine gun crews, and their ammunition carriers. A few mixed oddities were interspersed in their ranks: forward artillery observers; signalers with heavy rolls of telephone wire; military police to escort prisoners of war, not that there were many; graves-registration officers; an out-of-place chaplain; a few staff officers sent to assess the situation; and lowly of the lowly, a solitary private from the 52nd Lowland Sanitary Section.

The sanitary section worked alongside the Royal Army Medical Corps to prevent the spread of disease by ensuring trenches and billets were kept clean. They disinfected clothing and blankets, covered the dead in quicklime to mask the smell and speed decomposition, provided showers and potable water, and burned rubbish. Most of their duties were unknown, apart from the role they were most associated with—digging and cleaning latrines. Because of this, they were shunned and looked down upon. As the lone private passed by Harris smelling faintly of shit, sent forward with the stretcher-bearers to see what conditions existed and what latrines the Turks had left behind, Harris took absolutely no notice of him.

The private, on the other hand, stared at Harris below the lowered rim of his pith helmet at first in surprise and disbelief, quickly followed by intense loathing. Sergeant Major Skaig had stumbled across someone he truly hated, one of a handful of men he had vowed vengeance upon, and the focus of that hate was standing alone in front of him.

Skaig was no longer a sergeant major, nor was he serving in an elite highland regiment. For two long months, he had broken big stones into little stones in the Stirlinghill Quarry outside Peterhead Prison in Aberdeenshire, Scotland, serving out his four-month hard labor sentence. Peterhead's stone harbor was to be extended, and the local prison offered a convenient source of labor. So, along with other convict work gangs, Skaig had quarried and broken stone. He had done so silently, enduring the physical abuse bestowed on him as a former sergeant major by prisoners and guards alike. With each punch, with each kick, with each gob of spit hacked at his face, his hatred towards those he blamed for his downfall had grown and festered into a burning malevolence. Halfway through his sentence, he had been given the opportunity to swap prison for a pardon and frontline service.

By mid-1915, the British government knew it needed more soldiers, badly. Conscription was being considered. It was pointed out there were many soldiers and ex-soldiers safe and sound, malingering in jail while stalwart men served and died on the frontline. As a result, Sergeant Major Skaig, a former senior non-commissioned officer in the Seaforth Highlanders, found himself now Private Skaig, sanitary section. He'd been issued rubberized boots and an apron, a spade, and made 'senior shit cleaner and latrine digger' in the words of a sneering corporal who knew his former rank and position. Sent to Gallipoli with the Lowland Division, he believed himself hundreds of miles away from the men he had a personal vendetta against—until now.

Liam and Aiden struggled to squeeze past other men in the confines of the trench as they made their way towards the old strongpoint. They had volunteered to search for machine gun ammunition and take what they could find back to the section. They walked silently, each lost in his own thoughts, until Aiden said, "The Cuckoo Wrasse."

Liam turned to look at his friend. "What did you say?"

"The Cuckoo Wrasse. You were talking about the skiff and the day of the *Lusitania*, and it's got me thinking. We never named the skiff. Then I was thinking about Connor, how he caught that cuckoo wrasse and how we all laughed. So, I'm thinking we call it, *The Cuckoo Wrasse*, to remember the last day we were all together in the skiff." He looked over at Liam to see his reaction.

Liam smiled for the first time that day. "I like that. It has a nice ring to it."

Ordered by Angus to be quick and to find all the ammunition they could, they eventually came around an angled traverse in the captured trench, past men working to strengthen and repair it.

Harris saw them coming. As a solitary soldier passed him by, he took one last long drag of his cigarette, pulling the smoke into his lungs. He stubbed it out and waited until the two Irishmen came up to the bunker.

"All right, you two, enough dawdling. Search that bunker with a fine-tooth comb for ammo."

Out of breath in the stifling heat, Liam was about to nod his understanding when he heard Aiden shouting, "Grenade!"

Liam froze as Harris turned to see a circular grenade tumbling through the air towards them and yelled, "Down!" snapping Liam out of his trance.

As Harris dived to the trench floor he glimpsed, for a split second, the face of a soldier ducking away from where the grenade had been thrown. The grenade exploded as it struck the trench floor and blew apart into small irregular sections of jagged cast-iron that flew upwards and outwards within the margins of the trench. Liam and Aiden were beyond the immediate impact, but Harris was closer. His body took the full impact of the 100 grams of TNT exploding next to him. The crude fragmentation flew in a deadly arc above him, missing his prone body by inches, but the explosion rocked his head, sending a shock wave through his skull.

Liam and Aiden rose and staggered towards Harris who was bleeding from his ears, nose, and multiple small cuts to his face. He was losing consciousness. As Aiden yelled for stretcher-bearers, Harris reached up weakly, his lips moving. Liam knelt down, his ear close to Harris' lips. Men came running up the trench, rifles at the ready, only to find Liam and Aiden crouched over their sergeant, who had lapsed into unconsciousness.

Skaig slunk quickly away from the scene, unnoticed in the general alarm the grenade had caused. The arrival of the two Irishman had been perfectly timed, and he'd smiled maniacally as he'd lobbed the discarded Turkish grenade towards them. His only regret was that he hadn't the opportunity to smash their faces in with his spade, but it had still been a good day. He took solace in knowing if he hadn't managed to kill them all, his cold-blooded revenge had begun, and it tasted good. They'd be another chance—some other place, some other time. Of that, he was certain.

***

Liam and Aiden worked their way slowly back up the trench. Aiden had a sandbag half-full of loose machine gun ammunition over his shoulder they'd gathered up in the old strongpoint. As they approached the section Angus looked up. "Hurry up, you two. Harris will be back soon. You still need to shave and square those uniforms away!"

He was about to look away when something about the two soldiers made him hesitate. He stared at them and realized they were both covered in fresh blood from nicks and cuts. About to ask them what happened, he was stunned when Liam looked up and said, "Sergeant Harris won't be coming back soon, Corporal," before handing over Giles' pistol.

The section listened in silence as Liam and Aiden told them what had happened. Then they were bombarded with questions they couldn't fully answer: No, they hadn't seen who threw the grenade; No, they didn't see any Turks; and No, they didn't know if Harris would live. After a few of these, Angus called a halt to the one-sided question and answer session.

"There's just one thing," said Liam. "Before he lost consciousness, he was trying to say something, repeating it softly, but it didn't make any sense. I'm not even sure I heard right."

"What do you think he was saying?" asked Angus.

"Skaig."

"Skaig? That's impossible, Skaig's doing hard labor in prison back home!"

"I know, I know. We all know that, I'm just saying that's what it sounded like, Corporal," Liam replied with a shrug. "I must have heard wrong."

Angus weighed this up and shook his head. "If he was concussed, even if he did say Skaig, it could mean anything or nothing. We don't have time to dwell on it now."

He looked around and then back at the section. It was obvious that they were rocked by the loss of Harris from their downturned eyes. Harris was the veteran, the one who'd seen it all and done it all. He was the man they'd looked up to for advice and direction, even Second Lieutenant Morley, and now both he and their young officer were gone.

In their place was newly appointed Corporal Angus Rhuairi MacIntyre, and if that daunted him, he wasn't going to let it show.

"I'll tell Color Sergeant Rennie what's happened," he said in an even tone. Then he let his voice rise and directed it towards the section. "In the meantime, we still have our orders. Get those loose bullets into a machine gun belt, and make sure they're clean and folded properly into an ammunition container. Lance Corporal McReynolds, go and talk to the French. The rest of you get shaved and squared away. You have fifteen minutes, and we've just used up five of those being nice, so move it!"

Ten minutes later, the section was as squared away as it could be. They'd manage to salvage half a loaded belt of machine gun ammunition, most of it retrieved from the bunker by Liam and Aiden. Just as Angus appeared, so did Stuart, and behind him came the familiar beaming face of Innocent and a fearsome looking platoon of Senegalese Tirailleurs. They would man the trench to the immediate right and link in with the rest of the French soldiers. In among the tall West Africans moved the diminutive frame of a young man wearing a khaki version of a French Naval Midshipman's uniform. He had red hair and wore round-rimmed spectacles, which he pushed up his nose continuously. When he did so, his nose wrinkled and he showed his front teeth.

He looked about him, muttering continuously about the position being, "*C'est très, très dangereux*—this is very, very dangerous!"

Innocent, in broken English, introduced him as *L'Écureuil*—The Squirrel. Behind him followed two bedraggled and equally nervous naval ratings carrying a reel of telephone wire, a field handset, and various tubes containing charts, maps, and compasses. Before Angus could ask who he was, they heard Color Sergeant Rennie call, "Stand to! Stand to! Fix - bayonets!"

The Turks were attacking again, in force, all along the trench line.

Stuart took his position next to his brother and Liam. It had become a habit. They heard the Color Sergeant's voice cut through the air. "At two hundred yards, ra-pid fire!" and a few seconds later the line exploded into action. The Turks came forward in four great waves of men, throwing themselves against the rapid fire of the trained infantrymen. To their left, they heard a Vickers heavy machine gun burst into action and then light mountain artillery shells began impacting among the attackers, but still, they came on.

At 100 yards, Angus yelled at Liam and then pulled the side-cocking lever to the Turkish maxim. With Liam feeding in the belt of ammunition and swearing non-stop, Angus depressed the triggers. The gun rocked into action, sending out a stream of bullets into the leading ranks of enemy soldiers, mowing them down. It caused bloody mayhem within the attacking enemy ranks. Despite the carnage, they still advanced over the dead and wounded, shouting their battle cries to Allah, trumpets and whistles calling out for men to follow.

As the last beams of the sun faded, it became harder to pick out individual enemy soldiers, and that was exactly what they had planned. To Stuart's right, the maxim gun rattled to a standstill, all too soon out of ammunition. Both Angus and Liam grabbed their rifles to defend their position.

The machine guns, the artillery, and the rifle fire had taken their toll, but the Turks came on until they reached their old trench. As he had done so many times, Stuart felt both primordial fear and anger. He shot a Turk not ten feet away from him, and then braced for the deadly melee that was hand-to-hand combat.

A small wave of surviving Turks crashed into the trench. Stuart bayonetted the first as he leaped down, Stuart's bayonet going clean through his body. The Turk fell screaming to the trench floor. Stuart tugged, but his bayonet remained impaled, so he pulled the trigger and yanked his rifle free at the same time and in one continuous motion he brought the rifle buttplate back into the head of a Turk behind him fighting Ross, felling him instantly. He turned to face a Turk screaming towards him. The Turk's bayonet thrust by him, and then both men were locked together, straining to gain an advantage. The two men were evenly matched. Stuart felt bolts of pain shock through his head wound as he gritted his teeth and with all his might pushed the Turk backward and off balance. He kicked out and twisted and then felt the Turk fall backwards, tripping over a dead body, pulling him forwards as he fell.

Both men landed on the trench floor. Stuart lost the grip on his rifle and tried to strangle the soldier beneath him, but the soldier was strong and frantically fought off Stuart's hands. Desperate to end the struggle, Stuart reached his right hand down to his webbing and drew out the fighting knife Laffite had given him. In the gloom of the trench, the Turk didn't see the danger until it was too late. Stuart plunged the knife into the soldier's chest. The Turk screamed out in pain and alarm and kicked out, but Stuart plunged the knife again and again into his chest, yelling for him to die, screaming with all the anger and violence within him until he heard Ross calling his name.

"He's dead, Stuart. They're all dead," and he felt his brother's hand close more tightly on his own to still it.

Stuart was gently pulled to his feet. His right hand was slick with blood and his face was spattered with it. As he stood there he began to shake. Tears rolled down his face, clearing a trail through the blood and grime. "Haven't they had enough?" he pleaded. "How long can this go on? How many men do we have to kill for this to end?"

Ross took the knife out of his hands and drew his brother close. He wrapped an arm around his shoulders, feeling his brother's heart pounding through his chest. "I don't know, big brother. I honestly don't know."

If the enemy knew the answer, it didn't show. The Turks came twice more in the middle of the night. Aiden heard or sensed them both times, giving the men precious seconds to blast away into the darkness. The night fighting terrified Stuart. In the dark he couldn't tell friend from foe, and the fighting was chaotic, random, and vicious. On the second attack, Innocent and the Senegalese swept through their position with their dreaded *coup coup* fighting machetes, spreading blind terror among the Turks who retreated back out into the night. None of them slept. Stuart found himself willing the coming of the sun to end the darkness engulfing them.

As the first rays of dawn brightened the sky, the section slowly shuffled into position yet again and shared their last few precious drops of water. They looked out over a sea of dead bodies, torn apart and grotesque. Beyond them, they heard the trumpets blare and the cries of 'Allah!' and 'Allahu akbar' emerged into the still of the morning air.

"Stand to! Stand to!" cried the hoarse voice of Color Sergeant Rennie. The handful of Seaforths picked themselves up wearily to face the attacking enemy yet again. Stuart watched as waves of Turkish soldiers came into view. He felt his heart sink as he slowly worked his rifle's bolt to chamber a round into the breach. He was exhausted—they all were. They'd watched their friends die in front of their eyes and hadn't slept for the best part of two days. They'd run out of water and were precariously low on ammunition. The Turks had been fought to a standstill again and again, and yet they still came, willing to die rather than to have foreign invaders from the sea stay on their soil.

At 300 yards, the order went out for rapid fire. In the clear morning light, the Turks seemed closer than that, and behind them came fresh waves of men.

"Sweet Jesus," muttered Liam, firing over the lip of the trench. "There's just too many of the feckin bastards this time," he said with resignation. He quickly crossed himself while whispering, "Holy Mary, Mother of God, pray for us sinners, now and at the hour of our death."

Stuart fired his rifle slowly and deliberately, making each shot count. He was aware their rifle fire was having little effect, and it was already weakening along the line. They were all running out of ammunition.

"Fix-bayonets! Stand fast! Hold the line!" ordered Angus, empty rifle in one hand, Giles' pistol in the other. The desperation in his voice betrayed the fact that there weren't enough of them left. They could stand fast—and they would—but they couldn't repel another mass attack. The section could only die where they stood, exhausted, battered yet defiant to the end.

As a flare gun fired into the air behind him, Stuart raised his rifle and fired, again and again, reloading until his firing pin clicked on an empty chamber. He had no more bullets. Beside him, rifles slowly fell silent as they all finally ran out of rounds. He reached down, drew out his bayonet as another flare burst above him, and attached it to his rifle one last time.

He looked over at his brother next to him, "Together?"

Ross smiled despite the men charging towards them, raised his rifle with bayonet, and nodded, "Together."

The two brothers stood side by side and faced the charging enemy, ready to sell their lives as dearly as they could. Angus and Murdo paired off for mutual defense, as did Liam and Aiden, both shielding Seamus, who gripped his Luger in one hand with grim determination. Stuart thought of Nell so far away, her green eyes, upturned button nose, her smile, and how he loved her so very much. He wondered how much it would hurt—the dying—when the Turkish bayonets finally found their mark.

He gripped his rifle tightly and set his jaw, reciting Connor's battle prayer as he did so, "Defend us in battle, be our protection." Suddenly the air was rent in half by the screaming of a single incoming shell: not a light mountain artillery shell, but the deafening roar of a naval super-heavy caliber shell literally ripping the air apart.

The Squirrel was a French naval forward observer liaison officer. Throughout the night, he had plotted positions by torchlight under a canvas, muttering to himself and repeating precise instructions down the field telephone. By morning, he had fire-grids plotted and had pre-registered flare signals with the French offshore naval artillery support. It was all a question of geometry to him.

Despite the dangers, the French Navy had ordered one of its heavy battleships to steam overnight to provide infantry support. The Squirrel's offshore support came in the shape of the four-hundred-foot-long Charlemagne-class battleship *Saint Louis*. It had fired one of her four massive twelve-inch caliber, 48-ton guns, sending a shrapnel shell weighing 800 pounds into the air. It took the shell over seven seconds to reach Kereves Spur. It was so large it could be seen with the naked eye as it arced through the air over the peninsula.

Stuart instinctively recoiled back in fear as the shell screamed towards them and then exploded in midair, sending out eighteen thousand shrapnel balls into the tightly packed enemy soldiers. He gasped in shock and awe at the sheer overwhelming naked violence of it. The attacking Turks in front of them were obliterated in a gigantic maelstrom of steel balls that wounded, dismembered, or killed everyone in its path.

The surviving Turks stopped in their tracks, unable to comprehend the devastation as the *Saint Louis*, range confirmed by yet another flare arcing skywards, fired another shell with the same shattering effect. The ship's gunnery officer ordered her secondary five-and-a-half-inch guns to open up with high-explosive rounds. Then the *Saint Louis'* remaining twin twelve-inch guns joined in, firing the heavy-caliber shrapnel shells in unison, repeated within seconds by the first two guns. The massive guns took it in turns to rain their shells down onto the enemy soldiers, the gigantic twin explosions annihilating the Turkish attack in its tracks with lethal efficiency.

CHAPTER EIGHTEEN

Homeward

Cape Helles
Gallipoli, July 1915

Their proximity to both the French and to the Squirrel had saved the section. They had benefitted from both the French naval barrage and the acute self-preservation instinct within the Squirrel that made sure the area of most threat to him personally was swept clear of attackers first. As the smell of cordite hung in the air, Stuart and Ross looked out over the battlefield, strewn with the dead and dying. Enemy soldiers here and there were trying to make their way back to their own lines, limping, crawling, or being helped by their fellow soldiers. A few even crawled towards them, seeking shelter and safety, their rifles discarded. No one fired at them. They didn't have any bullets, and there was an unspoken agreement that anyone who had survived the naval bombardment deserved to live.

Stuart watched a finch flitter through the smoke and wondered how it had survived, where it had come from, and what nature made of the destruction wrought upon the land. The quietness that had descended upon the battlefield didn't last for long. Far off to their left, the British field artillery opened up, and a wave of soldiers emerged from the British rear trenches.

Despite being crippled from previous battles, the Royal Marine Light Infantry had been ordered to reinforce the line. The order had only reached two of three brigades, however, and no one had pointed out that at least one communications trench now existed between the old British frontline and the newly captured trenches. Instead of working their way up slowly but safely to the front, the marines charged over the old no man's land in full view of the Turks, who unleashed their artillery upon them.

"What in feck are they doing?" asked Liam. "Aiden and I saw men come up through a narrow comms trench. Why are they charging over the open ground?" If there was an answer, it was drowned out as the Turkish artillery poured high explosives and shrapnel down upon the naval infantrymen, who ran through the storm of artillery to reach the lines held by the light infantry and the borderers. And then they continued to advance.

Stuart looked on in horror and dismay as marines ran forward in search of the third trench. A trench that didn't exist, or at best was 12-inches deep and completely exposed to enemy fire. The section looked on in silence, too tired to say anything, too numb to be outraged anymore, already too used to the utter waste of men. They watched as the now-familiar scene repeated itself for a third time, and men were shelled and machine gunned until they eventually retreated.

"Poor sods," someone muttered. Angus broke the air of despondency, his throat parched, his voice croaky.

"All right; listen up. In case none of you have noticed, the Squirrel has scampered off. Unless you want to repel the next attack with well-aimed bad language, let me point out that we need rifle ammunition and water. Ammunition is the priority, so find some. Check webbing. You know the drill by now. The dead won't mind, but if you come back empty handed, I will. I want this trench squared away. You have ten minutes. After that, I want weapons cleaned. In the meantime, if any of you can find me a cup of tea, milk two sugars, I'll give you McReynold's stripe off his sleeve." The men smiled at the joke. It wasn't a good one or new, but it felt normal, and they broke into pairs to search for ammunition. As they gathered to distribute the few rounds they had, a familiar voice came from behind them.

"Ah, there you are." The men turned in surprise to see Major Sinclair holding a heavy-looking sandbag. He looked about him and then towards Angus. "Report."

Angus stood to attention. "Sir, we hold this section of trench. The French are beyond us. Color Sergeant Rennie and his men are back down the trench—you'll have passed through them. The enemy keeps coming at us, but we've held them so far; it's been a very close thing at times. We've only a few rounds left, and we're out of water and food. We have a captured Turkish maxim, but the crew is dead, and we have no ammunition left for it. The men haven't slept in two days. Our orders are to hold until relieved, sir."

As Sinclair listened to Angus, he looked about him and frowned. "Casualties?"

"Five, sir. One dead: Private Connor O'Connell; and two wounded: Lieutenant Morley and Sergeant Harris. The stretcher-bearers took them away. Lance Corporal McReynolds and Private Seamus O'Connell are both wounded but refuse to leave, sir."

Sinclair nodded, taking in the bad news. "Very well. Thank you, Corporal. At ease, please." He stared at the battlefield surrounding them and at the handful of men standing in front of him, noting the bloodied bandages on Stuart and Seamus. It was evident that they had all fought hard, and were close to being on their knees.

"I came up to see what was happening with my own eyes. There have been some conflicting reports regarding the third trench." He looked questioningly at Angus.

"It doesn't exist, sir," he said.

"It's on the maps, Corporal," countered Sinclair.

Angus tried to clear his dry throat. "It's not there, sir," he said, nodding his head towards the Turkish lines. "We've been out there. We found a trench a foot deep, incomplete and un-defendable, so Lieutenant Morley ordered us to re-treat back here, sir."

Sinclair pursed his lips as he digested the information. "And the attempts by the borderers, the light infantry, and the marines to find it?"

Angus didn't know what to say, so in the end, he shrugged his shoulders and said, "The Turkish artillery and machine guns had a field day, sir."

Sinclair's shoulders dropped. "I see, I see." He looked about and then up at Achi Baba rising above them. "I must tell Major General Egerton what's happened. He needs to be told. I've already seen enough." He swung the heavy sandbag towards Angus who caught it. "Share those out, Corporal. Hold until relieved as ordered, but be ready to go on my word."

"Yes, sir."

Sinclair turned and disappeared back down the trench. Angus looked inside the bag and saw clips of ammunition, four full water bottles, two packs of hard biscuits, and a tin of apricot jam. He handed out one bottle and let everyone take two large gulps. He handed a full bottle to Murdo and asked him to give it to Color Sergeant Rennie with the major's compliments. Then he gave one to Stuart to give to Innocent and his men. "They saved our arses last night. It's the least we can do." They drank the rest of the open bottle and shared out the biscuits and jam, hardly stopping to wave away the flies that returned each morning with the sun. The last bottle they kept for later—as Angus pointed out, they could be here for a long time.

Three hours later Color Sergeant Rennie and his men came to take over their position.

"The entire line is shifting to the left. The French will take this trench over, and we'll hold until then. Take your men and go, Corporal."

Angus looked at his section, beaten and battered, but not broken, and then at Rennie. "If it's all the same to you, Color Sergeant, we'll stay and go back together." He looked behind the senior non-commissioned officer to see six shattered men. "If you don't mind me saying it, your men look no better than mine, Color Sergeant."

Rennie looked at Angus and smiled. "If my men look like yours, you'd best stay."

An hour later, a French lieutenant came down the trench with a platoon of soldiers, and in halting English, relieved them of their post. Innocent and Lafitte were gone. Stuart wondered if they would ever meet them again, and if so, where.

Angus followed Rennie down the line, past men as exhausted, thirsty, and tired as they were. He wondered how long they'd have to hold their position. Where the trench hadn't been cleared, they walked on a carpet of dead bodies. At the old strongpoint, they slung their weapons on their backs and retrieved Connor's body, trying to ignore his blackened face and the smell. With Rennie clearing a path, they made their way back along the trench. At a traverse, they cut down the comms trench, towards the rear, away from the stench of no man's land, away from the fear and rage of the battle.

At the rear support trench, they parted from Rennie and his handful of surviving men. He shook their hands and wished them well, saying they could fight alongside the Royal Scots any time they wanted. Coming from a color sergeant in the oldest, most senior infantry regiment of the line in the British Army, it was meant as high praise and it was taken as such.

An hour later, they were back at their billet, a copse of scraggly pines with a small campfire in the middle. Angus went to find Major Sinclair to report their return as the men collapsed and passed around the last water bottle. Angus returned to say they should be ready to move at six, and until then, they had permission to bury Connor. With the sun rising higher in the sky, and the heat rising with it, the section staggered to their feet and shared the heavy burden between them, Angus carrying four spades.

It took a long time to dig the grave into the hard-baked ground, toiling under the sun, stripped to their waists, each taking a turn. Those that weren't digging helped fashion a cross, and then they lowered Connor into the soil of Gallipoli beside his older brother. Reversing the normal burial ceremony, they covered the body quickly, filling the grave first to avoid the flies and smell. They planted the cross and lowered their heads as Seamus stepped forward, holding his pierced bible in one hand.

He glanced at his friends. "I wish Father Foley were here. He'd know what to say and do, but here's something I wrote down." He pulled a scrap of paper from the bible and took a deep breath before continuing, looking down at the grave of his best friend.

"You're in the shade now, a good place to be, away from the flies, the heat, the dust, the pain. We can mourn you and we will, but we'll also remember you with a smile and a laugh. This hard-unyielding ground may not be the rich soil of home, but it's now made richer for you resting in it. Your fighting is over, you're in the shade now; a good place to be." He paused, unsure what to say next. Then he remembered a line from an old Irish blessing and added, "Until we meet again, may God hold you in the hollow of his hand."

He stooped and gathered a handful of loose soil and threw it over the grave, and one by one they all did the same. Stuart looked out over the blue Aegean Sea. It was so calm and turquoise, such a beautiful place to be. In the distance, he could hear gunfire and around him, he was surrounded by graves, countless rows of them. As they left, he noticed the mass grave he had seen just two days before was now full and already covered over. Stuart took one look back and wondered what McAvoy would think when he saw the fresh grave and realized who was buried there.

They spent the rest of the afternoon washing themselves and their clothes in the sea. They drank from a tepid water container by the stores' tent, stuffing their pouches with ammunition and then stripping and cleaning their rifles. By two, the sun became so hot Angus let them rest in the partial shade and sleep. He soon joined them himself, unable to stay awake. At six o'clock, Stuart felt something licking his face and opened his eyes to see Lucky and Major Sinclair standing above him. He jumped up muttering apologies as the rest of the section awoke from their sleep. Once conscious and standing, Sinclair told them to stand at ease. He had some news.

"First, Lieutenant Morley and Sergeant Harris have both been evacuated. I'm assured they will be well taken care of. Both of them are on a hospital ship to Malta as I speak, which is good news."

"Second, Major General Egerton is not best pleased with the use of his men. He has taken the matter up with Lieutenant General Hunter-Weston and General Sir Ian Hamilton. Whatever the outcome, the fact remains that the entire Scottish 52nd Lowland Division has now lost half its strength within days of landing. I suspect there is little he can do. As more reinforcements are now confirmed as being on their way and will arrive within days, he has made a small gesture, which is why I'm telling you this." He paused before continuing.

"As of immediate effect, we are released back to the 51st Highland Division. As such, we are free to leave Gallipoli, and he suggests we do so before someone interferes. He also adds his formal thanks for your service, which he described as exemplary. It's a judgment I fully endorse."

The section looked at each other in disbelief. "We're leaving, sir?" asked Liam.

Sinclair smiled. "Yes, we are, Private. Enough talk; pack up and be ready to move when I come back."

Lucky ran from man to man, looking for Connor, but Connor was no longer there to ruffle his ears and pat his back. In the end, the small dog sat and whined until Sinclair called him.

"I think he's really yours now, sir," said Seamus.

Sinclair reached down and patted the dog, who wagged his bum enthusiastically. "I'll take good care of him. I promise."

An hour later, Sinclair and Lucky returned with a brown envelope which he handed to Angus. "These are your orders to embark for Lemnos. Give these to the officer in charge of transportation. I'll meet you at the transit camp in Lemnos. I have to tie up a few loose ends for the general and will leave tomorrow. Keep out of trouble. Keep your heads low, and in two days' time we'll all be on a ship back to Britain." He looked at Stuart and Seamus. "You two, get a pretty nurse to look at those wounds. Actually, better still, get two pretty nurses to look at those wounds."

"Yes, sir," Stuart said with a smile as he looked over at Seamus. Seamus turned to his brother and grinned.

They were leaving Gallipoli with its flies and stench of death. Stuart's mind filled with thoughts of cold sea breezes, fresh bread slathered in fresh butter, food that didn't slop out of a tin can, and drinks with ice in them, lots of ice, lots and lots of ice. Then his heart leaped as he thought of seeing Nell again, and holding her close, touching her face and feeling the brush of her lips, the warmth of her touch, before he realized Sinclair was still talking.

"...and all of you, tomorrow, get a hot bath with lots of soap and clean those uniforms *properly*. You're going home."

***

Captain Campbell-Greenwood's dreams of assisting generals with their battle plans, conferring with them over predinner drinks and post-dinner port, before being swiftly promoted to aide-de-camp had been short-lived. Within hours of overseeing the awarding of medals, he had been offered the opportunity by a Major Sinclair to become transportation liaison officer for the lowland division. It had been offered so politely, and in such complimentary terms, that he hadn't realized he was being demoted to a tent on a beach strewn with rubbish and raw sewage from a latrine over-hanging the water until he was there.

His job was menial. He was to oversee troop movements out of 'Lancashire Landing,' as it was called after the fusiliers who had died assaulting the beach. When troops presented orders to his single aide, a corporal, he simply had to approve the corporal's choice of transportation and rubber stamp it. The choice of destinations was limited to three options: Imbros for rest and recreation; Lemnos for hospitalization or transportation on to Britain; and Anzac Cove further up the coast for inter-theatre troop movements. The third choice was proving busy, and rumor had it there was to be a big push in the predominantly Australian and New Zealand sector.

It took them two hours to reach the beach and find the correct tent. Transportation was all carried out at night under the cover of darkness. The light was already fading when Angus stepped into the tent, the section behind him. The transportation corporal sat behind a large field desk, separated from the rear of the tent by a half-curtain of canvas. Behind that Campbell-Greenwood was busy writing a letter to connections back in Britain to seek another posting when he heard his corporal say, "Seaforth Highlanders? I didn't know there were any Seaforths here."

"Well, we won't be soon!" said Angus with a laugh.

The corporal laughed along and content that the orders were genuine, looked up the next transport leaving for Lemnos, took their names and told them to come back in half an hour for their transportation tickets. He put the paperwork in an open brown envelope and walked it back to his new transportation officer for rubber stamping. "Seven men for Lemnos, sir, with orders for onward travel home."

"Thank you, Corporal. Why don't you take a ten-minute break before it gets busy, and I'll sort these out."

Not wanting to miss the opportunity for a cigarette, the surprised corporal muttered his thanks and disappeared, leaving Campbell-Greenwood alone. He worked fast. If he was rotting in some sewage strewn beach, he wasn't going to let the perceived source of his downfall leave if he could help it.

It was an easy matter. He removed the seven chits marked "Transport Lemnos, Dock A, 9 pm" and replaced them with seven others. Then he ripped their orders into pieces and threw them into the waste bucket. He sealed the envelope, scribbling 'Priority' on the outside and then stamped it. He then placed it on the corporal's desk, making sure the corporal's ledger still read 'Lemnos' as the destination next to the last seven names. On paper, that's where it would look like they went, and just as importantly, the corporal or the navy would shoulder the blame if none of the men arrived.

Stuart and Ross upturned their water bottles, swallowing the water in great gulps before swilling out their mouths and spitting out the grime, the stench and the blood of Gallipoli. They were sitting on the hard-baked earth overlooking Lancaster Landing.

"It's hard to believe we're actually leaving," said Stuart as he looked over at his brother.

"I know. It seems we've been here for ages. I feel sorry for the poor buggers that have to stay here, I really do." Ross replied, swatting the air.

Stuart smiled. "And I won't miss the bloody flies!"

"What do you want to do when we get back?"

Stuart closed his eyes and thought for a few seconds before replying. "Drink the tallest, coldest beer I can find. When the beer's so cold, condensation runs down the glass onto your fingers."

His brother groaned. "Ice cold lager. That would be a good start. I can just about feel the glass in my hand. Licking that mustache of foam away. God, that sounds good. You get the first round; I'll get the second."

Stuart laughed. "And a T-bone steak, medium-rare, pink in the middle, the biggest they have, with a dollop of mustard."

"Red wine?"

"A bottle each," agreed Stuart.

"Salad?"

"Maybe, or maybe just more red wine."

Ross chuckled. "And the girls?"

Stuart's heart jumped as he thought of Nell and imagined her smile and the gentle touch of her hand. "Yes, and the girls. Do you think Jo and Nell would drink beer?"

"I think they just might. Finding it cold enough would be the task."

Stuart looked over at his brother. "Let's do it. I mean it. Let's go to Edinburgh again, the four of us, and find a nice place that serves steak, cold beer, and red wine. Not too fancy, somewhere we can relax and laugh out loud. There has to be one somewhere."

Ross nodded, smiling at the thought of it. "That sounds like a good plan."

"And we want to come too!" said a voice behind them and they looked up to see Liam, Seamus, Aiden, and Murdo.

"And what would you order, Liam?" asked Stuart with a smile.

"Well, one of those feckin tall cold beers would be good for a start!" and they all laughed. "But then cured ham and cabbage."

"With champ," added Aiden. "A big mound of it," he said, referring to the traditional Irish dish of mashed potatoes, spring onions, butter, and milk.

"With colcannon," argued Seamus, referring to the equally traditional dish of mashed potatoes, kale, and butter.

"Aren't they the same thing?" asked Ross.

The three Irishmen looked at him in abject horror. "Now you may know a few things we don't," declared Liam solemnly, "but when it comes to potatoes, we're the experts."

Ross made a show of raising his hands in surrender.

"And a pint of Guinness XX, with soda bread," added Aiden.

"Now that's a good idea," declared Liam. "Maybe a couple of pints," he suggested, as if they'd never drunk more than one pint at a time in their lives.

"And what about you, Murdo?" asked Stuart.

Murdo sat silent for a while, and then asked, "Anything?"

"Anything you want, Murdo. It's all on the menu!" confirmed Stuart.

Murdo sat for a while, and then began to speak softly. "Well, there's this place back home, it's a barn really, we call it the cookhouse. It's run all by women, always smiling and joking with you, flirting with the men, calling everyone *honey*. They're always moving about, making sure you have what you need, serving the food. You sit at on long benches, next to each other, and when the table has enough folk, they bring out the food."

"What do they serve?" asked Seamus, envisioning the section all sitting down waiting to eat.

"Pancakes," Murdo said with a smile. "Huge stacks of golden buckwheat pancakes, each as big as a dinner plate. They just place them in the middle of the table, and you help yourselves. They're served with glass pitchers of maple syrup and freshly churned butter. They make it all themselves. The syrup is thick and rich and sweet and makes everything slide down and stick to your ribs. And when they're all gone, they just bring along another stack, until your sides and belly ache, and you can't eat no more. In late summer, they sometimes add blueberries to the batter. And pots of coffee, rich, fresh ground, and roasted. The women just walk about with a steaming pot, topping up your mug with a smile whenever it gets low." Murdo stared into the distance, licking his lips slowly.

"Did I mention the bacon?" he asked.

"No" replied Stuart in a hushed voice, his stomach rumbling.

"Their bacon is the simply the best," declared Murdo. "Sweet cured Canadian bacon, thick cut, slowly fried until it's browned and crisp. Like the pancakes, they just bring a big heaping plate of it and when it's gone, they bring some more."

Murdo raised his head, inhaling imagined aromas from far across the sea. "It's the smell of it all—the freshly made pancakes, the sweet maple syrup, the coffee brewing, thick bacon frying." He smiled and turned to his friends, who were all staring at him, entranced. "That's what I'd like to eat, and where I'd like to be."

The section sat, each lost in the wonderful vision of Murdo's cookhouse until Liam broke the silence.

"Well, that's it, we're all going home with you to Canada. And we're all going to eat those pancakes until the benches collapse beneath us. They'll have to pour some of that syrup all over us just to push us out the door!"

After a while, Angus gathered up his section and they returned to get their travel orders. The corporal handed him the sealed envelope. "Give this to the naval petty officer by the docks, he'll point you in the right direction," he said before turning to deal with an ever-increasing queue of soldiers.

It was almost dark when the section reached the makeshift docks and Angus gave the envelope to a bearded petty officer. It was the same bearded petty officer who had greeted them a few weeks ago. He tore the envelope open, took out the seven tickets inside, and then pointed to a small wooden dock built out into the sea, one of three. "Dock C, the transport is ready to go. You're late, run for it!" he roared, muttering, "Bloody colonials" before turning to the next group of soldiers approaching the docks.

Angus was about to point out that it wasn't even 9 pm and they weren't 'Bloody colonials,' but thought better of it.

The petty officer wasn't in a good mood. He wondered if he ever was.

"Follow me!" he shouted, and the section stayed close behind him and they ran for the third dock. They reached the transport just as sailors were beginning to haul in the gangplank; it consisted of a steam-powered pinnacle towing two tenders. The midshipman in charge hurried them towards the last tender cheerfully saying, "Better late than never, as I always say gentlemen. Although my father would always reply—better never late!" and he gave the order to cast off.

"G'day mates," said a deep Australian voice in the dark, "Light horse?"

Another voice came from behind, "Nah, mate, Kiwis for sure—they were holding hands and skipping when they came onboard!" and the men around them burst into laughter.

"Well, mate, what are you?"

"Highlanders," answered Angus hesitantly.

"I told you they were Kiwis!" declared the Australian.

"No, we're Seaforth Highlanders, 51st Highland Division," protested Angus.

"They're Scottish! Blimey, between them and the Kiwis, the sheep won't stand a chance!" and the boat around erupted into laughter again, even from the out-numbered New Zealand troops.

"Did someone say Seaforth Highlanders?" asked a voice from the back once the laughter had died back down.

"Yes," replied Angus.

"Out of the way, mates, I think I know these blokes," came a vaguely familiar voice from among a small group of New Zealand Mounted Infantry troopers halfway down the tender. One of the troopers came forward slowly through the darkened crowd, as the small steam pinnacle began to tow its pair of tenders offshore, the waves gently rocking the boat filled with soldiers.

"One of you isn't a bloody big bloke named Murdo is he?"

"Yes," replied Angus in amazement.

"Stone the crows, mates, I know these blokes, stood on the firing line with them on their first day here!"

It was Stuart who recognized the voice first, "Sunny Jim?"

"That's me, mate," the trooper said, coming forward to shake his hand. "What are you doing here, and why are you wearing slouch hats?"

"We're going home," replied Stuart with a big grin, feeling his head and removing the slouch hat, identical to the ones the Anzac troopers were wearing.

"Home? What are talking about, mate?" asked Sunny Jim with a hint of confusion his voice.

"We're going to Lemnos, then home," explained Stuart, the first clouds of doubt forming in his head.

Sunny Jim shook his head, "We've just come from Lemnos, most of us from the hospital there."

"Just come from Lemnos?" echoed Ross, the rest of the section crowding in. "But that's where this boat is going. That's where we have orders to go."

"Then you're on the wrong boat, Corp."

"The wrong boat?" repeated Angus in alarm. "But we have orders," and he searched in his tunic before realizing the envelope had disappeared back at the dock.

"Where's this boat going?" asked Stuart, but even as he asked it, he knew the answer. They were on a boat-load of Australians and New Zealanders, looking like them with their slouch hats still on. There could only be one destination.

"We're going to Anzac Cove, mate, for the big push, and by the looks of it, so are you," said Sunny Jim.

Stuart and Ross stared at each other in stunned silence.

"But we had orders—we're done with Gallipoli," said Stuart, a hint of desperation in his voice as thoughts of home, and Nell disappeared before his eyes.

Sunny Jim looked at the section with a touch of sympathy. There were fewer of them than he remembered, and no sign of their veteran sergeant. They were weathered and battered, their uniforms sun-bleached and torn, their features gaunt and tanned, bloodied bandages evidence of wounds and hand-to-hand fighting.

"Well, we're glad to have you with us, but I'm sorry mate—you may be done with Gallipoli, but I don't think Gallipoli is done with you."

Poet and Soldier,
could your land forget?
For you each morning
shall her fields be wet.

—*For Francis Ledwidge* (Killed in action, July 31, 1917),
Norreys Jephson O'Conor

Author's Notes

The sinking of the RMS *Lusitania* in May 1915 is still shrouded in controversy. At the time she was portrayed as an innocent victim of U-boat warfare, but subsequently it was shown she was carrying some munitions, and as a Royal Mail Ship (RMS), would be requisitioned by the government in time of war, making her a legitimate target, at least in the eyes of the German submariners. Recent research carried out by the High Explosives Applications Facility at the Lawrence Livermore National Laboratory in California on the likely cause of the violent second explosion pointed to a boiler explosion and ruled out gun-cotton, aluminum powder, or coal dust. Reports from survivors conflicted, with some claiming to have seen a U-boat surface and then move away, while others saw nothing.

The speed at which the Lusitania sank—just 18 minutes—lends its own tragedy to the event, and just as happens in the novel, there were eyewitness accounts of folk trapped forever in the elevators as the electrical power quickly failed. Many of those that survived owed their lives to the Irish fisherman who came to their rescue, including volunteer lifeboats rowed out from Courtmacsherry and Queenstown. Given the hundreds of people that went down with the ship, it disturbed me to read during my research that the wreck was regularly depth-charged by the U.S. Navy and the Royal Navy during World War II, ironically during anti-submarine practice. The Irish authorities have since listed the wreck as a protected heritage site.

The sinking of the Lusitania horrified a public unused to submarine warfare. Pre-war attempts to impose civilized rules upon submarine attacks had created 'prize rules' that obliged attacking submarines to halt and search a vessel before destroying it. It also imposed a duty of care upon the submarine captains to assure crews were allowed not only to abandon ship, but also to tow them to a relative place of safety. These prize rules were largely ignored when Germany announced its unrestricted submarine warfare early in 1915. The rules did continue in isolated instances until World War II, when following a deliberate allied attack by American bombers upon a U-boat towing survivors from RMS *Laconia* and openly broadcasting its humanitarian intent, Grand Admiral Karl Donitz issued the Laconia Order in 1942. It strictly forbade any further magnanimous gestures by his U-boat captains, stating that, "Rescue contradicts the most basic demands of the war: the destruction of hostile ships and their crews."

The sinking of the *Lusitania* moved public opinion in the United States away from their government's neutral stance towards the cause of the allies, which was not a forgone conclusion, given the high number of German and Austrian immigrants within the United States. In its aftermath, many Americans volunteered to join the American Ambulance Field Service, or, like Ernest Hemmingway, the American Red Cross. Pilots formed the American volunteer fighter squadron *Escadrille Lafayette,* and the larger, but less well known *Lafayette Flying Corps.* American volunteers living in France, who were initially banned from joining the French Army, instead were welcomed into the 2nd and 3rd Regiments de Marche of the French Foreign Legion.

For many Americans eager to fight for the allies, the easiest route to volunteer was by crossing their northern border to Canada, who openly recruited for the Canadian Army's *American Legion* despite the U.S. Government's neutral stance—American volunteers broke U.S. Penal Codes by enlisting in a foreign army and could have theoretically lost their citizenship. According to Chris Dickon in *Americans at War in Foreign Forces* (2014), 35,612 American-born citizens served in the Canadian Expeditionary Force. There they would serve until joined by the American Expeditionary Force in mid-1917. By the end of the war, an estimated 57,000 American residents served in the Canadian Forces.

This number includes British citizens living in America at the time (Richard Holt, *British Blood Calls British Blood*, Canadian Military History, Vol 22, Issue 1, 2015). In most cases, those killed in action would have been buried in British military commonwealth graves marked as Canadians, not as Americans.

Like Stuart and his brother Ross, thousands of Americans served in the British Army during World War I. "Great Britain attracted the largest number of volunteers, with tens of thousands of Americans serving in the British infantry or flying corps." (*The Volunteers, Americans join WWI 1914-1918*, AFS Intercultural Programs, 2016). Many survivors wrote books about their experiences, and have been republished: *Over the Top* (2017), by Arthur Guy Empey, who travelled to Britain and joined its army as a direct result of the sinking of the *Lusitania*; *A Yankee in the Trenches* (2017), by R Derby Holmes; *My Fourteen Months at the Front* (2018), by William Robinson; *Kitchener's Mob; the Adventures of an American in the British Army* (2018), by James Norman Hall; and *Shellproof Mack* (2018), by Arthur Mack—to name a few. Many served in the British Army's Scottish regiments (*Over There and Back, In Three Uniforms* (2018), by Joseph S Smith).

Americans who travelled to Britain were often first or second-generation Anglo, Welsh, or Scots-Americans, with close ties to their homeland. French, Polish, and Italian-Americans joined their respective homeland armies for the same reason. Many of the 8,282,618 Americans of German descent also returned to their homeland, but there's confusion over the matter. For instance, one source from the U.S. National Archives claims, "Relatively few Germans returned to their European homeland because their home now was America." Other sources talk of German-Americans joining the American forces to demonstrate their loyalty, and many German-Americans suffered persecution in America during the war. Contrasting with this, the U.S. National Parks Service quotes *500,000* German-Americans leaving the United States to enlist in Germany in their article found at www.nps.gov/articles/immigrants-in-the-military-during-wwi. This stance is backed up by David Laskin in his article *Ethnic Minorities at War (USA)* who states, "Young German-American men flooded the German Embassy in Washington with requests to be shipped back 'home' so they could join their co-nationals at the front." It's a fascinating subject, and would make a great research project.

According to Professor Keith Jeffery (*Ireland and The Great War,* in *The Irish Times*, August 2, 2014), at the outbreak of the war 28,000 Irishmen were serving in the British Army's Irish regiments and 30,000 reservists were called up to join them; an additional 148,000 men volunteered to fight in the conflict—there was no conscription in Ireland. Irishmen also served in military units from throughout the British Empire and later on, the United States. Many of these overseas units had Irish titles or affinities such as the London Irish Rifles, the Irish Canadian Rangers, the Irish Fusiliers of Canada, the South African Irish Regiment, and New York's "Fighting Sixty-Ninth." Although Victorian-era 'Irish Rifle' units existed in Australia and New Zealand, they lost their Irish titles by the outbreak of World War I.

Initially, Irish nationalists, unionists, and the all-pervading Catholic Church unanimously supported the call for volunteers for varying reasons, so Irishmen joined up by the tens of thousands. The wounded and the survivors soon returned to a completely changed country which was openly hostile to their service, and they were subsequently brushed-stroked out of Irish history, an inconvenient truth at odds with Irish nationalism both at home and abroad. Ireland's beautiful national war memorial at Islandbridge, Dublin, lay neglected and abused for decades—apparently the site was used as a rubbish dump in the 1970s by the city's refuse disposal office. It wasn't officially restored and dedicated until 1988. The first official Irish state memorial service for the estimated 49,000 Irishmen who died during World War I didn't take place until the 90th Anniversary of the Battle of the Somme, in 2006.

In 1707, the armies of Scotland and England amalgamated to create the British Army, serving under a combined flag—the Union Jack. As a result, if Ireland struggled to come to terms with military service in the British Forces, its Celtic cousin Scotland embraced it wholeheartedly. "Stern-faced 'Kiltie soldiers' came to dominate the Victorian Army, both in its Regular and Volunteer variants. Aside from a regular wage, aside from satisfying the old Highland love of fighting, the Army's regimental structure offered an acceptable substitute for the tight-knittedness of tribal life. Regiments were truly 'clannish.'"

There was something else: Swirling tartan kilts and skirling bagpipes also achieved the bleedin' obvious. Militarily, they looked fantastic. No one who saw a Scottish regiment on the march or on the attack was anything but moved. Or awed. (John Lewis-Stempel, *Scotland the Brave: Tough 'kilties' battled for Britain in WWI,* The Daily Express, March 23rd, 2014).

In many ways, Lewis-Stempel hits the nail on the head with his newspaper article. In Scotland ,it was a source of pride to be a soldier and always had been, as he goes on to explain: "...north of the Border, Caledonia way, soldiering was an honourable occupation. In Victorian England, soldiering was the male equivalent of street-walking." Thus, when the call to arms came in 1914, Scottish regiments were flooded with volunteers. During the war, 143 Scottish battalions were raised, and 557,618 men and women joined those Scots already in uniform.

Anglo-Scottish regiments based in England—the Scots Guards, the London Scottish, and the Liverpool Scottish all saw their numbers swell. To accommodate demand, new battalions were raised—the Manchester Scottish and the Tyneside Scottish. This pattern was repeated throughout the British Empire, with Scots or Scottish descendants joining the allied forces. Many of them served in Scottish-badged regiments in Canada (14 still exist), South Africa, India, Australia, and New Zealand. Their regimental names proudly declared their heritage: the Nova Scotia Highlanders, the Canadian Scottish Borderers, the Pictou Highlanders, the Transvaal Scottish, the Cape Town Highlanders, the Calcutta Scottish Volunteers, the South Australian Scottish, and my personal favorite, the Wanganui Highland Rifles to name a few (they were amalgamated just before the war, but I just like saying 'Wanganui'). They even included half a battalion of Scots-Americans recruited into Canada's 236th New Brunswick Kilties, also known as the MacLean Kilties of America—'Sir Sam's Own,' or simply, the MacLean Highlanders (I have a strong premonition we'll meet them in future novels...).

But Scotland's rush to war came at a heavy price. An estimated 147,609 soldiers died in the war, one fifth of the British Army's casualties, despite Scotland only accounting for one tenth of Britain's population. The disproportionate casualty rate was a result of enthusiastic self-inflicted over-representation in Britain's armed forces. It also reflects the opinion of Professor Tom Devine, historian and director of the Centre for Irish and Scottish Studies at Aberdeen University, that Scottish soldiers had built up such a fierce reputation that they were effectively used as shock troops. "From the 18th century onwards, the Scottish regiments were the military cutting edge of the British empire and were always used in a spearhead role, and that meant huge casualties."

The historical background to Murdo Munro's character is accurate, as is the fact that individual black men fought within the British Army and its Scottish regiments. This is evidenced by military regulations and photographs, and a recently published manuscript by Arthur Roberts, *As Good as Any Man* (2014), telling his story as a black soldier serving in the Royal Scots Fusiliers during World War I (edited and contextualised by Morag Miller, Roy Laycock, John Sadler and Rosie Serdiville).

While there was a restriction on promotion beyond sergeant, there was no such restriction against becoming an officer. Perhaps those updating the army's regulations never envisioned through their spectrum of social prejudices that any black man would ever apply, let alone pass selection and training to earn the King's commission. But they did. Walter Tull is often credited with being the first British black officer in World War I, but this is only partially true. He was the first black officer *in the British Army,* but by the time he was commissioned, David Louis Clemetson had already been an officer for two years *in the Territorial Force.* More would follow in their pioneering bootprints. Much is known of the black soldiers who served in the British West Indies Regiment, Canadian Construction Battalions, or American infantry units such as the 92nd 'Buffalo Soldiers' Division or the 'Harlem Hellfighters' of the 15th New York National Guard. Little was known about those who served individually in the British Forces during World War I until Stephen Bourne shone a much-needed light on the subject in *Black Poppies—Britain's Black Community and the Great War* (2014), followed by *Black Tommies: British Soldiers of African Descent in the First World War* (2015) by Ray Costello.

I use the term 'black' as its accepted current use in Britain, keenly aware other terms are used in other parts of the world—I mean no offense and ask forgiveness if any is taken. I also cite Staff Sergeant Drill Instructor Dossier, U.S. Marines, who made it crystal clear to us recruits he was black and proud to be black, not Afro-American, colored, or dark green (as recruits, we were told at the time—1990—to describe each other's ethnicity in shades of marine green).

The Quintinshill Disaster is little known, even within Scotland, although it remains the worst train crash in British history and killed or wounded close to 500 territorial soldiers from the Royal Scots, as well as civilians. By 1915, the war was not going as planned, and news of the disaster was suppressed. The signalmen, James Tinsley and George Meakin, were blamed, convicted, served reduced sentences, and then promptly returned to work for Caledonian Railways.

Tinsley's family were looked after by Caledonian during his imprisonment, and there is even some evidence that Meakin received compensation after his release. Every witness at their trial was an employee of Caledonian Railways apart from one policeman. Suspicion still exists today ("Quintinshill: was there a cover-up?," Adrian Searle, *Steam Railway* magazine, No. 439, March 2015) that a deal had been made between the accused and Caledonian Railways to sweep the incident under the carpet, so as to not embroil the government and further undermine public morale following the sinking of the *Lusitania*.

Caledonian Railways was not questioned on the use of out-of-date carriages traveling at express speeds, and the government was not questioned on the priority status given to troop trains while at the same time trying to maintain peacetime passenger and increased freight schedules as normal. Any semblance of modern day health and safety standards being raised were totally absent from the proceedings. Tragically, accounts of trapped Scots territorial soldiers committing suicide with pocket knives or bayonets or being shot by their own officers before burning to death are all too horrifyingly true.

Despite Napoleonic success with riflemen armed with the accurate Baker Rifle at the beginning of the war, the training of expert marksmen was limited to the Scotland's Lovat Scouts, the only such unit in the British Army, which drew its men from the ghillies and gamekeepers of the highlands and islands. The Germans had trained marksmen equipped with telescopic sights from the beginning, a legacy of their Jaeger troops. They wreaked havoc on the British and French frontlines in France, as did the Turks at Gallipoli. In response, individual British Army battalions, at the discretion of their commanding officers, began to identify their best shots and form them into small informal sharpshooting sections, equipped with telescopic-mounted Lee-Enfield III rifles. The first British Army "School of Sniping,

Observation, and Scouting" wasn't operational until 1916, halfway through the war.

Despite one of my great-grandfathers serving in the Royal Navy Trawler Service at Gallipoli, I confess I knew little of Cape Helles—the British and French sector, or the disastrous landings to secure it—until I began my research. The campaign has become synonymous with the Australians and New Zealanders who fought at Anzac Cove, which in turn became a watershed moment in both countries' national identities and a site of modern national pilgrimage. Sadly, it has less resonance in Britain.

Gallipoli. Whichever book you read, and there are many, the British military leadership during the ill-fated campaign comes in for an absolute slating, as does indeed the British Army officer cadre at the outbreak of the war. The Battle of Gully Ravine was deemed by the generals in charge as a huge success. On the left flank, up Gully Spur, backed up by artillery and naval gunfire, gains had been made up the Aegean coastline. In the center, again backed up with artillery and French heavy mortars, Boomerang Redoubt had been taken and modest gains made up Gully Ravine itself. At Fir Tree Spur, two lines of trenches had been taken at tremendous cost to the Royal Scots, but only partially. This so vexed Major General Henry de Beauvoir de Lisle, that he willfully ordered the destruction of the Cameronian territorials to achieve the impossible "...at all costs," against massed heavy machine guns.

By the end of their very first day in action, the Scottish Rifles Brigade, 52nd Lowland Division, had lost over half its strength: 1,563 men were killed, wounded, or missing, including the brigade's commanding officer. Both battalions of Cameronians and both battalions of Royal Scots ceased to exist as viable fighting units. The remnants had to be merged into two composite battalions and then taken out of the frontline.

General Sir Ian Hamilton's official dispatch regarding the battle stated that "Our casualties were very small; 1,750 in all."

Lieutenant General Aylmer Gould Hunter-Weston was the corps commander for the attack and a keen fox huntsman. On hearing the price paid by the territorial Scots at Fir Tree Spur, he was heard to comment that it had been a good opportunity, "...to blood the pups."

Characters such as Lieutenant General Hunter-Weston appear calloused and tactically obtuse. On hearing of the high casualties suffered by the depleted Royal Marines Brigade at Achi Baba Nullah, he echoed comments made by him on hearing of severe casualties during the initial landings, "Casualties, what do I care of casualties?" He then invited the Royal Marines' commanding officer to luncheon. (He declined.)

Excuses for the campaign's failure can be placed at many people's feet apart from those who actually fought on the frontline. Certainly, the land campaign was a hurried afterthought in response to the naval failure to breach the straits. The will and ability to fight shown by the Turks defending their own country was wholly under-estimated by British commanders used to fighting colonial campaigns. This was exemplified by General Sir Ian Hamilton's declaration that one British soldier was equal to eight Turks, Syrians, or Arabs, where in actual fact at Gallipoli the ratio was more like 1:1. The fall of Turkey, long regarded as 'the sick man of Europe,' was seen as inevitable, its collapse a foregone conclusion. Allied tactics and missed opportunities, "...depended for the most part on the assumption of an almost total absence of any further resistance from the Turks." (*Defeat at Gallipoli*, Nigel Steel and Peter Hart, 1995). The topography was against any sort of prolonged campaign and quickly favored the Turks. They ground the allied attack down to a stalemate early on in the campaign, containing the threat against them despite repeated frontal attacks by the British and French at Cape Helles and by the Australians and New Zealanders at Anzac Cove.

To overcome this stalemate Hamilton's general staff devised a credible plan to land British soldiers at Suvla Bay to out-flank and cut off the Turks. At the same time, the allies would launch a mass-breakout from Anzac Cove, sending the Turks into full retreat. But that, and the McReynolds' role in it, is another story to be found in the next Seaforths novel, *The Chosen Heroes*.

Acknowledgments

Hurrying to catch a train back to Scotland after a board meeting, I happened to glance down a side street in Manchester and saw a coffeeshop and bookstore called "Chapter One." I couldn't help but smile. The journey from writing those two words to becoming an author is a long one.

To start with, you have to write a book. I began mine on a laptop in front of the TV with three kids in pajamas by my side along with a cup of tea from my wife, and a dog stretched out on the carpet. I continued writing there, at times late into the evening, or while sipping a coffee while waiting for various after-school clubs and activities to finish. Sometimes, if I were lucky, I could even slip into a quiet village pub and tap away in the corner while sipping a pint. I ran the initial chapters past a dozen literary agents. I received 11 polite rejections and one request for the full manuscript. That request came from Robin Wade, who turned out to be a former Gordon Highlander. He liked the manuscript, but said it would be tough to find an editor for WWI historical fiction in London, where most of the British editors and publishers are based. "They don't have a military background," he explained.

I needed to find someone who understood the military angle. Cue Los Angeles-based military publishing specialists, Warriors Publishing Group—We publish books you like to read—and its founding editor, Julia Dye. If she were surprised to receive a submission from Scotland, it didn't show. A request for the full manuscript came and soon we were in business. So, my first thanks are to Julia. I promise, one of those days, I'll remember what a comma splice is.

Talking of comma splices, my wife Joanne has all my thanks for, well, being my wife. If that's not enough, she's also been forcefully conscripted into the role of head proofreader as together we try and recall long-forgotten rules on grammar and syntax to makes Julia's job a little bit easier. We don't always succeed; my English teachers would be very disappointed in me. You may only write a book once, but trust me, you'll proofread it a dozen times.

My thanks to Libby Jordan for her publicity expertise. I'd also like to acknowledge Dr Meg Bateman, Sabhal Mòr Ostaig, the National Centre for Gaelic Language and Culture, the University of the Highlands & Islands, Scotland, for translating the Gaelic Bible; and Ian McDonald, Special Counsel, Simpsons Solicitors, New South Wales, Australia, for steering me right on copyright laws. My thanks also to Amanda Merritt and Geoff Barker, who offered both encouragement and suggestions during a local creative writing class at Waid Academy, Anstruther, Scotland. Which, coincidentally, is where I went to school 40 years ago, before heading to California.

To cite websites I've used in my research would be never-ending. How else would you quickly find out the specifications of a German WWI torpedo, the weight of Lee-Enfield Mk III bayonet, or stumble across references to the Zion Mule Corps, the Ceylon Planters Rifles, or the Wanganui Highland Rifles? A thanks to all the reference sites will have to suffice, including Dan Snow's *WWI Uncut*, Ian McCollum's *Forgotten Weapons*; and Indy Neidell's wonderful canter through WWI in *The Great War*.

From the books I have used to further my understanding, I would recommend the following in addition to those already mentioned within Author's Notes: Erik Larson, *Dead Wake: The Last Crossing of the Lusitania* (2015); Patrick O'Sullivan, *The Sinking of the Lusitania* (2014); Diana Preston, *Wilful Murder: The Sinking Of The Lusitania* (2011); Adrian Searle and Jack Anthony Richards, *The Quintinshill Conspiracy: The Shocking True Story Behind Britain's Worst Rail Disaster* (2013); Andrew Rawson, *The British Army 1914-1918* (2014); Alan Moorehead, *Gallipoli* (2015); Edward J Erickson, *Gallipoli, The Ottoman Campaign* (2015); John Hamilton, *Gallipoli Sniper* (2015); Michael Chappell, *Scottish Divisions in the World Wars* (1994); Lt Col R.R Thompson, *The Fifty-Second (Lowland)*

Division 1914-1918 (2015); and Derek Young, *Forgotten Scottish Voices from the Great War* (2004).

I have to thank my wife, again, and my three children, for putting up with me tapping away on my laptop during evenings in front of the TV, and for sometimes disappearing into my own wee imaginary world. Finally, I would like to thank you, the reader. There are shelves, literal or online, of novels to choose from; I hope this one edged towards a good read—others will be coming your way. To find out more, please visit my website at www.rjmacdonald.scot or my Facebook page at @rjmacdonald.scot.

rjmacdonald.scot

About the Author

RJ MacDonald grew up in a small coastal fishing village in Scotland. He crossed the Atlantic and attended Cate School before studying at UC Berkeley, where his dissertation professor was Stephen Ambrose (*Band of Brothers*). After graduating with double BA in military history and social science, he enlisted in the U.S. Marines as a reservist. Boot camp in San Diego went well for five days until the drill instructors read his personnel file and discovered not only a "Berkeley hippy freak infiltrating their Marine Corps," but also one with an accent. "You speak funny, Private. Are you Russian?" Meritoriously promoted to sergeant, he served in a helicopter support squadron at NAS Miramar and as an expert marksman and marksmanship instructor. Returning to Scotland to complete two masters degrees, he was commissioned into the Royal Air Force Reserves. "You speak funny, sir. Are you Canadian?" Parachute qualified with jump-wings from Holland, the Czech Republic, and U.S. Special Operations Command Europe, he deployed as an operational intelligence officer with a Puma helicopter detachment during the war in Iraq, and then again to Cyprus during the conflict in Libya.

Now a director with a small research company, he also serves on a Royal National Lifeboat Institute volunteer crew tasked with a 24/7 all-weather maritime search and rescue role. He lives with his wife, three children, and a very cute but equally stupid cocker spaniel in the East Neuk of Fife where he grew up. *A Distant Field* is his debut novel and the first in The Seaforths series. His second novel, *The Chosen Heroes*, is underway.

Made in the USA
Las Vegas, NV
16 July 2022

51671747R00208